Edward Hayes Plumptre

The Life of Thomas Ken, D.D., Bishop of Bath and Wells

Vol. I

Edward Hayes Plumptre

The Life of Thomas Ken, D.D., Bishop of Bath and Wells
Vol. I

ISBN/EAN: 9783337095147

Printed in Europe, USA, Canada, Australia, Japan

Cover: Foto ©Raphael Reischuk / pixelio.de

More available books at **www.hansebooks.com**

My good Lord
your Graces most obedient humble servant
Tho: Bathebely

THE LIFE OF
THOMAS KEN, D.D.

BISHOP OF BATH AND WELLS

By E. H. PLUMPTRE, D.D.

DEAN OF WELLS

WITH ILLUSTRATIONS BY E. WHYMPER

"Of whom the world was not worthy."

"Isti sunt triumphatores et amici Dei, qui, contemnentes
jussa principum, meruerunt præmia æterna :
Modò coronantur et accipiunt palmam.

Isti sunt qui venerunt ex magnâ tribulatione et
laverunt stolas suas in sanguine Agni :
Modò coronantur et accipiunt palmam."

IN TWO VOLUMES

VOL. I.

LONDON
Wm. ISBISTER Limited
56 LUDGATE HILL
1889

WELLS CATHEDRAL.

A.D. 1710.

———

Weary and worn, and bent with years and pain,
  A pale form kneels upon that altar-stair;
  Long years have flown since from his pastoral chair,—
Hot thoughts, low sobs, half-choking protest vain,—
He stepped, nor thought within that glorious fane,
  Once more to tread, and breathe the words of prayer,
  Or hear sweet anthems floating on the air :
Then was it hard to balance loss and gain.
Now all is clear, and from his Pisgah height
  He sees the dawning of a brighter day,
And led, through clouds and darkness, on to light,
  Joins in the praise that shall not pass away.
"GLORY TO GOD: FROM HIM ALL BLESSINGS FLOW:"
  'One sows : another reaps'—yea, Lord, e'en so, e'en so.

August 22nd, 1888.

PREFACE.

It will be well, I think, to begin with a brief outline of the *genesis* and growth of these volumes.

In 1884 I was led to appeal to those who either revered Bishop Ken for the saintliness of his life, or simply loved him as the writer of the Morning and Evening Hymns, to join with me in an effort to place in our Cathedral at Wells some adequate memorial of one whose name was held in honour in all the Churches, but of whom, at that time, we had no outward and visible recognition, where it might most have been expected.

I was naturally led, in doing this, to study the life of Ken more closely than I had done before, and it was not long before I came to the conviction that there was more than room for another biography. I have no desire to undervalue the labours of my predecessors. The life published by the Bishop's great-nephew, William Hawkins, in 1713, contained much interesting material, which probably came to him from the Bishop's own lips. On the other hand it was singularly meagre, and often singularly inaccurate, transposing events in his great-uncle's life out of their right order.[1] It served, however,

---

[1] Hawkins omits, *e.g.*, all mention of Ken's work at Little Easton and his friendship with Lady Maynard, and of his appointment to Brightstone, gives a

together with a few notices of Ken's public life, as the basis of all biographical notices in Dictionaries and Encyclopædias—among them I may mention that in the *Biographia Britannica* as specially noticeable—and was republished, but with scarcely any notes or additions, in Mr. Round's edition of Ken's prose works in 1838.[1] In 1830 the work was taken in hand by Mr. William Lisle Bowles, Canon of Salisbury, and was published in two volumes. It was the fruit of some, though I am bound to say, not of much, research. Mr. Bowles's poetic feeling put him in sympathy with his subject. He brought out more fully than had been done before Ken's life at Winchester and Oxford, his own reminiscences as a Wykehamist giving life and interest to his pictures. As a whole, however, the book was disappointing. It was largely filled with the writer's views on the political and ecclesiastical topics of the day, with diatribes against Whig Reformers and popular Evangelicalism. Ken himself scarcely occupied more than half his pages.[2] The "Life" published in 1851 by "A Lay-

wrong date for his appointment as Chaplain to the King, and places the expedition to Tangiers (1684) as "some time" *before* the Chaplaincy at the Hague (1679). The only letter which he gives is that to Bishop Burnet, and of Ken's later relations to the other Non-jurors not a word is said. It may fairly be said in his excuse that the time for writing a fuller biography had not come.

[1] I am compelled to note Mr. Round's work as an editor as being more or less defective. He had in his hands the Malet and Prowse letters, the Williams MSS., and others in the Tanner and Smith MSS. in the Bodleian Library, and he was enabled to print forty-eight, as compared with Bowles's twelve. On the other hand the letters are given without a single note to explain their connexion with Ken's life, and without any attempt to fix the year in which they were written, where Ken, as was his custom, had given only the month and day. In many cases, as will be seen on a comparison with the sequence in which they are placed in these volumes, he gives them in what is demonstrably a wrong order, and thus involves the reader in almost inextricable confusion.

[2] When Mr. Bowles published his first volume, the only letter of Ken's of which he knew anything was that to Dr. Nicholas (No. I. in this volume). In

man " (whom I am now able, with the permission of his
family, to name as Mr. John Lavicourt Anderdon), possessed merits of a far higher order. It was the fruit of
the loving labours of many years, and of research, which,
as far as his opportunities went, was accurate and
thorough. While Bowles had lamented, when he entered
on his work, that there was only one letter of Ken's
known to exist, Mr. Anderdon, in his second edition,
published in two volumes in 1854, not only incorporated
some of the forty-eight published by Mr. Round in the
work above mentioned, but added, in whole or in part,
others which he had found in the Bodleian Library at
Oxford, and elsewhere. But that edition was out of
print. It was not easy to get copies at second-hand
booksellers. And in the interval that had passed since
its publication, the labours of the Historical MSS. Commission, of which Mr. Anderdon knew nothing, and of
the authorities of the Bodleian Library and the British
Museum, had brought to light many others in the Longleat, the Dartmouth, the Morrison, and other private
collections.[1] Our own records in the *Chapter Acts* of
Wells supplied also some new and interesting materials.
Facts communicated by others enabled me to tell the

the interval which followed he became acquainted with those to Mrs. Grigge in
the Malet MSS.; with those to Hooper in Mrs. Prowse's MS. memoir of her
father; and with the copious correspondence with Lloyd in the Williams MSS.
Of all these, however, he only prints twelve, and makes no attempt to trace out
with any fulness the history which they suggest. His chief contributions in
addition to these are (1) some fairly copious extracts from Mrs. Prowse's
Memoir, and (2) a copy of Ken's Will. Neither he nor Round thought it worth
while to give an Index.

[1] Anderdon, in his second edition, prints only twenty-four letters. The
present volumes contain eighty-five. His first edition, like Bowles's *Life*, was
without an Index, but the want was supplied in the second.

tale of some interesting episodes in Ken's life, notably
those in chapter xxiv., hitherto but little known.   And
so in the autumn of 1884 I entered on my work, and
wrote on till I had brought my story to the Bishop's
arrival at Wells, and the part he took in connexion with
the Duke of Monmouth's rebellion.   Then my labours
were, for a time, suspended.   On taking a survey of the
tasks I had in hand, I came to the conclusion that
another, on which I had been engaged, off and on, for
twenty years, had a prior claim on me.   I was unwilling
that it should be said of me in regard to that work,
" This man began to build, and was not able to finish."

When, however, my Dante labours were completed,
I lost no time in resuming those on the life of Ken, and
on the self-same day which brought me an early copy
of the second volume of the one, I sent off to the printer
the first chapter of the other.   The delay which has thus
been interposed between the beginning and the completion
of my work has had one result, not contemplated when
I began, on which I think I may congratulate myself,
i.e. that it has brought the publication of this volume
to 1888, the bi-centenary of the trial of the Seven
Bishops, and of the Revolution, of which that trial was the
starting point.   I can conceive no better contribution
to the commemoration of that bi-centenary than a fairly
adequate presentation of the life and character of one
who was foremost among the leading actors in it, who
was also foremost among the chief sufferers from it.[1]

---

1 Strictly speaking, of course, there has been no commemoration of either of
the two events.   Even in the proceedings of the Lambeth Conference, where one
might most have expected some recognition of the worth of the Seven Bishops,
and which held its first solemn meeting on the anniversary of the Trial, I have

How far I have succeeded in producing such a presentation it is, of course, for others to judge. I will
content myself with words which were once used by one
who entered on the like task of narrating what seemed
to him a great and glorious revolution, "If I have
done well and as is fitting the story, it is that which I
desired; but if slenderly and meanly, it is that which
I could attain unto."

I have felt, I need scarcely say, the difficulty of
dealing with a period of history so full of the strifes of
parties, so critical in its bearing on the life of the
English people. I cannot flatter myself that I shall be
able to satisfy the prepossessions of those who, though
far removed from that great drama in point of time,
have yet inherited, on either side, the principles and
emotions which were then dominant. I have found
myself unable to offer incense on the altar of Macaulay's
apotheosis of William III. While I rejoice in the
results of the Revolution of 1688, I cannot look upon
it as "glorious" as regards either the chief actors in it,
or the means by which it was brought about. As with
the parallel case of the Reformation, I see a great good
effected by men of very mixed motives, often unscrupulous and base in their use of means. And the view
which I take of that great good is not altogether the
traditional one. I cannot simply exult in our final sever-
ance from the historical continuity of Latin Christendom,
though I admit that this was inevitable. I find in it
something more than an onward step in the triumph of

---

failed to find a single word spoken referring to the issues of that fateful day.
One could scarcely find a more striking instance of the mutabilities of history.

Whig, or Liberal, or democratic principles. The gain of
the Reformation was that it saved England prospectively
from the dominion of Jesuitism; that of the Revolution was that it put an end then, and one may hope
for ever, to the long struggle which Jesuitism had made
to regain its ascendancy. But with the gain there was
also loss. The Revolution, like the Reformation, has
left its wounds, as yet but partly healed, in our own
ecclesiastical and religious life in England. It left to
the Church the inheritance of a cold and sceptical
Erastianism, of a worship in which there was little of
the beauty of holiness, of a theology which was neither
Evangelical nor Catholic, of a rivalry with Dissent in
which she has not always had the advantage. And here
also, as regards the gains which are to be set on the
credit side of the account, I distinguish between the
system and the men. The Society of Jesus has produced
saints and martyrs of whom the world was not worthy.
The system of Jesuitism has exercised a baneful
influence, wherever its power has been felt, on the literature, the art, the politics, the moral and spiritual
life, of Europe. Among the lessons which the recollection of 1688 ought to teach us, one, at least, is the
danger of once more coming under that influence.
Englishmen should learn not to build again the things
they have destroyed, to resist the temptation to "please
themselves in the children of strangers." [1]

[1] The mottoes which I have placed at the head of each chapter will remind
not a few readers of a time when the great leader of the Oxford movement,
which, for good or evil, has so largely affected the theology and the worship of
the Church of England during the last half-century, seemed to have learnt from
the history of the period that followed the Restoration, both in England and
abroad, the lessons which Ken learnt from them. I have shown in the closing

Nor can I hope that I shall altogether satisfy those who have been contented to accept the traditional estimate of Ken's character. I do not own to being, by one jot or tittle, a less reverent admirer of his saintliness than my predecessors, but I see that saintliness from a different point of view. They dismiss the four volumes of Ken's poetical works, including two epics, with supercilious indifference. I have found in them an almost priceless store of material. I accept as authentic, and as throwing light on his character, works ascribed to him in his own time, which they summarily reject as utterly unworthy of him. I can only say, by way of *apologia*, that when I entered on my work, I shared in the prejudices—the *præjudicia*, judgments formed prior to investigation—which I inherited from them, and that the conclusions to which I have been brought have been formed slowly and deliberately, and, as it seems to me, on adequate evidence.[1]

It remains that I should acknowledge my indebtedness to those who have contributed to the completeness

chapter of my work how largely Cardinal Newman's reverence for Ken entered into his thoughts and feelings in those memorable years of which we have the narrative in the *Apologia*. The more I read of the poems in the *Lyra Apostolica*, in which he gave utterance to his deepest emotions, the more they seemed to me to reproduce what Ken, in his time, must have felt and thought. We may mourn that, later on, the parallelism became one of contrast rather than of resemblance. Not the less, I believe, does it remain true that few words can help us to enter into Ken's mind and heart so fully as those which then came from one, far above him in intellectual force, but like him then, and, I will add, like him now, in the unworldliness of his life, in his strivings after holiness, in his yearnings for the beatific vision.

[1] Of other lives of Ken, that in Salmon's *Lives of the Bishops* (1733), that by Mr. J. H. Markland (1849), Miss Strickland in her *Lives of the Seven Bishops* (1866), and that by Mr. G. L. Duyckink (New York, 1859), I will content myself with saying that they have not been passed over, but that I have not gathered from them any material additions to what I had acquired from other sources.

of this volume. To give the names of all the correspondents, some hundreds of whose letters lie before me, with whom my work has brought me into pleasant and friendly contact is, I fear, impossible. I must content myself with forming, as it were, a 'legion of honour' out of the larger army of my Ken volunteers. The foremost place in that legion belongs to those who have given, or procured for, me, access to unpublished letters of Ken's or other records connected with him, and leave to publish such letters, to the Archbishop of Canterbury, the Marquis of Bath, the Earl of Dartmouth, Bishop Hobhouse, the late Sir Frederick Graham, Bart., of Netherby, Mr. A. R. Morrison, and Mr. T. M. Fallow. For the autograph letter reproduced in *facsimile* in this work my special thanks are due to the Rev. Canon Moor of Truro. I have to thank Lady Brooke, of Little Easton Lodge, for permission to engrave the portrait of Lady Margaret Maynard in her possession, and the Rev. G. C. Tufnell, Rector of that Parish, for photographs of the Church and House. For much valuable information I am indebted to Cardinal Newman, Cardinal Manning, and Bishop Abraham, to Mr. R. C. Browne, for researches in the Record Office and the Library at Lambeth, to Mr. C. L. Peel, C.B., and Mr. T. Preston of the Privy Council Office, to Mr. H. Maxwell Lyte and Mr. J. Cartwright of the Historical MSS. Commission, to Dr. Garnett and Mr. G. K. Fortescue of the British Museum, to the Rev. D. Macray and Mr. F. Madan of the Bodleian Library, to Mr. St. David Kemeys Tynte, and Miss Wolferstan. A large measure of obligation is due to those who have

undertaken to look at my proof-sheets as they passed
through the press, to my old and valued friend, Mr. G. H.
Sawtell, Mr. C. J. Pickering, the Rev. H. W. Pereira,
Mr. R. C. Browne, and Mr. John Kent,[1] for a supervision
extending through the whole work ; to the Dean of
Winchester, and the Rev. H. B. Fearon, Head Master
of Winchester College ; to Mr. J. H. Shorthouse, the
author of " John Inglesant ; " to the Rev. J. H. Overton,
the Rev. C. W. Boase, of Exeter College, Oxford, the
Rev. F. W. Weaver, for suggestions in the Chapters
belonging to those portions of my work that treat of
subjects in which they are recognised experts. Lastly,
I have to thank Mr. Pereira, yet once more, for the
loving labour which he has bestowed on the Index to
my volumes, and which makes it, as far as I have been
able to test , it a model of completeness.

E. H. P.

DEANERY, WELLS,
    August 21st, 1888.

---

[1] I find in Anderdon (p. 631) the expression of his acknowledgment of what
he owed to the last-named of these fellow-workers in the following words: " I
am anxious once more to acknowledge the indefatigable assistance of my friend,
Mr. Kent, in these and various other minute details, which he has continued to
afford me throughout the volume, and for which I find it difficult to express my
thanks." It is, I imagine, almost an exceptional fact in the history of literature,
that the same man should, after an interval of thirty-four years, be found doing
the same work for another labourer in the same field, but so in this case it is,
and my thanks to Mr. Kent for his loyal and ungrudging help are not less warm
than those of Mr. Anderdon.

TABLE OF CONTENTS.

VOL. I.

b

KEN'S LETTERS.

VOL. I.

ABBREVIATIONS.

A.—ANDERDON, *Life of Ken*, by A Layman. Second Edition.

B—BOWLES, *Life of Ken*.

R—ROUND, *Prose Works of Ken*.

LIST OF ILLUSTRATIONS.

VOL. I.

CHAPTER I.

" Like olive plants they stand,
Each answering each in home's soft sympathies,
Sisters and brothers. At the altar sighs
Parental fondness, and with anxious hands
Tenders its offering of young vows and prayers."

J. H. Newman.

THE genealogies with which it is customary for biographers
to begin their works have, in some instances, the merit of
throwing light on the doctrine of heredity. We see in the
subject of the memoir the working of transmitted tendencies
and capacities, modified by the environment in which they
were exercised, and by the individuality which is more or less
active in every man whose life is worth recording. If it is
true that a man is what his mother makes him, either by direct
transmission of temperament or by the influences of early
childhood, there is good ground for looking, us closely as may
be, into the records of the earliest years of one whom we seek
to know better than we have done. In the case of Thomas
Ken, however, inquiries do not help us much. He is said by
his great-nephew, and the statement has been accepted by his
biographers,[1] to have been descended from an ancient Somersetshire family, who took their name from, or gave it to, the village
of Ken, or Kenn,[2] near Clevedon, where the house known as

[1] Hawkins, p. 1. Collinson (iii. 592) gives John de Ken, temp. Henry III.
as the founder of the house. He connects the Bishop with the Kenns of Kenn.
His history was published in 1791.

[2] Ken himself adopts the former orthography, but Kenn is found in the
Royal letter that accompanied his *congé d'élire*, in all the records of the Diocesan

Kenn Court still attests their position among the gentry of the
county. In what relation Ken's father stood to the last representatives of the direct line, the daughters and co-heiresses of
Christopher Kenn, there is, so far as I have been able to trace,
no direct evidence to show,[1] but we can believe, without much
risk of error, that the fact that Lord Poulett, who married
one of them, took the Royalist side in the disputes between
Charles I. and his Parliament, and afterwards suffered severely
for his loyalty, would predispose the London branch of the
family, so far as they believed themselves to be connected
with him, in that direction. The occupation of Ken, the
father of the Bishop, who is described as being of Furnival's
Inn, and at once an attorney and a member of the Company
of Barber Surgeons,[2] indicates that he belonged to the professional middle class, but of his life we know little or nothing
beyond these few and not very suggestive facts.

On the mother's side, however, we meet with a name
of somewhat greater interest. Ion[3] Chalkhill, her father,
occupied a not unworthy place in the goodly company of
poets that were the glory of the Elizabethan period. He was
the friend of Spenser ; Izaak Walton quotes two of his songs[4]

Registry at Wells connected with his Episcopate, and is frequent in contemporary
publications, and even on the title-pages of his books after his decease. The
name appears in Ken (or Caen) Wood, Hampstead (Peck's *Hist. of Hampstead*).

[1] See Note A on *Ken Genealogies* at end of Chapter.

[2] Probably, as with other City Companies, membership had then, as in later
times, ceased, partially or altogether, to be connected with professional occupation, and was sought as a means of obtaining the freedom of the City and other
incidental advantages. The registers of the Barbers' Hall record the admission of Matthew Kenne in 1583 ; of Thomas Keene, son of Matthew Kene, in
1607 ; of Humfridus Kenn in 1629. The variations of spelling show how little
can be inferred in any case from the form of the name. The records of 1576
show that Matthew Ken and William Wyse, another member of the Hall, had
a quarrel, which ended in the latter "giving a breakfast to the Companie," and
"so they shook hands and were made friends."

[3] The name seems to have been more than a mere variant of John. Both John
and Ion appear in the list of the Bishop's brothers. The latter name is spelt
"Hyon" in the Register of Baptisms at St. Giles', Cripplegate. (See p. 13.)

[4]   "Oh ! the sweet contentment
        The countryman doth find."
                              I. ch. v.

     "Oh ! the gallant fisher's life,
        It is the best of any."
                              I. ch. xvi.

in the *Complete Angler*, and one of the latest employments
of his life was to bring out, in 1678, an edition of Chalkhill's *Thealma and Clearchus*, in the preface to which he speaks
highly of the poet's character, as honourable, refined, upright, and of which he clearly hoped that it would hand
down his half-forgotten fame to a future generation. The
memory of the poet-ancestor was, we may well believe, held in
honour in the family traditions, and may have tended to
stimulate the energies of one who, though not endowed with
the highest gifts of genius, might yet have had fair reason for
saying in his youth, *Anch' io son poeta.*

The future bishop was born at Great or Little Berkhampstead, in the county of Hertford, in July, 1637,[1] but as the
register of the former parish contains no entry of the name of
Ken, and those of the latter were destroyed at some time or
other, early in the eighteenth century, we cannot say how long
the family remained there. It seems probable that it was only
a temporary place of sojourn.[2]

The death of Ken's mother, in 1641, prevents our attribut-
ing to her any large share in the formation of his character ;
but a child's memory, even at the age of four, especially the
memory of such a child as Ken must have been, may well recall,
in after years, the first steps in the training by which his mind
and character were fashioned, the first dawning of the light
which was, in his after-life, to shine more and more unto the
perfect day. And such a recollection of those infant years

---

[1] So Hawkins. The Winchester register of his election states that he was
thirteen on October 20th, 1650 ; but this may have been based on the date of his
baptismal certificate. Writing on June 23rd, 1707 (Letter LXXII.), Ken says
that he " will be in his seventieth year next month."

[2] A solitary anecdote of later years suggests that Ken's father may probably,
at one time, have re-ided at Berkhampstead. "My father," he is reported to
have said, " was an honest farmer, and left me £20 a year, thank God." (Southey's
Omniana, i., 206, 1812.) Did he settle in the country in the later years of his
life? An indenture of Edward II. gives the name of Richard le Ken of Berkhampstead [Rev. F. Brown, deceased]. The Winchester registers give simply
Berkhampstead, as also does Hawkins. Most biographers give Little Berkhampstead, probably as an inference from the name not having been found in the
registers of the larger parish. The question is discussed by the Rev. J. W. Cobb
in two lectures on the *History and Antiquities of Berkhampstead* (p. 3, n.), 1883,
and decided in favour of the smaller parish, the registers of which, prior to 1712,
are lost.

we may find, if I mistake not, in the counsels which, as bishop, he gave to the " poor inhabitants " of his diocese, and which, for their exceeding beauty and tenderness, it is worth while to print *in extenso:*

" I exhort all you who are parents to instil good things into your children as soon as ever they begin to speak ; let the first words they utter, if it be possible, be these— 'Glory be to God :' accustom them to repeat these words on their knees as soon as they rise, and when they go to bed, and oft-times in the day; and let them not eat or drink without saying ' Glory be to God.'

" As their speech grows more plain and easy to them, teach them who made, and redeemed, and sanctified them, and for what end, namely, to glorify and to love God; and withal, teach them some of the shortest ejaculations you can, such as these—

> " ' Lord, help me, Lord save me.'
> " ' Lord, have mercy upon me.'
> " ' All love, all glory, be to God, who first loved me.'
> " ' Lord, keep me in thy love.'

" Within a little time you may teach them the Lord's Prayer, and hear them say it every day, morning and evening, on their knees, with some one or more of the foregoing ejaculations; and by degrees, as they grow up, they will learn the Creed and the whole Catechism.

" Be sure to teach your children with all the sweetness and gentleness you can, lest, if you should be severe, or should over-task them, religion should seem to them rather a burden than a blessing." [1]

I own that to me it seems absolutely impossible not to see in this passage the elements of an unconscious autobiography. I see the Hannah and the Samuel of those long past years, the sweet and gentle mother with her hand on his brow, and the devout and reverent child kneeling by her side, lisping that " All glory be to God," which, when he was old and greyheaded, was to stand at the head of well-nigh every letter that he wrote. What we read is as much, I believe, the tribute of a filial love and reverence to Ken's mother as were Cowper's well-known lines to the memory of his.

[1] *Directions for Prayer* in Round, p. 311. See ii. 175.

It was not given to the boy who had thus lost one parent in earliest childhood to enjoy the guidance of the other for more than a few years. His father died in 1651,[1] probably before his son had become a Scholar of Winchester, and the boy's home training fell into other hands. We have no formal **record** of what he thought and felt as to his father's influence. But here also the element of an unconscious autobiography comes in. The counsels from which I have quoted may refer to the father as well as to the mother. In a poem which, **as we** shall see, **bears** largely and more deliberately the character of self-portraiture, I find other words which are distinctly an **utter**-ance of personal thanksgiving.

> " E'er since I hung upon my mother's breast,
>   Thy love, my God, has me sustained and blest,
>   My virtuous parents, tender of their child,
>   My education, pious, careful, mild."

Hymnotheo,[2] p. 149.

It lies in the nature of the case that in a household such **as that of Ken's father** while he lived, and yet more after his death, the part played by an elder sister, who had gifts and character for **this** work, in the training of her orphan brother, could **not fail to** be an important one. All that we know of **Anne Ken** leads us to think that she possessed those gifts **in a more** than average measure, **and** that she did not fail **to** use them **at** once with wisdom and with tenderness. In 1646, five years after her step-mother's death and five before her father's, she had married Izaak Walton, **then** fifty-three, and

---

[1] He describes himself in his will, dated April 12th, 1651, as " a citizen of London, and member of the ancient Gild of Barber-Chirurgeons." The will begins after the manner of the time : " First and principally, I bequeathe my soul into the hands of Almighty God who gave it me." The formula was perhaps too common to allow us to infer much from it as to his personal piety. The fact that he leaves to his son-in-law, John Symonds, " a place in the circuits of South Wales to the value of 40 marks," implies a good professional position. One wonders whether his work in South Wales brought him into contact with the Kemeys family. (See Ch. xxiv.)

[2] One may compare Marcus Aurelius, i. 17. " From the Gods I have had good forefathers, good parents, a good sister, good teachers, good domestics, good friends, all, or nearly all, of them." (C. J. P.)

she herself, having been born in 1610, was seventeen years younger than her husband and twenty-seven years older than her brother, and thus served as a connecting link between the two, the disparity of whose years might otherwise have tended to obscure the brotherly relation by which, through this marriage, they were connected with each other. If I had anything like the artistic skill which we admire in works like *John Inglesant*, or, *longo intervallo*, the *Diary of Mary Powell*, I should portray her as entering alike into her husband's angling and her boy-brother's studies, hearing the latter say his Creed and Catechism and Collects, as his mother used to do, training him with all the " remarkable prudence " and the " great and general knowledge " which her husband ascribes to her,[1] into the pattern of that " primitive piety " of which she was herself so bright an example; going with him, while yet she could, to church services[2] and communions; and then, when the Westminster Directory had taken the place of the Prayer Book, and those who still worshipped God after the manner of their fathers had to meet, as it were, in the dens and caves of the earth, contenting herself with keeping up, in

[1] The Epitaph in Worcester Cathedral is worth copying *in extenso*.

Ex. Terris.

D.

M. S.

" HERE LYETH BURIED SO MUCH AS COULD DIE
OF ANNE, THE WIFE OF
IZAAK WALTON,
WHO WAS A WOMAN OF REMARKABLE PRUDENCE,
AND OF THE PRIMITIVE PIETY,
HER GREAT AND GENERAL KNOWLEDGE
BEING ADORNED WITH SUCH TRUE HUMILITY,
AND BLEST WITH SOE MUCH CHRISTIAN MEEKNESS,
AS MADE HER WORTHY OF A MORE MEMORABLE MONUMENT.
SHE DYED (ALAS! THAT SHE IS DEAD!)
THE 17TH OF APRIL, 1662. AGED 52.
STUDY TO BE LIKE HER.

The D. M. S. (*Diis Manibus Sacrum*) is noticeable as a curious touch of classicalism in the author of the *Complete Angler*.

[2] Within easy reach of Walton's house in Fleet Street, at the corner of Chancery Lane, a Church of England congregation used to meet in Blackfriars, and the services were conducted by Dr. Peter Gunning (afterwards Bishop of Ely), Dr. Timothy Thuscross, and Dr. Mossom, names that will meet us again later on, p. 72. These services were suppressed in 1648.

the worship of her home, the sacred traditions of the past. From
her also, as the "Kenna," whose skill in song and music are
commemorated in the *Complete Angler*,[1] the scholar-brother
may well have derived the taste for music and song which
was the joy and nourishment of his inner life in his busiest
years, and his consolation in the time of pain and solitude and
homelessness.   I do not know whether, as I write, I shall
have occasion to mention Anne Ken's name again.   Enough
has, I think, been said to show that she must have been as
a sunbeam in the house, illumining its dark places, speaking
"words of hope and comfort" to those who needed them; the
guardian angel of the boy who had been committed to her
charge, striving by acts and words, and yet more by her
prayers, that he might be kept pure from evil, and daily increase in all wisdom and holiness.   It was given to her to
see, as the growth of the seed which she had thus sown, the
"blade," and the "ear;" but the "full corn in the ear," the
ripened holiness of the pastor and the confessor, she did not
live to witness.   And so we part from her.   Farewell, dear
sister of a saint!   Though "one soweth and another reapeth,"
there shall come a time when thou shalt not lack thy meed
of praise for that which thou didst contribute to his holiness.

A still more important element in Ken's early life is to be
found in the close contact with his brother-in-law, Izaak Walton,
into which he was brought by the marriage of which I have
been speaking.   Presumably that contact may have begun
before the marriage, during the years in which Anne was
presiding over her widowed father's household (1641-1646).[2]
After the marriage it must have become closer.   On the death
of Ken's father, in 1651, there is a probability, amounting to

---

[1] "Hear, hear my Kenna sing a song."—i. ch. v.
A marginal note indicates that the song was to be—

"Like Hermit poor in pensive place obscure."

The line in which *Kenna* is named is from a song, obviously by Walton himself, which appears in the third and fourth editions, with "Chlora," possibly an
anagram on Rachel, the Christian name of Walton's first wife.   In the fifth
edition this is displaced for *Kenna*.

[2] The registers of St. Giles, Cripplegate, record the death of Martha, wife,
and the baptism of Martin, son, of Thomas Ken, on March 16th and 19th, 16⁴⁷.
Apparently she died in child-bed.

something like a moral certainty, that Walton's house must
have been the boy's home, to which he came during his school
holidays and his University vacations.[1] The importance, according to the estimate which I have been led to take of it, of this

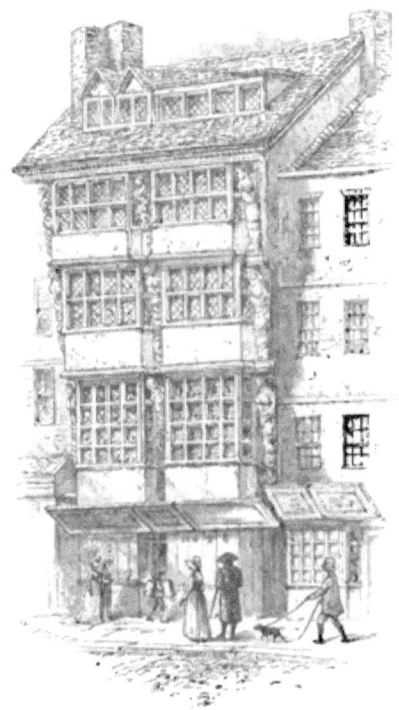

THE HOUSE OF IZAAC WALTON.

new influence, calls for a separate treatment of it, which I
reserve for the next chapter.

I have not undertaken to write a history of Ken's "times"
as well as of his "life," and I shall, as I proceed, notice

[1] It was about this time that Walton left London and settled in his cottage
near the river Dove. Morley, it is well known, often visited him there, as
before in London, and may therefore have known his future chaplain in earliest
boyhood.

the contemporary events only so far as they more or less directly affected him. Our thoughts of his childhood would, however, be incomplete if we did not call to mind some outline-image of the years of strife and civil war, of chaos and confusion, in the midst of which the child passed into the boy. A few dates will be sufficient for this purpose. The year of Ken's birth, then, was memorable as the beginning of that strife which afterwards led men to draw the sword and cast away the scabbard. In 1637 Laud made his ill-advised attempt to force upon the Presbyterians of Scotland a liturgy which was at least so far reactionary in its character as to seem to those who compared it with that of the Anglican Church, a step backward towards Rome. In England that year was memorable for Charles I.'s impost of ship-money, and for Hampden's trial on refusing payment of it. In 1640 the Long Parliament met and gave an indication of its temper by impeaching Strafford and Laud. In the following year the Star Chamber was abolished, and Strafford was attainted and executed. In 1642, Charles's daughter, the Princess Mary, was married to William of Orange, grandson of the "Taciturn" one, to whom the Netherlands owed their freedom, and became in 1650, after her husband's death, the mother of the greater William who was in after years to exercise so memorable an influence on Ken's life. The 30th of January, 1649, when he was a boy of eleven, witnessed the execution of the king, on whom he and his looked with a loyalty and reverence into which we now find it hard to enter, as one who had died a martyr's death in defence of the faith and polity of the Church, and of the divine right which from their point of view was a divine trust, for which the king would have to render an account, though, as trustee, he was responsible to no human tribunal. We can picture to ourselves the thrill of horror which that day must have sent through the Walton household, the antipathy and dread with which it must have led the boy to look on all persons, books, principles that seemed to favour the movement of which this had been the outcome.

Note A.—Ken Genealogies.—There is abundant evidence from parish registers, the archives of Wells Cathedral, Heraldic Visitations, and the like sources, of the existence, in the fifteenth and sixteenth centuries, of a family named Le Chen, Ken, Kenn, or

Kenne (the three last forms appear indiscriminately), of Kenn Court, in the parish of Kenn, near Clevedon.[1] This, the elder branch of the family, ended in the two daughters of Christopher Kenn, *Armiger*, of whom it may be mentioned that he appears as contributing £50 towards the national subscription for resisting the Spanish Armada in 1588. One of these, Margaret, married Sir William Guise, of Elmore, Gloucestershire, the other, Mr. afterwards Lord, Poulett, of Hinton St. George, Somerset. The Kenn property passed with the latter into the Poulett family. John Kenn, a brother of Christopher's, is commemorated by an altar-tomb in the chancel of the old church at Clevedon. He died April 12th, 1593.

The Bishop's ancestry, on the other hand, cannot be traced farther back than his grandfather, Matthew Ken, who was in 1596 settled in the parish of St. Giles, Cripplegate, London.[2] The spelling varies as before, but there is absolutely no direct evidence proving the connexion of this family with that of Somerset. One of our best local experts in these matters, the late Rev. F. Brown used to say, indeed, that the common tradition was "a fond thing vainly invented."[3] On the other hand, the fact that William Hawkins, the Bishop's great-nephew, states that his uncle the Bishop was descended from the Kenns of Kenn Court, is at least evidence of a family tradition likely to be correct, as is also the fact that when Ken became bishop he impaled their arms, with those of his diocese, on his episcopal seal.[4] I have not been able to discover whether they were borne by his father or by himself before his episcopate. The arms appear to have been granted to the Kenns of Kenn in 1561. It seems useless, under these conditions, to give anything like a genealogy of the Somerset Kenns, but I append one of the London family, indicating the contemporary members of the other branch, which may be useful. If connected, the Bishop's ancestors must have migrated to London not later than the early part of the sixteenth century, and there is no trace of any subsequent intermarriages. The Rev. F. W. Weaver, Vicar of Milton, Somerset, who is an expert in these studies, thinks that

---

[1] The name appears in charters from 1205 in other parts of England—Essex, Lincoln, Devon, Cumberland. (J. Esdaile, *Notes of Charters, &c.*)

[2] His will was proved in 1596; his widow's in 1628.

[3] *Report of Som. Arch. Society*, 1881, p. 55.

[4] The arms will be found on the cover of this volume. Technically they are described as "*ermine*, three crescents, *gules*." The same arms, with a different crest, are given in Burke's *General Armoury* as belonging to the Kenns of Langford.

they may have branched off before 1500. He notices, among other things, the unusual frequency with which the name Thomas occurs in the pedigree of the Kenns of Kenn Court. One of them, a Thomas, son of Thomas, son of Thomas, is described as a mercer in London, who was twice married and was living in 1643, which is tantalisingly near in point of time, but the Bishop's father's wives (he also was married twice) bore names which are not those of the Thomas of the Kenn pedigree. A Thomas Ken appears in 1642 as one of the clerks of the House of Lords, but I have not been able to connect him with either branch.[1] He may possibly have been Ken's father. There was also a John Ken, Mayor of Bridgwater, *circ.* 1686.

The register of St. Olave's, Silver Street, London, gives the marriage of Thomas Ken and Martha Carpenter, in December, 1625. John Chalkhill, in his will, dated August 1, 1615, simply names his "daughter Martha." Presumably Carpenter was her first husband. She was Thomas Ken's second wife.

Elizabeth Ken, widow, of St. Giles's, Cripplegate, the grandmother of the Bishop, gives legacies in her will, dated October 6, 1628, to "Thomas my son," and to "his children, Thomas, Ion, Anne, and Jane," and then one to "Martha, the wife of my son, Thomas Ken." It would appear from this that there was a son Thomas by the first marriage of the Bishop's father, with Jane Hughes, who must have died young, and that the name was given by him, as was not uncommon in such cases, to a son by the second marriage.

It may be noted, as illustrating the variations of spelling, (1) that the register of St. James's, Clerkenwell, gives on April 23, 1647, the marriage of Mr. Isaak Walton to Anne Keene: (2) that Caen Wood, Hampstead, appears in documents of the last century as Ken Wood; and (3) that the Churchwardens' accounts at Frome (1764) call the Bishop Dr. Can. (See p. 170.)

The Registers of Baptisms in St. Giles's, Cripplegate, give names and dates as follows. All are described as children of "Mr. Thomas Kenn, gentleman: "—

1626, January 1st, John; 1628, June 23rd, Martha; 1629, February 23rd, Mary; 1631, March 26th, Margaret; 1632,

---

[1] Hist. MSS. Comm. *Rep.* v. 58. An Edmund Kenne appears as a prisoner in the Fleet in 1635. He petitions the Privy Council for release. His offence was "unadvised behaviour at election of Knights of the Shire and scandalising Sir Robert Phelipps of Montacute." It is probable, therefore, that he was of the Somerset branch. (H. M. C. *Rep.* i. 57.)

Kenn Branch.

London Branch.

MATTHEW KEN = ELIZABETH BENNET, OF LONDON.[1]

(1). JANE HUGHES = THOMAS KEN, = (2) MARTHA CARPENTER,[2]
daughter of | of Furnival's | daughter of Ion
Rowland | Inn, Attor- | Chalkhill, of St.
Hughes, of | ney in Court | Giles's, Cripple-
Essendon, | of Common | gate, ob. March
Herts. | Pleas. | 19, 1647.

CHRISTOPHER KENN, = 1. (22 Eliz.) ELIZABETH,
of Kenn Court, by | daughter and co-
his marriage with | heiress of Sir Roger
Elizabeth got the | Cholmeley, relict of
manor of Little | Sir Leonard Beck-
Oakley, Kent, | with, of Selby,
which he sold. | Yorkshire.
Ob. 21 Jan., 1593,
buried at Kenn.

= 2. FLORENCE,
afterwards m.
Sir N. Staley.

MARTHA = JAMES BERKMAN JOX, =
| Treasurer
| of East
| India Com-
| pany, 1683.

ANNE = IZAAK
ob. 17 Ap- | WALTON,
ril, 1662, | the Aug-
bur. Wor- | ler, ob.
cester Ca- | 15 Dec.,
thedral, | 1683.
at 52.

ROSE, = THOMAS, MARTIN,
daughter of | Bishop died in
Sir Thomas | of Bath infancy.
Vernon, of | and
Coleman | Wells.
Street,
London.
Living in
1707.

1st daughter = Sir
WILLIAM GUISE,[3]
Kt., of Elmore,
High Sheriff co.
Glos. 6 James I.

1st daughter, ELIZABETH = JOHN,
| 1st Ld. Poulett,
| of Hinton St.
| George, ob. 29
| March, 1649.
= JOHN ASHBURN-
| HAM, ob. 1671.
(Qu. If Charles
I.'s faithful fol-
lower who died
in that year.)

JANE,
m. John
Symonds.

JOHN, THOMAS.
died
1651.

ISAAC,
B.A., Ch. Ch.,
Oxon., Canon of
Sarum, 1719.

ANNE = DR. WILLIAM HAWKINS, Canon of
Winchester, ob. 17th July, 1691.

WILLIAM,
Middle Tem-
ple, ob. 29
Nov., 1748.
Author of a
short account
of the life of
Bishop Ken,
8vo, 1713.

ANNE,
ob. unm., 27
Novem., 1728,
buried in Salis-
bury Cathedral.

[1] In the volumes of the Harleian Society, xxiv. p. 124, we find a marriage license for John Keene, of St. Giles's, Cripplegate, Bachelor, to Mary Noble, of Abingdon, September 28th, 1672; and in xxv. p 1582, one for that of Christopher Keene, of the City of London, Taylor, to Suzanna Idvell, at St. Martin's in the Fields. The Christian name "Christopher," points to a connexion with the Kenn branch.

[2] Martha Carpenter's brother, John Chalkhill, was a Fellow of Winchester College when Ken went there.

[3] In 1679 Rouge Croix, Herald's College, certified to forty-two quarterings in the Guise arms. Amongst them are those of Kenne.—*Gloucestershire Notes and Queries*, iii. 361.

July 10th, Hyon;[1] 1635, April 14th, Elizabeth; 1638, August 17th, Mary; 1640, March 16th, Martin.

It may be presumed that the younger Mary replaced the older, as was also the case with the younger Thomas. The mother died, apparently, in giving birth to Martin, and the child died with her.

A few miscellaneous facts remain to be noted.

(1.) The Registers of the Parish of Kenn show a singular intermixture of the names of Kenn and Walton between 1569 and 1580. May Somerset claim any share in the ancestry of Izaak? There is a parish of Walton not far from Kenn.

(2.) A carved oak chest is in the possession of Mr. A. H. Raikes, of Windermere, with the inscription—

> "Izaak Walton and Anne Ken
> Was (*sic*) joined together in Holy Wedlocke,
> Yᵉ Eve of Saint Gregory, Año MDCXVI.
> 'Comfort ye one another.'"

The year is an obvious blunder of the carver's, nor does the day agree with that in the Register of Clerkenwell given above. I am unable to explain the discrepancies.

(3.) The name Ken is given as of Frisian origin in Brons. *Friesische Namen*, Emden, 1878 (J. K.).

(4.) Essenden, the birth-place of the first wife of Ken's father, was close to Berkhampstead. Probably the future bishop was born when the latter was, with his second wife, visiting the relations of his first.

---

[1] "Hyon" is clearly a variant of the "Ion" of the genealogical table, and shows, therefore, that it was treated, as in the case of the two Chalkhills, as a distinct name from "John."

CHAPTER II.

A.D. 1637—1683.

> " There are no colours in the fairest sky
> So fair as these. The feather whence the pen
> Was shaped that traced the lives of these good men,
> Dropped from an angel's wings."
>
> *Wordsworth.*

I AM about to claim for the author of the *Complete Angler* a larger share in the formation of Ken's character than the biographers of either have assigned to him. It may be questioned, perhaps, whether one in a hundred of those who use the Morning and Evening Hymns knows of the close tie by which the two men were connected with each other; whether one in a thousand of those who look to Walton for their guidance in catching roach or grayling, or enjoy the pleasant, cheerful, just a wee bit garrulous, talk in which that guidance is conveyed, has ever thought of the author as the virtual foster-father, the actual brother-in-law, of the non-juring bishop. To me, after a careful study of the lives of the two men, it seems scarcely an exaggeration to say that the surroundings of the home in which Ken found a refuge after his father's death left an indelible impression on his character, and determined the direction of his mental and moral growth ; that his whole after-life was fashioned by the atmosphere which he there breathed, and by the books which he read there. I find in Walton's *Lives* the unconscious prophecy of all into which that life was, as it were, destined to develop, in proportion as it followed the vocation which was thus conveyed to it.

I doubt indeed whether any but a few students of English social or church history have formed any adequate estimate of the position which Walton occupied among the leading ecclesiastics and men of culture of the time. We think of him as a "sempster" (something, I presume, in the hosier or linen-draper line), a middle-class tradesman whom his friends of a higher rank (*e.g.* Bishop King) used to address, somewhat condescendingly, as "honest Izaak;" who went out for his holiday walks by the New River, and angled for his trout in the Lea, the Itchin, or the Dove. We forget that there was scarcely a theologian or man of letters with whom he did not correspond on friendly and familiar terms; that the list of those friends included such men as Archbishops Ussher and Sheldon, and Bishops King, of Chichester, and Morley, of Worcester and Winchester, and Sanderson, of Lincoln; and Donne and William Chillingworth, and Hammond, and Hales, the "admirable," and Sir Henry Wotton, and Abraham Cowley, and Drayton, of the *Polyolbion*, and the Elias Ashmole, to whom Oxford owes its Museum.[1] He was, in the Church life of his own generation, in spite of his very different social position, what Evelyn was to that which came next, and Robert Nelson to the next but one, what Joshua Watson and Sir Robert Inglis were within the memory of our more immediate fathers, or Mr. Beresford Hope within our own. If he was not, as men then deemed, a man of letters, he had, at least, associated with those who were so. If he was not the rose, he had, at least, caught something of its fragrance by living among the roses. Into such a companionship Ken was brought in early boyhood, and the friendship continued unbroken till little more than a year before Ken was consecrated, when he was forty-six, and Walton fell asleep at the ripe age of ninety.[2]

I do not imagine that Ken was ever a proficient in the art which we associate with Walton's name. If he had been, we should probably have found some notice of him, if not in Walton's own work, at least in Cotton's *Supplement* to the *Com-*

---

[1] Walton's first wife, Rachel Flood, was a great-niece of Archbishop Cranmer. This probably put him in the way of clerical companionship. He chose his early friends well, and they rose to eminence in after years. (G. H. S.)

[2] I cannot resist quoting the words in which Cotton speaks of Walton: "the worthiest man, the best and truest friend any man ever had, who gives me leave to call him father."

plete Angler.[1] He did not become an expert in barbel fishing
like Sheldon, or think of angling hours as "idle time not idly
spent" like Sir H. Wotton, or find in it, as did George
Herbert, a "season of leisure for devout meditation." We
may perhaps fancy that the boy shrank with the refinement, the sympathy, the unwillingness to cause pain, which
afterwards characterized him, from handling the ground-bait, or
impaling his minnow on the hook as "though he loved him."
But not the less may those walks by the Lea have been
useful in building up the boy's character—the character of the
future bishop.[2] They stamped upon him the love of nature and
retirement, rather than of courts and crowds. To live *procul*
negotiis, to pursue the *fallentis semita vitæ*, instead of "seeking great things"[3] for himself, became in this way the great
ideal of his life. Beyond this those walks brought him into
contact with nature, and taught him to observe. They gave him
the open eye to see the actual phænomena of things as they
are, which is the necessary condition of the higher spiritual
vision that reads the parables of nature. In that sphere the
companionship of such a man as Walton was invaluable.
Every page of the *Angler* shows how he watched the habits
of everything that lives, the adaptation of their structure to
their environment, their instincts of self-preservation or
aggression, the things in which they foreshadow the self-
seeking or the altruism of humanity.[4] I am drawing no

[1] This conclusion is, perhaps, traversed by a passage in one of Ken's *Paraphrases* of Horace, where one of the joys of the retired life is described :

> "Where he delights, in his own Stream,
> To Angle for Trout, Pike, or Bream."
>
> *Works*, iv., p. 533.

I incline to look on the *Paraphrases* as belonging to Ken's school or college days.

[2] Comp. an interesting dialogue between Stillingfleet and Frampton, on the
Amusements of Clergymen, in which the former argues against live bait, in Overton's *Life in the English Church*, p. 316, 1886. (C. J. P.)

[3] The words of Jer. xlv. 5, *Et tu quæris tibi grandia? Noli quærere;* were
afterwards, as we shall see (p 139). Ken's favourite text, written by him in his
Greek Testament, and other books in daily use.

[4] I note a few examples from the *Complete Angler*—(1) of the song of birds,
"Lord, what music hast Thou provided for the saints in heaven, when Thou
affordest bad men such music upon earth?" (2) "Doubtless cats talk and reason
one with another." (3) The pet dog named Bryan, probably after Bryan Duppa,

imaginary picture in assuming that these influences contributed
to Ken's after character. His tenderness of feeling towards
animal life is seen in the fact that in the portrait which he
draws, in his *Hymnotheo,* of one with whom, more or less
consciously, he identified himself, he brings to light one of the
obscurer traditions of St. John :—

> " The youth, of David's mournful cell possessed,
>   Allured a widowed dove with him to rest,
>   Like John who, when his mind he would unbend,
>   With a tame partridge would few minutes spend." [1]
>
> *Works,* i., p. 79.

His sense of the teachings of nature is seen in another pattern
of the saintly life :— [2]

> " Three volumes he assiduously perused,
>   Which heavenly wisdom and delight infused,
>   God's works, his conscience, and the Book inspired."
>
> *Works,* ii., p. 76.

His habits of observation, in which he seems almost to have
surpassed his master, find their fullest, though not their only,
example, in the account he gives of the habits of the ant. It
will be admitted, I think, by those who are experts in such
matters, that it may challenge comparison, in its minuteness
and accuracy of detail, with what we find in the works of
Huber, or Sir J. Lubbock, or Romanes. The whole passage
is somewhat too long for insertion, and I content myself
with a few extracts. Walton, it may be noticed, contents
himself (I. c. i.) with speaking briefly of the " little pismire who,
in the summer, provides and lays up her winter provisions."—

> " In multitude they march, yet order just ;
>   No adverse files each other stop or thrust.
>   They have presensions of the change in air,
>   And never work abroad but when 'tis fair ;

Bishop of Winchester. (4) The taming of an otter by Nicholas Seagrave, of
Leicestershire, and of a lamprey, by Hortensius. (5) Miscellaneous notes on
bees, hawks, carrier-pigeons, and the longevity of pikes.

[1] The story is told by Cassian, *Collatt.* xxiv. c. 2.

[2] Did Walton stand for Sophronio ?

> They take advantage of the lunar light,
> And only at full moons they work by night." [1]

And so he goes on to paint the whole order and polity of the ant community : how some are seen nipping the grass, and others carrying it to their barns ; how they bring it out to dry when it has been wetted by the rain ; how they lay up " triennial stores ;" how they clean their feet as they enter the gates of their city, and erect a bastion round it to prevent inundations. Lastly he notices, what has sometimes been questioned, sometimes announced as among the most recent discoveries, the burying habits of the ants, in his sketch of the structure of the ant-hill, intersected as it is by a long street from end to end :

> " That Square they for their Cemetery keep,
> Where with dead Parents their dead Children sleep :
> The teeming females in this space remain,
> And there the youth they up to labour train ;
> The granary is there . . . ."
>
> *Works*, iii., p. 11—13.

Nor ought we to pass over the advantage it must have been to a studious and thoughtful boy to have the run of a library such as Walton's, or to listen to the conversation of the friends —such as those named above—who came to visit him, attracted by the conspicuous cheerfulness of his home, or seeking refuge there from the strife of tongues that raged around them. There, on those shelves, he would find, to say nothing of the books which Walton does *not* name, the works of Donne and Bishop Hall, of George Herbert, Christopher Harvey (author of the *Synagogue*, which is often bound up with Herbert's *Temple*, and belongs to the same school of devoutly meditative verse), and Du Bartas, and Josephus, and Montaigne, and Plutarch's *Lives*, and Dean Nowell's *Catechism*, and the *Devout Considerations* of John Valdesso, which Herbert commends so warmly, and Sibbes' *Bruised Reed* and *Soul's Conflict*, and Cowley's *Davideis*, which afterwards served as the model of Ken's own epic, *Edmund*, and Fletcher's *Purple Island*, and Camden's *Britannia*, and Mendez

---

[1] The parallelism with Dante (*Purg.* iii. 12), is worth noting, as also that with Shakespeare on bees in *Henry V.* (i. 2).

Pinto, and E. Sandys' *Travels*, and the works on Natural History by Gessner and Rondeletius (botanists, whose names survive in the genera of *Gessneria* and *Rondeletia*), and Topselius' *History of Serpents*, and others, *quæ nunc perscribere longum est.*

But more than all the books that he thus had the opportunity of reading were the traditions of which Walton, as belonging to a previous generation (he was, it will be remembered, Ken's senior by four-and-forty years), was the depository, and of which his *Lives* are the treasure-house.[1] To have been the intimate friend of such men as Donne and Wotton, to have at least seen Herbert, to have known and reported the ascetic saintliness of the life of Nicholas Ferrar, at Little Gidding, was enough to rivet the attention of the thoughtful boy as he listened to the old man's manifold reminiscences. There is scarcely one of those lives (I am tempted, as I write, to alter that "scarcely" into "absolutely not one") in which I cannot trace, beyond the shadow of a doubt, the influence which it exercised on his character, facts which were actually reproduced in his own after-life. Donne may have been his first master in what has been expressively, though not very accurately, described by Johnson as the "metaphysical" school of poetry, modified in this instance by intense personal devotion, the pattern after which, with the exception of the epic of *Edmund*, in which he followed Cowley, nearly all his own poetry was fashioned. It is not unreasonable to conjecture that Walton's selection of Hart Hall for his brother-in-law's residence at Oxford, while he was waiting for a vacancy at New College, was determined by the fact that it was there that Donne had studied. Even in the last-recorded act of his life I trace a distinct reminiscence of what he must have learnt from Walton. Donne, according to his biographer, when he knew that his end was near, had himself wrapped up in a winding-sheet, and gave instructions to a sculptor to represent him on his tomb as he thus appeared. Ken, in the same spirit, but without the theatrical element which slightly mingled with Donne's act, when he learnt from his physician that he had but

---

[1] The *Lives* themselves were not written till Walton was an inmate in Morley's house after the Restoration.

a few hours to live, took the shroud which for years before he
had always carried with him in his portmanteau, put it on with
his own hands, and so calmly lay down to await the end.[1]   The
continuity of spirit which united the two men, and the channel
through which that continuity was maintained, was not without
a fitting symbol linking the three together.   Donne left by his
will to a few special friends a gold signet-ring, in which was set a

heliotrope, *i.e.* blood-stone, with a figure of the Crucified One, not on the cross, but on an anchor, as the em-
blem of hope.   One of these rings he left to Walton;
from him it passed on to Ken, who wore and used it to
the latest years of his life.[2]   His will was sealed with it.

In Sir H. Wotton, Ken had before him a pattern of a different
type;   a man reared in the diplomacy of courts, skilled in the
speech and literature of France and Italy, whose maxims of social
wisdom, upright statecraft, and ecclesiastical moderation were
often on Walton's lips, as they were afterwards recorded in his
Life of his friend.   Here too the friendship affected even the
outward facts of Ken's life.   Wotton had been trained at the
two St. Mary Winton Colleges, and almost the last fact that
Walton narrates concerning him is his visit to Winchester, in
1639, two months before his death, and the touching memories
of past years which that visit brought back to him.   There were
the same scenes, the same school-rooms, cloisters, playground,
almost, it might seem, the same boys, as he had known in his
youth, and it was pleasant to look back on those days as a time
of hope and purity and promise, which had not altogether failed
of their fulfilment.   With the impression of that former intercourse upon him, we can well enter into the feeling which led
Walton, as the friend and adviser of the Ken family, probably
after the death of the boy's father, to select Winchester,
rather than Eton or Westminster, as the school to which his
brother-in-law was to be sent.[3]   When in after years his own son

[1] II. 202. Herrick, who wrote a charming little poem, *To His Winding Sheet*,
did the same. (C. J. P.)

[2] One such seal is now at Longleat. A smaller seal, with the same design,
probably that referred to in the text, also used by him, passed to Miss Hawkins,
the daughter of his great-nephew, and is now in the possession of the Rev. E.
C. Merewether. It is from this that the woodcut is taken.

[3] Ken's uncle, John Chalkhill, however, was, as has been said above (p. 12), a
Fellow of Winchester, and this may have helped to determine Walton's choice.

travelled under that brother's care to France and Italy we may think of him as giving them at second hand the maxim of *Viso sciolto, pensieri stretti,* with which, as we know, Milton had been fortified by Wotton for his wanderings among a strange people and the members of an alien church. So, in like manner, amid the strifes of tongues and hot debates that raged around him Ken would call to mind the golden saying of which Wotton had said that all that he desired to have written on his tomb was that he was its author,

Disputandi pruritus, ecclesiarum scabies,

and it would keep him, and did keep him, and almost him alone, of all the divines and prelates of his time, from preaching polemic sermons and writing controversial treatises.[1]

In George Herbert, as in Donne, the young Ken would find a spirit like-minded with his own, calm, meditative, musical, finding in quaint, devout verse, the natural channel for the thoughts that were working on his mind, and singing hymns to his lute, and in all those points we may think of Ken as a kind of Herbert *redivivus,* taking that life for the pattern of his own. They started indeed from a very different point. Herbert belonged to one of the noble families of England ; Ken was the son of a reputable citizen and attorney. All the more would he be likely to reverence one who presented in his Cambridge life, before he took orders, the ideal of what an Englishman of high birth might be. When Ken came into contact with court life, as it was in the days of Charles II., with all its foul profligacy and godless rowdyism, it was some-thing for him to remember that the aristocracy of England had, at times, at least, produced examples of a nobler life.

It is not, however, in any of these respects, only or chiefly, that I point to the life of George Herbert as having influenced Ken. It is in the Bishop's work as a parish priest that I trace Herbert's influence most distinctly. The *Country Parson* might almost seem to pass from precept to practice, from the

---

[1] Two more maxims of Wotton deserve notice, as illustrated by Ken's life and character : (1) that in which he summed up his experience as a statesman, *Animos fieri sapientiores quiescendo ;* and (2) the motto which he chose for his *In Memoriam* rings to the Fellows of Eton, *Amor unit omnia.* (C. J. P.)

abstract to the concrete, as we see Ken in his parochial and other labours. I will not anticipate the details, which will find their natural and fitting place farther on. It will be enough to note here one or two striking instances of parallelism. Does Herbert lay stress on the importance of training boys and girls to be confirmed and become communicants at an earlier age than was then, or is now, customary, as soon, in fact (to use his own words), "as they were able to distinguish sacramental from common bread, at what age soever" (c. xxii.) ? We find Ken, in his *Manual for Winchester Scholars*, assuming, at a time when boys left school sooner than they do now, that many of them would be, or ought to be, communicants. Is Herbert's *Country Parson* one who, while open-hearted to all real suffering, is chary of giving to "beggars and idle persons," lest by so doing he should do more harm than good ? It is Ken's first care, as we shall see, on coming to his diocese, to endeavour (not, as it chanced, successfully) to work out the scheme of something like a Charity Organization Society (p. 252), and the echo of Herbert's teaching on this matter is found in the picture of an ideal king in Ken's *Edmund*, of whom he says that in his kingdom—

> "No sturdy beggars in his lands could lurk,
> But were in proper houses forced to work."
>
> *Works*, ii., 50.

Does Herbert dwell on the duty of daily service ? Ken made that service his rule as a parish priest, and enforced it as a bishop, however small might be the congregation that could be brought to attend it. All that we know of his life as rector of Little Easton, and, practically, chaplain to Lord Maynard, is based upon the lines which we find in the *Country Parson* (c. ii.). I close my induction with the noticeable fact that Herbert lays special stress (c. xi.) on his Parson inviting the poorer members of his flock to dine with him on Sundays, to sit down with them and carve for them, and that this was precisely what Ken did, even as the occupant of his palace at Wells (p. 252).

Passing from Herbert to Hooker, it will be obvious to every one who studies Ken's character as a divine, that his theology was essentially on the lines of the *Ecclesiastical Polity*, Anglican, as distinguished from the two extremes of Romanism and Puritanism, with, as will be seen here-after,[1] a leaning to a wider hope as to the extent of the love of God and the work of Christ than we find in his master; and that this was so at a time when Hooker's work was comparatively a recent book, not as yet recognised in bishops' examinations or university lectures. We note further that Ken's thoughts habitually turned, as did Hooker's on his death-bed, to "meditations on the ministry of angels." But, if I mistake not, the chief influence which Walton's *Life of Hooker* exercised on him must have been negative rather than positive. I fancy that the story of the great mistake of Hooker's *Life*, the one instance in which he was not "judicious," must have been often told at Walton's table, and we can enter into the feelings of a boy even then, in one sense, precociously ascetic and devout, as he listened to it. That picture of the author of the *Ecclesiastical Polity*, as he sat tending his sheep in a common field because his servant was gone home to dine, or rocking the cradle, while the harsh nagging voice of his wife was heard, calling "Richard, Richard," in dictatorial tones; the feelings of the old pupils, George Cranmer and Edwin Sandys, both of them connected with Walton by marriage,[2] who, unable to veil their impressions in silence or conventional courtesies, were constrained to offer him their condolences "that he had not a more comfortable wife;" all this must have seemed to the young student sufficiently humiliating. One who was naturally of what we may call the celibate temperament, disposed, in regard to the other sex, to friendship rather than love, could scarcely fail to say to himself, on hearing such a tale, "If that is what a man may sometimes get in the lottery of marriage, I for one will choose the other part and not that." The outcome of his thoughts, over and above the fact of his choice of celibacy, may be found in two lines, written in after years—

---

[1] Hooker had insisted on the salvability of Papists (*Serm. II*). Ken included the Heathen who lived according to their light within his hopes. (See ch. xxviii.)

[2] Walton's first wife, Rachel Flood, was descended from the Cranmer family, as also was Sandys. The two visitors sought another and quieter lodging for the night.

"A virgin priest the altar best attends;
Our Lord that state commands not, but commends."

That may have been the starting point of what was afterwards a matter of mild pleasantry among the Bishop's friends, that he made a vow every morning as he rose, that "he wouldn't be married that day."[1] I am disposed to think, from the stress laid on promissory vows in Ken's *Exposition of the Catechism*, that he may have had some such resolve present to his thoughts at his ordination, if not before.

The last of Walton's *Lives*, that of Sanderson, belongs to too late a date (1677) to be numbered among the influences by which Ken's character was fashioned, and Sanderson himself had left Oxford before Ken entered it. The latter, however, may have heard Walton's account of his interesting conversation with Sanderson in 1655. All that need be said under this head, therefore, is that the "casuistry" (I use the term in its truest and noblest sense) by which Ken was guided in the intricate labyrinth of questions which the political crisis of the time brought before him, a casuistry as unlike as possible to that of Jesuit confessors or time-serving statesmen, was, as will be seen hereafter, precisely what might have been expected from one who had laid the foundations of his ethics under the teaching of Sanderson. It led him to be faithful, at whatever cost, to the supreme authority of conscience, and when he was in doubt and the scales were nearly balanced, to decide in favour of the conclusion which brought least of the profit and pleasure by the hope of which most men allow their judgments to be biassed.

One point more remains to be noticed, and then I have completed my case as to Izaak Walton and his influence on Ken's life. The will of the former contains, as was common with devout persons of that period, a confession of his faith, and the confession runs thus :—

"Because the profession of Christianity does at this time seem to be subdivided into Papist and Protestant, I take it to be at least convenient to declare my belief to be, in all points of faith, as the Church of England now professeth, and this I do, the rather because

---

[1] Southey's *Omniana*, p. 206.

of a very long and very true friendship with some of the Roman Church." [1]

I do not quote these words wholly or chiefly on account of their striking parallelism with Ken's own confession of faith, which will find its proper place at the close of this biography, though this is singularly suggestive, but for the fact to which the last words point. Roman Catholics, we may well believe, as those words show, of the highest and best type, were among Walton's cherished friends, and may well have been frequent visitors at his house.   One who was brought up in the midst of such surroundings may well have learnt to shrink from the hot anathemas and præternatural suspicion with which ordinary Englishmen looked upon a Papist. His personal experience must have given force to that other maxim of Sir Henry Wotton's, that "men were surely in error if they thought that the farther they were from Rome the nearer they were to truth."   To have known and loved men of what we regard as an alien or corrupted Church, though it does not take away the sadness of controversy, at least deprives it of its bitterness.   This helps also to explain the attitude consistently maintained by Ken in the midst of the unhappy divisions of his time.   It accounts for the hopes of James II. that he might even win the most loved and honoured of English bishops to his side, and for the suspicion which ever and anon dogged Ken's footsteps that he really inclined to Rome.   Looking at his character all round, I know nothing that more helps one to understand it than the portrait that has been drawn, with a master's hand, by Mr. Shorthouse, of one more or less of the same type, and growing up under somewhat of the same influences, in his *John Inglesant*, and worked out with a more subtle analysis in the *Introduction* to his edition of George Herbert's *Poems*.

---

[1] I conjecture that among these may have been Crashaw, the poet, Christopher Davenport, better known as Francis à Sanctâ Clarâ, an Oxford convert, who wrote a treatise more or less anticipating Cardinal Newman's treatment of the Thirty-nine Articles in *Tract XC.*, and Hugh Serenus de Cressy, whom Mr. Shorthouse brings into his *John Inglesant*. (See page 275, chap. xix.) I find works by the first two in the catalogue of Ken's books at Longleat, and by the third among those which he left to the Cathedral Library at Wells.

How far that portraiture is a satisfactory representation of
the type after which I believe Ken to have been fashioned—
how far the analysis of character, which seems to Mr. Shorthouse a sufficient account of George Herbert's excellence, is
adequate—are questions which may admit of more or less difference of opinion.[1] It may, I think, be contended that Mr. Shorthouse has laid too exclusive a stress on the refinement, the
gentlemanliness, as it were, of the religious character of the
Laudian, or so-called Anglo-Catholic school, of which the
Oxford movement was a revival. Doubtless that was prominent
in it. It accounts, in part at least, for the almost invincible
antipathy with which the middle-class Englishman, tradesman
or farmer,—the " Philistine " of Matthew Arnold's classifica-
tion—has from the first regarded it. It seemed to him an
aristocratic form of religion, and therefore, over and above his
suspicion of its Popish tendencies he opposed it and disliked it,
as he disliked other aristocratic characteristics. It accounts
also for the fact that that school of thought has never as yet
exercised, as Wesley and Whitefield exercised, a power over
those of a yet lower social *stratum*—the artisans and the
working-men of England—outside the range of agricultural
labourers. The sweetness and light and tenderness of the
Country Parson might win individuals, but it was lacking in
the intensity of power which can wield at will the multitudes of a spiritual democracy, and move the miners of Cornwall or the colliers of Bristol, as Wesley moved them, to the
tears of penitence. But there was with all this refinement, this
love of music and of song, this union of the temper of the
ascetic and the man of letters, a certain heroism of conscience
in Ken and his fellows which is not, I think, portrayed in
John Inglesant, or recognised adequately in the introductory
analysis of Herbert.[2]

[1] See article by the Rev. H. Wace, D.D., Principal of King's College, London,
in the *Churchman* of May, 1883.

[2] I venture, with Mr. Shorthouse's permission, to reproduce part of a letter
on this chapter as it stood in my first proof:—" I do not think that any one
could suppose that I meant John Inglesant to stand as a typical churchman of
his day, seeing that he was brought up by a Jesuit in a most exceptional manner ; but what is infinitely more important than any reference to my writings
can be, is an expression, which I fear may be misunderstood, in what you say

These men might have wide sympathies on either side—
might feel that there was much in the system of Rome and
in the lives of Romanists which they could admire and love;
but they did not, when they had to make their choice between
truth and falsehood, right and wrong, halt between two
opinions. They saw the thing that ought to be done, and
they did it, regardless of consequences. If they had a weak
element of character in this respect, it was that their fear of
following a multitude to do evil led them almost instinctively
to start with a bias to the cause that was not the multitude's.
They would not tune their voice according to the time to gain
the favour of princes or of people. There are men, not without a certain measure of honesty—men who would not consciously descend to baseness for the sake of gain and honour,
and who rise to the high places of the earth in Church and
State amid the plaudits of their fellows—who seem to act on
the rule given to inexperienced whist-players, "When in doubt,
take the trick." Most of Ken's contemporaries belonged to this
class. They passed from régime to régime, from one form of
worship to another, unconscious of reproach. They took oaths,

about the antipathy of the middle-class Englishmen, tradesmen, and farmers, to
the Anglo-Catholic School. I fear this may be understood by some people to
mean 'antipathy to the Church of England.' If it means only antipathy to
those called ignorantly and vulgarly 'Ritualists' it may be true to a certain
extent, but, in this case, it is not applicable to my Introduction to *George
Herbert*, because all I claim of refinement there refers simply to the Church of
England as a whole. I expressly point out that Herbert himself was not even a
Laudian, neither were any of the men I mention—Donne and Wotton, and
George Wither, Francis Quarles, and Henry Vaughan. Religion is a 'refiner's
fire,' and that religion which is coarse and vulgar is so far an imperfect religion,
though it may be a real one. My experience has led me to note a wonderful
refinement in those of the working classes who have been brought under the
influence of the Church of England. I should regard it as a national mis-
fortune, should it appear, by any misunderstanding of a single phrase, that you
thought that the Church of England was not attractive to, or had lost touch
with, the lower, or working, classes, though, of course, a Church which main-
tains a lofty standard cannot compete with *all natures* and at *all times* with such
as avowedly descend to a lower level." Another friend (R. C. B.) writes :—" Is
not the Philistine hatred to Anglo-Catholicism rather called forth by the true
democracy of the Church, the witness which she bears against the mean estimate
of their poorer brethren which the middle-class too often take? . . . . Surely,
Herbert's ploughmen at Bemerton and the Holborn artisans who attend St.
Alban's were, and are, not inaccessible to refined and refining religious influences."

from that of the League and Covenant, under the Long Parliament, to that of abjuration under Queen Anne, with a facility
which reminds one of Talleyrand's "aside" when he swore allegiance to Louis Philippe: "It is the thirteenth; Heaven grant it
may be the last!" With Ken and his fellows it was just the
opposite of this. The rule on which they appear to have acted
was, "When in doubt, take the losing side. Follow the path
which leads, not to wealth and honour, but to loss, privation,
contumely." We can think of them as giving thanks, as Mr.
Maurice did in the later years of his life, that they had always
been on the side of the minority.[1]

The inquiry which has furnished the materials for this
chapter has at least taught me something over and above its
immediate object. As I have dwelt on that home of Walton's,
retaining its calm and cheerfulness and even mirth in the midst
of the confusions of the age, I seem to myself to have understood, almost for the first time, what it was that led the poet
of our own age whose spirit was most akin to Ken's, to fix on
it as an oasis in the dreary wilderness of controversy. The
succession of the witnesses for a higher and serener life seems,
at first, a somewhat strange one. First St. Jerome, and then
St. Louis, and, to complete the series—

"A fouler vision yet; an age of light—
    Light without love,—dawns on the aching sight;
        O who can tell how fair and sweet,
            Meek Walton! shows thy green retreat,
    When, wearied with the tale thy times disclose,
The eye first finds thee out in thy secure repose?"[2]

[1] *Life*, by Col. Maurice, ii. 69.
[2] *Christian Year.* Advent Sunday.

CHAPTER III.

" Blessings in boyhood's marvelling hour,
    Bright dreams, and fancyings strange ;
Blessings, when reason's awful power
    Gave thought a bolder range."

J. H. Newman.

THE analysis of the elements in the surroundings of Ken's early years which was the subject of the last chapter anticipated, as was inevitable, some of the facts that belong to a later period in his life. We have now to go back to the time, to give the precise date, January 30, $165\frac{1}{2}$, the third anniversary of Charles I.'s execution, when "Thomas Ken of Berkhampstead, in the county of Hertford," was admitted on the foundation of Winchester College as a scholar. His election had taken place on September 26, 1651.

Biographers for the most part record the fact as if it were of much the same character as that of any other boy going to any other school at any other time. They forget to take into account that the public school-life of that period was utterly unlike anything that had preceded or that has followed it. It was the school of the Puritan Revolution, and the change which passed over the methods of English education, so far as it affected the religious life of boys, was nearly as great, though of a different character, as that which passed over the education of France under the influence of the anti-Christian, if not atheistic,[1] French Revolution. There, at Winchester, as elsewhere, there had been a great upheaving of the traditions of

---

[1] Robespierre's discourse on the *Être Suprême* leads me to insert the qualifying words.

the past.[1] The soldiers of the Parliament profaned the Cathedral with their rough horse-play, and paraded the streets in surplices till their disorders were stopped by their commander, Colonel Fiennes. The Cathedral services and those of the school chapel, if not suspended altogether, must have been entirely altered in their character.[2] The Westminster Directory had taken the place of the Prayer Book, the Westminster Catechism had superseded that of the Church of England. The Warden of Winchester, Dr. John Harris (1630—1658), formerly Professor of Greek at Oxford and Prebendary of Winchester, was a member of the Westminster Assembly of Divines, appointed by Parliament in 1643, by which those two documents were framed.[3] The Warden, however, then as now, exercised only a general superintendence over the College, and the actual instruction of the boys was in the hands of the *Informator,* or head-master, Mr. Pottenger (1651), and Mr. Burt (1654), who became Warden on Harris's death in 1658, and Mr. Phillips, the *Ostiarius,* or second master. In the absence of adequate *data* of information as to the school-life of England during the period of the Commonwealth, one is left in some measure to construct for this period of Ken's life an ideal biography; but assuming the average conditions of boy nature, it is probable enough that the strife which had rent asunder the social life of England reproduced itself in the school at Winchester, and that the boys whom Ken found there on his admission were ranged under opposing banners as Roundheads and Cavaliers, each trying to assert itself against the other. Under such circumstances a boy whose antecedents were like Ken's, who still said his Collects in the dormitory and observed fasts and festivals, would be likely enough to find himself pointed at as a formalist and prelatist, as a Papist or a "follower of Canterbury," even if this were not followed up by more

[1] At Sherborne, *e.g.,* the captain of the Parliamentary forces, after taking the castle in 1650, compelled the governors of the school to remove the royal arms. They were of course replaced at the Restoration.

[2] I am told, however, that the College accounts show that a musical service of some kind, was kept up during the Parliamentary and Commonwealth regime.

[3] There is no evidence, however, that Harris made more than a single appearance at the 1163 Meetings of the Assembly. Neal (ii. 702) says that he took the Covenant and so remained in his office.

active persecution.[1] Even then the young *Philotheus* (I use his own term for his ideal Winchester scholar) may have had to pass through some of the trials that were as the training for that suffering for conscience' sake, which was afterwards, even if we think that he suffered for an unworthy cause, the glory of his later life. If the child is the father of the man, and if, therefore, we may idealise backward from the Bishop to the boy, it may be that he found among the boys of the other side some whom he could learn to love, pure, devout, truthful, and whom I can picture him as protecting from the rough handling of his Cavalier playmates. In these trials it is probable that he found a friend and companion, probably also a protector, in Francis Turner, afterwards Bishop of Ely (one of the seven bishops who shared Ken's deprivation), with whom he was united in after years in the bonds of a life-long friendship of the David and Jonathan, or Pylades and Orestes type, or, to take a parallel from the more recent records of Winchester, like that which bound together Lord Hatherley and Dean Hook from their earliest boyhood at that school to their death.[2]   Other school friends were John Nicholas, elected in the same year with Ken, afterwards, in succession, Warden of New College and Winchester, whom we shall meet again (p. 124), and, for his last two years, Edward Young, afterwards Fellow of the College and Dean of Salisbury.

[1] So, in a later generation, the boys of Winchester arranged themselves as Jacobites or Hanoverians.—Adams, *Wykehamica*, p. 112.

[2] Turner will meet us so often in the course of this narrative that it may be well to give the principal facts in his career. He was born in 1636, and was therefore a year older than Ken. His father was successively chaplain to Charles I. and Dean of Rochester and Canterbury. He went to New College a year before Ken. In 1664 he was presented to the living of Therfield, in Hertfordshire; in November, 1670, he was elected Master of St. John's College, Cambridge, where he was the intimate friend of Peter Gunning, who had brought him to Cambridge (1666) with a view to his succeeding him in the Mastership, and whom he succeeded also in the Bishopric of Ely, in 1684, having in the meantime been chaplain to the Duke of York, Dean of Windsor (February, 1684), and Bishop of Rochester. (See Baker's *History of St. John's*, 1689, p. 273.) Like Ken, he was a poet, and wrote hymns. He also published a life of Nicholas Ferrar, of Little Gidding. His later life will come before us once and again, as closely connected with that of his old schoolfellow. In many ways he and Ken had much in common, but he was more vigorous and impulsive, and their friendship rested on qualities in which each was complementary to the other.

He was the father of the author of the *Night Thoughts*, and preached Ken's Consecration Sermon.

So far as the instruction element of education was concerned, Ken's position was not unfavourable. Harris was a good scholar, and Savile (the editor of Chrysostome) spoke of his preaching as second only to that of the " golden-mouthed " one.   So far as the power of the preacher depends on training, whatever natural gifts Ken had been endowed with were under fair conditions for their culture.

How far the boy shared in the sports of the school, or what under the Puritan régime those sports were, is again a matter on which we are left to guess.   One pictures him to one's self as not much of an athlete—meditative, studious, devout, shrinking alike from the roughness of those of whom Matthew Arnold used to speak as " barbarians," and from the Pharisaism of the " Philistines," from the sons of the " King's men " and the " Parliament men " with whom he was associated.[1]

When Ken went to Winchester, in January, $165\frac{1}{2}$, he was probably an orphan.[2]   Those who have passed through a like experience will acknowledge that such a bereavement at that age makes all the future different from all the past.   The boy stands more alone, is more dependent on himself.   According to his character, he becomes the better or the worse for it.   He asserts a false independence, or drifts about aimlessly for want of guidance ; or he forms the habit of acting with greater foresight, and learns the secret of self-mastery, or, it may be, finds refuge in the thought of the Eternal Fatherhood, and seeks there for the counsel and the comfort of which the death of his earthly father has deprived him. It is something more than a legitimate conjecture to assume that Ken chose the " better part " of the latter alternative, that his life became more inward and therefore stronger ; more self-sustained, because he was resting on the support of the Everlasting Arms.   One result of the sorrow would, in the

[1] A tradition, which I am unable to trace, reported by the late Rev. H. L. Dodd, speaks of him as having been among the earliest and best cricketers of Winchester.   See Trower's *Sussex Cricket, past and present.*

[2] His father's will is dated April 12th, 1651.   I have been unable to ascertain the precise date of his death.

nature of things, be to knit his affections more closely to those who yet remained to him, and the house of Izaak Walton would be more and more a home to him.[1]

Anyhow, whatever were the trials and sorrows of that period of his life, it is true of boys, as of men, that—

"Time and the hour runs through the roughest day."

Life had to be lived, lessons learnt, games played; there were walks in Winchester and in London and by the Lea, or perhaps in Staffordshire by the Dove, which the *Complete Angler* has made famous, with his sister and with Walton. There was the boy's eagerness as a devourer of books finding its satisfaction in what we have seen to have been his brother-in-law's well-stored library. He would form his taste in poetry on Donne, Herbert, Cowley, and perhaps even then deepen the foundations of his faith in Nowell and Hooker and Bishop Hall. And so the years passed on till he was in the highest form of the school and all but superannuated, and the important day came when the Warden of New College (Dr. Stringer) and two Fellows came on the election Tuesday (September 6th, 1656) to examine the candidates for admission to the higher of the two St. Mary Winton Colleges, better known as New College, Oxford. The result was that Ken was chosen to the second place on the list, after founder's kin, but as there was at the time no vacancy in the Fellowships there, he had to wait and take his chance of what might happen in the year that followed.[2] In the meantime he was entered by Walton at Hart Hall, probably, as we have seen (p. 20), because it was associated with the latter's memories of Donne.

Scanty as our knowledge is of the actual life of the school at Winchester in Ken's time, we can at all events believe that some of its older traditions were not altogether interrupted, and can picture to ourselves the impression which they must have

[1] Ken's maternal uncle, John Chalkhill, was, as we have seen (p. 12), Fellow of Winchester from 1633 to 1679, but whether he resided there is doubtful.

[2] Strictly speaking, boys from Winchester took their place at New College not as Scholars, but as Fellows. The present Head Master of Winchester was the first ever elected under the former title.

left on a mind like Ken's.   It was, perhaps, believed that the
old Latin morning hymn—

Jam lucis orto sidere,

had been composed for the scholars of Winton.[1]   There was,
perhaps, the *Dulce domum*, dear to the heart of all Wykehamists,[2]
with its cheery verses—

> "*Musa! libros mitte, fessa ;*
> *Mitte pensa dura,*

[1] The statement has, I need hardly say, no historical foundation, but it is
given by Bowles (I. 16), who was an old Wykehamist, in his *Life of Ken.*
The hymn, *Jam lucis*, belongs to the fifth century, and was, perhaps, written by
St. Ambrose.   It had been used from an early date in the Roman office for *Prime*,
and, therefore, had been sung daily at Winchester to the time of the Reformation.   It would seem to have held its place in the School Services in the sixteenth
and seventeenth centuries, to have been disused in the eighteenth.   A scholarly
Warden, like Harris, was likely, I think, to combine its use with the Westminster Directory.   Its occasional use has been recently revived.   It can scarcely,
I think, be questioned that Ken's Morning Hymn for his *Philotheus* was an echo
of what he had learnt at Winchester in his own boyhood, and I therefore submit
the *Jam lucis* itself, and a translation, to the reader who may wish to compare
the two :—

JAM LUCIS ORTO SIDERE.

"Jam lucis orto sidere,
Deum precemur supplices,
Ut, in diurnis actibus,
Nos servet à nocentibus.

"Lo! sunrise floods the world with light,
Let us to God as suppliants pray
That He will guide our way aright,
In all we think or do this day.

"Linguam refrænans temperet,
Ne litis horror insonet :
Visum fovendo contegat
Ne vanitates hauriat.

"May He our heedless lips restrain,
That strife's loud clamour sound not thence;
May He hide from us all things vain,
And veil our eyes with innocence.

"Sint pura cordis intima ;
Absistat et vecordia,
Carnis terat superbiam
Potus cibique parcitas :

"Pure let the heart's deep fountain be,
And idle sloth be driven afar ;
In all we eat or drink may we
Tame lusts that with the soul make war.

"Ut, cum dies abscesserit,
Noctemque sors reduxerit,
Mundi per abstinentiam
Ipsi canamus gloriam."

"So, when the day shall vanish hence,
And on it falls the gloom of night,
May we, made pure by abstinence,
Praise Him, His glory and His might.'

[2] I speak with some doubt.   Adams (*Wyk.* p. 410) says that it came into use
between 1675 and 1700.   Bowles (I. 18) says it was used before the Reformation.
John Reading, who composed the tune to which it is now sung, was organist,
1681—9.

Mitte negotium,
Jam datur otium,
Me mea mittito cura.

" *Ridet annus, prata rident,*
  Nosque rideamus ;
Jam repetit domum
Daulias advena ;
  Nosque domum repetamus." [1]

For one who in later years idealised himself under the name
of Hymnotheo these fragments from the music and hymnology
of the past must even then, I take it, have had an almost priceless value.[2]   They were witnesses of something better than the
jarring strife of tongues and the bitter mutual anathemas in
the midst of which he found himself.   Even if, as is possible
under the Puritan ascendency, the Latin hymns were no longer
sung, they may still have lived in the traditions of the school.
He would read the warning words, *Aut Disce aut Discede : Manet*
sors tertia, cædi.[3]   The motto of William of Wykeham—

"𝔐𝔞𝔫𝔫𝔢𝔯𝔰 𝔐𝔞𝔲𝔶𝔱𝔥 𝔐𝔞𝔫,"

was still the watchword of the college.   His statutes—which

---

[1] I venture here also on a translation of three verses, including the two given
in the text :—

> " At last the hour is drawing near,
>   Hour of joy and pleasure,
> After months of wear and tear
>   Comes the longed-for leisure.

> " Away with tasks, away with books,
>   Away with toil and sadness,
> Our holiday no lesson brooks ;
>   After care comes gladness.

> " The year, the fields, with smiles are drest,
>   Let smiles, too, deck our faces ;
> Seek we, as swallow seeks her nest,
>   Our home's familiar places."

[2] Yet earlier traditions may have come before him.   In his epic of *Edmund*
he identifies Winchester with the Arthurian Camelot.   The whole poem is full
of interesting reminiscences of Winchester, traditions of Arthur, St. Swithin,
and the like.

[3] In their present position, the words belong to the generation that followed
Ken, but they have an earlier ring about them.

D 2

contained for juniors this rule, "*præfectis obtemperato*," and
for præpostors, "*legitimè imperato*," and for both, "*uterque
a mendaciis, ostentationibus, jurgiis, pugnis, et furtis abstineto*"
—must have been impressed on Ken's mind as a counsel for
the guidance of his life. The strange symbolic figure of the
Trusty Servant, familiar to all Wykehamists, could scarcely
fail to be interpreted by a mind early trained to understand
parables.[1] In the *Manual for Winchester Scholars*, which he
wrote in after years, in the directions which he gives to his
young Philotheus (the choice of the name for the ideal
scholar is singularly suggestive) for morning prayers in the
chapel "between the first and second peal," to avoid the interruptions of the "common chamber" or dormitory,[2] and for
evening prayers as he went *Circum;*[3] for reading "before second
peal " " some short psalm, or piece of a chapter out of the Gospel
or historical books, because they are most easy to be understood ; " for listening devoutly when Scripture was " daily read
in the hall before dinner and supper; " for profiting by the
hymns and psalms which were " sung so frequently in his
chamber, in the chapel, and in the hall; " for preparing for
the "blessed sacrament " and "rightly approaching the holy
altar ; " by withdrawing into his chamber or the chapel, and
there "communing with his own heart," we may legitimately
trace, in part (making due allowance for the changes caused in

---

[1] The present painting dates from the early part of the eighteenth century
but the figure is known to have existed in 1560.—Adams, *Wyk.*, p. 42.

[2] I may note, as a feature in the school-life of the time, that the scholars of
Winchester then slept in truckle-beds on the floor. They owed their bedsteads
to Bishop Trelawney, who succeeded Peter Mews in 1707. At 5 A.M. the pre-
fect of the chamber gave the order to rise. The boys said some Latin psalms
before dressing, combed their hair, and made their beds (till 1540 they had only
bundles of straw), and said their private prayers.—(Adams, *Wyk.*, p. 83). Trelawney substituted 6 A.M. for 5 A.M. during the winter half-year.

[3] The phrase refers to the practice, now discontinued, of a procession round
the cloisters, to a bench in the ambulatory, where the boys said their prayers
before they went to bed. (Adams, *Wyk.*, p. 39.) Bishop Charles Wordsworth,
in his *College of St. Mary, Winton* (pp. 42–46), prints two Psalms for morning
and evening use by the scholars of Winchester, *in cubiculo*, which were printed
at Oxford (1616) in a volume of *Preces*, &c., compiled by Dr. Hugh Robinson,
then Head Master. They are mainly from the Vulgate Psalms. They may
have been continued to be used under Harris. Warton, Head Master from 1766
to 1793, states that they were still used then.

some of these matters by the Puritan discipline), what had been his own practices in striving after the higher life, in part also, perhaps, his recollection of the omissions through which he seemed to himself to have fallen short of it.[1]

I must not close the story of Ken's boy-life at Winchester without touching on the fact, familiar as it is, that he left one outward and visible record of his presence there. On the stone buttress of the south-east corner of the cloister we still read the name "THO. KEN. 1656."[2] It was the last year of his sojourn there. It was probably, as it were, his farewell to the school, to which he then little dreamt that he should ever return in another character. We speak sometimes harshly of that English name-cutting habit (not exclusively English though) which leads boys or men thus to commemorate their existence. We are shocked, as Ken must afterwards have been in his own cathedral,[3] to see the stately monuments of prelates and nobles disfigured from head to foot with the initials or names of nobodies; but there are instances in which, as the walls and desks of all our public schools show, we look on the graven letters as with a strange fascination. The hand that cut them

[1] A question meets us which I wish I was able to answer. Confirmation is so important an epoch in a boy's religious life that we should gladly learn when, and by what bishop, Ken was confirmed. Under the Puritan regime it is obvious that it could not have been at Winchester. Even Evelyn (*Diary*, June 7, 1657) had to get his child baptized in secret by Jeremy Taylor. Bishop Hall of Norwich (died 1656), and Bishop Skinner, however, continued to ordain during the Commonwealth, and probably therefore confirmed also. It is likely enough that Walton may have had Skinner or other episcopal visitors in his house in Staffordshire, and one of them may have laid hands on Ken. Hall published a *Treatise on Confirmation* (1645), in which he complains of its being generally neglected in all the reformed churches, England included. Devon and Cornwall, curiously enough, are named by him as counties in which the common people still desired it. The Bursar's accounts at Winchester show that Holy Communion was administered, when Ken was there, at Christmas and Easter, and on All Saints' Day. A choral service of some kind was also kept up.

[2] The name is also found in the north-western corner of the cloister, as is that of Ken's friend, Francis Turner. The initials, T. K., also occur twice in the same positions. If the second occurrence of the name be Ken's work—though less clear than the first, Mr. Whymper is, I think, right in engraving "Ken" there also—it would show that he had revisited the school in the year after his election.

[3] I find on the ancient monuments of Bishop Ralph of Shrewsbury, and Bishop Beckyngton, in Wells Cathedral, names and dates which carry the practice back to 1676; but there are probably earlier undated instances.

there wielded afterwards the pen, the sword, the pastoral staff, and did great things with it. The rough carving becomes an unconscious prophecy. The boy left his mark in the school, the man will leave it in the world.

NAME IN CLOISTERS, WINCHESTER.

CHAPTER IV.

"Few though the faithful, and fierce though the foe,
  Yet weakness is aye Heaven's might."

J. H. Newman (p. 76).

HERE again, at Oxford as at Winchester, our first step towards
any clear apprehension of Ken's education must be to realise
the fact that university life with him was very different from
that life as we commonly picture it to ourselves in the present
or the past.   Here also the Puritan revolution had triumphed,
and when Ken entered on his career at Oxford, there had been
a great upturning of all things.   The colleges had, as is read in
every history, devoted themselves, with rare exceptions, loyally
and heartily, to the King.   He had held his courts and parliament within their walls.   The younger members had enlisted in
his army, under Prince Rupert.   College plate, flagons, salvers,
cups, that would now be of priceless value among the treasures
of South Kensington, were cast into the melting-pot to supply
his treasury.[1]   His bishops and chaplains, the high churchmen
of the school of Laud and Montague and Hammond, the
staunchest preachers of the divine right of kings and of passive
obedience, were then of paramount authority.   But a change
had passed over Oxford.   The King's cause waned as that of
the Parliament waxed strong, and the University had to pay the

---

[1] I note, as a fact, which, as yet, I cannot explain, that New College, though
conspicuously loyal, does not appear in the list of the contributors. (Gutch,
i., 227.)   The plate was coined into money at New Inn Hall, and the coins bore
the legend, "*Exsurgat Deus; dissipentur inimici*"—Cromwell's prayer, we
remember, before Dunbar—and was commonly known as *Exsurgat* money.—
[C. J. P.]

penalty of its devotion. After the battle of Naseby, Fairfax laid siege to Oxford, and the town and University capitulated. It is no part of my work to trace the details of even that corner of the great history of the rebellion. It will be enough to note, in briefest outline, that the Lords and Commons assembled in Parliament had, on May 1st, 1647, passed an ordinance for "the Visitation and the Reformation of the University of Oxford, and the several Halls and Colleges therein.' As the first step of this decree twenty-four Visitors were appointed, fourteen laymen and ten Puritan divines, with Lord Pembroke at their head (appointed Chancellor in Feb., 1648), with all the wide authority of what one might almost call a roving commission. The whole power that had before been vested in the Visitors recognised by the statutes of the several colleges was transferred to them. They were to enforce the solemn League and Covenant, the "negative" oath, and the observance of the Westminster Directory, and further to "inquire and report upon all such persons as had borne arms against the Parliament.' As a Court of Appeal and Direction a standing Committee was appointed, consisting of twenty-six lords and fifty-two members of the House of Commons. The Visitors were for the most part men of little mark, but one or two deserve special notice. The chairman was Sir Nathaniel Brent, who as Vicar-General of England, and Judge of the Prerogative Court, as well as Warden of Merton, had at first been a strong supporter of the Royalist cause, but had afterwards joined that of the Parliament, had taken the Covenant, and, as a consequence, been displaced by the King from his Wardenship to make way for William Harvey, the King's physician, and famous to all ages as the discoverer of the circulation of the blood. On the surrender of Oxford to the Parliamentary forces Brent was reinstated in his office, and now took his place at the head of the Visitors in a smarting and vindictive temper.[1] With him were William Prynne, of Lincoln's Inn, whose *Histriomastix* had marked him out as a man of omnivorous erudition, and Thomas Cheynell, of Merton, who had worried Chillingworth on his

---

[1] He is said to have taken down the rich altar-hangings of Merton Chapel and used them for his bedroom (Ant. à Wood in Anderdon, p. 21).

death-bed in prison, and had anathematised his *Religion of Pro-testants* as that "cursed book," that "rotten and corrupted book," which "had seduced so many millions of souls."[1]   The rest, as I have said, were nobodies ; but it may be assumed of most, if not all, of those who belonged to the University, that they had winced under the Laudian régime, and now felt that the hour of revenge had come.   The Committee of Lords and Commons included nearly all the best known names of the sup-porters of the Parliamentary cause, but, as there is, as far as I can trace, no record of those who, from time to time, took part in its proceedings, it will be enough to note the name of Francis Rous, who had been prominent in the House of Commons under James and Charles, and was almost its leader in the Long Parlia-ment.   He was one of the lay members of the Westminster Assembly of Divines, and had been made Provost of Eton by the Parliament, was the chief "Trier of Preachers," the author of several theological works, and one of Cromwell's "Lords."   His name appears as its Chairman at the foot of all the resolutions of the Committee.

I must not enter fully on the tale of the way in which the Visitors began and carried on their work.   At first, as was natural, they were, as far as men dared, snubbed and thwarted. Sheldon, as Warden of All Souls, and others, notably including Sanderson, protested against their jurisdiction and against the League and Covenant.   They were treated superciliously by the Vice-Chancellor, burlesqued and satirised in pamphlets, flouted at by undergraduates.   These things, however, did but serve to irritate them.   They had the irresistible logic of the *force majeure* to back them, and they set to work in a "root and branch" style which was as thorough as the "thorough" of Laud and Strafford, on a wider scale of action, had been be-fore them.   They expelled right and left with an unsparing severity.   Reynolds was appointed Vice-Chancellor.   Heads of houses, and fellows and scholars and commoners, down to the very cooks and butlers and scouts, were summoned to appear

---

[1] It is right to add that Cheynell, who was appointed as President of St. John's, was expelled for not taking the "engagement" oath.   Reynolds forfeited the Deanery of Christ Church for the same reason, and was succeeded by John Owen.

before them, and if they refused to submit were summarily deprived.[1] The Westminster Directory, issued by order of Parliament in 1645, was enforced; "superstitious ornaments" (one knows what a wide latitude of interpretation would be given to those words by such men and at such a time) were removed from college chapels. The organs and the anthems were for the most part silenced. Sheldon, Hammond, Morley, and Sanderson were ejected from their respective posts, and the first two were imprisoned for not taking the Covenant and Negative Oath. Those who were thrust into the headships, canonries, fellowships, thus vacated, 497 in number, were many of them illiterate. They were, in the nature of the case, Puritans (whether Presbyterians or Independents, at first chiefly the former) of the severest type.[2]

Such was the Oxford into the life of which Ken entered as a member of Hart Hall in 1656. That society, one of the smaller bodies known as Halls, which served, as in Ken's case, as a place of sojourning for those who were waiting for admission to a college, or, sometimes, as in later days, as a city of refuge for those who had failed to obtain admission into, or had been ejected from, one, has had the singular destiny of having passed through four successive transformations.[3]

All that we know of the condition of this institution at the time when Ken entered into residence is chiefly to be inferred from the *Register of the Parliamentary Visitors,*[4] edited by Professor Burrows, and published by the Camden Society in 1881. It would appear (1) from the fact that only

---

[1] 375 Fellows and Scholars were deprived; 180 withdrew.—Neal, ii., 479.

[2] Burrows, p. lxxxix.

[3] Founded in 1282 as Hart Hall, it was chartered as Hertford College in 1740, dissolved from insufficiency of endowments in 1805; the site and part of its endowments transferred in 1816 to Magdalen Hall, when that institution, founded as a dependency of Magdalen College, 1480, and becoming an independent Hall in 1603, was burnt out of its old quarters; and finally, by the exertions of the Principal, Dr. Michell and the munificence of Mr. Thomas Baring, M.P., it was again chartered as Hertford College. with a splendid foundation for fourteen fellows and twenty-nine scholars"—(Burrows, p. 117). A brochure by Father Goldie, S.J., *A Bygone Oxford*, represents Hart Hall and St. John's Hall (now Worcester College), as places of refuge for Catholics. [C. J. P.]

[4] Wood, in his *Colleges and Halls*, gives some curious particulars in 1651—2 (C. W. B.). It was full before the Civil Wars began, but the members left Oxford when the King entered it, apparently as being on the other side.

three members of it were summoned to appear before the
Visitors, that it had fallen to a somewhat low level as regards
numbers ; and (2) from the immediate and full submission of
those three members to the Parliamentary Visitors, that they,
in common with the members of all the Halls, who seem to
have been in opposition to the majority of the Colleges, belonged
to the Puritan party. Of the three who are thus named
nothing further is known, and we may conclude that they
were persons of no special mark.[1]

Our ignorance in this matter is, however, of not much consequence. Ken remained at the Hall for a few months only,
and was admitted at New College to the longed-for fellowship
in 1657. I content myself with recording the names of the
fellows admitted at the same time, Richard Parsons, Edward
Colley, Ambrose Phillips, Edward Spenser, Christopher Min-
shull, William Darell, and John Nicholas, afterwards Warden
of New College, and then of Winchester.[2]

Here we know more, and what we know is sufficiently suggestive. Of all the Colleges in Oxford the foundation of
William of Wykeham was that on which the strong hand of
the Visitors fell most heavily, and, as we shall see, not without
cause. In the early stages of the struggle between the
King and the Parliament, its Warden, Dr. Robert Pink, had
formed a regiment of militia out of the fellows, scholars, and
other members of the society. The College became something
like a fortress, and helmets, and pikes, and muskets were
routed out and furbished up for use. Scholars were so
attracted by the activities and gaieties of military life that
they could never be brought to their books again.[3] Pink
himself belonged to the school of Laud, and his appointment of
such men as Isaac Barrow,[4] Peter Gunning, and Richard Sher-

---

[1] Burrows, p. 11.

[2] The rooms of the scholars of New College were known by distinctive names,
such as the "Vine," the "Baptist's Head," the "Star." Each chamber had four
beds and a small study, under the superintendence of a Fellow. Ken was in the
"Rose," and his old school friend, Turner, was one of his "chums."

[3] A. Wood, *Life*, p. 13.

[4] Not the famous Isaac Barrow, Master of Trinity College, Cambridge,
but his uncle, afterwards Bishop of St. Asaph, memorable among other things
for the inscription on his tomb in that cathedral, *Orate pro conservo vestro.*
The three Chaplains were all refugees from the Puritan oppression at Cambridge.

lock, father of the more famous Dean of St. Paul's, as chaplains, indicates that he was "thorough" as a member of that school. He, however, had died in 1647, in the early days of the rule of the Visitors, after being seized by the Parliamentary generals, and imprisoned in the Gate-house at Westminster. The Visitors, according to Walker,[1] thrust in a Major Jordan, but there is no mention of any such appointment in the register of their proceedings, though the name occurs later on in the list of the Fellows whom they nominated. So in like manner Wood's statement, that they named to the vacant place a former fellow of the college, White, a Vicar of Trinity Church, Dorchester, and known as the "Patriarch" of that town, and that he, from a sense of loyalty to his old college, declined the honour, is wanting in any official confirmation. Wood's report apparently indicates nothing more than rumoured intentions on the part of the Visitors, even if that. What is certain is that the Fellows, on the death of Dr. Pink, in deference to an order from the Visitors to proceed to an election, met according to their statutes in 1647, and chose Dr. Henry Stringer, a scholar of some repute as Greek lecturer of the University, whom we have seen as taking part in the election to scholarships at Winchester, as Warden.

Under his rule the college took its place in the foremost ranks of the opposition to the Visitors. He avoided as long as he could the service of the summons, and was "not at home" when their officer came to the college. When the policy of delay was played out, he refused to admit their jurisdiction, and was followed by all the members of the foundation with one solitary exception. Even the very cooks and butlers of the College were staunch in their allegiance. The case of New College differed in some respects from that of most other colleges, and gave them, from a legal standpoint, a stronger position. They were bound by William of Wykeham's statutes not to submit to the jurisdiction of any member of the University as a Visitor. Now they found themselves face to face with a body which consisted largely of such members, and which claimed the fullest plenitude of

---

[1] Walker, *Sufferings of the Clergy*, in Bowles, i. 32.

visitatorial authority. Their conscience compelled them, at any cost, to refuse to submit. And so one and all, fifty-four fellows and eight chaplains, with the exception of one solitary fellow (we can scarcely, under the circumstances, though he states that he, too, is "convicted in conscience" to come to an opposite conclusion, call him an Abdiel among the faithless or an *Athanasius contra mundum*), they appeared, protested, and were ejected. They at least had the courage of their convictions, and were content to bear the penalty. The list of seventy-five appointments to the vacant fellowships shows how entirely the whole construction of the college was changed. Stringer was deprived, and, on January 25, $164\frac{8}{9}$, George Marshall, not a Wykehamist, not even an Oxford man, but a clergyman who, after a Cambridge training, had acted as Chaplain to the Parliamentary Army, was appointed Warden in his place. The muniment room and college chests which had been left locked were broken open, and their contents handed over to his keeping. The college was for the time the most deeply dyed with Puritanism in the whole of Oxford. Edward Clarke, the pseudo-Abdiel referred to above, was well-nigh the only link with the traditions of the past. One touching instance of a reluctant submission was to be found in the conduct of William Haxney, the college barber, who, after having accepted the jurisdiction of the Visitors unreservedly, afterwards qualified his assent.[1] "Soe farre as I may, without breach of my oath, I shall humbly submit to this Visitation." It is touching to think that the tonsorial casuist may have cut Ken's hair or trimmed his beard, if he had one.

This then was the college life on which Ken entered in 1657,[2] and it will be admitted, I think, that he must have found himself in a sufficiently alien element. There, as before at Winchester, instead of the services which he loved with a love like that embodied in Herbert's words "The Church's prayers —there are none like hers," there were either no services at

---

[1] Burrows, pp. 60, 116.

[2] If the second name in the woodcut of p. 38 be Ken's, he was probably at Winchester for the election, and travelled with his comrades, on foot, like Hooker, or on horseback.

all in the College Chapel which all Oxford men associate
with the chants and anthems that have made its fame—(this
seems probable from the resolution passed by the Visitors in
1654, reminding tutors that they ought to gather their scholars
round them and pray with them between the hours of 7 and
10 P.M.)—or, if this was meant in addition to the Chapel services, only meetings for extemporary prayer after the fashion of
the Westminster Directory.[1] Instead of scholars and theologians
whom he could respect, the tutors and fellows were men comparatively illiterate,[2] even as regards the scholarship of the schools,
and yet more as regards the wider culture with which Walton s
library and his friends had made Ken familiar. Hugh Peters
and others of a like type, were among the appointed University
preachers at St. Mary's. At the risk of seeming to indulge in
paradox I venture to express my belief that it was better for Ken,
even happier for him, at that period of his life, that this should
have been so, than that his student-years should have been passed
at Oxford either in the period that preceded the triumph of the
Parliament or that which followed on the Restoration. If it
seemed hard for him thus to "bear the yoke in his youth,"
by being associated with men with whom he had little or no
sympathy, it would, I imagine, have been still harder for a man
of Ken's temperament, to find himself among those who, while
outwardly, in their politics and their party-cries, on the same
side with himself, were yet, in mind and morals, even more
alien from his character. The undergraduate Cavaliers who
followed Prince Rupert's standard, and caught the infection of
the dissolute roystering manners of his courtier-officers, with

[1] Burrows, pp. 302, 359, 372.
[2] Anderdon (p. 19) quotes some amusing verses from John Allibone:—

> "Conscendo orbis illud decus,
>   Bodleio Fundatore,
> Sed intus erat nullum pecus,
>   Excepto janitore.

> "Neglectos vidi multos libros,
>   Quod minimè mirandum ;
> Nam inter bardos tot et stultos,
>   There's few could understand 'em."

In July, 1651, however, Evelyn records a visit to the Bodleian. Barlow, afterwards Bishop of Lincoln, was then Librarian and apparently active in his office.
Probably Allibone's verses were hardly more than a squib.

their lovelocks and their oaths and their shameless licentiousness ; the fellows who came back to the places from which they
had been expelled in the temper of an exulting, but too natural,
vindictiveness, the type of undergraduate life which was pre-
dominant under Charles II., to which all piety was Puritanism,
as afterwards, in the days of the Wesleyan revival, all devotion
was Methodism, would, I take it, have been more distasteful
even than the rigorous Calvinism in the midst of which he had
found himself.   Wherever there was the element of a true
personal religion, the fear of God and the love of man, Ken
would find even then, as the kindly relations in which he
lived with Non-conformists show that he found in after life,
some point of contact and fellowship.   We cannot altogether
ignore the testimony of Philip Henry, the gentle saint of Non-
conformity under the rule of the Restoration (b. 1631, d. 1696),
and the father of Matthew Henry, the commentator, that
the Oxford men of his time—and that time must have been
nearly coincident with Ken's—if they were less scholarly
than their predecessors, were also men who led a purer and
more devout life.[1]   He would, I imagine, approve the ordinance
by which Owen abolished the scurrilous, and often obscene,
railleries of the *Terræ Filius* at the *Saturnalia* of the annual
Oxford Act, or Commemoration.[2]

And it may be added that at the time when Ken became a
student at New College the tyranny was in some measure over-
past.   The axe had lost the keenness of its edge, the " root and
branch " work had been accomplished, and expulsions had ceased
to be the order of the day, partly, of course, because there were
now very few " malignants " to be expelled, but partly also, it
must be acknowledged, because the later acts of the Visitors
showed that they were now striving (*circ.* 1654) to raise the

---

[1] Burrows, p. lxxiv.   Among the " seekers " whom Wood describes after his
manner (*Fasti.* ii., 61), with "mortified countenances, puling voices, uplifted eyes,
hands on their breasts, and short hair," there must, I conceive, have been some
who were neither hypocrites nor fanatics.

[2] On one occasion Owen actually pulled down the *Terræ Filius* from the
rostrum, and sent him to the Oxford prison known as Bocardo.   Lancelot Addison,
Joseph's father, two years after Ken came up, was compelled to make a formal
apology for attacking the hypocrisy of the then rulers of the kingdom.   He was
but seventeen.   (C. J. P.)

standard both of scholarship and religion. The ordinances to which I have already called attention, together with other resolutions establishing sermons and lectures in divinity in several colleges[1] are sufficient evidence as to the latter. Their zeal in regard to the former was shown in their repeated decrees directing that fellows and students should in their meals in Hall speak Latin or Greek, so that "their ignorance in this matter might not bring discredit on the University in their publique discourses with forreignors."[2] Even the regulations against "excesse and vanitie, in powdering of hair, wearing knots of ribands, walking in boots and spurs, and bote hose-tops," which indicate the revival of Cavalier costumes, would probably not be unwelcome to a student of Ken's temperament, to whose influence a like sumptuary regulation after the Restoration was probably in great measure due.[3]

But above all there was, shortly after Ken's entrance, a relaxation of the rigour which had deprived those who were loyal to the old order of the English Church of that on which they had depended for the sustenance of their religious life. The original commission lapsed in 1652, and a new one, representing the Independent rather than the Presbyterian element, was appointed in June, 1653.[4] In that instance, as in so many others—as, *e.g.* in the wide comprehensiveness of the Royal Declaration (probably drawn up by Laud) prefixed to the Thirty-nine Articles—the old Virgilian quotation comes in aptly enough—

Via prima salutis,
Quod minime reris, Graiâ pandetur ab urbe.

When Cromwell had triumphed over the Parliament, John

---

[1] Burrows, pp. 374, 382, 390, *et al.*

[2] Burrows, pp. 249, 266, *et al.*

[3] I refer to the letter issued by the Duke of Monmouth to the University of Cambridge, and reproduced in Latin by Ralph Bathurst (afterwards Dean of Wells), against the secular apparel which the clergy and scholars were beginning to use. Some Oxford readers will remember like sumptuary regulations in the Laudian statutes. The letter also condemned the indolent and discreditable practice of reading written sermons, in which also the influence of Ken and of his school may be traced. We have a contemporary MS. copy of Monmouth's letter, possibly written by himself, in our Library at Wells. It was probably among Dean Bathurst's papers. (See p. 201).

[4] Burrows, pp. 353—8.

Owen, his chaplain,[1] an Independent of the strongest type, was made Dean of Christ Church, and was the ruling mind on the Board of Visitors. Cromwell himself was Chancellor, and Owen, Vice-Chancellor. It was precisely under the régime of the latter that there was the first dawn of freedom. Though he himself was so great an enemy to forms, that he would sit down and put on his hat, when the Lord's Prayer was used even by Presbyterian preachers, yet with his full acquiescence, if not approval, Dr. John Fell, afterwards famous as his successor in the deanery, was allowed on Sundays and holy days to hold Church of England services, including Holy Communion, in the house of Thomas Willis, Fell's brother-in-law, within, or in closest neighbourhood to, the walls of the college, at which the officiating ministers wore surplices, and the order of ritual was at least decent and reverential. These services were attended by not less than three hundred members, graduates and undergraduates, from Christ Church and other colleges.[2]

It would be interesting, could we obtain anything like a roll-call of those who welcomed the opportunity thus afforded them, after a long privation, of worshipping God after the manner of their fathers, to trace, as Mr. Masson has traced, in his *Life of Milton*, the history of those who were his companions and tutors at Christ's College during his Cambridge life, the careers of those who were thus associated with Ken during his Oxford years, and speculate on their points of contact, in their previous or their later history, their family or ecclesiastical relationships, with the subject of this memoir. As that opening for research is not given us, we must content ourselves with one or two of the more memorable names among those who were Ken's contemporaries, and who may probably have been thus connected with him.

---

[1] Owen astonished the University by a costume "like a young scholar," which might well come under Monmouth's censure. "Powdered hair, snake-bone band strings, large tassels and ribbons pointed at the knees, and Spanish leather boots, with large lawn tops, and wore his hat cocked."—Wood's *Athen. Oxon.*, ii. p. 738.

[2] Burrows, p. xlvi. It is right to state that Owen denied the accusation of treating the Lord's Prayer with disrespect, and said that he thought it the most perfect prayer that was ever composed (*Sermons and Tracts*, p. 619). Apparently he objected only to its pulpit use. The hat seems often to have been worn during sermons, and Owen's act, perhaps, simply implied that he treated the prayer, so used, as part of the sermon. [C. J. P.]

We can scarcely be wrong in assuming that he, at least,
was one of that congregation. John Locke was a student at
Christ Church, matriculated in 1651, but it is scarcely probable, I think, that he would have attended the services in
question, or that if he and Ken ever came into contact with
each other, they would find many points of sympathy.[1] Of
Robert Boyle, afterwards memorable as one of the early members of the Royal Society and as the founder of the Boyle
Lectures, we may, I think, feel sure that he would have been
a devout member of that Christ Church gathering, and may
believe that he and Ken, did they become acquainted with each
other, would find, in much that they held in common, a ground
of fellowship and friendship. Of three, however, who were then
at Christ Church we have something more than conjectural
surmises. There, a year or two younger than Ken, was Thomas
Thynne, the eldest son of a family conspicuous for its devotion
to the Royalist cause, whose father had suffered for that devotion at the hands of the Parliament in the form of a heavy fine,
which included, by a singular coincidence, looking to the after
relations of the two men, a charge of £20 per annum for the
benefit of St. John's Church at Frome, where, after eighteen
years spent at Longleat under his protection, Ken was to
find his final resting-place. Thynne's education had been
directed by Hammond and Fell, and he was therefore prepared to sympathise with the young Fellow of New College.
There also was George Hooper, fresh from Westminster School,
full of manifold promise of intellectual gifts and high-toned
character, of whom Busby, the Master of that school (we
may remember that he was Dryden's master also), had said
that, unpromising as his exterior might be, he had more in him
than any other of his scholars, to whom others bore their
witness that he united "all that was most characteristic
of the scholar, the English gentleman, and the divine,"[2]

[1] On the other hand, in 1691 we find Ken writing to Mrs. Grigge, who was a
cousin of Locke's, and Locke's mother was daughter of Edward Keene, of Wrington (ii. 52). Keene was one of the many variants of Ken, and the two facts suggest
the possibility of some family connexion. In later years Locke was a visitor at
Longleat, and Mrs. Grigge resided with Francis Turner when he, then a
widower, was Bishop of Ely, as governess to his daughter. See ii., p. 52.

[2] Miller, of Highclere. Anderdon, p. 87.

and whose life was to be linked, as we shall see, in its
many changes and chances, and in ways so memorable, with
that of Ken.   There also must have been Francis Turner,
senior by a year to Ken at New College, who had been among
his chosen friends at Winchester, and who was afterwards to
be associated with him in the most memorable crisis of their
lives, and in the sacrifices which they had to bear, through many
years, for what seemed to the conscience of each the imperative
obligation of his duty.   Among Ken's friends at Oxford, and
therefore probably a member of the congregation who thus
worshipped after the ritual of the Church of England, we may
also note John Fitzwilliam, Fellow of Magdalen, whose life-
long intimacy with him will meet us again more than once in
this history.[1]   Among his contemporaries were many men
more or less famous, Wilkins (afterwards Bishop of Chester),
Dr. Wallis (the mathematician), Seth Ward (afterwards Bishop
of Salisbury), William Petty, and Christopher Wren.[2]

The mitigation of the rigour of the Puritan régime indicated in these services at Christ Church, was seen in other
matters in which Ken was more or less a sharer.   Evelyn
visits Oxford in July, 1654 and reports that he finds the

[1] A few facts in Fitzwilliam's life may fitly find a place here. In 1651 he
entered Magdalen College as a servitor, and was elected to a demyship in 1656.
At the Restoration, according to Antony à Wood, he "turned about" and
"became a great complier to the restored Liturgy." He was Fellow of Magdalen 1661—70, and Librarian in 1662, being at the same time University Lecturer
on Music. In 1664 he was Chaplain to the Earl of Southampton, father of Lady
Rachel Russell, and there began the friendship of which their later correspondence is the record. He published a Thanksgiving Sermon after the discovery
of the Rye-House Plot, which led, it will be remembered, to William, Lord
Russell's execution. He was Chaplain to Bishop Morley, as also in 1666 to the
Duke of York, and succeeded Ken at Brightstone in 1669. He was Vicar of
Tottenham and Canon of Windsor, became a Non-juror in 1690, and died in 1699,
leaving Ken as his executor, with a life interest in £500, which he bequeathed to
the library of his college. He was also a friend of Izaak Walton's, who sent him
presentation copies of his works. Like other students of the time, like Ken him-
self, he often wrote his favourite texts or mottoes on the fly-leaves of his books.
Two of these are specially characteristic. "*Reddenda est ratio villicationis tuæ*"
("Thou must give an account of thy stewardship"), and Φιλοτιμεῖσθε ἡσυχάζειν
("Study to be quiet").

[2] Oxford men may, perhaps, like to think that Josiah Pullen, who planted
the elm at Headington which still bears his name, was Vice-Principal of Hart
Hall in 1657. He died in 1714. (C. J. P.)

chapel at New College in "its ancient garb," "Mr. Gibbons, the famous musician, giving a taste of his skill" upon the organ, reverence for the *genius loci* having apparently triumphed over the dominant tendencies of the new members and the intruded fellows, as about the same time it availed to protect the chapel at Winchester College from a sacrilegious desecration. Antony à Wood relates how, in 1656, a musical society had been established at Oxford, the members of which met once a week in the house of William Ellis, formerly organist of St. John's. He gives a long list of the members, among whom we note Crewe, afterwards Bishop of Durham, Kenelm Digby, Fellow of All Souls, and in 1658 "Thomas Ken of New College, a Junior," who "would be sometimes among them and sing his part."[1] The choral training of Walton's home and of the school at Winchester was thus revived, and, as we shall see hereafter, became the perpetual solace of his life. It is natural to assume that his taste for music led him about this time, if not at an earlier period, to the skill in instrumental music which was shown afterwards by his having an organ in his room at Winchester, and by his daily practice, later on in life, of always singing his Morning and Evening Hymns, even when alone, to his own accompaniment on the lute. A characteristic trait of his Oxford life is given by Hearne, who describes him as habitually going out on his walks with a pocketful of small cash, which, before he returned, had commonly been distributed in casual alms.[2]

And so the years passed on, and the youth grew into manhood, gravely, thoughtfully, devoutly, in all purity and godliness and honesty. Lectures were attended and books read, classical, historical, and theological, or in the lighter regions of literature, of which we have no record and scarcely even materials for conjecture. Students of science, Locke, Sprat, Boyle, Wilkins, Petty, Wren, and Bathurst, met in each others' rooms, and were known as the *Virtuosi*, developing at the

---

[1] Wood, *Life*, p. 88, 1772. Evelyn records a musical meeting at All Souls, July 11, 1654.

[2] MSS. *Journals* in Bodleian Library, cvi. p. 27 (Anderdon, p. 52). The same habit is recorded of Mrs. Rowe, who, as Elizabeth Singer, was much under Ken's influence.

Restoration into the *Royal Society of London*. In November, 1658, Marshall, the intruded non-Wykehamist Warden, died, and the fellows this time were allowed to elect freely; and, by their choice of a former fellow, restored, in Dr. Woodward, the interrupted continuity of Wintonian traditions. The unusually long interval between Ken's matriculation in 1656, and his B.A. degree on May 3rd, 1661, may probably be accounted for by the fact that he shrank from taking any oath of obedience, even as to a *de facto* Government, to the Commonwealth authorities, and that the signs of the times, on Cromwell's death on September 3, 1658, began to give notice of the impending change. At last, after more than a year of uncertainties and intrigues and faction fights under Richard Cromwell, the Restoration came, and its immediate effects were probably felt more powerfully at Oxford than at most other places. Well-nigh every historian has dwelt on the general reaction of the time from Puritan preciseness to Cavalier licence, that licence having largely taken a darker character than before from the life which the exiles with Charles II. had led at Paris, at Brussels, and at the Hague. The nation threw off all restraint and sobriety in its rampant exultation. We can picture to ourselves without much difficulty the effect of such a sudden change in a society so largely consisting of young men as that of Oxford; the revival of oaths, love-locks, and "foolish talking and jesting" about the things that are "not convenient;" the bursts of boisterous derision at whatever savoured of the now vanishing order of things; the absolute delight in saying and doing evil things because they would shock the susceptibilities of the "godly." The University, as Antony à Wood said, went "stark-staring mad" in its new freedom. According to the conclusions which I have been led to form, Ken has left on record in two distinct forms the impressions which this state of things made upon him; but, as these conclusions rest on circumstantial evidence which may seem to some, not without reason, more or less of an imperfect character, I reserve the first of the two documents for a note to this chapter, and the second for a separate discussion in that which follows.

Here I will only note the fact that though there is no evi-

dence as to when or by whom Ken was ordained, it may be
assumed that, as he was presented to a living in 1663, he was
probably ordained by Bishop Skinner, of Oxford, in 1661 or
1662, with his Fellowship as a title.[1] New College records
show (1) that in 1662 he received certain emoluments, which
he could not have received without being in orders; and
(2) that in 1661 he held office as a College tutor, and
lectured on Logic and Mathematics. With what feelings he
entered on the ministry to which he, if any man, had a true
vocation, we are, unless I am right in my more or less contingent
inferences, left to conjecture. If I am not wholly wrong they
show that those feelings included a large element of melancholy
forebodings, such as marked the whole tenor of his after life.
To him it may have seemed then, as it did when he preached his
Whitehall sermon on April 1, 1688, that the bishops and clergy
of the Church of England, and the statesmen who controlled
her actions, had learnt nothing that was good and forgotten
nothing that was evil, in the discipline of their exile. As he
looked forward with a dreamer's prophetic glance, he could
hardly help feeling that a further and severer discipline of
chastisement, nothing less than a Babylonian captivity of
seventy years, could eradicate her besetting evils.

[1] Skinner, Bishop of Oxford, is said to have ordained between four hundred
and five hundred priests during the revolutionary period. Ralph Bathurst and
Lamplugh, afterwards Bishop of Exeter, finally Archbishop of York (1688),
assisted him, the former acting as archdeacon, the latter as chaplain. Lamplugh
made not less than three hundred journeys from Oxford to Launton, where the
Bishop lived, in connexion with his ordinations, confirmations and other pastoral
work. Evelyn (May 6, 1656) relates how he had procured ordination for a
young Frenchman who had been trained at the Sorbonne, through Jeremy
Taylor, at the hands of the Bishop of Meath, then living in great poverty, in
London. Patrick was ordained by Hall "in his own parlour" at Higham, near
Norwich.—Patrick, *Diary*, pp. 23, 24, 1839.

NOTE on *Ken as a Student of Science.*—My attention has been called, as these
sheets are passing through the press, to the Catalogue of the Aylesford Library
(Christie's, 1888), which contains a copy of Agricola *De Re Metallica*, given by
Ken to Sir Heneage Finch, August 5th, 1707. For other traces of a like line of
study, see p. 201. The Longleat Catalogue gives Galen, Gassendi, Galileo,
Ray as among his books.

DID KEN WRITE "EXPOSTULATORIA?"

Within two months after Ken's death, a small volume appeared with the title of "*Expostulatoria*, or the Complaints of the Church of England against (1) Undue Ordination, (2) Loose Prophaneness, (3) Unconscionable Symony, (4) Encroaching Pluralities, (5) Careless Non-residence, now reigning among the clergy. By the Right Rev. Father in God, Thomas Kenn, D.D., late Lord Bishop of Bath and Wells." It was printed and sold by J. Baker, at the Black Boy, Paternoster Row, 1711. It is of 12mo size, of about 120 pages. The Editor states that "the spirit of devotion which shines through the whole is enough to convince the reader, if he has any knowledge of the late Bishop of Bath and Wells, Dr. Kenn's composures, that he is the incomparable author," but that his own opinion is that it "was written some years since." He assures the reader that "it is genuine, and taken from a manuscript lately presented to one of our Universities by a Person of Learning and Quality."

The editor then gives a life of Bishop Ken, not without errors, giving 1645 as the year of his birth instead of 1637, 1659 for his election at Winchester, and 1662 for that at New College; but he obviously knows something of his subject, and reports, though without names, the whole of the Zulestein story, which had not then been published, though it is given by Hawkins in his *Life of Ken* in 1713. It ends with quoting, as applicable to Ken, and written, indeed, as his portrait, Dryden's *Character of a Good Parson*, based on Chaucer's *Poor Persone of a Toune*. The contents of the book are sufficiently startling. I give a few extracts under each head. The Church is introduced as lamenting over the evils of the time; she can vindicate her doctrine, discipline, constitution, ceremonies, but she cannot justify her sons and ministers: they are guilty of the sins stated in the title-page.

(1) *Undue Ordination.*—Orders have, "through inadvertency, been bestowed on the Young, the Unlearned, the Debauched, the Profane. We have young ministers unstable in all their ways, impudent in their carriage, weak in their discourses" (p. 31). "Are you not afraid," the writer asks, as the mouth-piece of the Church, "to ascend that pulpit which Luther said he never came into without fear and trembling?" (p. 32). He complains that "men have been ordained who have been expelled from College for licentiousness" (p. 34); that the clergy were for the most part "unlearned;" that religion has been "exposed to a prophane world" by the "ridiculous impertinence" of men "zealous, but not according to knowledge." "What empty discourses do I hear?" (p. 36). The Church could but sigh when she saw "so many weak shoulders, such unwashed hands, such unprepared feet, such rash heads, such empty souls" (p. 40).

(2) *Scandalous Prophaneness.*—"Oh! your carelessness; Oh! your indifference in matters of religion." And then, after dwelling on other scandals, he names, as too often seen, that of "a minister, and yet given to wine" (p. 44).

(3) *Unconscionable Symony.*—He quotes the Statute of 31 Elizabeth against simony, and adds, "Yet still you truck for livings, you market for benefices; still you buy and sell in the Temple" (p. 46). The Church may well ask, "Have I no true ministers, but a generation of Demases?" (p. 47).

(4) *Encroaching Pluralities.*—He contrasts the present with the past. Once each parish had its own minister, ... now two or three cannot suffice you . . . . Why is that preferment engrossed by one which might maintain twenty ?" (p. 51). "Must all the industrious ministers be stipendiaries ? . . . . "Our fathers, in 632, divided England into parishes. . . . . Our times unite those parishes again " (p. 58).

(5.) *Non-Residence.*—"The Church," we are told, "might almost say with Augustus, when he heard of the defeat of Varus, ' *Redde legiones* ' " (p. 63). "The harvest is great ; the prebends are many, the priests are many, the impropriators are many, the labourers are few " (p. 65). "You say, 'we have curates, and they perform our duties.' Curates ! What new generation of men are these curates ?" p. 67). [1]

The book ends—after a quotation from Gildas, *de Excidio Britanniæ,* " *O Inimici Dei, non sacerdotes ! O Licitatores malorum, non Pontifices ! Traditores et non Apostolorum successores !* "—with the statement that of 12,000 livings in the Church 3,000 were impropriate, and that 4,165 suffered from non-residence (p. 71).

All this was, as I have said, enought to startle men as coming from a Bishop of the Church. William Hawkins, Ken's great-nephew and executor, inserted advertisements in the London papers (*The Post Boy,* May, 29th, 1711), denouncing it as spurious. It was only a reprint of a book that had been first printed under the title of *Ichabod,* in 1663, and afterwards in 1691. Hearne at first speaks of it in his *Diary* as an " infamous book." [2] "Nobody of understanding and honesty could think that Ken wrote it." He accepts Hawkins's statement that it was a reprint of a "fanatical book" entitled *Ichabod.* A few days or weeks later, he modifies his judgment. The book was " far better done " than he had thought, it was but "too true a representation of the condition of the Church." It was "writ in the style of Bishop Ken," and though he still "questioned whether it be really his," he thought it "very well done," and saw "no hurt why it may not bear so great a name." It is obvious, therefore, that, in the judgment of one of the most learned of Ken's contemporaries, the book, as far as internal evidence went, might well have been his. I am able to state that that judgment is confirmed by the opinion of the late Rev. W. J. Copeland, Fellow of Trinity College, Oxford, closely connected, as such, with the leaders of the Oxford movement in our time, pre-eminent as an expert in Anglo-catholic literature, and by that of Bishop Wordsworth, of Lincoln, both of whom were inclined to accept it "as probably an early piece of Ken's." [3] I incline, with very little hesitation, to adopt that conclusion myself. If the question were one which affected only the genuineness of a work, published as Ken's after his death, it would find its fit place under the general head of ' Ken Bibliography.' But its identity with the *Ichabod* of 1663, reprinted in 1689 under the title of *Lachrymæ Ecclesiarum,* gives it, it will be admitted, an entirely new character. If Ken wrote it then, at the age of twenty-six, it throws a light on what were at that time his views and aspirations, which places them in a hitherto unsuspected aspect. My explanation of the phænomenon, which I give with a full recognition of its conjectural character, is, that the Restoration had seemed to him

---

[1] The passage may be noted as an early instance of the use of the word "Curate" in its modern sense.

[2] Bodleian MSS. in Records. p. vi.

[3] Letter from Rev. Charles Nevile, rector of Stow, to E. H. P.

as it did to others, to be a new starting point from which a golden age for the English Church and people might well be looked for, if only the Church were faithful to herself. Charles II.'s declaration from Breda, and again that of 1662, anticipating later Declarations of Indulgence, his own in 1672, James II.'s in 1686 and 1687, had given scope for the dreams of idealists of many different kinds. The Presbyterians thought of the re-establishment of their system, modified by a limited episcopacy such as they were willing to accept, with a Prayer Book expurgated from all that had been as stumbling-blocks to them and to their fathers. Independents, Baptists, and even Quakers, looked forward to a deliverance from the persecutions to which, under canon and statute law they were still liable, and which, even before the Act of Uniformity, had thrown John Bunyan into the gaol at Bedford. And the Anglican idealists had also their dreams of the future. The phœnix might rise from its ashes to a new and mightier life. The Church of England might become the link between the Churches of the East and West; and there might yet be a re-union of Christendom. Old strifes and discords might be hushed even in England itself. Those who differed from her might be drawn as with "the cords of a man," by gentler methods than those of the Court of High Commission, or the excommunications, fines, and imprisonment to which more regular procedure still made them subject, and by the removal of scandals which an honest judgment could not but acknowledge to be flagrant. Thorndike's *Epilogue to the Tragedy of the Church of England* was one example of such an ideal.[1] I take *Ichabod* to have been another, written, however, not in the flush of hope, but in the first bitterness of disappointment, a bitterness which I can only compare to that which rose in Cardinal Newman's mind when he found that the bishops of his day would not accept his ideal of Anglicanism. My theory of *Ichabod*—I give it with a *valeat quantum*—is that Ken was vexed in his soul when he saw the old evils re-appearing, the old scandals and unwisdom perpetuated, the insolent triumph of success showing itself where there ought to have been the penitence of a Church in sackcloth and ashes. That tone, I conceive, would have been quite in harmony with the sermons which he preached in 1687 and 1688, with the feelings with which he looked on the Revolution. He wrote *liberare animam*. Having done so he relapsed into silence, took the path of obedience, did what he could, as his position in the Church enabled him, to remedy the evils; protesting against Rome, but never reviling Romanists; treating Dissenters, as his dear friend Frampton did in his diocese of Gloucester, with courtesy and tenderness. When the book appeared, in 1689, under the title of *Lachrymæ Ecclesiarum*, the editor presents it to the reader as a book which, "after a careful and delightful perusal," he had thought it not improper to reproduce in these times as a useful piece. Apparently, therefore, Ken did not authorise its republication. After his death it may have been published under its new title by some one who was in the secret.[2]

The repudiation of the *Expostulatoria*, by William Hawkins, is, of course, a serious difficulty; but it is traversed I think by two considerations: (1.) The aged

---

[1] Thorndike's treatise was a plea for bringing the Church of England back to a primitive pattern. The clergy of each diocese were to take counsel of the bishops. The Communion Service was to be restored as in the first Prayer Book of Edward VI. The discipline of penance was to be revived.—(Stoughton, i. p. 35.)

[2] I have not been able to meet with a copy of the *Lachrymæ Ecclesiarum* in either the British Museum or Bodleian Library. Round says (p. viii.) on the authority of Archdeacon Todd, that it was identical with *Ichabod*. Hawkins, in his advertisement, speaks of an edition of *Ichabod*, in 1691.

bishop was not likely to talk much of that unacknowledged episode in his life to his young great-nephew. Hawkins's disclaimer proves nothing more than that he did not believe that the work was by the Bishop. (2.) His life of the Bishop is disfigured by general inaccuracies (see Preface), which diminish the value of his evidence. On the whole then I rest on the conclusion that Ken was responsible for the *Ichabod*, and therefore for the *Expostulatoria*, and that they throw a light on his inner life and character, which we cannot afford to ignore as we trace the chances and changes of his life. If not by Ken, I note the *Ichabod* and its reproductions as one of the unsolved problems of the history of the Church of the Restoration, and invite suggestions for its solution. Whose, we may well ask, was this *vox clamantis in deserto*, heard uttering its prophetic warnings at intervals during half a century, lamenting and rebuking the vices of the Ministers of the Church, in the tones of Ezekiel and Jeremiah, when others were exulting and triumphant, or were railing against Rome on one side, and Nonconformity on the other? An article reviewing Round's *Prose Works of Bishop Ken* in No. 47 of the *British Critic*, the first number under Cardinal Newman's editorship, gives the writer's opinion that *Ichabod* represents "precisely that view which one might fancy that a young person might describe, who saw vividly the contrast between the theory and the practice of the Church." That contrast may, I conceive, have been painfully impressed upon Ken by the prevailing tone and temper of those who were ordained with him. The fact that it was printed at Cambridge seems to the reviewer against Ken's authorship. This, however, may be traversed by the conjecture that Ken had friends at Cambridge, and that he may have preferred publishing where his authorship was less likely to be identified. Cardinal Newman does not remember who wrote the article. Internal evidence would lead me to conjecture Mr. W. J. Copeland as the author. (See p. 56.)

I cannot close this account of *Ichabod* without noticing the singular parallel presented to it by Rosmini's *Five Wounds of the Church*, a translation of which has been published with a preface by Canon Liddon. Rosmini's counts in the indictment are (1) the division between the people and the clergy in public worship; (2) the insufficient education of the clergy; (3) the divisions of the bishops; (4) the nomination of bishops by the lay-power; (5) the enforced infringements of the full rights of ecclesiastical property. The resemblance is, it will be admitted, so close as to suggest the thought of derivation. I am assured, however, by Father Lockhart, the representative of the English branch of Rosmini's Order of Charity, that the Superior General of that Order (Father Lauroni), to whom he kindly passed on my inquiry, tells him that the modern Italian reformer knew nothing of the work of his English predecessor.

I may add that the *Ichabod* is quoted somewhat fully in Stanford's *Life of Joseph Alleine*, pp. 187 . . . He speaks of the writer as "a beneficed clergyman." (J. K.)

CHAPTER V.

" Lord, who can trace but Thou
The strife obscure, 'twixt sin's soul-thralling spell
And Thy keen spirit, now quench'd, reviving now."
                                        J. H. Newman.

THE change of which I have spoken must, I imagine, have had its dark as well as its bright side for Ken. On the one hand, the return to the old order of the Church services, not by connivance, as in an "upper room," but in college chapels and cathedrals, the return of the old Wykehamist Fellows, and the extrusion, in their turn, of the intruders who had usurped their places, would be simply matters for rejoicing. On the other hand, however, if the Restoration life of Oxford partook, in its measure and degree, of the characteristics of the Restoration life of London and the rest of England, a man like Ken must have felt, as I have said in the preceding chapter, that he was brought into contact with an element that was lower, in its moral and spiritual life, than that in which he had passed his undergraduate years. The strong current of licence in speech and act, of licentiousness in practice, and of a rampant, exulting, undevout churchmanship set in with a force which threatened to carry everything before it. If I am not mistaken, he felt in after years, as he looked back upon that period, that it had been to him a time of temptation and of trial,—I will even venture to add, of temptation to which, as he judged himself in the tribunal of his conscience, however blameless he might have seemed in the eyes of men, he had yielded overmuch. Here, also, as in the case of nearly all who have attained to a holiness like Ken's, there had been something like the crisis of

a conversion, a "stumbling," if not a "fall," from which there
had been, through God's great mercy, an entire restoration. He
too had known what it was to "rise to higher things" as on
the "stepping stones of his dead self," perhaps had felt, in
Cardinal Newman's words, in his own soul,—

> "The miserable power to dreams allowed,
> In mockery guiling it to act again
> The revel or the scoff in Satan's frantic train."

It is right, that I may not seem to be writing an imaginary
biography, that I should give my evidence for presenting an
aspect of Ken's life on which no previous writer has ventured.

Ken's biographers have contented themselves, for the most
part, with speaking of his two Epics in terms of almost contemptuous disparagement. I respectfully demur to that judgment. Whatever may be the merits of *Edmund* and *Hymnotheo*
as works of art, they were, I believe, those in which Ken most
delighted, not as such, but because they gave him a channel for
the outpouring of his deepest thoughts and feelings. *Edmund*,
as will be seen in due course, embodied his convictions as to an
ideal polity in Church and State. *Hymnotheo*, the more I read
it, seems to me, beyond a doubt, to have been, essentially and
deliberately, under the thinnest possible disguise, an idealised
autobiography. As the basis of his poem he takes the well-
known story told by Clement of Alexandria[1] of St. John and
the catechumen of Smyrna, who afterwards fell into evil ways
and became the captain of a band of robbers, whom the apostle,
when he heard of his downfall, followed in eager zeal to his
haunts at the risk of his own life, and rescued and brought back
to the true flock and to the safe-keeping of the fold.[2] To this
youth, who is without a name, as Clement tells the story, Ken
gives the ideal name of Hymnotheo. That was to describe his
gifts and his vocation, just as it described what Ken may well,
at a comparatively early period, have recognised as his own.
The boy has been trained in all the blessedness of a holy home,
and it is from the part of the poem which describes that train-

---

[1] *Quis Dives Salvetur*, c. 42.

[2] The story has been poetically treated by T. Dale in his *Outlaw of Taurus*,
and by the present writer in his *Lazarus*.

ing that biographers have quoted some of the lines which have
been given in Chapter I. as describing Ken's own boyhood.
From my present point of view, the passage, both evidentially
and otherwise, is of sufficient importance to be quoted more at
large. Hymnotheo *loquitur* :—

> " E'er since I hung upon my mother's breast,
> Thy love, my God, has me sustained and blest ;
> My virtuous parents, tender of their child,
> My education pious, careful, mild,
> My teachers, zealous well to form my mind,
> My faithful friends and benefactors kind,
> My creditable station and good name,
> My life preserved from scandal and from shame,
> My understanding, memory, and health,
> Relations dear and competence of wealth ;
> All the vouchsafements thou to me hast shown,
> All blessings, all deliverances unknown,—
> To hymn thy love my verse for ever bind,
> And yet thy greatest love is still behind."
>
> *Hymnoth. V.* p. 149.

It is Hymnotheo who observes and describes the habits
of the insect world, as quoted in p. 17. On his restoration
he passes through a process of discipline in the dwelling of
Ecclesia, which reminds us of the Red Cross Knight of the
Faerie Queene in the House of Holiness. And every precept of
life is identical with those on which Ken habitually acted.
Ferventio, his hermit-teacher, warns him against the peril of a
life spent overmuch in books :

> " Know, son ! 'tis not bare reading I commend ;
> You must choice hours in meditation spend."

Sophronio, another teacher of a calmer type, perhaps an
idealised Walton, tells him of the threefold revelation of
nature, conscience, and the Word, in the passage already
quoted. Vigilio (the names are all of the Bunyan type of
allegory) bids him act as Ken afterwards acted throughout his
life.

> " A harp Davidick on his desk was placed ;
> With that away he ghostly slumber chased."

For him the tree of knowledge, which was the occasion of
man's fall, was none other than the vine which had been the
cause of so much misery and shame.[1] Hymnotheo, after this
discipline, is received back again by St. John and the seven
bishops of the Asiatic Churches who had been faithful in persecution (was there a reminiscence of the seven of whom Ken
himself was one ?[2]), and prepares for admission to the priesthood by a fast of forty days.   The old gift of minstrelsy comes
back to him as with a new power of consecration.   The apostle
comes to visit him, and

> " With love divine John warmed Hymnotheo's heart,
>   Who ne'er without a song let John depart." ·

It is from the beloved disciple that he derives the ideal of
the pastoral life which he sought to realise.

> " Bless'd Jesus' past'ral love to his lost sheep,
>   Upon his spirit made impressions deep."[3]

Hymnotheo finishes his course by leading the Smyrniotes to
see in Homer (Ken, in this matter, anticipating a favourite
theory of Mr. Gladstone's) the half-conscious depository of the
traditions of a primitive revelation, by singing to them the old,
yet ever new, story of creation and redemption, and so leading
them to find in Homer a " schoolmaster leading them to
Christ."   He fulfils the ideal of his name, and hymns are the
one chief product of his life, and that by which he expects his
name to live in the age that was come.

It will scarcely be questioned, I imagine, that the features
on which I have dwelt are essentially autobiographical.   One
side at least of the life of the good old man[4] is seen by us, in its
completeness, as painted by himself.   But if this be so, is it not

---

[1] *Hymnoth.*, xi. p. 323.

[2] It was said that the seven bishops rather rejoiced in Frampton's not
arriving in time to sign the petition before it was presented to the King.   They
wished to preserve the sacred number.   The sermons, medals, engravings of the
time abound in references to the seven angels of the seven Churches of
Revelation i.—iii.

[3] We remember Ken's motto for his episcopal coat-of-arms : *Pastor bonus dat
animam pro ovibus.*

[4] The poem seems to me of the nature of the retrospect of age, but there are
no distinct passages, as in *Edmund*, proving a date subsequent to Ken's
deprivation.   Perhaps even in *Edmund* there were after-touches.

equally legitimate and natural to recognise the autobiographical element elsewhere also? And here the framework of Ken's story is at least sufficiently suggestive. In the story of the catechumen, as told by Clement, he simply falls into evil courses and takes to a life of licence and of plunder, like that described in the first chapters of the Book of Proverbs and of the Wisdom of Solomon. Ken takes his hero to Antioch as the seat at once of culture and of luxury. He drinks of the poisoned cup of pleasure in the groves of Daphne.[1] Angels and fiends are contending for the possession of his soul, and through the loving care of the former he stops short of the point at which his fall would have become hopeless and irretrievable. But then, as at all times, the loss, even the partial loss, of purity of soul involved also the loss of clearness of spiritual vision and steadfastness of faith, and it is to recover these that the long ascetic discipline was needed.

Is it not a legitimate conclusion from all this to infer that in the reaction from the strain of Puritanism which then poured in on the land, in the new companionships that were opened by the return of men of the Restoration stamp, Ken had passed through something of the experience which he thus describes? The morals and manners of the court of Charles II. were certain, in the nature of things, to affect for evil those of the society of Oxford, and there, or in London, where his vacations were probably spent, he may possibly have felt for a little time, and, as we should count it, in scant measure, the spell of its fascination. It is not necessary,—it is, we may well say, impossible,—to suppose that he sank, even for a moment, to the level of the swine of Circe, but it may well have been that he too had listened to the voice of the Sirens, and had asked himself the question which even Milton asked—

> " Were it not better done as others do,
>   To sport with Amaryllis in the shade,
>   Or with the tangles of Neæra's hair ? "

---

[1] It is a more or less suggestive fact that the groves of Trinity College, Oxford, including a labyrinth, shown in old plans, which, as recorded in *John Inglesant* (ch. ix.), were used as a promenade for the gay and frivolous, were known colloquially as Daphne. For the Daphne of Antioch compare Gibbon, c. xxiii.

The old habits which led him

> " To scorn delight and live laborious days "

may have been broken down, and his gifts of song and music
turned to secular uses. He too, like Bunyan's pilgrim, may
have wandered in the Enchanted Ground, or entered, not
altogether as a pilgrim, within the precincts of the Fair of
Vanity, or, like Spenser's knight, Guyon, may have passed the
borders of the perilous garden of Acrasia, and seen, recoiling
when he saw it, how it led on to the valley of the shadow of
death. (*Faerie Queene*, ii. 6.)

If such things were, and I think I have shown that they were
probable, that other peril of a weakened faith in the Unseen,
and of uncertainty of belief in the Eternal, could not be far
distant. And this also Ken has shadowed forth in the history
of his Hymnotheo. The demons of hell are deliberating on
the best means of securing his destruction (the machinery seems
to me to make it possible that a reminiscence of the *Paradise
Regained*,[1] as well as of the *Davideis*, was floating in his mind),
and Belial rises, as the subtlest of all the spirits of evil, with
his suggestion. And it takes a sufficiently curious form :

> " Let latitudinarian spirits strive,
> All heresies long buried to revive,
> Atheism to the licentious youth suggest,
> Urge them consideration[2] to detest,
> With opposite religions to comply,
> And Christ, for gain or safety, to deny."

Considered as poetry, there is, of course, something almost
ludicrously incongruous in thus bringing the *bête noire* of the
closing years of the seventeenth century into the perils of the
first. But for that very reason, looked at from the point of
view from which I am now studying it, the passage which I
have quoted is all the more significant. The controversy between faith and unfaith, the peril of what, in successive periods

---

[1] I find both Milton's great poems among Ken's books, the *Paradise Lost* of
1674, the *Paradise Regained* of 1705.

[2] *I.e.*, in the half-technical sense in which the word was often used, " devout
meditation." Horneck wrote a book on *The Great Law of Consideration*.

of English thought, has been known as latitudinarianism, freethinking, indifferentism, scepticism, rationalism, agnosticism, was a factor then, as it has been ever since, in the university life of England, and Ken may have felt, in some degree, the power of its benumbing touch. The memory of that conflict may have been one of the elements, over and above all legal and constitutional objections, which led him to look with suspicion on the simulated liberalism of James's Declaration of Indulgence.

Was Duessa[1] altogether absent from those years, or, it may be, only months, of trial? Had the wave of a revived Catholicism which had set in over the whole of England in the previous generation, and had not yet ebbed, threatened to carry him, as it had carried others, into the deep waters? We know how eagerly the Jesuit propagandists dwelt, when they came in contact with young minds that were vacillating and uncertain, on the assertion that in Rome alone was to be found the one refuge of belief, the haven of rest for tempest-tost and shipwrecked souls. For a time they enthralled even the clear intellect of Chillingworth, till he took refuge in the not very accurate statement, however popular as a catchword, that "the Bible, and the Bible only, is the religion of Protestants." That there were such souls at Oxford, longing then, as Ken longed to the end (ii. 209), for the reunion of Christendom and the faith of the undivided Church of the East and West, about the time when he was growing to man's estate, we have one quaint illustration in the gossip of good old Anthony à Wood.[2] It was in 1658, under Richard Cromwell, when Ken was just twenty-one, that a grave stranger, with long beard and hair overgrown, appeared at the Mitre Inn in Oxford. He announced himself (we are not told in what language) as a patriarch, by name Jeremius, of some far-off Eastern Church. He had come to confer with theologians at Oxford with a view to a new "modell" (that was then the fashionable term for what we should now call an "ideal") or programme of reformation for his own and for other Churches. It must be remembered that the communications which had passed not many years before between Laud and Cyril Lucaris, the patriarch of Constantinople, and to

[1] Spenser, *F. Q.* i. 8. [2] *Lives of Leland, Hearne, and Wood*, ii., p. 132.
VOL. I. F

which we owe our possession of the great Alexandrian Codex
of the LXX. and New Testament, gave to the advent of such
a visitor at least a colourable credibility. The "sensation"
through the university was immense. "Divers Royalists"
repaired to him and "craved his blessing on their knees." In
the long absence of a benediction from bishop or archbishop, it
would be something to have that of an Eastern patriarch.
John Harmar, Professor of Greek, "appeared very formally
and made a Greek harangue before him." Even Owen, then
Dean of Christ Church, and some of the Puritan Canons and
students of that house, themselves also probably not without a
longing for a wider unity, came to hold conference with him.
Suddenly,—as a matter of fact, through an irrepressible
burst of laughter in the midst of the Greek oration,—the
bubble burst, and the great theologians and ardent idealists
found that they had been the victims of a hoax. The Greek
patriarch was a London merchant of the name of Kinaston.
The deviser of the hoax was a William Lloyd, then living at
Wadham as a private tutor (afterwards in succession Bishop of
St. Asaph, and, as such, associated with Ken in the trial of the
seven bishops, of Lichfield and of Worcester). The wrath of
the tricked Vice-Chancellor (Owen) waxed hot, and Lloyd, to
avert worse fate, had to run away and hide himself.

It is, I venture to think, probable, in the nature of things,
that a young man of Ken's training and temperament would
be among those who were interested in this transaction,
possible that he was among its victims. That antecedent
probability is strengthened by one or two coincidences not
without interest, which it may be well to note. (1.) Harmar,
the Greek professor, was an old Wykehamist, afterwards head
of Magdalen College, Oxford, and, as such, was a man to whom
Ken would be likely to look up. (2.) When Harmar died, in
1670, he was buried at the cost of Nicholas Lloyd (also a
Fellow of Wadham), who was more nearly of Ken's age (seven
years older), like-minded with him, a writer of meditations
and prayers which might almost be taken for his, and which,
though never, I believe, published, have come before me in MS.

But there was a more serious element working at Oxford
which could hardly have been without its influence on a cha-

racter like Ken's.   Strange as it may seem, Oxford, under the Presbyterian régime of the Commonwealth, was the centre of an active Romanist propaganda. Christopher Davenport had entered at Merton in 1613, and after two years there, went, under the influence of a Roman Catholic priest in or near Oxford, to Douay, and joined the Order of the Franciscans at Ypres. After some time he became a missionary in England under the new name of Franciscus a Sanctâ Clarâ.[1] Under Charles I. he held the post of chaplain to Queen Henrietta Maria, and after the Restoration, discharged the same functions in the court of Catharine of Braganza.   He was known to Laud and Chillingworth, and applied to the former for his sanction in printing a work entitled *Deus, Natura, Gratia;* and his correspondence with that prelate afforded some of the materials for the counts of the indictment against Laud, which charged him with Romanising tendencies.   "During the Rebellion," say the editors of Wood's *Life*[2] "he lived in an obscure manner, *but was sometimes at Oxford,* for the use of the public library."   He died in 1680.   The Jesuit priest, Father Sancta Clara, of Mr. Shorthouse's *John Inglesant,* may fairly serve to represent the character and influence of the Davenport of history.

It can scarcely be doubted that such a man as Davenport, of singular gifts and attractive presence, would be likely to be on the look-out for all promising undergraduates; and of all the undergraduates then at Oxford few could have seemed so promising as Ken. Trained in Anglicanism of the Donne and Herbert and Ferrar type, brought up in a household in which Romanists were frequent visitors, where Davenport, who was a friend of Chillingworth's, may well have been one of those visitors, it is, I conceive, almost a moral certainty that the two must have come into contact, and that such a contact was not without its peril for Ken's inner life as an English Churchman.

[1] See note, p. 25.

[2] Like most Roman Catholics of his time in England, he had to pass, not unfrequently, under an *alias*, Hunt or Coventry. (Wood, *ut supra*, p. 225.) Davenport was noted chiefly for a work on the Thirty-nine Articles (*Paraphrastica Expositio . . .*) on much the same lines as Newman's *Tract XC.* Like most mediating books it was condemned from very opposite quarters. In England it was thought Jesuitical. At Rome the Jesuits tried to suppress it and get it burnt. It was, however, licensed at last. The *Deus, Natura, Gratia* is among Ken's books at Wells.

The hypothesis, at least, has the merit of explaining many of the phenomena of his later life. It accounts for the prominence in his library of Spanish and Italian devotional books of the ascetic type;[1] it explains the suspicions of a leaning to Rome which more or less followed him throughout his life; it suggests a reason for James II.'s choice of him as chaplain to his daughter, the Princess Mary, at the Hague, and as chaplain to the fleet in the expedition to Tangier; it furnishes, partially at least, a key to the language used by that king to the Vice-Chancellor and doctors at his visit to Oxford in 1688: "I must tell you that in the King my father's time the Church of England's men and the Catholicks loved each other and were, as 'twere, all one; but now there is gotten a spirit which is quite contrary, and what the reason is I cannot tell." (See p. 295.)

Of all the champions of Duessa there were few so silver-tongued and dexterous of fence as Davenport; and all we know leads us to think of him as being something more than the average Jesuit propagandist as pictured by our English imagination. There was an element of real enthusiasm which sustained him through the changes and chances of his pilgrimage; a touch of the poetry of feeling, if not of form, of which we find an illustration (not unlike that of the snapdragon on the wall of Trinity, Oxford, stamped on Cardinal Newman's memory) in the feeling which led him to return ever and anon to the old haunts at Merton and in the Bodleian, still more in his dying wish that he might be buried in the churchyard of St. Ebbe's, Oxford, because that was on the site of the old house of the Franciscan Order to which he had attached himself. Such a man, I conceive, must, if they met, have cast something like a spell of fascination over a character like Ken's.[2]

We know, however, at any rate, that he resisted this temptation as he had resisted temptations of another kind. He was

[1] Mr. Shorthouse (*John Inglesant*, c. iv.) represents Nicholas Ferrar as having bought many such books. I sometimes wonder, as I look at the catalogue of Ken's books in those languages, whether any of Ferrar's are among them, or whether they were entirely his own choice. See p. 259.

[2] It is a curious fact that there was among the writers of the time a John Ken, a Jesuit, who wrote in 1672 a controversial book, *The Truth of Religion Examined*, which was answered by Burnet. I cannot ascertain whether he was related to the Bishop.

appointed to the Rectory of Little Easton, in Essex, in 1663, and this implies that he must have been admitted to deacon's orders in the previous year, when he was twenty-five, and a year after he had taken his degree in 1661. We can well believe that, as he represents the preparation of Hymnotheo, who was as the shadow of his own personality cast on the cloudlands of fancy, so he prepared himself for that solemn time by a retreat, perhaps a forty days' retreat, of fasting and prayer, of self-conse-cration and ascetic thought. I have already stated (p. 23) that it seems to me probable that as part of this preparation there was a solemn resolve, if not a formal vow, to devote him-self to the pastoral office by a life of celibacy. That resolve was something more than an accident of temperament and circumstance, something more than the result of an early recol-lection of Hooker's experiences. He deliberately felt that this was, for him at least, though he dared not judge others, the highest and safest life, that in which he could most effectually follow in the footsteps of St. Paul, and in those of the many saints whom his early training and his later studies had taught him to reverence and love.[1]

[1] See quotation from *Edmund* (*Works*, ii. p. 169), in p. 24.

CHAPTER VI.

" Noiseless duties, silent cares,
　Mercies lighting unawares,
　Modest influence working good,
　Gifts, by the keen heart understood :
　Such as viewless spirits might give,—
　These they love, in these they live."

J. H. Newman.

MR. ANDERDON has shown, with the painstaking accuracy as to facts which distinguishes his *Life of Ken*, that he was appointed in 1663 to the Rectory of Little Easton, in the hundred of Dunmow, in Essex, and not, as previous biographers had stated, to a chaplaincy in the family of William, Lord Maynard. Lord Maynard was, however, the patron of the living, and it is natural to ask how the young Fellow of New College came to be chosen for this preferment. In the absence of direct information, we are left to inferences more or less conjectural, but the inference in this case assumes, if I mistake not, the character of a high degree of probability.

Lord Maynard, of Easton Lodge, then about the age of thirty-five, a widower with two children, the head of a conspicuous county family in Essex (an uncle, Sir John Maynard, had been impeached by the House of Commons for High Treason in

---

[1] Ant. à Wood. Ath. Oxon. ii. p. 939. So Anderdon quotes the following, which is decisive. "EASTON PARVA : P. Dunmow, Thos. Ken, 20 Aug., 1663, per mortem Dockley. Wms. Doms. Maynard. Br. Easton." (Records of the Diocese of London in the Faculty Office.) The same Records show that David Nichols, of whom I have not been able to learn anything, was appointed to the chaplaincy in 1662.

1647, and was sent to the Tower in 1658[1]), had just married his second wife, Margaret, a daughter of the Earl of Dysart.[2] In the short account of her life which Ken gives in his funeral sermon, preached in 1682, we find that she died at the age of forty, and that she was therefore not more than twenty-one when he first made her acquaintance. Her mother had died when she was eleven years old, in 1654, when the Puritan

LITTLE EASTON LODGE.
From a Photograph by Mr. W. Stacey.

policy was in the ascendant, and the "priests and service of God were driven into corners," but she had "continued stead-

---

[1] I have not been able to ascertain whether we may reckon Sergeant Maynard, who was knighted by Charles II., and was prominent through the whole period in Parliamentary debates, and who told William III. that he had survived not only the race of lawyers with whom he had started, but "nearly all law," among the members of the family.

[2] Her father had been in exile during the Commonwealth; her sister, a woman of very different type, was wife of the Duke of Lauderdale, of persecuting infamy in Scotland, and was reported to have been Cromwell's mistress. (Reresby, p. 116.) Maynard's first wife was daughter and heiress of Sir Robert Banastre, of Passenham, Northants.—Bramston, p. 405.

fast in the communion of the Church of England," and even
at that early age she had "daily resorted, though with great
difficulty, to the public prayers," "visited and relieved and fed
and clothed the suffering Royalists," and set apart a "certain
sum yearly out of her income that she might be able to succour
them."[1]   Among those whose ministrations, under these conditions of difficulty, she attended, Ken names Dr. Thruscross
and Dr. Mossom ; Peter Gunning, afterwards Bishop of Ely ;
and Brian Duppa, then Bishop of Salisbury, and afterwards of
Winchester.   Each of these names, famous in their day, though
now but little known except to students of Church history,
presents some points of contact with the life of Ken, and what
we know of them may perhaps serve to explain how the living
of Little Easton came to be offered to him.

Peter Gunning, whose name survives in the records of
Anglo-Catholic theology as the author of a treatise *On Lent*,
and who was ejected from Cambridge by the dominant Puritan
party, because he refused to take the Covenant, found refuge at
Oxford, and had been one of the chaplains of New College
under Dr. Pink's wardenship.   The action of the Parliamentary visitors probably drove him from Oxford, and Evelyn's
Diary (December 25th, 1657, March 7th, 165$\frac{7}{8}$) shows that he was
then in London ; but it is at least probable that he renewed
his intercourse with the College after the Restoration, and
would thus hear of the devout and ascetic character of young
Ken, and see in him one who would carry on to completeness
the spiritual training of the high-born girl who had been so
promising a disciple.   He was a conspicuous patron of Ken's
friend, Francis Turner, and brought him to St. John's College,
Cambridge, of which College Gunning was Master, Turner
succeeding him both there and at Ely.   The name of Timothy
Thruscross,[2] successively Prebendary of York, Archdeacon of
Cleveland, Preacher of the Charterhouse, and Fellow of Eton,

---

[1] Ken's *Funeral Sermon* in Round, *passim*.

[2] The name appears in many different forms—Thrisco, Thristcross, &c.   I am
indebted for the facts that follow to a MS. *Life* by the Rev. J. Ingle Dredge.
See also Prof. Mayor's *Life of Nicholas Ferrar*.   Evelyn (December 9th, 1659)
meets him at Gunning's, with other "devout and learned divines and firm confessors."   He adds, at a later date, that most of them were afterwards made
bishops.

though less known in the nineteenth century even than Gun-
ing's was, in the seventeenth, sufficiently conspicuous among
the members of the great Anglo-Catholic brotherhood. He
had been the friend of Nicholas Ferrar, of Little Gidding, and
had recorded his wish that such examples of the "common
life" might be multiplied in England. Men grouped him in
their common speech with Herbert Thorndike and Barnabas
Oley, the latter of whom had published Herbert's *Country
Parson* in 1652, and has, within the last few years, been made
more familiar to us than his fellows as the friend of John
Inglesant in Mr. Shorthouse's historical romance. When the
Restoration came they were actually grouped together in a
royal mandate directing the University of Oxford to confer
on them the degree of Doctor of Divinity. In September, 1655,
he seems to have been in London, holding Church services and
preaching. In 1660 he was living at Westminster. Such a
man was obviously one of those whom all good Churchmen,
like Izaak Walton, would delight to honour. He in his turn
could scarcely fail to know something of Walton and his surroundings. He also therefore may have had opportunities for
judging of Ken's character, for helping him on to a position
of trust and responsibility. There may have been a yet more
immediate link between the two men. Thruscross was of
Magdalen College, Oxford, and, though much the senior of the
two, may thus have known Fitzwilliam, whose life-long friendship with Ken has been already noticed as a memorable fact
in the latter's Oxford career.

In Dr. Robert Mossom, after the Restoration, Dean of Christ
Church, Dublin, and subsequently Bishop of Derry, we have
another of the confessors who maintained, as far as they could,
the continuity of Church of England services in spite of all pro-
hibitions of Parliament or Protector. In 1642 he had been chaplain in the royal army at York. In 1649 (March 25th) Evelyn
records that he attended the Church of St. Peter, Paul's Wharf,
of which Mossom was rector, and heard ("a rare thing now-a-
days") the Common Prayer. It was frequented by "a great
concourse and resort, both of the nobility and gentry," among
others, we may note, by Sir John Bramston, an Essex baronet
and a friend of the Maynards of Easton Lodge. The services

were not carried on without occasional interruptions and threats
and insults on the part of "Independent" soldiers and other
rioters, and in 1655 they were suspended by a more rigorous
edict on the part of the Protector, making the holding of such
services, or otherwise preaching or teaching, an offence punish-
able by exile or imprisonment.   After that time we may well
believe that Mossom, as the pastor whom she had loved and
honoured, was one of those whom the young Lady Margaret
helped in their struggles and privations.   Last among Lady
Maynard's advisers Ken names Brian Duppa, then Bishop of
Salisbury, afterwards of Winchester, "an exemplary confessor
for the King and for the Church," whom she often visited, and
who "seemed to be designed on purpose to be her spiritual
guide, to confirm her in all holy resolutions, to satisfy all
those scruples, to becalm all those fears and regulate all those
fervours which are incident to an early and tender piety." [1]

The facts which I have brought together seem to me to indicate with sufficient clearness that when Ken became rector of
Little Easton he was no stranger to either Lord Maynard or
his wife.   They started with a sufficient groundwork for mutual
respect and trust, and the relations into which they were now
brought did not end in disappointment.   As regards the prospects of advancement in the world the two years which Ken
spent with the Maynards were not without their influence on
his future career.   Lord Maynard held an honourable position
in the county, "kept good correspondence" with its gentry,
and "joyned his interest with theirs in all elections." [2]   He
had been loyal to the cause of the Crown in dark times, had
been impeached by Parliament in 1647, took a large part in
bringing about the Restoration (for which Charles II. thanked
him in a letter still in possession of the family), and through
the influence of his brother-in-law, the Duke of Lauderdale,
he obtained the honourable and lucrative position of Comptroller of the Household to Charles II., and was also a Privy
Councillor.   He appears to us as the type of a kindly, high-

---

[1] Duppa, it may be noted, had been with Charles I. at Carisbrooke, and was
thought to have had a hand in the *Ikon Basilike.*   Charles II. came to see him
when he was on his death-bed in 1662, and asked his blessing.

[2] Bramston, p. 405.

principled English nobleman whom Ken could justly honour, and who was able to understand and appreciate him. When James II. entered on the fatally rash policy which issued in the Declaration of Indulgence, he tried to secure Lord Maynard's support by promises and threats at a private interview, but was met by a steadfast resistance, such as Ken would have admired, and dismissed him from his office.[1] Through the influence of Godolphin Maynard obtained a pension, which was

LITTLE EASTON CHURCH.
From a Photograph by Mr. W. Stacey.

continued under William III. till his death in January, 1699. In the crisis of 1688 he voted in the House of Lords with Ken for the theory of a regency, as for a king incapacitated from personal sovereignty, rather than for that of a throne which the King had "abdicated," and which was therefore vacant. His position at Court under Charles II. may obviously have contributed, combined with other influences, to help Ken's somewhat rapid progress in later years up the ladder of promotion.

[1] Bramston, p. 269.

The chief interest presented by these two years at Little
Easton is found, however, in the bearing they had upon Ken's
inner life.   It was, we may feel quite sure, the first time that
the young rector had ever come across a woman of such a type
as that which he found in Lady Maynard.   When twenty
years afterwards he paints her portrait with all the loving
reverence of memory, we can picture to ourselves what she
was in the brightness of the earlier years of her married life.
The seventeenth century was indeed fruitful in noble patterns
of an almost ideal womanhood, of which we have examples in
Lucy Hutchinson, Mrs. Godolphin, the Countess of Warwick,
and Lady Rachel Russell, and which Thackeray has reproduced with a master hand in his Lady Esmond.   Such
characters may vary in opinions or in creed, according to their
political or theological surroundings.   What they had as the
groundwork of their life was the fear and love of God as a
living personal reality, and the intense purity of soul which,
even when it comes in contact with evil, as Lady Maynard
and Mrs. Godolphin came in contact with it in the court of
Charles II., remains untainted.[1]   And with this there was the
wisdom that meets the duties and difficulties of daily life with
a right judgment in all things, and the wide sympathy that
meets the wants of rich and poor—the poor especially—with
loving words and acts.   The conditions of undergraduate life
at Oxford, as they then were, were not likely to have brought
such a type of character within Ken's horizon.   Excellent as his
sister was in her way, she belonged to the middle, not the noble,
class of society, and could hardly have presented the refined
culture with which he now came into contact.   That sister, too,
was now lost to him, and her death, in April, 1662, the very
year before he went to Little Easton, must have left a gap in
his affections, which would make a friendship like Lady Maynard's doubly precious to him.   And he was six years her
senior, so that he might well feel that he was able to offer to
her, in the somewhat difficult position which she occupied as a
stepmother to her husband's children by his first marriage,

---

[1] I suggest the *Devout Women of the Court of Charles II.* as not a bad subject
for a special study in biography, or even, in contrast with the undevout women,
for art.

something of the guidance of an elder brother. Of the impression which she made on him, and the relations in which they stood to each other, he has himself told us with sufficient fulness in his funeral sermon. To him she was emphatically the "gracious woman" of whom the sage of Israel had spoken (Prov. xi. 16), "inflamed with heavenly love," full of all inward and outward graces, keeping herself unspotted from the world, in the midst of all the corruptions of the court.

LADY MAYNARD.

Studious and thoughtful as well as devout, able to give a reason for the hope that was in her, writing letters to her friends and relations, that came as a message of comfort and "subtle-pacéd counsel in distress"—the highest ideal of saintly womanhood, such as Ken had read of in Proba and Monica, seemed to be reproduced in her.[1]

---

[1] A confirmation of Ken's estimate, if any were wanted, is found in one or two passages of the Diary of Lady Warwick, sister of Robert Boyle, who will

To such a soul as this it was the young priest's privilege to act as guide and counsellor, and he knew more than any one else the secrets of her inner life. He received her confessions and directed her conscience when she was in doubt, and guided her in her choice of books. Morning and evening she was seen at the daily prayers which he, the first rector after the Restoration, must have introduced in the Parish Church. She observed, with reverential thankfulness, all the fasts and festivals of the Church's order. She took notes of his sermons, and abstracts of them were found among her papers on her death. It is reasonable to assume that the quotations given in the funeral sermon are from letters which she wrote to Ken after he had left the parish, and that he thus continued to act as her spiritual guide, as his friend Fitzwilliam did to Lady Rachel Russell, to say nothing of their opportunities for meeting, when they were both in London, during the remainder of her life. And the character of their correspondence may be inferred from some of the passages thus quoted. She was ever "making it her business to fit herself for her change, knowing the moment of it to be uncertain, and having no assurance that her warning would be great." So far from "being solicitous for riches for herself or her children," she looked on them "as dangerous things which did only clog and press down our souls to this earth." When sorrow and bereavement fell on her she could write : "Since God gives us all, let us not be sorrowful though we are to part with all ; the kingdom of heaven is a prize that is worth striving for, though it costs us dear. Alas! what is there in the world that links our hearts so close to it ? " She had learnt that "all blessings are given on this condition, that either they must be taken from us or we from them ; if then, we lose anything which we esteem a blessing, we are to give God the glory[1] and to resign it freely." Instead of turning to the "varieties and divertisements which most of her sex do usually admire," her rule of life was that "we are to seek for comfort and joy from God's ordinances and the converse of pious Chris-

meet us again. She also lived in Essex, and records (in 1663–1671) some of her visits to Lady Maynard, in which they exchanged their thoughts on the spiritual life, and held "sweet converse," as in "the house of God," as friends (p. 151).

[1] We note the familiar phrase of Ken's own letters in his later years.

tians, and not to take the usual course of the world, to drive
away melancholy by exposing ourselves to temptations." It
was no wonder that such an one should bear her " pains and
sicknesses, which were sharp and many," without " one symp-
tome of impatience." She reflected rather "how apt we are to
abuse prosperity." She asked " where our conformity is to the
great Captain of our salvation, if we have no sufferings ? " she
professes " that God, by suffering our conditions to be uneasy,
by that gentle way invites us to higher satisfactions than are to
be met with here," and acknowledges that "God was most
righteous in all that had befallen her, and there had been so
much mercy mixed with his chastising that she had been
but too happy." Her feeling for her husband to the last was
that of the "most affectionate thanks imaginable, for his invaluable and unparalleled kindness towards her." He allowed her,
" when she was a wife, to retain the accustomed devotion which
she had practised when a virgin." For the two children that
had been given her she desired that "the chief care should
be to make them pious Christians, which would be the best
provision that could be made for them." For her son in
particular (not, it will be remembered, heir to his father's title)
her express desire was that "he should be good rather than
either rich or great ; " that he should be " bred in the strictest
principles of sobriety, piety, and charity, of temperance and
innocency of life that could be ; " that he should "never be
indulged in the least sin, that he should never be that which
these corrupt days call a wit or a fine gentlemen, but an honest
and sincere Christian she desired he might be." And when the
end of that saintly life was near, she professed "that there was
nothing hard to be parted with but her lord and her dear
children ; yet from them she was content to part, for, by the
letters she left behind her for them, she 'took care of their
souls,' and she comforted herself with an entire acquiescence in
the good pleasure of her Beloved, with hopes that she should
still pray for them in heaven, and that she should ere long
meet them."[1] And this "put her into a transport which makes
her cry out, in one of her letters, ' O how joyful shall we be,

---

[1] It is suggestive to note the correspondence of this feeling with Ken's own
teaching (p. 233).

to meet at Christ's right hand, if we may be admitted into that elect number.' "

I have dwelt, at what may perhaps seem almost disproportionate length, on the character of this saintly lady. Those who have followed me in the wish to examine the various influences which were working on Ken's life and moulding his character to a like type of holiness will not, I think, blame me. No moment of a young clergyman's life is more critical than that of his first parochial charge and his first female friendship. If I have been in any measure right in what I have sketched as the "temptations of Hymnotheo," such a friendship was at once the corrective of those temptations, and, I will add, at the risk of being thought to affirm a paradox, that which was certain to confirm whatever vows of self-dedication to a celibate life he had made at his ordination. What may have begun in his shrinking from the possibility of falling to a lot like Hooker's would be confirmed by his contemplation of an ideal excellence of so rare a type that there was not the remotest chance of his ever meeting with it again, or if so, of its being, in any measure, within his reach. For him she was to the end of his life as much a transfigured and glorified ideal as Beatrice was to Dante.[1]   By a strange coincidence he quotes, as applicable to her, the very words of the *Veni, Sponsa de Libano*, with which, in Dante's vision, the appearance of his beloved one had been greeted by her angelic attendants.[2]

---

[1] See Ch. xxviii. p. 255.

[2] *Purg.* xxx. 11.   I give Ken's words as an instance of the poetry of strong emotion :—" Do but imagine you were in the Spouse's garden, where, when the south wind blows (Cant. iv. 16) the several spices and gums, the spikenard and the cinnamon, the frankincense and the myrrh, send forth their various smells, which meeting together and mixing in the air, make a compounde odour ; such a composition of all virtues. such an universal and uniform agreeableness, is there in a *gracious* soul, which, in a manner, whether we will or no, engages our affections."   Curiously enough the Maynard motto was what heralds call " canting " and laymen " punning "—*Manus justa nardus*.   Was the passage suggested by the motto ?   [We may trace a reminiscence, if I mistake not, in *Edmund*, b. vi. p. 169, where the " ruby " spirit (Edmund) and that of the pearl (Hilda) meet in Paradise.]   It will be remembered that Margaret means pearl—

" By conversation they a friendship made :
As on the Spouse's Garden's flow'ry Beds,
Where Rays benign the heavenly Bridegroom sheds ;

Of his parochial work at Little Easton, what he has said of Lady Maynard's share in it gives us a sufficiently clear view. Daily prayers and frequent communions, the regular observance of the Church's fasts and feasts, the instruction of the children by catechising in church, after the pattern of that more excellent way in which he has taught us that the *Exposition of the Church Catechism* can be made also a *Practice of Divine Love ;* teaching them to pray not with the lips but with the heart, not with the spirit only but with the understanding also ; with this we may believe that he began, as we know that he ended, his pastoral care of souls.[1]   Herbert's *Country Parson*, which I have already shown seemed as his model in that work, had been published in 1652 by his friend Barnabas Oley, and there can be little or no doubt that Ken set himself to reproduce what he there read, in whatever, in act or word, was lovely and excellent and of good report.[2]

Where the blest Spouse and Virgin oft repose,
Spring Valley Lilies, and the Sharon Rose,
One Scarlet Red, the other Snowy White,
And the sweet Odours which they breathe unite.

  * * * *

Ah! thought the Ruby, will good God our eyes
With views remote of Heaven thus tantalise?"

[C. J. P.]

[1] Ken's name does not occur in the registers of Little Easton, but it was not common then to sign the entries. The handwriting from 1663 to 1665 is said to be very like his. There are many Maynard monuments in a mortuary chapel. Easton Lodge is at present occupied by Lady Brooke, granddaughter of Viscount Maynard, who died there in 1865. I am indebted for the portrait of Lady Margaret to Lady Brooke's kindness. It has no name on it, but the family tradition is that it represents her.

[2] It is not without interest to note that a copy of Ken's *Funeral Sermon*, bound in morocco, still lies on the Communion Table in the chapel of Ilam House, Twickenham, which was occupied, when it was preached, by Lady Maynard's sister, the Duchess of Lauderdale, and still belongs to the Dysart family.

CHAPTER VII.

" But Thou, dear Lord,
Whilst I traced out bright scenes which were to come,
Isaac's pure blessings, and a verdant home,
   Did'st spare me, and withhold Thy fearful word :
Wiling me year by year, till I am found,
A pilgrim pale, with Paul's sad girdle bound."

J. H. Newman.

THE position in which Ken found himself at Little Easton
would seem so ideally adapted to a man of his temperament,
the work so exactly suited to him, that we might have expected
that he would have stayed there until there was a manifest call to
a higher work and greater responsibilities. As a fact it was not
so. Within two years he resigned the living, and we find him
at Winchester. And there was no summons, such as I have
spoken of, to account for his resignation. He was not elected
to a fellowship at Winchester till December, 1666. He was
not appointed to his first living in the diocese till July, 1667.
It is possible (for the dates of such appointments are not
entered in the diocesan registries, like those to livings and prebendal stalls) that Bishop Morley may have offered him the
post of chaplain, but episcopal chaplaincies were probably
then, as now, unsalaried appointments, the holders of which
were content to dwell for a while in the shadow-land of expectation. I do not say, and I do not imagine, that this last fact
would have had much weight with Ken in coming to a decision ;
but in the absence of some weightier inducement, a comparatively uncertain position like that of a bishop's chaplain, was
hardly a thing for which a sensible man would resign a parish
in which everything went well with him. And so far as we

know everything was going well. There were no parochial troubles, no interruption in the friendship which bound him to the family at Easton Lodge. In the absence of outward *data* we are left to look to circumstantial evidence and to the motives which might probably be working on such a mind as Ken's. And looking to the character of that mind, it does not seem to me an extravagant hypothesis to believe that he almost shrank, as it were, from the completeness of the bright and happy surroundings in the midst of which he found himself. In proportion as Lady Maynard met his conceptions of the perfect excellence of womanhood, opening to him, as Beatrice did to Dante, the mysteries of a *Vita Nuova*, he, in whom the poetic temperament was strong, though he lacked the clear vision and the master-hand of the supreme artist, might come to feel that he was exposed to the risk of finding his rest where he ought not to find it, of dwelling on that fair vision of the beauty of holiness until he became dependent on its presence for the peace and joy which ought to come to him from a diviner source. To the inward man of such an one in such a state there might come the whisper of the inner voice, "Arise and depart, for this is *not* thy rest."

And if any outward circumstances came in at the same time, which tended to a change of dwelling and of work, they would appear to one who, like Ken, saw in the changes and chances of life the leadings of a providential guidance, to confirm what might have before been only a vague and undefined feeling, not yet ripened into a purpose. And just at this point of Ken's life there were these outward circumstances. Izaak Walton had lost his wife, as we have seen, in April, 1662, and as she was buried at Worcester, though there is no trace of his ever having had a home in or near that city, his biographers have inferred with a sufficient show of reason that he had found a refuge in the palace of his old friend Bishop Morley, who became bishop of that diocese in 1660. But in 1662 Morley was translated to Winchester, and he took Walton and his son, Ken's nephew, then about eleven years old, with him, and his palace there was the old angler's home till his death in December, 1683. Walton was then seventy, and it may well have seemed to Morley that it would be an arrangement that

would work well for all concerned, if Ken also were to live with
him in the palace as his chaplain, look after his aged brother-
in-law, and superintend the education of his young nephew.[1]
All the memories of what his sister or Walton had done for him,
when he had been left first motherless and then fatherless, would
plead loudly for Ken's acceptance of such a proposal, and he
was not likely to let any considerations of income affect his
decision.   He had his fellowship at New College ; he had made
up his mind not to marry, and what he had was enough for a
man who had learnt the lesson of "plain living and high
thinking."

Bishop Morley, who thus appears for the first time in connexion with Ken's personal history, was thrown into such
close companionship with him during the next eighteen years
that it will be necessary to dwell, for a little space, on his life
and character.   Of his parentage and early life but little, so
far as I know, is recorded, but the first fact that stands out
clearly connects him with one of the great names in English
literature.   He was one of those familiarly known as the
"sons" of Ben Jonson, and this implies a certain measure
of literary culture and an acquaintance with many of the men
of letters of the period.   He had known Walton as far back as
1644, and must therefore have seen something of Ken's boyhood.   He had introduced Walton to Chillingworth and Hammond and Sanderson.[2]   When the Parliamentary Visitors entered
on their work at Oxford he was, with Henry Hammond and
John Fell, a Canon of Christ Church.   As a staunch royalist he
refused to acknowledge their authority, and though, through
the intervention of friends in high quarters, he was offered,
through Izaak Walton, the choice of retaining his preferment, without taking the Solemn League and Covenant, if
he would simply acquiesce and adopt the policy of silence,

---

[1] Anderdon (p. 53) refers to a letter of Ken's, at New College, dated Aug. 6,
1663, in which he asks for leave of absence till the following Easter, saying that
his "absence is contrived by my Lord of Winton himself," as suggesting that
even then he may have been chaplain.   It seems to me more probable that it
refers to his residence at Little Easton, and, if so, it suggests that his appointment to that living was due to the Bishop's influence.   The Warden of New
College, Dr. Sewell, informs me that he cannot find the letter referred to.

[2] Walton's Dedication to *Life of Sanderson*.

he preferred to share the fortunes of his comrades and left the university, as they did, for a life of concealment, of wandering, and of exile. He had the courage to attend Lord Capel when that nobleman fell into the hands of the Parliamentary army and was beheaded. Walton is said (but the evidence is not quite satisfactory) to have sheltered him for a year in his home on the banks of the Dove.[1] After a while he made his way abroad, joined Charles II. first at Paris and afterwards at the Hague, was appointed his chaplain, and kept up the services of the English Church, twice a day, for those who shared his exile. When the Restoration came he was naturally among the first whom Charles selected for preferment, and was appointed to the Deanery of Christ Church, and then to the see of Worcester in 1660, from which in 1662 he was translated, as has been said above, to Winchester. In theology he was one of those who, following in the footsteps of Whitgift and Davenant, were at once Calvinists and High Churchmen.[2] Unfamiliar as that combination is to us, it must be remembered that Hooker in the sixteenth century had shown, as Professor James Mozley has done in the nineteenth, that there is an aspect of Calvinism which, as in the case of Augustine, the fontal source from which both systems were derived, was compatible with what is commonly thought of as the Catholic doctrine of the sacraments and ecclesiastical polity. Though siding with the High Church party in the Act of Uniformity and other like measures, he showed much personal kindness to the Dissenters in his diocese, asked one of their ministers to dinner, and declared openly that they would never be won by rigour. Like Ken he never married; like him also he was indifferent to money,[3] and fulfilled Charles II.'s prophecy that he would never be richer for his bishopric. As it was, he spent his revenues in the repair and enlargement of

---

[1] Bowles, i. p. 96—112, where we find an imaginary conversation between Walton, Kenna, and Morley, which may be read with interest.

[2] Some one once asked him, under the Laudian régime, what the Arminians really held. "What do they hold?" was his reply. "Why, they hold all the best livings and canonries in England."—Clarendon's *Life*, i. 50.

[3] I notice, but only to reject, the calumny that in his last days he hurried on the renewal of leases that he might get the fines. If this were done at all, it must have been the act of relations who took advantage of his illness. See p. 177.

the episcopal palace at Wolvesey, near Winchester, and gave
liberally all round.

This, then, was the man into whose friendship and constant
companionship Ken was now thrown, probably, as I have said,
as chaplain. We can well believe that it must have been
pleasant for him to return to the scenes in which he had passed
his boyhood, to hear the services of the Church in the cathedral
as he had never heard them then, to watch the growth of the
new generation of boys whom he found within the walls of the
college. In what way his thoughts and sympathies with them
bore, in due time, their fruits, will come before us at a later period
of his life. For the present his duties as chaplain, sometimes
at Winchester, sometimes at Farnham, sometimes at the old
Winchester House in Chelsea,[1] occupied his time fairly. But it
would seem, though here again dates are not easily verifiable,
that they were not allowed to occupy it wholly. There was a
poor, neglected parish in the outskirts of the city, known as St.
John in the Soke.[2] The income was so small that it was difficult to find anyone to accept it. In 1665 Ken undertook the
duty *gratis*, and seems to have made it his peculiar charge as
long as he remained at, or when he returned to, Winchester.
During the period of the Rebellion and the Commonwealth,
church ordinances had fallen into disuse, and there, as in other
parts of England, there were many who had grown up un-
baptized. Ken left his mark on the place by giving his
special care to these cases; and the Office of Adult Baptism,
which the revision of the Prayer Book in 1662 had provided
for the purpose, was brought into frequent use.[3]

[1] The house was bought by Bishop Morley for £4,000, was annexed to the see
of Winchester, and so remained till the days of Bishop Tomline, when it was
superseded by the Winchester House in St. James's Square. It stood exactly
opposite the present Chelsea Pier. (G. H. S.)

[2] The " Soke " was a signiority or lordship, endowed by the king with the
liberty of holding a Court of Tenants or soc-men (defined by Stubbs as " coorls,
free land-owners, not noble "). The " Soke " was free from local customs duties,
but could impose its own. At Winchester it lay outside the walls, chiefly from
the N.E. corner, where St. John's parish is situated, to the S.W., and in the
seventeenth century had come to be a poor and neglected suburb. (E. W. K.
and T. F. K.)

[3] It may be noted that the traditions of the parish of Croscombe, near Wells,
report that Ken looked after such cases, when he was bishop, and, where he had
the opportunity, baptized them with his own hands.

The activity with which these pastoral duties were discharged marked him out as one who was worthy of a higher and
more definite position, and on December 8th, 1666, he was
elected unanimously to the position, all but the crowning
honour of a Wykehamist career, of a Fellow of Winchester.[1]
This was followed by Bishop Morley's collating him, in July,
1667, to the Rectory of Brightstone in the Isle of Wight, a

BRIGHTSTONE CHURCH, ISLE OF WIGHT.
From a Photograph by Mr. J. Milman Brown.

village about six miles from Carisbrook, which was memorable, in
Ken's time, for Charles I.'s imprisonment and attempted escape.
Of his work in that parish we have no distinct record, but looking
to the fact that the Bishop laid stress, in his government of his
diocese, on the observance of the fasts and festivals of the
Church's Calendar, and on the rubric as to daily prayers, we
have no reason to doubt that his ministrations were conducted
on the same lines as at Little Easton.   His signature is found

---

[1] This involved, of course, his resigning his Fellowship of New College, to
which he made a parting gift of £100 towards the New Buildings then in progress.

in the Parish Registers once only, according to Bishop Moberly, who held the living from 1866 to 1869, but, as we have
seen in the case of Little Easton, it was not usual at that time
for the clergy to sign each entry. A yew hedge at the bottom
of the Rectory garden is still traditionally known as Ken's
walk, in which, according to local belief, he composed his
Morning and Evening Hymns, dividing the historical interest
of the place with a pear-tree, under which Bishop Wilberforce,
when he was rector, wrote the whole of *Agathos*. A room in
the Rectory is still known as Ken's. Beyond these scanty
records we know nothing, with the exception of the fact, not
without its interest, that when Ken left Brightstone, in May,
1669, he was succeeded by Dr. John Fitzwilliam, who was also
one of Bishop Morley's chaplains, and who had been, as we
have seen, one of Ken's friends at Oxford. (See p. 51 and *n.*)

During this period, however, Ken's reputation as a preacher
was gaining a wide range. The *Diary* of Lady Warwick,[1]
one of the " devout and honourable women " of the period,
who was a sister of Robert Boyle, and who has already
met us as a friend of Lady Maynard, records her visits to
the Old Church at Chelsea in 1667—68,[2] and the impressions
which Ken's sermons made on her. They moved " her heart
to long after the blessed feast " of the holy communion ;
to " weep bitterly ; " to " bless God and have sweet communion with Him." They stirred her up to speak to her
husband " about things of everlasting concernment," to " persuade him to repentance and to make his peace with God."
" With strong desires and tears," when Ken preached on the
words, " Sin no more, lest a worse thing come unto thee," she
was " able to beg power against sin for the time to come." We
may well believe that she was not alone in these experiences,
and that Ken, at that comparatively early age—he was then just
thirty—had made his mark as one of the great preachers of the
day. There seems good reason to believe, as will be shown
hereafter, that he did not read his sermons, but either preached

---

[1] Published in part by the Religious Tract Society, in 1847. The entire MS.
is in the British Museum.

[2] The position of old Winchester House in the parish of Chelsea would
naturally lead to his preaching in that church.

extempore, or adopted the then dominant continental practice of first writing, and then preaching them from memory.[1] These visits to London would also, in the nature of things, introduce Ken to the notice of some of those in high places, with whom he was afterwards to be more closely connected. Morley had acted as confessor to the Duchess of York, daughter of Lord Clarendon, in her youth, and, though she joined the Church of Rome in 1669, was still on terms of intimacy with her and with the Duke.

WINCHESTER COLLEGE.

In resigning Brightstone, Ken was probably meeting the wishes of his bishop, who was naturally anxious both to provide for Fitzwilliam, and to have the chaplain on whom he most depended nearer to him. In April, 1669, Morley appointed Ken a prebendary of Winchester,[2] and as a living on the main-

[1] This probably accounts, in part, for the fact that only three of his sermons are now known to be extant; notes, sketches, and, perhaps, fully-written discourses may, however, have been destroyed by him in the first days of his fatal illness at Longleat.

[2] The Bishop's Register records Ken's appointment to another prebend, on May 29th of the same year. This may have involved some increase of income, or, perhaps, a better house. I am indebted to Mr. F. J. Baigent, of Winchester, for the extracts from the Register which give these dates.

land was obviously more compatible with his cathedral duties
and his residence as a Fellow of the College than one in the Isle
of Wight, transferred him to the rectory of East Woodhay, in
Hampshire, vacant by the resignation of Robert Sharrock, his
former tutor at New College, on the 28th of May, 1669—
his resignation of Brightstone is dated on the same day—and
that living he held till November, 1672,[1] when he vacated
it, in this instance without accepting any other preferment in
its place, to make way for another Oxford friend (Dr. George
Hooper, of Christ Church), who also was a chaplain of Bishop
Morley's, and with whom Ken was afterwards connected in
some of the most critical episodes of his life.[2] At present it
will be enough to say of him that he was one of the best scholars
of his time, with a far wider range of knowledge than either
Ken or Morley, well read in Hebrew, Syriac, Arabic, which
he had studied under Pococke, and quite up to the highest
point of the mathematical science of his time.   Morley, who
must have known him in former days at Oxford, had for some
time past had his eye on him, and had written to him in May,
1670, to tell him that he was only waiting for the power to offer
him some reasonable provision in place of his studentship and
tutorship at Christ Church, to ask him to become his chaplain.
This he was able to do in 1672 by giving him the rectory of
Havant; but Hooper found the place unhealthy and suffered
severely from ague, and Ken, with his usual disregard for personal interests, made way for him at Woodhay.[3]

[1] The Register of Woodhay contains the entry of the birth of Rose Ken,
daughter of Ion Ken, and his wife, Rose, daughter of Sir Thomas Vernon, June
3rd, 1670. Apparently, therefore, Ken was visited there by his brother's family.
Ion Ken was Treasurer to the East India Company, and his daughter, Martha,
married Frederick Krienberg, Resident for the Elector of Hanover in London.
In 1707, the Bishop mentions his 'sister Ken,' whose only son had died in
Cyprus (ii. 284). Ion appears, as I have said (p. 2, *n*, and 13), to have been a distinct name from John.

[2] Hooper, in the meantime, had, at the Archbishop's special request, been
made Chaplain to Sheldon, and was admitted to his fullest confidence in matters
of Church and State.   Morley sent for him to attend his deathbed.

[3] In connexion with Ken's life at Woodhay, we may mention the facts, (1)
that Sir Robert Sawyer, afterwards famous as one of the Counsel for the Seven
Bishops, then lived at Highclere in the next parish ; (2) that the rector of
Highclere, Mr. Thomas Milles, was as much a model priest as Ken himself.
Anderdon (pp. 82—85) gives an interesting account of him, based on the *Life*

From 1672 to 1675, accordingly, Ken had no other duties than those of chaplain, prebendary, and Fellow of the College, together with the pastoral charge, which he resumed, of the parish of St. John in the Soke.[1]   Such a period of comparative leisure was one in which a man of Ken's character would naturally strive to work out something of the ideal in which he recognised his own special calling and vocation.   And we have seen that, in his autobiographical poem of *Hymnotheo*, he

ST. JOHN IN THE SOKE.

has shown with sufficient clearness what he conceived that calling to be.   He felt that it was in him to exercise his gifts of

written by his son Thomas, Bishop of Waterford and Lismore, who reports that his father " admired Ken beyond all others in the Church of Christ," and never spoke of him " without raptures of veneration " (p. 119). Of Hooper, Milles used to say that he never knew any one who united in equal measure " the character of the perfect gentleman, the thorough scholar, and the venerable skilful divine " (p. 120).

[1] A strange story is told in a MS. printed by Anderdon (p. 97) of a boy of St. John in the Soke, who, for the first five years of his life, was subject to fits and never walked or spoke. Ken baptized him by the name of Matthew. A few days afterwards one of his playmates called him by what had been his nickname of

song and his spiritual experience so as to help others forward
in the higher life. And so, while continuing his unpaid work
as a preacher to the poor of St. John in the Soke, his thoughts
turned to the "children" of William of Wykeham, of whom
he had himself been one, and he wrote for them the *Manual of
Prayers* which has been used by many generations of scholars
at Winchester, and possibly[1] the Morning and Evening Hymns
which have made his name famous throughout English-speak-
ing Christendom.

The *Manual*, however, deserves a special Appendix to itself;
and now that Ken has reached, at the age of thirty-five, *il mezzo
del cammin di nostra vita*, it will not be an unfitting time to see
him, so far as we can picture him to ourselves, as he appeared to
his contemporaries, to ask what were the daily habits of his life,
how he spoke and acted. The portraits which are now extant
belong, all of them, to the period of his episcopate or his deprivation, and we have therefore to read backward from what
they present to us to what he was at an earlier period of his
life. I seem to see him, "little Ken," the "little black fellow,"
as Charles II. called him, rather below than above the middle
height, spare in frame, with a face in which the lines of asceticism were already marked, an expression wanting somewhat of
the sturdiness and strength of many of his distinguished contemporaries, but more than compensating for that defect by
meditative dark eyes and a singular sweet courtesy of manner
and expression. He wears no beard nor moustaches, and
altogether eschews the full flowing perukes which were then
becoming common even among the clergy, and his own hair is
somewhat thin, is short in front, is allowed to fall in slightly
curling locks over the collar of his coat. His life is one of

---

"Tattie," and he, who never spoke before, replied, "My name is not Tattie;
my name is Matthew, Dr. Ken has baptized me." From that time forward he
walked like other boys. The story is signed by the boy's mother, Sarah Cante.
Baker, in whose collection the MS., now in the Malet MSS. in the British
Museum, is found, adds, "This I had from the Master, Dr. Jenkin, who was
much with Dr. Ken, in Lord Weymouth's family." Ken himself told the story
to James II. in a conversation on alleged modern miracles (*Evelyn*, Sept. 16,
1685). The *Diary* gives "Westminster," but this is obviously a mistake (p. 266).

[1] I use the adverb advisedly. Several editions of the *Manual* were published from 1674 onwards, but the first in which the three hymns for Morning,
Evening, and Midnight appears is that of 1695. But see Chap. xxvii.

rigorous temperance, probably of total abstinence from wine,[1] and for him the Church's fast days are very serious realities. He has trained himself, following Morley's example, to take but one meal a day, and one sleep when he lies down to rest, and he habitually rises at two or three in the morning for prayer and meditation, and begins the day with singing his own, or some other, hymns, accompanying himself on his lute. At five A.M., as a Fellow of the College, he attends the school matins in the chapel, or else, as Prebendary, waits for those of the Cathedral. The day is given to study, to his duties as chaplain, to correspondence, and to pastoral visits among the poor. More and more he finds in music his comfort and delight, and has an organ in his own room, as almost, if not altogether, his only luxury.[2] When evening comes he gives a few hours, weary as the long day has made him, to companionship with the Bishop and his brother chaplains, with his aged brother-in-law, and his nephew, Izaak Walton, junior. The words in which his great-nephew, William Hawkins,[3] tells us that, at such times, "so lively and cheerful was his temper that he would be very facetious and entertaining to his friends in the evening, even when it was perceived that with difficulty he kept his eyes open," give one the impression of a quiet, quaint humour, sometimes passing into a not unkindly irony, with here and there an apt quotation, or a word of counsel and comfort, or the questions of one who seeks to draw out from others what they have seen and known in regions to which he himself is a stranger. The attempt to describe a man's familiar converse is, however, an almost hopeless task for any but a Boswell, and I have no sufficient dramatic power to follow Bowles, in attempting to present to others in the form of an imaginary conversation, after the manner of Landor, what I seem to picture to myself with sufficient vividness. Something of what I thus imagine, I have seen in Frederick Maurice and John Henry Newman, and there, *mutatis mutandis*, with all imaginable allowances for

---

[1] The "forbidden fruit" of the temptation of Genesis iii. is represented in *Hymnotheo* as the vine.—B. xi. p. 323. (See Hawkins, p. 3.)

[2] The organ is mentioned by Thomas Warton as shown at Winchester in his time (*circ.* 1735), and I have not been able to discover when it disappeared.

[3] Hawkins, p. 3.

differences in time, circumstances, character, I must be content
to leave it.

We are on somewhat firmer ground when we ask what were
Ken's studies at this period of his life, what books he read, to
what objects he looked forward, how far and in what direction
he contemplated authorship? When he was deprived of well-
nigh all other earthly possessions, he kept his library as "a
dukedom large enough," and took it with him to Longleat.
On his death he divided it by his will as follows: his French,
Italian, and Spanish books to the library of the Abbey Church
at Bath; the bulk of the remainder to his host, Lord Weymouth;
duplicates, and such others as he did not care to keep, to the
Cathedral Library at Wells. Excluding those which were
published at a later date than that of his residence at Winchester, we may reasonably infer that we have, in the rest, a fair
evidence as to what were at that period the favourite objects of
his study. What one notes chiefly on looking over the cata-
logues is the comparative absence of controversial theology.
The works of the great reformers of the Continent, Luther,
Melancthon, Calvin, Beza, of the great divines of the English
Reformation, of the Puritan theologians who had published
their voluminous commentaries and treatises, are simply conspicuous by their absence. Greek and Hebrew Grammars show
that he kept up his Oxford studies in those directions. Homer,
and Horace, and Tacitus, and the younger Pliny, and Cæsar,
and Isocrates, and Marcus Aurelius, and Plato, and Hesiod and
Virgil, seem to have been his favourite classics. Histories of
the Council of Trent and the Synod of Dort stand side by side,
as do the *Defensio* of Charles I., by Salmasius, and the *Defensio
pro populo Anglicano* of Milton, in reply to it. A Hebrew
Old Testament and a Septuagint show that he read that portion
of the Bible in the original and in the earliest version. The
two most striking groups in his books now at Longleat, and
Bath Abbey, and in the Cathedral Library of Wells, are,
however, (1) those that are the utterances of devout minds in
different communions, tending, some of them in the direction
of mysticism, such, *e.g.*, as Luis de Grenada, and Juan de Avila,
and Francis de Sales, and Erasmus, and Gerhard, and à Kempis,
and Molinos, and Francis of Assisi, and Fenelon, and St. Cyran,

and, (2), those which bear upon the early history of England and the English Church, such as Bede, and Spelman, and Matthew Paris, and the collected edition of the *Rerum Anglicarum Scriptores.* All these are, I believe, sufficiently characteristic, and point to the directions in which his mind was working. Ken was so spare a writer, contrasting in this respect with most of his contemporaries, such as Taylor, and Burnet, and Tillotson, and Barrow, a man to whom silence was as gold and speech as silver, who shrank in his humility from publishing what was in his mind, unless he could recognise something like a special call to publication, pursuing the even tenour of his way and unwilling to expose himself to the temptation, from which even the best and wisest among authors find it hard to escape, of thinking what acceptance his book will meet with, whether it will encounter the rough north-west of censure or the soft south-west of praise, that we cannot, save in scant measure, trace, as we can do with many authors, the connexion between his studies and his writings. In much of what he did write, however, we can trace the outcome of these two lines of reading. The study of the masters of the spiritual life helped him, in addition to his own personal experience, in the preparation of the devotional Manuals, which seem to have been the only books that he much cared to publish. In the epic poem of *Edmund,* the King and Martyr of the Anglo-Saxon Church, we may find the fruit of many weeks, or months, or years, given to the history of that Church. Whether the idea of that poem was even then floating before him, or whether it belonged altogether to a later period of his life, we have no sufficient data to determine.[1] When a man dies at the age of seventy-four, having published only three hymns as his contribution to the verse literature of his country during his lifetime, but leaves behind him, as Ken did, a mass of MSS. sufficient to fill four fair-sized octavo volumes, with no dates, and in most cases with but scanty internal evidence as to their order of priority, it is not easy to say when he first became, rightly or wrongly, conscious that he too had a gift of song. Some writers, such *e.g.* as Young, who is said to have

---

[1] Parts of the poem, as will be seen in Chapter xxvi., imply a date subsequent to Ken's elevation to the episcopate.

begun his *Night Thoughts* after he was sixty, take to poetry late
in life.   And if we were to take the date of the first published
edition of the *Winchester Manual*, that contained the three hymns
for Morning, Evening, and Midnight, that of 1695, it might
be contended that even they were not written till Ken also had
reached the same measure of three score years of age.   The few
attempts that have been made to fix the dates of any of the
poems on subjective grounds show how uncertain all such conjectures are.   I postpone, however, the full discussion of this
question till I come to deal specially with Ken's poems as a
whole.   What seems to me probable, partly from the autobiographical indications suggested in his *Hymnotheo*, is that he began writing verse at an early age, perhaps even in boyhood, that
the three famous hymns were written at Winchester before the
publication of the *Manual* in 1675, and that he then began the
habit of singing them daily to his lute or organ.   In the later
years of his life, in the enforced leisure of his residence at
Longleat, and as a relief in many weary days of suffering, he
appears to have looked over all the mass of MSS. that had
accumulated in the lapse of years, to have fair-copied what he
thought worth preserving, and to have destroyed the rest.   On
this assumption it is not without interest to note the fact that
the presence of *Paradise Lost* (1674) and *Paradise Regained*
(1705) among his books shows that he was among Milton's early
readers.   We can think of him as feeling, when he read the
former, that he too had it in him to write an epic, that he
would take the period which Milton had at one time contemplated and then abandoned, as his subject ; that, on comparing
the blank verse of Milton with the heroic couplet of the
Davideis of Cowley, which had been the object of his youthful
admiration, he would say "the old is better," and work upon
the model which he there found presented to him.

Of one book at any rate, the *Manual for Winchester Scholars*,
we know, with absolute certainty, that it belongs to this period
of Ken's life, and bears the impress of his character.   It
deserves, however, and will receive a fuller treatment than can
conveniently be given here.

THE "MANUAL FOR WINCHESTER SCHOLARS."

THE fact that this was Ken's first publication was in every way characteristic. There was little prospect of fame or profit from such a book. It did not appeal, as a controversial treatise or volume of sermons might have done, to a wide circle of readers who might be led to see in him the apologist for the position of the Church of England in its attitude towards Popery and Puritanism, or recognise him as one of the great thinkers of the day. It was simply an endeavour to meet a spiritual want which he knew to be a very real one, and to such a work he might well feel that he had a distinct calling. The recollections of his own boy-life at Winchester, the peculiar sympathy with children which is often the special inheritance of the childless,[1] the feeling that, though he was not a Master in the school, they were, in some measure, a flock committed to his care, the recollection of the Master's words "Feed my lambs," would all work upon his mind and lead him to do what lay in him to make their life a holier, and therefore a happier, one.

These motives might have actuated any one, in any time or place, who occupied Ken's position in relation to a great school. But if I mistake not there were some special elements in this case which it is not difficult to discern. Ken's boyhood at Winchester had been passed under the Puritan régime. Whatever drawbacks and defects Ken may have discerned in that régime then or afterwards, it can scarcely be questioned that, after its fashion, wisely or unwisely, it laid more stress upon personal religion than was likely to be found in the families of English country gentlemen and clergy in the years that followed the Restoration. A change for the worse had affected the whole social order. The type of character

---

[1] I anticipate an anecdote belonging to a later period of Ken's life, as illustrating what I speak of. Barbara, wife of Viscount Longueville, of Easton-Mauduit, Northamptonshire, was left a widow with seven children in 1704. Ken was requested to pay her a visit of consolation. He begged to see all her children, who were very young. He made them stand before him in a line and said, "It was very grateful to him to be able to see so many beings who had never wilfully offended God." The story was told by the late Robert Wilberforce, whose mother was descended from Lady Longueville, to Mr. Anderdon (p. 734).

which was represented by Walton and Wotton and Herbert
had all but passed away. The Cavalier of the days of Charles I.
had been replaced by the lower type of the Restoration. The profligacy of the Court of Charles had tainted the fathers and mothers
of the rising generation. Households like those of Colonel and
Lucy Hutchinson were hardly to be found. Where there was
more culture it was drifting into a worldly, latitudinarian indifference. The very Presbyterians were fast passing into Uni-
tarians. Where there was less profligacy, whatever there was of
religious feeling in the middle classes too often took the form of "No
Popery" fanaticism, rabid against all teaching and practices that
seemed to them to tend towards the doctrine or the ritual or the
polity of Rome.

All these facts we have to take into account when we think of
Ken as sitting down to write his *Manual*. And it is not a little
suggestive, as we do so, to find that its opening sentence is a distinct
echo of the first words of the *Catechism* of the Westminster Assembly,
which has been the backbone of the religious education of Scotland
ever since.[1] Men as different in their theological position as
Carlyle, Erskine of Linlathen, and Frederick Maurice, have seen in
those words, stamped as they are in early youth on the minds of
the Scotch people, the secret, in great measure, of its strength and
excellence.

I am not dealing with the *Manual* as a critic, not even as measuring
it by the standard of other like devotional books, but as it shows us
what Ken was, what thoughts were in his heart as he planned the
book, what cares and prayers were with him in the writing. His
choice of an ideal name for the boy-scholar is, obviously, sufficiently significant. He is not only a Timotheus, "one who honours
God," but a "Philotheus,"[2] one who loves God, who is the friend
of God. That, and nothing lower or less than that, is his ideal of
boyhood. To keep that in view from the first will make the life
safe, consistent, happy. In words in which we may trace something like a personal confession, for which, as we have seen, we,
however, can find a parallel in the story of "Hymnotheo,"[3] he

---

[1] "If you have any regard, good Philotheus, to your own eternal happiness,
it ought to be your chiefest care to serve and glorify God. It is for this end God
both made and redeemed you."—*Ken.*

"The chief end of man is to glorify God and to enjoy Him for ever."

Shorter Catechism.

[2] The name occurs also in *Edmund.*

[3] We note this name also as framed after the same pattern.

himself being his **only accuser**, he wishes his ideal boy to be better and purer and stronger than he himself had been.

> "O Philotheus, do but ask any one old penitent, what fruit, what satisfaction he hath purchased to himself by all those pleasures of sin which flattered him in his youth, and of which he is now ashamed. Will he not sadly tell you he has found them all to be but vanity and vexation of spirit? . . . . How bitterly will he, with David, lament the sins of his youth?"

The high-pitched ideal, however, does not lead him into vague generalities when he is dealing with the boys for whose souls' sakes he writes. He realises the precise position of each single boy, as a "commoner," or as a "chorister," or, in the technical language of William of Wykeham's statute, a "child" of the house, *i.e.* a boy on the foundation. The former are advised to say their prayers in their own chamber, the others, who have a common dormitory, are counselled, for greater quietude, to go to the chapel "between the first and second peal in the morning" (*i.e.* between 5 and 5.30 A.M.), and to repeat their evening prayers when, in the old Winton language, they "go *circum*," *i.e.* when the whole society, at 5 P.M., Warden, fellows, masters, clerks, scholars and choristers went in procession round the cloisters, returning to a supper in the hall, followed by evensong in the chapel at 8 P.M. In the absence of fuller information, it may be assumed that there was a short interval between the procession and the supper which the young Philotheus was advised to pass in the cloister or the chapel, saying his own evening prayers. The youngest boy was to learn his catechism without book, not as a task, but as the groundwork of his own faith and practice. Prayers were given for daily use; special meditations on "the Holy Child Jesus" for Sundays and holydays. All were to "*sing*" (not *say*) the "Morning and Evening Hymn[1] in their chamber devoutly." Those who were old enough to be communicants (the age is not specified, but an early admission to communion, say at twelve or thirteen, after the rule of George Herbert's *Country Parson*, seems implied throughout), have longer prayers and ejaculations provided for them. They are counselled "before second peal" (5·30 A.M.) to read "some short Psalm, or piece of a chapter out of the Gospel

---

[1] The words, which appear in the first edition of the *Manual*, seem to imply that the hymns were already in existence. They were probably printed separately, with music, and were therefore not reproduced in the *Manual*, in which they do not appear till the edition of 1695. Possibly, however, Ken may refer to some earlier anthems then in use (see Chap. xxvi.). It may be worth noting that the earliest recorded use of Morning and Evening Hymns is found in the Pythagorean Societies of Italy. Porphyry, *Vit. Pythag.*, p. 40, in Biggs' *Bampton Lectures on The Christian Platonists of Alexandria.*—(C. J. P.)

or historical books," and, when they hear it read in chapel, to
prepare themselves with short prayers that it may give them light
and wisdom. Self-examination as to sins of "idleness, or un-
chastity, lying, stubbornness, or quarrels," becomes a prominent
part of the spiritual exercises at the close of each day. If Philotheus cannot sleep at night, he is to "guard himself against idle
and unclean thoughts which will then be apt to crowd into his
mind" by repeating Psalms cxxx. and cxxxix., and by special
ejaculations of midnight praise. He is to look to "the receiving of
the blessed sacrament," as "the most divine and solemn act of our
religion," and therefore is to "approach the holy altar" with
devout preparation in his own chamber or in the chapel, according
to circumstances, as before. Fuller rules of self-examination than
before are given him in relation to sins of thought, word, or deed.
If he "finds this examination too difficult" for him, or is "afraid
that he shall not rightly perform it, or meets with any scruples or
troubles of conscience in the practice of it," his counsellor advises him,
"as the Church does," to "go to one of his superiors in this place, to
be his spiritual guide." He is "not to be ashamed to unburthen his
soul freely to him, that besides his ghostly counsel, he may receive
the benefit of absolution : for though confession of our sins to God
is only matter of duty and absolutely necessary, yet confession to
our spiritual guide also, is by many devout souls, found to be very
advantageous to true repentance."

I have thought it right (changing only for the sake of uniformity
the second person into the third) to give this passage *in extenso*, as
showing the importance which Ken attached to personal intercourse
of this kind as an element in the right guidance of the inner life,
and the consistency with which he acted on this conviction now, as
he had done at Little Easton at the beginning of his ministry, as he
did afterwards to the closing years of his life. He was not deterred,
either by what he may have seen of the evils of compulsory confession in the practice of the Church of Rome, still less by any
clamour on the part of the representatives of popular Protestantism
against the "abominations of the confessional," from acting on the
rule which had been commended to him by the law of the Church,
by the lives of saints, and by his own personal experience.

Self-examination is followed in due course by forms of confession,
which the penitent is to fill up for himself, and by "acts" of
shame, abhorrence, and contrition. These in their turn are succeeded by resolutions, and an oblation, or act of self-dedication, to
God's service. Petitions for pardon, for grace in general, for
particular graces, lead on to what is the crown and completion of

the book, its "Meditations on the Holy Eucharist." The language of those Meditations is after the manner of most of the Anglo-Catholic divines of the seventeenth century. It lays stress upon the actual communication, through the outward signs, of the spiritual presence of the body and blood of Christ, without formulating theories, Romish, Lutheran, Calvinistic, or Zuinglian, to explain the manner of that presence. It uses the term "altar" frequently and without reserve for the "holy table," but in its teaching dwells almost exclusively on the commemorative rather than the sacrificial character of the ordinance, on its bringing us into communion with the life of Christ rather than on its being the re-presentation of the one great offering. One passage in the *Meditations* is noteworthy as having given occasion of offence and having been altered by the author in a later revision. The early editions, from 1674 to 1681, had contained the words,

"Help me, then, O ye blessed Host of Heaven, to celebrate that unknown sorrow, that wonderful love which you yourselves so much admire ; help me to praise my crucified Saviour."

The edition of 1687 contained a prefatory advertisement :—

"Whereas a late Popish Pamphlet[1] has injuriously affirmed that in a *Manual of Prayers* for the use of the scholars of Winchester Colledge, I have taught the scholars of Winchester to invocate the whole court of Heaven, citing these words, page 93, 'Help me, then, O ye blessed host of Heaven,' &c., I think myself obliged to declare that by that apostrophe, I did no more intend the Popish Invocation of Saints and Angels than the holy Psalmist did, when he calls upon the Sun, Moon, and Stars, Fire, Hail and Snow, &c., to praise God (Psalm cxlviii.), and to prevent all future misinterpretations, I have altered, not the sense, but the words of that paragraph, and I do solemnly profess that I believe the 'Invocation of Saints and Angels, as it is practised in the Church of Rome, to be a *fond thing vainly invented, grounded on no warranty of Scripture, but rather repugnant to the Word of God,*' as the Twenty-Second Article of the Church of England styles it, to whose judgment I humbly submit.

"THO. BATH AND WELLS."

The passage as revised runs thus—

"O ye blessed Host of Heaven, who rejoice at the conversion of one single sinner, adore and praise my crucified Saviour, who dyed for the sins of the world ; adore and praise that unknown sorrow, that wonderful Love, which you yourselves must needs admire."[2]

[1] I have not succeeded in finding the pamphlet referred to. It was apparently of the same type as the letter addressed to him on his Bath Sermon (see p. 275). The language of the Evening Hymn was revised afterwards in the same direction (see ii. p. 213).

[2] We note the parallelism, conscious or unconscious, with Dante, *Par.* xviii. 124—6. (C. J. P.)

It will be seen, when we come to the period of Ken's life to which this revision belongs, that it was symptomatic of a more definitely anti-Romish cast of thought, brought about, we may believe, in part by the responsibilities of the episcopate and the imminent perils of the time, and partly by the impression made on him by the travels in France and Italy, which will come before us in the next chapter.

As the *Manual* proceeds, devotions are provided for use before and after communicating, and then there come forms of thanksgiving and intercession, the latter including prayers for the defence of " the Church of England from all assaults of schism, or heresy, or sacrilege," and for the conversion of " all Jews, Turks, Infidels, Atheists and Heretics." If the ideal Philotheus is a " child of the College " in the technical sense of that term, he is to use also a thanksgiving for " our founder, William of Wykeham, and all other our benefactors." He is warned not to neglect the " orders or duties of the school " on the plea of devotion ; to let " fasting and alms " accompany his acts of self-examination ; the fasting, however, being limited to abstinence from any additions, such as would seem to have been usual, to the short "commons" of certain days in the week, such as Friday and Saturday. Lastly, the *Manual* concludes with special prayers and ejaculations for a time of sickness, and in the editions from 1695 onward the three Hymns for Morning, Evening, and Midnight, follow as an appendix.[1]

We ask, as we close our survey of this spiritual guide for boyhood, how far the ideal which it contemplates was attainable? Can we think of a life so regulated developing after what we are accustomed to regard as the normal and healthy growth of a schoolboy, taking his place in school-work and the cricket field, and mingling cheerily with his companions? The experience of most schoolmasters would lead them, if I mistake not, to think the directions of the *Manual* too high-pitched for the average boy. That experience would also, I believe, teach them that in each generation of schoolboys there is at least a small percentage who, without being morbidly introspective or ostentatiously devout, after the Puritan or Seminarist type, are yet capable of at least appreciating and aspiring after such an ideal as Ken set before them. He himself, with his own boyhood still clearly present to his memory, in daily contact with those who were then at Winchester, probably himself

[1] It is, perhaps, worth noting that the editions of the *Manual* from 1688 to 1709, contain prayers for our Sovereign Lord, the King. I can scarcely doubt that Ken, from his position as a Non-Juror, meant James II.

acting as spiritual guide to many of them and receiving their confessions, did not despair of finding a Philotheus or two among
them.[1]   And even for the average boy it is better to have an ideal
that is beyond his reach, than to be left to the schoolboy's sense of
honour or to his natural scorn of 'sneaks' and 'snobs' and 'cads,' a
scorn not always resting, it may be feared, on purely ethical considerations. I cannot doubt, different as were the religious characteristics
of the two men, that Ken, in his day and generation, was acting on
the same general principles as those which guided Arnold. He
was content if he could influence the few, that so the few in their
turn might influence the many. The presence of one Philotheus in
a dormitory might be a light shining in a dark place. If there
were two they would discern and recognise each other, as by the
attraction of an elective affinity, and one would help his brother,
and each would, at times, as in the old Homeric words[2] keep an
outlook on the future for the other as well as for himself. And
if one more was added to that brotherhood of souls then would
that saying be true, that a "threefold cord is not easily broken."[3]
Ubi tres, ibi Ecclesia, is a rule that holds good of the world of
school as well as of the wider world of Christendom. So Arnold
found it, and the life of holiness and prayer to which Ken would
have led his ideal boy was probably not more difficult of attainment
by those who sought it than the "moral thoughtfulness" which
was the ideal of Rugby, and led them to a higher level. The lives
of men like Bishop Selwyn and Bishop Patteson at Eton, of Arthur
Stanley and other pupils of Arnold's, have shown in our own time,
to say nothing of those who, though unknown to fame, have
served God faithfully in their generation, that such an elevation of
the life of boyhood above the average standard is not impossible.
And the results would seem to testify that Ken's aspirations were
not disappointed. Edition followed upon edition in rapid succession
in his lifetime. The book which had been designed for Winchester
was accepted and used widely elsewhere.[4] When the hymns, which
are the groundwork of Ken's fame in Christendom, were added, it
gained a yet wider influence. Through generation after generation

---

[1] He did not expect too much, however. Compare the tenderly pathetic passage in Round, p. 427. "Be not afflicted, good Philotheus, if you cannot come
up exactly to the rules here given you. Believe me, it was never imagined that
you would."—(C. J. P.)

[2] *Iliad*, x. 224—6.

[3] *Eccles.*, iv. 12.

[4] The *Century* Magazine for January, 1888, records an instance of three
dozen copies being ordered from Philadelphia in 1751.

it served to keep alive the memory of better things than were found in the current maxims of the ethics and religion of the eighteenth century. The fact that Bishop Moberly, when he was head-master of Winchester, republished the *Manual*, with a brief but interesting life of Ken, shows that he believed it had not lost its power for good. It is still, I am informed, freely given by the masters there to the boys who are preparing for Confirmation, and I am not without sufficient evidence that the boys value it and profit by it.

CHAPTER VIII.

THE GRAND TOUR.

" Oh, that thy creed were sound !
For thou dost soothe the heart, thou Church of Rome,
By thine unwearied watch and varied round
Of service in thy Saviour's holy home.
* * * * *
There, on a foreign shore,
The home-sick solitary finds a friend."

J. H. Newman.

In 1675, just after the publication of the *Manual*, Ken made up his mind, for the first time in his life, to see something of the wider world. His nephew, the younger Izaak Walton, had attained the age of twenty-four, and both his father and his uncle may have thought it desirable that he should enlarge his mind, after the manner of other young men who could afford it, by taking what was known as the "grand tour" of Europe. Their recollections of Sir Henry Wotton's maxims, and of Bacon's *Essay on Travel*, would lead them to adopt Shakespeare's generalisation that

"Home-keeping youths have ever homely wits."

If they did not seek, as the heroes of the Elizabethan age did, "to discover islands far away," it might yet seem to them that it was well worth while to make their way to the " studious universities " of Europe, and to gather, after the pattern of Ulysses, whatever wisdom was to be gained from seeing " cities and manners of men." With Ken himself another motive was probably at work. He had known many Roman Catholics in England (p. 25). He had studied, doubtless, the arguments of English converts, like De Cressy[1] and Davenport. He may

---

[1] De Cressy's *Exomologesis*, a work giving the history of his own conversion (1653), is found in the catalogue of Ken's books left to the Cathedral Library at

have felt some leanings towards practices which he recognised as
ancient and Catholic in the Romish system, and which the popular Protestantism of England had rejected. His old schoolfellow
and friend, Francis Turner, was chaplain to the Duke of York,
continuing to hold that office in the Duke's household even
after the Duke's avowal of his conversion to Rome in 1669,
and when Ken compared the characters of the royal brothers it
may well have seemed to him that the younger, with all his
many sins, was yet the better and more lovable of the two.
Though, like Laud, not prepared to make overtures to Rome,
or to accept them from her, until " she be other than she is,"
the question whether a re-union were possible on the basis
of mutual concessions and re-adjustment, may well have
seemed to him to be one that called for an answer.   But this
would naturally be followed in its turn by yet another question :
Was it not well that he should see with his own eyes and hear
with his own ears, what Rome actually was, instead of trusting to
ex parte statements on either side ?   If that purpose formed an
element in Ken's plans of travel, it must be admitted that he
could not have chosen a more favourable time for such a tour of
observation.   The year 1675 was, according to the later Roman
practice of fixing the festival at intervals of twenty-five instead
of fifty years, a year of Jubilee, and the reigning Pope,
Clement X., had issued proclamations, which were circulated
throughout Roman Catholic Europe, for its observance with
more than ordinary splendour.   Such a time would serve the
inquirer as a kind of crucial experiment.   Did the system tend,
in proportion as men were under its power, to integrity and
industry, to holiness and purity, or to the reverse of all these ?
Were the influences which were ever emanating from its
centre, and were to be felt there at the maximum of their
intensity, favourable or unfavourable to the development of the
Christian life ?

     There is, perhaps, no one period of Ken's life on which we

Wells. He had been a Fellow of Merton (1627), Chaplain to Strafford and
Falkland, Canon of Windsor, and Dean of Loighlin (1648). He was converted
by what he saw of the holiness of the Carthusians at Paris, in 1650, published
his book, and was afterwards Chaplain to Catherine of Braganza.—Foley,
Records of the English Province of the Society of Jesus, ii. p. 305.

should more welcome information than this. To know what
things he then saw, what lessons he then learnt, would help us
to understand much of his after-life more clearly than we do.
Unhappily there is no period of which we know so little. Not
a single letter or fragment of a journal has come down to us.
Hardly a single reference to his travels occurs in his later
writings. We may, perhaps, infer from one casual remark
of his, that he went to Rome. A chance passage in Cotton's
sequel to Walton's *Complete Angler* records the fact, that
"young Master Izaak" (Ken's companion) "has been in
France, and at Rome, and at Venice, and I can't tell where."

In this dearth of information one has to make one's choice
between two alternatives. We may simply say nothing, record
the bare fact that he thus travelled, and pass on to what followed on his return to England; or we may venture on something of the nature of an 'ideal biography.' We can, without
much risk of error, conjecture what route the two travellers
took. We know what things must have come under their
observation in the cities through which they passed. We have
a sufficient knowledge of Ken's character to judge what impression they were likely to make on him. If we find that
judgment confirmed by what we find in his later writings or
actions, the chances of error will be almost, if not altogether,
eliminated. We may legitimately, I think, under such conditions, indulge in this account of imaginary travels as other
writers, such *e.g.* as Walter Savage Landor, have indulged in
"imaginary conversations." For my own satisfaction I follow
this course and not the other. Readers who prefer to confine
themselves to a record of actual facts can skip this chapter and
pass on.

In the work on which I now enter I find myself helped by
Bishop Burnet's *Letters to R.B.* (beyond a doubt, Robert Boyle),
giving an account of his travels in France, Switzerland, and
Italy in 1685, and by Boyle's account of his own travels in
1638—40, as given in Birch's *Life of Boyle*, pp. 35—48, and by
John Locke's Journal, as given in his *Life* by Lord King.[1] All

[1] Evelyn's *Diary*, 1641—1652, takes a wider range, extends over a longer
time, and is written from the standpoint of one who is professedly a connoisseur

these travellers took much the same route, and it may easily be
inferred that it was that commonly taken by English travellers
who started on the "grand tour."   Assuming that Ken took
it,[1] we have to think of him as reaching Paris by way of
Calais and Amiens, or Dieppe and Rouen.   In that city Ken
would have an opportunity of seeing what the Court of the
Grand Monarque was like.[2]   Bossuet was at that time forty-
eight, and Bourdaloue forty-three, and he may have heard them
preach, and have been confirmed by the effect of their eloquence
in the habit, which we have reason to believe he had adopted at
an earlier date, of preaching his own sermons from notes or
memory, and not reading them.   At Paris, at this time, he
would naturally visit the Carthusian house, the ascetic holiness of which had so impressed De Cressy.   We have to remember, however, that one great event in the political history of
Europe and the religious history of France came between the
date of Ken's travels and that of Burnet's.   The latter passed
through the country the year after the revocation of the Edict
of Nantes.   The reformed churches had been ruthlessly dispersed,
and their members, of whom we popularly, though somewhat in-
accurately, speak as the French Protestants (" Reformed " was
the more correct description), had been forced by a propagandism
of terror, which had begun in the persecution of the Cevennes
and culminated in the outrages of the Dragonnades, to choose
between apostasy and exile.   Many of them, as we shall see,
found a home in England.   Others, as Burnet records, were
received with open arms by their brethren in Switzerland.
When he journeyed from Paris to Lyons, he noted the depopu-
lated state even of considerable towns, the abject poverty and

in works of art, and is, therefore, I think, less serviceable in its supply of
materials.
    [1] The fact that the other route to Italy by the Netherlands, through Brussels,
Cologne, Augsburg, and Innspruck to Venice, was through a country at that
time the seat of war, and impassable for ordinary travellers, confirms, as Anderdon has pointed out (p. 83), this conjecture.   The greater part of the tour was
probably, as was then common, made on horseback.
    [2] Among other things he may have seen, or heard of, what Locke describes
as Louis XIV.'s levée.   The word was then used literally.   The king rose from
his bed, put on his clothes, and then knelt by his bedside for some time, priests
kneeling with him, and said his prayers, the room being full of courtiers, who
buzzed and talked all the time.—King, i. 151.

misery which met his eyes at every turn. His pictures of desolation, his forecasts of evil, are almost as graphic and prophetic as were those of Arthur Young at the close of the following century. But when Ken passed through France the descendants of the old Huguenots were still there, as the very salt of the nation's life, preserving it from utter putrefaction.[1] I cannot for a moment doubt that he would feel and act as Cosin had felt and acted before him, that he would admire their steadfastness, their integrity, the purity of their lives, their readiness to suffer for their faith, that he would attend their services and join in their communion.[2] The large-hearted, open-handed sympathy which he manifested afterwards to the refugees who sought shelter in England (see p. 243) must have rested on an antecedent and intelligent admiration. He could not regard their position, placed as they were, as schismatical, or their want of episcopal orders as anything else than an involuntary defect. I take it, then, that his first impressions as he passed through France tended to confirm his Anglican convictions, and probably gave them a more distinctively Protestant character.

Following in Burnet's track,—I do not, of course, take him as representing what Ken was likely to think or feel; often, indeed, looking to the strong contrasts of their temperaments, I reason by the rule of contraries,—we may think of Ken as he passed through Lyons, visiting the church dedicated to St. Irenæus, reading the inscription of the heathen husband on the tomb of his Christian wife—

" *Quæ dum nimis pia fuit, facta est impia,*"

and asking himself whether that was not a representative instance of the judgment which the world at all times passes on those who are not conformed to it. Aix-les-Bains, Chambéry, Grenoble, would follow naturally in the travellers' itinerary,

---

[1] There were, however, premonitory symptoms of the coming persecution. The Protestants of Uzes, Nismes, Montpellier, had had to pull down their "temples," their 'consuls' were not allowed to receive the sacrament in their official robes, their consistories lost the power of examining witnesses on oath (King i., 103—110). This was in 1676, one year after Ken's travels.

[2] *Life of Cosin*, prefixed to his *Works* in *Anglo-Catholic Library.*

and we can hardly think of a man of Ken's temperament looking back to the ascetic holiness of the saints of the past, and
himself walking in their footsteps, as turning back from the
ascent of the Grande Chartreuse, in which the ascetic holiness
of Rome, which had converted De Cressy, was believed to reach
its culminating point.   Robert Boyle, who had been a contemporary of Ken's at Oxford, has left on record a striking account
of the effect of such a visit on his own mind.[1]   The storm and
terror and sadness of the place, the " deep raving melancholy "
with which its scenery impressed him, the " strange stories and
pictures he found there of Bruno, the father of that order," all
these " suggested such strange and hideous distracting doubts
of some of the fundamentals of Christianity, that, though his
looks did little betray his thoughts, nothing but the forbidden-
ness of self-dispatch hindered his acting it."   I do not imagine
that what he saw of the Grande Chartreuse or its inhabitants
had this effect on Ken.   He had passed the age at which the
spiritual life is ordinarily exposed to this kind of crisis.   He
would look, we may believe, on the self-denying life which he
witnessed with something of a reverential sympathy, but all his
subsequent career bears its witness that he was content with
such forms of holy living as were compatible with home life
such as he had seen in England.   The piety of the Walton and
the Maynard households, of the brotherhood of Little Gidding,
and of the palaces at Winchester and Farnham Castle, would
seem to him of a healthier and safer type.   His efforts should
be given to helping to strengthen and deepen the religious life
of the family in England as he had found it, not to endeavour
to impress on it that which was a survival of mediævalism and
the inheritance of an alien Church.

From the Grande Chartreuse to Geneva was to pass from one
extreme of the Christian life to its opposite.[2]   We can hardly

---

[1] Birch, p. 41.

[2] Anderdon (p. 133) suggests Avignon, Vaucluse, and the Riviera as the
probable route.   If so, we may conjecture that it brought Ken within the range
of the influence of the saintly Nicholas Pavillon, Bishop of Alet, then nearly
fourscore, to whose character and life his own presented so striking a parallelism
(see Chap. xxix).   The fact that one of Pavillon's works (*Statuts Synodaux du
Diocèse d'Alet*) is found in Ken's library, as are also the works of Jansenius, and
the *Lettres Chrétiennes* of St. Cyran, and a translation of the *Lettres Provinciales*,
—all connected with the controversy in which Pavillon took an active part on

imagine that what Ken saw there would inspire him with the fervour which animates Burnet in that portion of his travels. The Scotch divine would naturally feel at home in a Christian society which was so closely connected in doctrine and discipline with that of his own country. He was content almost to rest the controversy between Romanism and Protestantism on the test "By their fruits ye shall know them," as applied to the contrast between the two cities which were respectively the representatives of the two systems on the Continent of Europe. On his second visit there he asked and obtained leave from the authorities to hold a Church of England service, which was attended by a large number of residents, including professors and ministers, and on the last Sunday he "gave the sacrament according to the way of the Church of England," to the great joy of the inhabitants, who were glad to take this "opportunity of expressing the respect which they had for our Church" (p. 275). When he left the city it was "with a concern that I could not have felt in leaving any place out of Great Britain."

I do not imagine that Ken's feelings quite rose to this height of admiration. Probably he reverenced the memory of Francis de Sales[1] more than that of Calvin, but there was much in the state of Geneva at the time calculated to enlist his sympathy. Calvinism was beginning to expand there, as it was expanding at that very time among the Presbyterians of England, as it has expanded within the last half century among those of Scotland. The leading theologians—Turretin and Tronchin—were Universalists, in the sense of teaching an universal, and not a particular or limited, redemption, and these wider thoughts of the Love and Fatherhood of God had not yet passed, as they did afterwards, both in England and Geneva, into Unitarianism. And what he saw there of the "strong hand of

the side of the Port Royalists, is, perhaps, in favour of this view. In any case we can scarcely suppose that Ken, in travelling through France, could turn away from the dispute between the Jesuits and Jansenists which then filled all men's minds in that country. See Note to Chap. xv. for a further account of Pavillon's influence on Ken.

[1] The Bishop of Geneva's *Introduction to a Devout Life* is among Ken's works at Longleat. His own *Practice of Divine Love* is, as will appear in Chap. xv., largely imbued with the spirit of St. Francis.

purity" with which the Reformed Church of Switzerland guided her children, its sumptuary laws restraining prodigality and profligacy, its criminal code inflicting death for a third adultery and the like, would, we can scarcely doubt, enlist his sympathy. It is at least suggestive that when, in his poem of *Edmund*, Ken sketches out an ideal polity, he introduces laws after this pattern as framed by the Saxon king, and reproduces one sumptuary regulation which Burnet singles out for special praise in his account of the constitution of Geneva, *i.e.* the provision by the Government of a reserved store of corn as a safeguard against famine, or monopoly on the part of private dealers. So in like manner Edmund's laws against mendicancy are obviously after the pattern of those of the Protestant cantons of Switzerland rather than of those which were within the obedience of Rome, and in which, as in all cities and villages of Italy, the plague of beggars "for the love of God," or, as then seems to have been the popular plea, "for the souls in purgatory," reigned without let or hindrance.[1]

I do not think of Ken as caring, as Burnet, the historian of the Reformation, cared, for the letters of the English Reformers, preserved in the archives of Zürich; but when he passed on to Chur, on his way by the Splügen Pass to Italy, one whose studies had led him, as his *Edmund* shows, to the *Origines* of the British and English Churches, could hardly fail to take note of the traditions which connect that city with Lucius, the first Christian British King, who was said to have left his fatherland to become the apostle of the Grisons. From Chur, if Ken followed the normal line of travel, he would pass to Milan, and thence to Padua and Venice. I do not care to indulge in any sensational rhetoric on the first feelings with which Ken, with his poetic tastes and scholarly culture, may have looked down on the fair plains of Lombardy or sailed on the waters of the Italian lakes. To be in the land of Virgil and Horace and Livy, of Dante and Petrarch and Tasso, to walk among the monuments of the great dead, and over the battle-fields of mighty armies, was, doubtless, for him, as for most of us who have known it, a thing never to be forgotten. I confine myself deliberately to the more limited

[1] *Edmund*, Book ii. pp. 49, 50. See i. 22, 336.

region of his thoughts as a student of Church history and a
seeker after truth, applying the law that systems, like men, are
to be known by their fruits, and seeking a basis for that
knowledge in as wide an induction as lay within his reach. In
matters of taste and feeling he would probably look on many
things with very different eyes from Burnet's. He would
scarcely dismiss the Duomo at Milan with saying that " it hath
nothing to commend it of architecture, being built in the rude
Gothic manner," or of St. Mark's, at Venice, that it also " hath
nothing to recommend it but its great antiquity and the vast
riches of the building."   He would, I conceive, be more stirred
with reverential admiration for the saintliness of St. Carlo
Borromeo, and would look with tolerance on many things which
to Burnet seemed to indicate an abject superstition.   The
Sunday-school in the Cathedral of Milan, instituted by St.
Carlo Borromeo, and in full activity then, as it is now, would,
we may well believe, attract the sympathy and admiration of
one who, when he became a bishop, looked on the spiritual
education of the lambs of the flock of Christ (*Pasce agnos
meos*) as one of the chief objects of his care.[1]   But on the great
plain questions of public morals, of uprightness in the administration of justice, of purity of life, the two English theologians
could hardly fail to be of one mind, and the impressions which
the one records we may well believe to have been shared also
by the other.   And so we may judge what Ken would have
thought of the practical influence of the Romish system when
he came in contact, at Venice, with the misery of the peasants
and the " old and unsubdued insolence of the nobility," and
the pervading espionage of the Inquisition, " so undermining
all natural confidence," that " none dare to trust another with
a secret of such consequence " as any attempt to assert their
freedom ; still more when he saw the " great libertinage "
which was " unblushingly practised by men of all orders
and degrees," extending itself to the clergy to such a degree
that though ignorance and vice were the only " indelible cha-

[1] I find Godeau's *Vie de St. Charles Borromée*, 1663, among Ken's books at
Bath Abbey. It seems to have been his habit, wherever he went, to buy
devotional books, or the lives of devout men. Controversial literature does not
seem, then or afterwards, to have attracted him.

racters" that they carry generally all over Italy, " they reached their highest point of baseness at Venice."[1] So it was that most of the nunneries, especially those into which women of the higher class entered, were an open scandal, and the young men, instead of serving their country in the wars against the Turks, "stayed at home, managing their intrigues in the Broglio, and dissolving their spirits among their courtesans." A " horrible distrust made it very rare to find a friend in Italy, but most of all at Venice." He who remembered what he had seen of the better type of English women and English homes would turn with loathing from the " ignorance," the " dull superstition," the " downright lewdness and beastliness," without even the gilding which vice wore in France, of the women of Venice. Not all his reverence for the real excellence of St. Antony of Padua could prevent his being shocked with the universal mendicancy which was practised in that Saint's name throughout Lombardy, or with the blasphemous inscription that was to be read on the *Ex-votos* in his Church : *Exaudit quos non audit et ipse Deus.*[2]

Burnet does not appear to have stayed long enough at Florence[3] to do more than note the chief buildings, libraries, and the like ; but if the state of things there in 1675 was not much altered from what it had been when Robert Boyle stayed there in 1641, Ken would find in it no great improvement upon Venice.[4] It had sunk to a lower depth of degradation than it had reached when Savonarola preached there. The shameless publicity of its prostitution had placed its brothels in the list of the " lions" of the city which strangers, even when they were not vicious, went to see, as travellers who were not gamblers have gone to the saloons of Baden-Baden or Monaco, and exhibited " the impudent nakedness of vice" which " description cannot reach and the worst of epithets can-

---

[1] The passages in inverted commas are taken from Burnet's *Letters*, iii., pp. 150—170.

[2] Burnet, p. 135.

[3] I note, not without a natural regret, that I do not find Dante among Ken's books. At the time he travelled Jesuitism was triumphant, and its conspiracy of silence to stamp out the poet's influence had been only too successful.

[4] Birch, p. 45.

not but flatter." Its monks and friars had fallen to the lowest imaginable depths of infamy. We can without much difficulty picture to ourselves, if this was what Robert Boyle and Burnet saw in quiet times, when life was running on in its usual grooves, what must have met Ken's eyes in the excitement which then prevailed, when companies of pilgrims—men, women, and children—were streaming from every town and village in Roman Catholic Christendom, and overcrowding every inn, in the year of jubilee. Does anything we have ever known of such pilgrimages, from Chaucer onwards, lead us to think of them as characterized by any serious devotion, any true repentance? Must we not rather picture them as aggravating all existing evils, plunging men into profound depths of superstition, exhibiting a more thoroughly paganised idolatry, narcotising conscience with the promise of cheap indulgences, ministering opportunities to every form of sensual licence?

Would matters be better when Ken entered the gates of Rome itself and stood in the very central seat of Latin Christianity? Ruins, churches, pictures, Capitol, Forum, Colosseum, catacombs, all these would of course have for him the attraction which they have had at all times for all travellers.[1] But the main question which such a man would ask himself in that place and time would be, What evidence is to be found here that the Church which claims to be the one true Church on earth is doing its Master's work, that the vicar of Christ, the successor of St. Peter, the infallible guide, has, in any appreciable measure, the mind of Christ? In answering that question we are not left to conjecture. We have Ken's own statement, in reply to James II., that whatever disposition he might have had in

---

[1] Two reminiscences of Italian travel may, perhaps, be traced in the *Hymnotheo*—

(1) The Maremma.
   " Ev'n ravenous beasts will never harbour there;
   Ev'n noxious plants die in that pois'nous air."—(p. 268.) ;

(2) The Catacombs.
   " Dead Rome, of living Rome the spacious drain,
   Where walking ghosts ne'er find their way again."—(p. 269.)

Had Ken lost his way in them? [C. J. P.]

favour of Rome had disappeared in that visit.[1] We have
Hawkins's report that he was " often heard to say that he had
great reason to give God thanks for his travels, since (if it were
possible) he returned rather more confirmed of the purity of the
Protestant religion than he was before." [2] Nor does he con-
ceal from us in his own writings what it was that mainly led
him to this conclusion. What struck him most was the way
in which the Roman clergy had sold themselves to Mammon
worship. The nepotism of Popes was the chronic scandal of
the Church. Five occupants of St. Peter's chair had been
conspicuous for their avarice. If they did not enrich their
favourites they heaped up treasures for themselves. The taxa-
tion of the Papal territory was so oppressive that a fourth
part of the inhabitants left the city. The pre-emption of corn
by the Papal officials (which Burnet contrasts with the plan
followed at Geneva) deprived the owners of the soil of the
profit of their labour.[3] From the Curia downwards there was
nothing but venality. Their eyes and their heart were but
for their covetousness. Their one object in dealing with the
myriads who crowded the city for the jubilee was—

" To wring
From the hard hands of peasants their vile trash,"

to rake up the gold and silver and copper which were poured
out at their shrines and on their counters, for candles, and
ex votos, and indulgences. To lead them by earnest preaching
to the kingdom of God and His righteousness was not in their
thoughts at all. What Ken thought of all this he has left on

[1] " Bishop Ken went to Rome with Dr. Walton : part of his design was to
inquire into the Roman religion, and if he found it sound, to profess it and continue at Rome. He returned about 1675, after six years' stay abroad (*sic*). In
King James's reign, upon his complimenting him upon some passages in his
writings for their nearness of opinions, he told the King what little reason he
had to do so ; that he had once been inclined to his religion, but that the New
Testament and his journey to Rome had cured him." (Spence, *Aneed.* p. 329,
1820.) Wood, *Ath. Oxon.* ii. 989, says that Ken "on his return found that he
had lost the favour of many of his former associates, who supposed that by this
journey he had been tinged with Popery," and adds that "they were altogether
mistaken."
[2] Hawkins, p. 6.
[3] Burnet, *Letters*, p. 196.

record in his *Edmund*, when (after the manner of Milton) he
introduces Mammon as speaking in a council of demons—

> "I of the Vatican the power assume,
> I only am infallible at Rome."
>
> *Works*, ii. p. 105.

I do not say that even then Ken wrapt the whole body of
the Church of Rome in one sweeping condemnation. The
affinity which holy souls have everywhere for each other must
have brought him into contact with the ten righteous men who
were left, even in the Papal Sodom. There might be found
much love even where there was little light. There might be
some truths to which the teaching and the worship, even of a
corrupted church, bore their witness, and which the professors
of a more intelligent Christianity had been contented to ignore.
The memories of St. Francis de Sales and St. Charles Borromeo were very precious to him. He collected, wherever he
went, the works of devout Roman Catholics, Nieremberg,
Drexelius, Pavillon, and others. He probably looked on Pascal
and the Port-Royalists as giving hope of better things (p. 258).
And, from this point of view, there was one fact, even in that
year of jubilee, which ought not to be passed over. Molinos,[1] the
preacher of the mystical quietism with which the author of
John Inglesant has lately made English readers familiar,
was then nearly at the height of his fame and influence.
It was in 1675, the very year of Ken's visit to Rome, that
he published his *Spiritual Guide*. The aim of his teaching
was to insist less on compulsory confession and formulated

---

[1] Molinos was born 1627, and educated at Coimbra. He was at first supported
by Innocent XI., but the Jesuits commissioned Paul Segneri to write against him,
and his work was put in the Index. His opponents stirred up Louis XIV.
against him, as they had done against the Port-Royalists, and through his confessors, Père la Chaise and Cardinal D'Estreés, denounced him to the Inquisition. He was imprisoned for twenty-two months, and tortured, and recanted,
after the manner of Galileo, with "a face full of scorn and defiance." Among
other charges the Jesuits accused him of impurity of life. He was again imprisoned till his death, December 28, 1696. He taught with Gerson that "the
spirit should become as a little child, or a beggar," that "faith and silence
brought the soul into the presence of God," and with Theophylact that "he
always prays who does good works."—J. H. Shorthouse. *Golden Thoughts from
Molinos.*

devotion, and more on the intercourse of the soul, through the
Eternal Spirit, with the Father and the Son.   Burnet (p. 211)
tells us that he was "much supported both in the kingdom of
Naples and in Sicily, and had also many friends and followers
in Rome." The Jesuits, as was to be expected, opposed a
system which threatened to undermine their influence, and
backed by "a great king, that is now extremely in the interests
of their Order" (Louis XIV.), threw him and hundreds of his
Quietist followers into the dungeons of the Inquisition.[1]

It is not, I think, an overbold stretch of imagination to think
of Ken as watching this movement with a profound interest.
One whose sole purpose as a writer was to lead men to a spiritual communion with God, to a life conversant with the Unseen
and the Eternal, whose studies lay, as we have seen, largely in
the regions of mystical theology, could not fail to be attracted
to one who was, in great measure, like-minded with himself.
There is every reason to believe, from the number of Spanish
books in his library, that Ken knew that language, and this
would facilitate, assuming that they met, the intercourse of the
two kindred souls. Ken may have learnt some lessons from
him which appeared in his *Practice of Divine Love*, and in yet
fuller measure in the more transcendental hymns which were
published posthumously.[2]   In practice, however, as himself the
spiritual guide of others, he did not adopt the principle which
was dominant in the teaching of Molinos.   Quietism may well
have seemed to him adapted to the Spanish or the Italian temperament rather than to the English.   When he answered the request
which must have been often put to him, "Teach us to pray," he
did not say, "Fold your hands; open your minds passively to a
supernatural influence; wait for the advent of an ecstatic fellow-

[1] Burnet gives not a bad story of one of the Pasquin satires of the time.
About the same time as that of Molinos' imprisonment, one man had been sentenced to the galleys for something he had spoken; and another hanged for
something he had written. And so the pasquinade ran, "*Si parliamo, in
galere; si scrivemmo, impiccati; si stiamo in quiete, all' Sant' Uffìcio: e che bisogna
fare?*" ("If we speak, there are the galleys for us; if we write, there is the
gallows; if we stand quiet, there is the Inquisition. What then must we do?")

[2] It is not without interest to note that an English translation of Molinos'
Spiritual Guide was among the books which Ken left to the Library of Wells
Cathedral.

ship with the Eternal." He knew that his penitents, like those who came to the Baptist, needed helps of a humbler and a safer kind, and he told them to use their Prayer Books, and wrote acts of intercession, contrition, thanksgiving, and the like, for their personal devotions, and gave them simple rules of soberness, temperance, and chastity for their daily life.

And so Ken left Rome at once sadder and wiser. He had seen Duessa in her own palace and was not likely now to mistake her for Una. If he had ever felt the fascination of her spells, those spells were at length broken. What remained for him? Popular Protestantism, as seen in Switzerland, France, Germany, Scotland, in the theology and worship of the English Puritans, did not altogether satisfy him. Even the Church of England must have seemed to one, to whom the *Expostulatoria* could, with any show of plausibility be ascribed,[1] far from perfect, defective in her discipline, exposed more and more to the perils of a latitudinarian Erastianism. There remained for him the ideal, in contemplating which he lived and died, and found his peace and joy. There was "the faith of the Undivided Church of the East and West." To that faith, as distinguished from the corruptions and half-truths of Rome and Geneva, he would be true and steadfast; it would be an anchor of the soul amid the storms of doubt and unbelief. It would supply all that he needed for the attainment of that holiness without which no man shall see the Lord.[2]

I have dwelt thus fully on Ken's travels up to this point because they had a manifest bearing on his life. By what route he returned from Rome, what he saw on his way from it, is of less importance for us. The common route for the homeward bound would seem to have been from Civita Vecchia or Leghorn to Marseilles or Genoa. I am inclined to think, however, from a passage in Ken's *Edmund*,[3] in which Nuremberg is described, and its two rivers, the Regnitz and the Pegnitz (hardly likely to have been known, even by name, except to those who had visited that city), that he came back by Innsbruck, and, passing

---

[1] See Note to Chap. iv.
[2] See Ken's Will (ii. p. 209), and *Practice of Divine Love*, p. 48, ed. 1686.
[3] *Edmund*, Book iv. pp. 69, 70.

through Nuremberg, made his way to England by the Rhine and the Netherlands.[1] Anyhow, he returned to Winchester some time in 1676 or 1677, and resumed the normal course of his life there, till, after three years of quiet retirement, he was called to a post of higher dignity and greater responsibility.

[1] The first letter in the next Chapter is dated October 24th, 1677. There are no *data* for fixing the time of his return precisely. Assuming that he did not reach England till the spring or summer of 1677, there would be time for a visit to Spain, and so for the acquirement of the knowledge of its language and literature implied in the presence of many Spanish books in his library.

NOTE.—KEN AND CARDINAL NEWMAN.—It is not, I think, without interest to note, as an instance of the parallelism of contrast, the impression made on J. H. Newman by his Italian travels. "The churches," he says, "calmed my impatience." On the other hand, what he saw of Rome impressed him with the feeling that "all, save the spirit of man, is divine." It was at this time (June 16th, 1833), distracted by conflicting emotions, that he wrote "Lead, kindly Light," in the Straits of Bonifazio.—*Apolog.*, pp. 96—100. See ii. 268.

CHAPTER IX.

> " Then, all thy meekness from thy hearers hid
> Beneath the Ascetic's port, the Preacher's fire
> Flow'd forth."
>
> *J. H. Newman.*

THE three years that followed on Ken's return to England must have been, if I mistake not, the calmest and happiest of his life. He had returned, as men who travel for the first time, and have known how to use their opportunities, commonly return, with the consciousness of enlarged knowledge and wider thoughts. Regions of culture were now open to him to which he had previously been a stranger. French and Italian, and, probably, Spanish, literature also, became familiar ground to him. His faith in the rightful claims of the Church of which he was a minister had been strengthened by what he saw of the defects and the corruptions of other Churches. It had not embittered his relations with members of those Churches, the Reformed of France or the un-reformed of Rome, or turned him into a vulgar or vehement controversialist. Rather had it led him to look on all but those who were avowedly indifferent to truth of any kind, with an enlarged sympathy and tolerance.

And his life at Winchester offered all that was congenial and attractive to such a mind as Ken's. Morley was still there, whom he honoured with a filial reverence ; and Walton, in the green old age of an octogenarian, hearty and hale, and full as ever of the recollections of the past ; and Walton's son, who had shared his travels, and was to him both as a nephew and a younger brother ; and Walton's daughter and her husband, William Hawkins, who before long became a Prebendary in the same Cathedral body as himself. And he had his organ in his rooms in the college, on which he could accompany himself, as he sang his own or other hymns, and could find leisure for larger excursions into the fields of poesy. The outlines of the two great epics on which perhaps he counted, so far as he dreamt of fame, as likely to perpetuate his name to later generations, may already have occupied his thoughts. He had time for reading the writers in mystical and ascetic theology, à Kempis, Gerson, Gerhard, De Sales, Molinos, St. Cyran, and the Spanish and Italian authors with whom he had lately made acquaintance, and storing up thoughts in his mind, as a treasure of things new and old, out of which he was afterwards to set them forth as a wise master-scribe instructed unto the Kingdom of Heaven, for the good of others. Above all there were the boys of the college, for whom, before he travelled, he had written his *Manual of Prayers*, and over whose use of that book he was now able to watch, with the satisfaction of knowing that his work had not been fruitless, that it had been accepted and welcomed there, as elsewhere, as a help to the higher life, that the hymns for morning and evening which had been printed, not at first with the *Manual*, but on a separate broad-sheet,[1] already rose as from the lips of the " babes and sucklings," out of which not seldom God " has perfected His praise."

The earliest of Ken's extant letters belongs to this period, and though dealing only with private matters, is sufficiently characteristic to deserve insertion :—[2]

LETTER I.

" FOR THE REVEREND DR. JOHN NICHOLAS, VICE-CHANCELLOR OF THE UNIVERSITY OF OXFORD.

" MY GOOD FRIEND,

" It pleased God to take away Mr. Coles between 10 and 11 of y[e] o'clock yesterday night about y[e] very time we were commending him to God in the prayers ; *Cujus anima requiescat in pace.* His sisters have lost an excellent brother, and y[e] society a very sincere and

---

[1] See Chap. xxvii.

[2] Anderdon (p. 58) speaks of a letter in New College as early as 1663, but the present Warden has been unable to trace it.

understanding man, but, to recompense his losse, as soon as ever
he was dead, ye Warden was persuaded to go to an election of a
successoure immediately; and just as we went into the chappello
Mr. Harris appeared, and was chose, *nemine contradicente*, before
dinner.   You may perhaps suspecte that we of this colledge might
have a design against you, in taking your friends away, and leaving
you all your honours; but, to convince you of the contrary, I will
endeavour to rid you of Bampton, whom Dr. Clutterbuck is willing
to recommend to his kinsman, upon some discourse I had with you,
but I intend he shall receive the favour from you early, (*only* ?)
or not at all; and I hope the New Colledge are now resolved that no
one who offers disrespect to you can be acceptable now.   I thank
you kindly for your favours to *my little boy*.   (If) it is fitt for me to
appere at Oxford, I shall, God willing, be ready.   In ye mean time,
you would do me kindnesse to *exchange* offices with me, for I would
willingly be Vice Chancellour *a month*, provided you would be
Bursar!   In regard to the death of my colleague ye present account
of the whole yeare lies on me.   Read to B. what follows : Dr.
Clutterbuck desires me to send to you for a scholar who is prudent
and welle-behaved, to live with a Knight at Greenwich, of his owne
name, and of kin to him.   His employment will be only to read
prayers, and to have a young gentleman's company, who is about
17 yeares of age, but, having lived in Italy, scarcely knows the
customes of England, and to read some parts of learning which are
most suitable to him.   I doubt not but you are able to recommend
several fitt for him, but, if I might guide your choice, I would wish
you would propose it to Mr. Bampton.   I know very welle that you
have not any reason to be kind to him, but I am of opinion, as they
soon go abroad for some time, you would soon learne to like him
better at his returne than before; besides, he told me the other day
that he was desirous of a schoole, and soome friends did recommend
him to Mr. Nowell for a chaplaine; but I am afraide he will not
suit him, and though his behaviour to you has made me much less
concern'd for him than, I own to you, I should have bene, yett I
like him so welle, that if he has a mind to this employement I desire
you to recommend him, for without your recommendation I shall be
able to doo him no good.   Dr. Clutterbuck is now in London,
lodging att Mr. Roger Newton's, in Little Brittaine.   Send your
resolution by ye nexte post to him, for he expects it.   Excuse this
very long letter.

" Deare Sir,
" Yours most affectionately,

"*Oct.* 24*th*, 1677.   " T. KEN."

[Dr. Nicholas, who had been elected to New College in the same year as Ken
(p. 31), succeeded Woodward as Warden of the College in 1675. Gilbert Coles,
whose death Ken writes to report, had been elected with them as a Fellow of
that College in 1637, and of Winchester College, first by the Parliamentary
Visitors, and then, on the Restoration, by the Fellows. He held in succession the living of East Meon, in Hampshire; of Ash, Surrey; and Easton,
near Winchester. In 1674 he published "*Theophilus and Orthodoxus*, or several
Conferences between two Friends, the one a true son of the Church of England,
the other fallen off to the Church of Rome, Oxford, 1674." The epitaph on his
tomb at Easton gives June 19, 1676, as the date of his death. Possibly the
discrepancy between this and the date given in the letter (October 23, 1677),
may be explained by supposing that Ken left his letter undated, and that it was
at some later period wrongly endorsed. Round, who prints both dates, makes
no attempt to reconcile them. Bampton would seem to have been a young
Fellow of New College. Dr. Clutterbuck was of Magdalen College, Oxford,
rector of South Stoneham, Hants, and succeeded Sharrock, Ken's predecessor at
Woodhay, as Archdeacon of Winchester. The "Knight at Greenwich" may
be identified with an Alderman Clutterbuck mentioned in Pepys's *Diary*, February 4, 1663—4, as one of the Mercers' Company, whom he met on a speech
day at St. Paul's School, one of the proposed Knights of the Royal Oak, or with
a Sir Thomas Clutterbuck, also of London, *circ.* 1670. Ken had probably become acquainted with the "young gentleman" during his Italian travels, and
found himself now, as in later life, consulted as a family adviser.

   What is chiefly noticeable in the letter, is (1) the *Requiescat in pace*, as showing
that Ken did not look on such a prayer as condemned by the Church of England.
It will be seen that the epitaph which he wrote for himself, but which was not
placed on his grave (ii. p. 203), included a request for such a prayer for his own
soul. That which appears on the monument of Bishop Barrow of St. Asaph (it
well be remembered that he had been Chaplain at New College, under Dr. Pink),
with its *Orate pro conservo vestro ut inveniat misericordiam in die Domini*, is another
notable instance of the same feeling. This also was written by the Bishop
himself, and bears the date of 1680. (2) We note throughout the letter a
characteristic graciousness and tact. Ken wishes to oblige the Warden, who
apparently had reason to be dissatisfied with Bampton, by giving him an
opportunity to get rid of his presence, and at the same time to help the young
man, against whom there would seem to have been nothing very serious, with a
suitable employment, and, in doing this, to meet the wants of the two Clutter-
bucks. (3) The youth of whom Ken speaks affectionately as his "little boy"
was probably one of his two nephews, sons of his sister Martha and John
Beacham. One of them, William, became fellow of New College, and died in
1711. The other, John, was probably of Trinity College, Oxford, and was made
Prebendary of Wells in 1687, and Vicar of East Brent in 1689. (4) We note,
with something of a smile, the groan which escapes from the ascetic student
at the prospect of being plunged into all the mundane business of the
bursar of a college. Leases, and fines, and ledgers were as unwelcome an
interruption to him as they were to J. H. Newman when he was bursar of Oriel,
or to the late Dean Stanley when he had a like office in the Chapter of
Canterbury.]

   The halcyon days of calm at Winchester were, however,

drawing to a close, and greater cares than those of a bursarship were looming in the near distance. The drift of circumstances had been bringing Ken gradually, year by year, within the range of Court influences. He had become popular as a preacher. The publication of his *Manual* had marked him out as qualified more than most men for the spiritual guidance of the young, and the outcome of it all was, that in 1679 he was offered the post of chaplain to the Princess Mary of Orange at the Hague. We are able, without much risk of error, to trace the path by which he was thus brought into contact with the family of the Duke of York, in the fortunes of which, in one way or another, his own were, for the rest of his life, inextricably interwoven.

It will be necessary for this purpose, without attempting a full history of the political transactions of the times, to note some of those transactions so far as they affected the Prince, with whom Ken was, now and for so many years afterwards, to be connected. James, Duke of York, had been brought up in the faith of the Church of England, and had in early youth resisted the pressure which the counsellors of his mother, Henrietta Maria, had put upon him, to adopt that of the Church of Rome. He had shared his brother's life at Paris and Cologne, and in Holland, and his habits of life were tainted with the same licentiousness. Charles, however, was content to be vicious where vice was safe and easy. It was otherwise with James. Within six months after the Restoration the English public was startled by the rumour that he had seduced the daughter of Lord Clarendon, the Chancellor of England. The baseness of the act was aggravated by its having been committed under cover of a promise of marriage written with his own blood, which the prince afterwards, it was reported, had stolen from Anne Hyde's cabinet. A child was born—a boy, who died young—on October 14th. Under pressure from the King, and in fear of the odium consequent on a public exposure, he consented, about December 21st, to make reparation by acknowledging a private marriage.[1] The consent of the Queen Dowager, who had other views for her

---

[1] Burnet, B. ii. 1660 ; Clarendon's *Life*, continuation, ii. 27 ; Pepys, Oct. 7, Dec. 21, 1660.

son's marriage, was obtained, after some difficulty, by the
influence of the Chancellor being exercised in her favour in
the matter of some pecuniary claims.

And with it began the chain of circumstances which brought
Ken into the position of chaplain to that Princess.   Bishop
Morley, Ken's patron, had been in old days on intimate terms
with Clarendon.   They had been in the circle of Lord Falkland's friends, whom he was wont to gather at Great Tew.   They
had been together during the exile at the Hague, and Morley
had kept up the services of the Prayer Book among the somewhat wild company of courtiers and exiles that were gathered
there.   The hand of Morley, who told the Presbyterians, who
came over with the invitation to Charles to resume the throne
of his father, that he also was a Calvinist, may be traced, without much risk of error, in the wide comprehensiveness of the
Declaration of Breda, commonly ascribed to Clarendon, by
which they were reconciled to the restoration of episcopacy.
It was probably not the fault of either that the promises of that
Declaration were not fulfilled.

It was natural enough, looking to these antecedents, that
Morley, as Bishop of Winchester, should watch the fortunes of
his friend's daughter in her new position.   He had been in the
habit of hearing her confessions from her girlhood.[1]   He would
try to keep her and her children and her household as free as
might be from the corruptions that surrounded them.   For a time
the Duchess persevered in her Anglicanism, and she and Morley
appear in one curious story as aiding to support a worthless
adventurer of the name of Macedo, whose only claim was that
he was a convert from Romanism.   At first the shameful
faithlessness of James must have made his wife's position
sufficiently painful.   But with the birth of his children, Mary
and Anne, the better side of his nature came out.   He loved to
pass his leisure in playing with them,[2] and fell into domestic
habits which provoked the sneer of his more cynical and more
profligate brother, who professed to see in him an almost dramatic exemplification of the character of the " hen-pecked
husband."   With this change in his private life there was also
something like a sense of public duty, which was never seen in

[1] Burnet, *O. T.*, Book ii. 1662.   [2] Pepys, Sept. 12, 1664.

Charles. As Admiral of the English fleet in the war against the Dutch, he covered himself with laurels in the battle of Solebay. In the administration of the Admiralty, as Pepys's *Diary* bears witness in almost every page, he introduced something like order, honesty, and economy, and maintained the character of a reformer who was, at least, free from the pecuniary corruption which infected well-nigh all other departments of the State.

What has been said will account for the interest with which Morley watched the course of events in the Duke's household, and for the hopes which he cherished that he might exercise some influence for good over them. The downfall and exile of Clarendon in 1667 would not diminish his anxiety to do what he could for his daughter and her children. And those children were now every day more and more conspicuous in the eyes of the nation as being in the line of succession to the throne. There seemed no prospect of any legitimate issue to Charles, and he set himself steadfastly—it is almost the only act in his life in which we trace anything like a sense of duty—in spite of all his otherwise doting fondness, against every proposal for legitimatising Monmouth, or otherwise taking measures which might give him a legal heir.[1] Before her death, however, the Duchess of York was believed to be a convert to the Church of Rome. Shortly after her death (1672)[2] it was noticed that James ceased to receive the communion and afterwards with-

---

[1] The measures suggested were singularly characteristic of their authors. Buckingham proposed that the Queen should be carried off to a convent, and so leave her husband free. Shaftesbury, that he should divorce her, and marry another princess. Burnet, following Luther, thought a second marriage without a divorce permissible.—Burnet, *O. T.*, Book ii. 1668, Note p. 177 in ed. of 1838.

[2] The death was miserable alike in its physical and spiritual aspects, "full of unspeakable torture, in doubt of her religion, without the sacrament or divine by her, like a poor wretch, none remembered her after one week, none sorry for her ; she was tost and flung about, and everyone did what they would with that stately carcase " (Evelyn, *Godolph.* p. 13.) The Duchess, for some months before her death, had been observed to withdraw from Communion, which she had previously received once a month. Morley remonstrated, but was put off with excuses, and did not know of her conversion till her death. On her deathbed the bishop who attended her expressed his hope that she was " steadfast in the Truth," and her only reply was " What is Truth ?" James showed Burnet a letter from her, giving her reasons for her conversion, which was afterwards published by Maimbourg.—Burnet, *O. T*, Book ii. 1672.

drew altogether from the services at the chapel at Whitehall. Charles, who in 1670 had entered into a secret treaty[1] with Louis XIV. to introduce Romanism into England, continued, as we know, to conform outwardly to the established Church up to the last hour of his life, when Huddleston was called in to complete the work of conversion which he had begun, more or less effectually, after the King's escape from the rout at Worcester. He was only so far not a hypocrite, as Burnet notes, that he showed ostentatiously, by look and manner, in all his attendance at the services of the Anglican Church, that he was contemptuously indifferent, and cared for none of these things.[2] He pressed James to follow his example, but that prince had personally the courage of his convictions, and held out even against the arguments of Sancroft and Morley. On one point, however, the King was peremptory. He had gauged the temper of the English people, and insisted that the two Princesses should be brought up as Protestants, though the choice of instructors and chaplains was probably left mainly to James. The responsibility for their education would seem to have fallen naturally upon Morley, and so we find among the leading members of the Duke's household those who were conspicuous as his friends, and therefore as Ken's also. Francis Turner, whom we have seen as the chosen companion of his school and college life, was chaplain to the Duke. Fitzwilliam, the friend of Kettlewell and Ken, and the spiritual guide of Lady Rachel Russell, was tutor to the Princess Anne, and Compton to Mary. Lord Maynard, Ken's first patron-friend at Little Easton, was Comptroller of the Household. Colonel James Grahme (or Graham), whose name will meet us farther

[1] The history of the treaty is curious enough to deserve a note. It was kept so profoundly secret that, though signed by Arlington, Arundell, Clifford, and Bellings for England, and by Colbert for France, its existence was unknown till 1830, when Lord Clifford allowed Lingard to publish it from the original MS. (ix., 503). It has been, I think, somewhat hastily inferred from it that Charles was a Romanist by conviction in 1670. I only find that for the sake of money he told Louis that he was one, as, for the same reason, he told the House of Commons that he was a Protestant. The root-element of his character was a profound unveracity. The " princely David " of Dryden's poem said, not in his haste only but in his leisure, that all men were liars, and resolved that he would be the master-liar among them all—the king " whose word no man relies on."

[2] Burnet, *O. T.*, Book ii. 1660.

on in 1695 as connected with an interesting episode in Ken's life, held an office of the " Privy Purse " nature in it.   George Hooper, also an Oxford friend of Ken's, who had succeeded him at Woodhay, was made chaplain to the Princess Mary after her marriage with the Prince William Henry of Orange.   Thomas White, afterwards Bishop of Peterborough, was, at a later date, appointed domestic chaplain to the Princess Anne on her marriage with Prince George of Denmark.

Of Ken himself, in connexion with the Court circle into which one after another of his friends thus found their way, we have no direct trace till his appointment (1679) as chaplain at the Hague, in succession to Hooper.   But that appointment implied a previous knowledge, and that knowledge may have been brought about in many ways.   First, the presence of the friends who have just been named in James's household would lead naturally to their sounding his praises to their master. Secondly, Ken's visits to London, when he stayed with Morley at Winchester House, and his growing fame as a preacher, would attract attention, and his abstention from controversy would, under the circumstances, count as a special recommendation.   Lastly, there was the fact that both the King and the Duke were frequent visitors at Morley's palace at Winchester, and at Farnham Castle, when they went to hunt in the New Forest.   So frequent, indeed, were their visits that the old prelate was once provoked (this, however, was at a later date) to speak unadvisedly with his lips, and to ask whether the King meant to " turn Farnham Castle into an inn."[1]

It lies in the nature of the case that this intimacy with the clerical members of James's household would lead to an acquaintance with other notabilities.   Pepys, as secretary to the Duke at the Admiralty, could scarcely fail to know something of Ken.   Evelyn, with his strong Church feeling and his pure and upright character, the friend of the Colonel Grahme above mentioned, knowing everybody and everything about the Court, may have often come in contact with him. It is at least probable that during these years Ken may have begun to recognise in John Kettlewell, the friend of Fitzwilliam, and like him intimately associated with Lord Russell

[1] Prideaux, *Letters*, p. 141.

and his wife, a man like-minded with himself, one whom he
learnt, as the years passed on, to love and honour more and
more for his unworldly saintliness, that he may have come in
contact with Margaret Blagge, Maid of Honour first to the
Duchess of York, and afterwards to the Queen, better known as
the Mrs. Godolphin,[1] whom Evelyn reverenced as maintaining
the habits of a devout purity in the midst of all the profligacy
of the society in which her lot was cast. It is even, I think,
possible that he may have known something of one who, of
all his contemporaries, was most like himself. Sir Elisha
Leighton,[2] himself a Roman Catholic and secretary to the
Duke of York, was brother to Robert, who, shortly after the
Restoration, was made Bishop of Dunblane, and afterwards Archbishop of Glasgow. The Bishop was consecrated in 1661 at
Lambeth by Sheldon and four other bishops, of whom Morley
would naturally be one.[3] He was introduced by his brother to
the King, and probably also to the Duke, for, as Burnet
states, "he loved to know men in all varieties of religion."
In this respect we may note a strong resemblance to Ken.

[1] Evelyn's *Life* of Mrs. Godolphin was published by Bishop Wilberforce in 1848.
Her spiritual director at this period was the Dean of Hereford, George Benson
(1672—1692). There may probably have been an earlier acquaintance between
her and Ken. When Charles II. was leaving England after the battle of Worcester, he placed his 'George' set with diamonds (probably that with the Queen's
portrait, which Charles I. had worn at his execution) in the hands of Colonel
Blagge, Mrs. Godolphin's father. He concealed it for the sake of safety, and
shortly afterwards was himself taken and imprisoned in the Tower. It was
afterwards conveyed to him there " by the trusty hands of Mr. Izaak Walton."
It is natural to infer from this that there was an acquaintance more or less
intimate between the two families (Evelyn, *Life*, p. 236). A new edition of the
Life has recently (1887) been published by Mr. Harcourt of Nuncham.

[2] The name is disguised in Pepys's *Diary* as Layton. The phonetic variations
of the orthography of this period are often a serious difficulty to the biographer.
Thus, *e.g.*, Pepys himself is found as Peepes, Creighton in its old Scotch form
of Crichton, or Creeton or Cryton, Graham as Grahme, Graeme, and even Grime,
Querouaille as Carwell, and so on in many other instances.

[3] It is noticeable that Leighton was scandalised by the costly stateliness of the
banquet given by Sheldon at his consecration. He told Burnet, that the "feast-
ing and jollity . . . . had not such an appearance of seriousness and piety as
became the new modelling of a church " (Burnet, *O. T.*, Book ii. 1661). It is worth
noting (1) that Evelyn estimates (November 30th, 1662), the cost of the banquet
at Earle's consecration as Bishop of Worcester at £600. (2) That it was probably
the consecration dinner at the Nag's Head Tavern that gave rise to one of the
charges which Romish controversialists were never weary of bringing against
the Church of England. (3) That Ken, when his time came, broke through a

Like Ken, he chose the celibate and contemplative life. Like him, he delighted in the study of mystical and ascetic writers, and drew largely not only from the *Imitation of Christ*, but from the other works of Thomas à Kempis. Like him he held it to be all but essential to the efficiency of a preacher that he should speak and not read his sermons. Like him, he was suspected of being a Papist in disguise.[1] Lastly, we may remember that antipathies as well as friendships may have had their starting-point about this period. Gilbert Burnet was then about the Court, not without influence as a Scotch Episcopalian, pushing, bustling, self-asserting, depreciating others, always talking of the great people he had known, and of the confidence in matters political and ecclesiastical with which they had honoured him. Of all the prominent Church personages of the time who had a decent reputation, I know no one whose character was so utterly unlike Ken's. We shall see how they thought and spoke of each other in later years, when each had been led to take his own line, and they had chosen widely divergent paths. I can scarcely doubt that there must have been something of a mutual repulsion from the first hour in which they came in contact.

In the meantime the section of the clergy to which Ken belonged were not inactive in endeavouring, as far as in them lay, to check the rampant licentiousness of the Court. Creighton, who had been Charles's companion in exile, and therefore much in contact with Morley, who was afterwards

custom of which it might be said with truth that it was "more honoured in the breach than in the observance." See p. 191.

[1] Leighton's reasons for resigning the Archbishopric of Glasgow—"the sense I have of the dreadful weight of whatsoever charge of souls . . . . and withal of my own extreme unworthiness and uselessness; the continuing and daily increasing divisions and contentions, and the little or no appearance of their cure for our time; the earnest desire I have long had of a retired and private life, which is now much increased by sickliness and old age"—present a suggestive parallelism to those which led Ken to his cession. (*Life of Leighton*, by J. N. Pearson, *Works*, 1835, p. 57; comp. *Letters*, liv., lvii.) Another point of resemblance is found in the width of Leighton's sympathies. It is recorded of him that he once went to visit a sick Presbyterian minister on a horse which he had borrowed from a Roman Catholic priest (*Ibid.* p. 66). The later years of his life were spent at Horsted Keynes, in Sussex. He died June 25, 1684, at the Bell Inn, Warwick Lane. He was not unfrequently in London, and I would fain hope, looking to the fact that they were in the same circle, that he and Ken may have met.

made Dean of Wells, and succeeded to the bishopric of that
diocese in 1670, startled the courtiers and concubines at Whitehall by a sermon against adultery, in which he told them
almost in Hamlet's language, that "for all the pains the ladies
took with their faces,"[1] they must "come at last to the same
end as Rosamond and Jane Shore," and the whole succession of
Court mistresses.[2]

A brief review of the political events which by bringing
about the marriage of the Prince of Orange and the Princess Mary
of York were to affect Ken's subsequent life, will be sufficient
for our present purpose. As elsewhere, I remember that I am
writing the life of Ken and not the larger history of his times.
The death of James's first wife was followed, as we have seen,
by the avowal of his own conversion to Romanism. His marriage with Mary Beatrice of Modena, in 1673, increased the
alarm with which the great mass of the English people looked
forward to his succession to the throne. They had before them
the prospect of a Popish dynasty, allied with the dynasties of
the Continent that were at once Popish and despotic. There
was with this the probability, amounting almost to a certainty,
that, under a Popish king, all high offices in the State would be
filled by the enemies of the Church and of the liberties of England. The disposition which Charles had shown to relieve the
Dissenters from some of the disabilities imposed by the Act of
Uniformity, the Five Mile Act, and other like laws, by the
exercise of the royal prerogative in the Declarations of Indulgence of 1662 and 1672,[3] in which it was known that James
heartily concurred, and which it was believed that he had
prompted, was viewed with suspicion as part of a covert plot for
introducing toleration for the sake of Popery, and men were
not without good grounds for believing that the toleration

[1] Pepys, March 16, 166⅔.

[2] The Duke of Monmouth's letter against written sermons, addressed to the
University of Cambridge, mentioned in p. 48, and a similar letter, in Latin,
addressed by Bathurst, President of Trinity College, Oxford, and Dean of Wells,
to that University, may probably be traced to the influence of Morley and his
friends.

[3] The later Declaration, it may be noted, was that which set John Bunyan
free from his twelve years' imprisonment, and released also many of George
Fox's followers.

would not last after it had served its purpose. The Test Act (1678), which excluded from offices, political or municipal, all who did not receive the Lord's Supper according to the order of the Church of England, was hurried through Parliament by large majorities, and was followed by the Duke of York's resignation of his office as Lord High Admiral and his retirement from public life. In 1679, after a temporary residence at Brussels, he withdrew to Scotland, and remained there, with the exception of a short visit to the King in February, 1680, until March, 1682.

As the star of the house of Stuart was thus waning, another actor in the drama of history, who was destined to work out its overthrow, appeared on the stage. In 1641, memorable as the year of the outbreak of the war between the King and his Parliament, the Princess Mary, daughter of Charles I., had been married to William II. of the house of Orange-Nassau, Stadtholder of the States of Holland. In November, 1650, the year that followed Charles's execution, William died. A few days after his death his widow gave birth to a son and heir, the William III. of the future history of England. He succeeded to the titles and patrimony that were hereditary in his house, but the States, jealous of the power of the house of Orange, which had succeeded in making the office of Stadtholder almost a part of its inheritance, took advantage of the opportunity thus presented, to abolish that office, and constituted themselves a republic pure and simple. The education of the young Prince, who lost his mother at an early age, was confided by John de Witt, who was at the head of the executive of the States, to his paternal grandmother, the Princess Augusta of Solms. Under these conditions the boy, naturally of a sickly constitution, but firm, reticent, and wary, grew up, presenting even in his early years a character that men found it hard to understand. In the wars between the States and England under Cromwell in 1652 and under Charles II. in 1664, he was of course too young to take part. The ambitious schemes of Louis XIV., who in 1667 laid claim, in virtue of the right of his wife, Maria Theresa, daughter of the King of Spain, to the succession of the Spanish Netherlands, which he had renounced on his marriage, gave, however, a new prominence to the youth who represented the

house that had, in its contest with Spain in a former generation, secured the fortunes of the Republic.   The balance of
power in Europe seemed threatened by the triumphant success
that followed the assertion of the claims of France.   The war
against Holland, in which England had taken part, as subservient to the policy of Louis, and in which the English fleet had
defeated the Dutch in 1666, and the Dutch had retaliated in
1667, by sailing up the Medway and destroying the arsenal
and stores at Sheerness and Chatham, was brought to a close
by the Peace of Breda in the latter year.   This was followed, in 1668, by the Triple Alliance between England,
Holland, and Sweden, as against France, negotiated by Sir
William Temple as the English envoy at the Hague, and by
John de Witt as the Grand Pensioner of the States.   The
young Prince meanwhile was watching the course of events,
concentrating every resolve on the re-assertion of the independence of his country, and on repelling the aggressions of the
French king.   For a time he did not seem likely, in spite of
the Triple Alliance, to gain much help from England.   The
ministers of the Cabal (Clifford, Ashley, Buckingham, Arlington,
Lauderdale), the first and fourth of whom were Roman Catholics,
directed the counsels of England and sold themselves to France.
Charles's sister, the Duchess of Orleans, came over on a mission of
political intrigue, and brought with her Mdlle. de Querouaille,
the fairest and most fascinating of the dames of France, that, as
the King's mistress, she might help to keep him and his advisers
in the line required by the policy of Louis.   The plan succeeded,
and, as Duchess of Portsmouth, she retained her influence over
Charles to the end of his life, and for the most part used that
influence as she was expected to use it.   If these adverse influences, however, were dominant in England, William gained in
the same year (1670) a step towards the accomplishment of his
designs, in his election by the States, in spite of the opposition
of De Witt, to the office of Captain-General.   In 1672 came
the crisis in which he took the position, never afterwards abandoned, of the champion of the liberties of Europe against the
French king, Louis XIV., who during 1671 had employed Vau-
ban in fortifying towns in the Netherlands as the base of his
operations, declared war against the United Provinces, and was

supported by the English Court, the Duke of York commanding the fleet, and the Duke of Monmouth taking part under Turenne in the last campaign. On the 12th of June Louis crossed the Rhine at Tolhuis, took city after city, and conquered the provinces of Utrecht, Guelderland, and Overyssel. The Dutch began to suspect De Witt of incompetency, if not of complicity with France, and, in the cruelty which springs out of panic, murdered him and his brother Cornelius (1672), with circumstances of horror that have hardly a parallel in history till we come to the massacres of September in the French Revolution. In that dark hour William found his opportunity. He at least would not despair of the Republic. He was appointed Stadtholder (the office, it will be remembered, had been abolished by the Perpetual Edict), and by opening the sluices of the great dyke, inundated the country and checked the progress of the invader. If nothing else remained, he was ready to "die in the last ditch" rather than surrender. He succeeded in forming an alliance against Louis, which included the Emperor of Germany, the King of Spain, and the Elector of Brandenburg. The tide of public feeling in England began to turn. The House of Commons, alarmed by the marriage of James with Mary of Modena, addressed the King against the French alliance and the Dutch war (November 4, 1673), and, though the King prorogued Parliament to restrain its further action, it had the effect of modifying his policy. Louis, after endeavouring to seduce William from his allies by the offer of the sovereignty of part of the United Provinces, guaranteed by England and France—an offer which the Prince rejected with a magnanimity which Ken, or one who shared Ken's mind, remembered long years afterwards to his honour,[1] in the midst of much personal and political antagonism,—stopped his course of conquest after the reduction of Maestricht, and returned to Paris, leaving the conduct of the war to Condé and Turenne. The temper of the Parliament, which met on January 7, 1674, led Charles to change his tactics. Peace was made with Holland in February, and Sir William Temple, who had always been a firm supporter of the Triple Alliance, was sent again as Minister

---

[1] Letter to Archbishop Tenison, commonly ascribed, at the time, to Ken. See note at end of Chap. xxi.

to the Hague, and co-operated loyally with William.   In the battle of Senef (August 1) the Prince showed himself no un-equal match even against the generalship of Condé.   The death of Turenne (July 27, 1675), the surrender of Trèves to the Allies, the capture of the Marshal de Créqui, the retirement of Condé from active service at the end of that year's campaign, led him to enter into negotiations for peace, which were carried on at Nimeguen under the mediation of England.   The negoti-ations dragged on slowly during 1676, and William did not suspend his military operations, but the death of De Ruyter in an engagement with the French in the Mediterranean was probably felt as a serious loss, and the defeat of the Prince himself at Mount Cassel, on April 11, 1677, by the Duke of Orleans and Luxembourg, made him anxious to secure a peace, if that peace could be obtained on terms consistent with the independence of the States.   For this purpose it was necessary to secure the influence of England, and with this view William came over in October, accompanied by his friends and counsel-lors, Bentinck and Zulestein, to propose a marriage between himself and his cousin, the Princess Mary.   Charles, who saw in such a marriage the means of regaining some of his lost popularity, the nation welcoming it as a security for Protes-tantism, gave his consent and overcame the reluctance of his brother and of the Princess herself, and the wedding took place accordingly on November 4, which, as it chanced, was the birthday of the Prince.

It was not a marriage that promised much for the happiness of the home-life of those who were thus united. It was the outcome, not of personal affection but of political plans, which, probably, even then had a far-reaching future. Mary wept bitterly when she was told that it had been decided for her. The days before and after the wedding were occupied with discussions between the Prince and the King as to the terms of the coming peace. The former was at one time on the point of leaving the country in disgust and breaking off the match, because the negotiations did not prosper as he wished. The Princess received the congratu-latory addresses that poured in from Parliament and corporate bodies with sad and downcast looks. The week was clouded over by the illness of her sister the Princess Anne, who was attacked with small-pox, and by the death of Archbishop Shel-don. Men and women about the Court began to note even then that the Prince treated his young bride—she was only fifteen and he was twenty-seven—with a coldness and sullenness that augured ill for the future, and this want of heart was hardly compensated by the jewels, of the value of £40,000, which he sent to her by Bentinck, the friend whom, apparently, he loved better than his wife. Before her departure the Princess opened her grief to the Queen, and was hardly comforted by her re-minding her that she too had had her troubles, and had known what it was to leave her native country for a home in a strange land : "Yes, madam," was the reply, "but you came to England, and I am leaving it." The weeks, however, ran their course, and on November 19th, the Prince and Princess sailed for Holland and entered on their life there.[1] And here for the present we will leave them.

The marriage, among its other consequences, was destined to affect the whole of the after-life of Ken, and for that reason it seemed desirable to trace the course of events which led up to it, and to note the character of its beginning. For the time, however, he was left at peace, so far as any one could be at peace in the stormy years that followed, in his work at Winchester. We can think of him as watching from afar, with horror and amazement, in 1678, the national madness of the Popish plot, the infamous perjuries of Oates and Dugdale and Dangerfield, against which hardly any one but Burnet had the courage to protest, the trials in which the lives of innocent men were sworn away, culminating, in 1680, in the condem-nation of Lord Stafford, though he was tried, not by a middle-class jury under the influence of panic, but by his own peers in the House of Lords. Though he was then in Holland, Ken must have shared, we can hardly doubt, in the feelings that led Morley, in conjunction, let us remember, with Halifax, to oppose the Exclusion Bill, pushed with all their power by

---

[1] They were accompanied, among others, by Sir Gabriel Sylvius (he had Latinised his original surname of Wood for the sake of diplomatic dignity), and his wife. The former was Chamberlain (*Hof-Maester*) to William. The latter was a friend of Mrs. Godolphin, whose life Evelyn dedicates to her, and sister to Mrs. Graham, or Grahme, who will meet us farther on (Chap. xxiv.)

Shaftesbury and his party, by which the succession to the crown was to be altered to secure a Protestant Sovereign.

It was, perhaps, somewhat of a relief to him when, towards the close of 1679, he was invited to accept, as successor to his friend Hooper, the Chaplaincy to the Princess Mary at the Hague. What had preceded his arrival there and in what surroundings he found himself, how his days passed there, and how they affected his after-life, will be our next subject of inquiry.[1]

---

[1] It may be noted, in passing, that Ken had taken his B.D. July 6th, 1678, and his D.D. June 30th, 1679. On May 20th, 1679, he lost his maternal uncle, John Chalkhill, who was a Fellow of Winchester, elected in 1633.

> " Next, as he threads the maze of men,
>   Aye must he lift his witness, when
>   A sin is spoke in Heaven's dread face,
>   And none at hand of higher grace
>   The Cross to carry in his place."
>
> J. H. *Newman.*

To most men the position on which Ken now entered would have been attractive, as bringing him within the more immediate range of Court influence, and therefore opening a prospect of Court preferment. Persons in such positions were thought to have a preferential claim to canonries and deaneries and bishoprics. Ken's own feelings may be inferred from the text which about this time he seems to have taken as the watchword of his life. In the fly-leaf of a copy of Grotius *de Veritate* (an Elzevir edition, published at Leyden, and therefore probably bought while Ken was in Holland), now in the Cathedral library at Wells, I find, in his writing, the words which the prophet Jeremiah addressed to his too ambitious scribe : " *Et tu quæris tibi grandia ? Noli quærere.*" " Seekest thou great things for thyself ? seek them not."—Jeremiah xxxv. 5. The same text appears in the Greek Testament which was the constant companion of his later years, and which is now in the possession of the Rev. Wyndham Merewether.[1]

Whatever stirrings of ambition, whatever wish to bear his part in the drama of history, or at least, to do as others did,

---

[1] Other texts written on the same fly-leaf in Mr. Merewether's copy are (1) Ταῦτα μελίτα, ἐν τούτοις ἴσθι (" Meditate upon these things ; give thyself wholly to them ")—1 Tim. iv. 15, and (2) "Ἱνα ἐν ἡμῖν μάθητε τὸ μὴ ὑπὲρ ὅ γίγραπται φρονεῖν (" That ye might learn in us not to think of men above that which is written ")—1 Cor. iv. 6.

such, *e.g.*, as Burnet, and mingle with the actors in that drama and hear what they said and did behind the scenes, and, it might be, pull some of the wires that moved the puppets in the play, may have been working in Ken's mind, and tending to shake his singleness of purpose, were thus repressed by him. He accepted the work to which he was now called simply because he was called to it, because it gave an opening for some possible influence for good on those who were likely, in the natural course of things, to exercise a greater influence than himself. What he may have heard from those who had preceded him in his office was not very encouraging. The education of the Duke of York's daughter had been confided, under the direction of Compton, Bishop of London, to Dr. William Lake, from whose *Diary*[1] we derive the information as to the Princess Mary's marriage given in the previous chapter. He notes, with a plaintive sadness, that she was given to card-playing on Sundays. Under his remonstrances she had given up the practice in England, but he heard that she had resumed it on her arrival at the Hague. Her first chaplain, recommended probably either by Compton or Morley, was Dr. William Lloyd, afterwards Bishop of St. Asaph, whom we identify as the perpetrator in his Oxford days of the practical joke recorded in p. 66. Of him, Lake complains that he allowed the Princess to leave the services of the Church of England for those of a body of Dutch religionists of the Brownist or Congregationalist type. He did not hold office long, and was succeeded (in this case we trace Sheldon's and Morley's influence) by George Hooper, Ken's friend at Oxford, who had succeeded him at Woodhay, and who, after being chaplain to Morley, was promoted to the same office under Sheldon. His report of domestic matters in William's household gives a somewhat unpleasant picture. The indifference of his conduct before marriage had passed into harshness. We can scarcely avoid the conclusion that the Prince of Orange had deliberately adopted, with the far-sighted forecast which commonly characterized his actions, what we may call a Petruchio policy. His Katharine was to be trained to bear the yoke in small things so that she might learn to be subservient in great, when

---

[1] *Camden Miscellany*, vol. i.

the time was ripe for demanding such subservience.[1]   In
what Hooper records, accordingly, we may recognise something
more than a casual outbreak of ill-temper or ill-manners.
There was no chapel in the Prince's house, and, as he never
dined with the Princess, she gave up her dining-room to be
fitted up for the purpose. The Prince came in to see the altered
room, and kicked contemptuously at the steps on which the
Communion Table stood, asking, "What was the use of them?"
Hooper found that the Princess had been set to read Dissenting
theology, and gave her Hooker and Eusebius to study by way
of balance. The Prince looked at them with a sneer, "I suppose
Dr. Hooper persuades you to read these books." When he
talked with Hooper on the state of Church matters in England,
and urged a larger comprehensiveness in the treatment of
Dissenters, he met the chaplain's plea for uniformity with the
remark, "Well, Dr. Hooper, you will never be a bishop," and
observed to a friend—the words are significant enough of plans
at least half-formed—that "If he ever had anything to do with
England, Dr. Hooper should be Dr. Hooper still."[2]   It would
seem too that the Prince had not provided for the payment of
the chaplain as part of the disbursements of his household.
Hooper's colleague, who had no private resources and expected a decent stipend, "never got a shilling," ran into debt,
and died of worry and vexation. Hooper was more fortunate,
but during the year and a-half of his residence at the Hague,
he received nothing till the night before he sailed for England,
when Bentinck sent a servant to him with £70, and excuses
for its not having been sent sooner. The chaplain of the
Princess was apparently supposed to be "passing rich on £40
a year."[3]

[1] So Covell, who succeeded Ken as chaplain, writes (in 1685) that "the
Princess's heart is ready to break, and yet she counterfeits the greatest joy."
"The Prince hath infallibly made her a slave, and there's an end of it." The
later history of her behaviour, when she joined William at Whitehall after
James's flight (ii. 35), will show us how effectual the discipline had been.

[2] When Mary, during William's absence from England, appointed Hooper as
Dean of Canterbury, she had to encounter her husband's strongly marked dis-
pleasure. (*Strickland*, x., p. 193.) The anecdotes are from the MS. Memoirs of
Hooper, by Mrs. Prowse.—Anderdon, p. 159.

[3] Prowse.

Looking to the intimacy between Ken and Hooper, it is probable that these facts had come to the knowledge of the former before he accepted his appointment. When he arrived at the Hague he found the Hon. Henry Sidney, son of the Earl of Leicester, and brother of the more famous Algernon, as envoy at the Court of the Stadtholder. He had been Master of the Horse to the first Duchess of York, and was in great favour with her, and had, therefore, known the Princess from her childhood, and may have had some previous acquaintance with Ken.[1] With him was Sir Gabriel Sylvius, one of the respectable diplomatists of the time, a friend of Evelyn's, who had married Anne, daughter of Mrs. Howard, "exceedingly loved by" Mrs. Godolphin.[2] Another daughter had married Colonel James Grahme, of Levens, with whom Ken was afterwards, partially even then, on terms of intimate friendship, and who will meet us again when we come to the *Episodes* of his private life. Here, therefore, were some congenial associates. Among the Princess's female attendants he found Anne Trelawney, daughter of Sir Jonathan, afterwards Bishop of Bristol, Exeter, and Winchester, who had held an appointment in the household of the Duke of York at Deptford. She had been associated at an early age with the Princess as her maid of honour, was the only female friend she ever admitted to intimacy, and remained with her till she was dismissed by William, as standing in the way of the complete subjection to which he had determined to reduce his wife. Another maid of honour was Jane Wroth, daughter of Sir Henry Wroth, of Durants, Enfield, whose mother was sister to Ken's early patron, Lord Maynard, and whom he may therefore have known, more or less intimately, at Little Easton. As she was grand-daughter of the first Earl of Leicester, and niece of Sir Philip Sidney, she must also have been a cousin of the Envoy.

[1] At a later date, Sidney, in conjunction with Compton, was one of the most active promoters of the Revolution, and, after it was accomplished, William made him Earl of Romney.

[2] Evelyn, it may be noted, dedicates his life of Mrs. Godolphin to Lady Sylvius. The former was married to Mr., afterwards Lord, Godolphin by Dr. Lake, in the Temple Church, on May 16th, 1675. Berkeley House, where Mrs. Howard lived, was a kind of second home to Mrs. Godolphin before her marriage, and she went there on resigning her place in the Queen's household. It was afterwards, in William's reign, occupied by the Princess Anne.

Sidney kept a diary,[1] and it is from the entries in it that we gain our chief knowledge of Ken's life at the Hague. He records the fact that he preached on December 14, 1679, and that he dined with him on Christmas Day.[2] In the following spring we have two entries of more serious import, which it will be well to give in his own words :—

"March 31, 1680. Dr. Ken was with me; I find he is horribly unsatisfied with the Prince, and thinks that he is not kind to his wife ; he resolved to speak with him, though he kicks him out of doors."—*Diary*, ii. p. 19.

Whether the chaplain acted on that resolve the diary does not record, but a few days later we have another entry, which shows that he was not alone in his opinion of the Prince's conduct ;—

"April 11. Sir Gabriel Sylvius and Dr. Ken were with me, and both complain of the Prince, especially of his usage to his wife; they think she is sensible of it, which doth contribute to her illness; they are mightily for her going to England, but they think he will never give his consent."—*Diary*, ii. p. 19.

It is probable enough from Ken's character that he did venture on some remonstrances. In addition to William's general neglect and ill-treatment of his wife, there was the *liaison* between him and the Lady Elizabeth Villiers, who was also in the Princess's household ; a scandal which began early and continued through the whole of his married life, and which he acknowledged, with some professions of penitence, in answer to Archbishop Tenison's expostulations after Mary's death.[3] The example of William's licence was, however, followed by others, and in one of these cases Ken felt himself bound to interfere. Among William's chief ministers and associates was a

[1] Published under the title of *Diary of the Times of Charles II.*, by R. W. Blencowe, 1843.

[2] *Diary*, i., pp. 201, 211.

[3] Mary herself, who seems to have borne her wrongs silently during her life, left a letter, written on the first night of her fatal illness, to be given to him after her death, in which she reproached him with his infidelity. The result was that William separated himself from his mistress when he was in England, and that she joined him at Loo when he went to Holland.—*Strickland*, xi. p. 306.

Count Zulestein, whose father was the illegitimate son of
Frederick Henry of Nassau, Prince of Orange, and who was
therefore cousin to the Prince. During his minority the
Count's father had accompanied William to England, in 1670,
when he paid his first visit to the King, his uncle.[1] It came to
be known that he had seduced one of the maids of honour, the
Jane Wroth with whom, as we have seen, Ken had many ties
of association in the memory of old days at Little Easton, under
a promise of marriage. It was the old story of James and Anne
Hyde acted over again. Ken, with the courage of a Christian
pastor and the spirit of an English gentleman, pressed Zulestein,
who was inclined to hold back, as it would seem, through fear
of offending William, to follow James's example and to avert
the scandal of an open shame. His remonstrances were successful, and Sidney's Diary records significantly, on January
28, 168$\frac{0}{1}$, the two facts that "the Prince went to Amsterdam,
and that Monsieur Zulestein was married."[2]

On William's return to the Hague he showed by his ex-
asperation that there had been a good reason for hurry-
ing on the marriage in his absence. He threatened Ken
with dismissal, but was met with a bold front. The chaplain " resented the threats," and would not accept a dismissal
at the hands of William, who had not appointed him, but was
ready to beg leave of the Princess, and retire as soon as might
be. He withdrew at once from his attendance at the Court,
and " warned himself from the service," *i.e.* gave formal notice
of his resignation. William, however, thought better of it
and restrained his irritation. It would not be wise to risk the
loss of popularity in England, which would naturally follow on
the abrupt dismissal of such a man as Ken, already widely
known and honoured, especially at the English Court, for such
a reason. He accordingly entreated him to resume his duties,
and treated him with a greater share of favour than before.

[1] Evelyn, December 15, 1670. The *Diary* gives (November 4) the impression
which the Prince, then twenty years old, made on those who saw him. " He has
a manly, courageous, wise countenance, resembling his mother and the Duke of
Gloucester."

[2] The story is told by William Hawkins, but without names, which were
naturally suppressed while the parties concerned were still living. The names
were first given by Bowles (ii. 43), who probably learnt them from the traditions
of the Hawkins family.

Ken consented to remain for one year longer, and so the matter ended. As far as we can trace, the marriage turned out well. Zulestein continued to hold a high place in the circle of William's counsellors, came over with him to England in 1688, was employed in the delicate negotiations with James at Rochester and Whitehall,[1] was made Master of the Robes, and raised to the peerage. The maid of honour, who might have been left to an ignominious and dishonoured life, became Countess of Rochford, and her eldest son succeeded to the earldom, now extinct.

The relations between William and Ken seem, as we have said, to have been bettered by the courage which the latter had displayed in these embarrassing circumstances. William knew how to respect the strength of character which had been shown in a righteous cause. Sidney records a visit from Ken (December 19, 1680) in which he told him "what enemies the Prince had in England," and so set him on his guard against their machinations. Ken acknowledges in August, as in the letter that follows, that he was "in much favour with the Prince," and as "obligingly treated" by Bentinck and all others as he could wish. The later months of his residence at the Hague were probably happier than the earlier. And during them we find him occupied in two matters of some importance, of which his own letters preserve the record.

I. The first of these transactions has the interest of being one of the series of abortive attempts to bring about the union of Protestant Christendom. The bishops who, then and afterwards, showed themselves eager to conciliate the English Nonconformists by concessions, looked with sympathy on their brethren of the Dutch Churches, and Ken was commissioned, first by Lloyd (afterwards Bishop of St. Asaph), who had preceded him in his chaplaincy, and who had then scandalised Lake by encouraging the Princess to attend the Dutch services, and afterwards by Compton, Bishop of London, to whom the education of James's two daughters had been mainly confided, and who was already known as being *par excellence* the "Protestant" Bishop, to make overtures with a view to union. Ken addresses his report to the latter. His letter to Lloyd, in which he had "freely told" his thoughts, has not come down to us.

[1] Macaulay, Chap. x.

LETTER II.

To the Bishop of London (Compton).

"Dieren, Aug. 19th, 1680.

"My very Good Lord,

"How it came to passe I know not, but I receiv'd not your Lordshippes letter till about ten dayes since, when wee lay at Soesdyke, in oᵘ Passage to Dieren ; & knowing Mʳ· Sidney would meet us heere, I referred my answer to be sent in his pacquett, wᶜʰ I knew to be yᵉ most secure way. As to your Lordshippes proposall, it is, in a manner, yᵉ same yᵗ Dʳ· Lloyd sent me not long before ; & I, looking on it as an effect of his owne private zeale, did freely tell him my thoughts, but not so fully as I could have done had I been to have discourst with him. But to give your Lordshipp a more perfect account, though it is extreamely fitt to have yᵉ concurrent sentiments of their professours, yett I cannot apprehend yᵉ judgments of yᵉ generality of those Dutch divines, with whome I have converst, to be worth yᵉ asking, or very creditable to urge, should they give it for us, they, for yᵉ most part, rather despising than studying Ecclesiasticall antiquity ; & yᵉ classicall authours wᶜʰ many of them read with most deference are oᶠ English Nonconformists ; so yᵗ if yᵉ factious party should countermine us in this particular, I am perswaded yᵗ more of oʳ Divines here would be for them whom they call their Brethren, & esteeme as yᵉ great Doctours of yᵉ Reformed Church, than for us whom they censure for at least halfe papists. Besides I know some of them so well, yᵗ I dare say, should they give their hands for us, they would hardly thinke any preferment under a Deanery could reward their service. But yᵗ wᶜʰ most swayes with me, & wᶜʰ I most humbly offer to your Lordshippe, is this, yᵗ should I desire their approbation of oʳ communion : I foresee yᵗ yᵉ next thing they will expect from us will be oʳ subscription to yᵉ validity of their orders, and, as a further confirmation, a demand yᵗ yᵉ Princesse may come to their sacrament, wᶜʰ hitherto she has never done, & if ever she does doe it, farewell all Comͦonprayer here for the future. And I have reason to feare this, because yᵉ resentment they have at our reordaining them sticks in their stomach ; & it has been urg'd to me by them, & I have, at present, so far laid yᵉ controversy asleepe & satisfyd them, yᵗ I would be loath it should start up againe ; for if it does, I must either desert yᵉ Church, or be so far deserted here yᵗ I must leave yᵉ place, and how far this is reasonable wᶜʰ I say, Dr. Hooper, who undeservedly fellt yᵉ effect of something like it, can best informe your

Lordshippe. *I am at present in as much favour with y*^e^ *Prince, & am as obligingly treated by M*^r.^ *Benting & all here, as I can desire,* & therefore if I am scrupulous *quieta movere,* I hope your Lordshippe will pardon me. But if your Lordshippe thinke it absolutely necessary, I will entirely submitt to your judgment, & shall act as your Lordshippe directs me at my returne to ye Hague, wch will be about ye beginning of ye next moneth, for at this distance I am able to doe nothing; but I request of your Lordshippe to send me your com̃ands in Mr. Sidney's pacquett.

      " My Honoured Good Lord,

          " Your Lordshippes most humble and most

                obedient Servant,

                          "THO. KEN."

[Ken writes, it will be seen, from Dieren, a town on the Yssel, where William had a country house, not far from the celebrated field of Zutphen, to which he had apparently gone for change of air during the August heats. He was expecting to be joined by the English Envoy, Henry Sidney, and we may perhaps indulge the thought that one of their objects was to visit the scene that had been made famous for all time by the "cup of cold water" which Sir Philip Sidney, (the great-uncle of the Envoy and of the newly married Countess Zulestein) had passed from his own lips to one whose need was greater than his own. As to the proposals for union, Ken appears to take no very sanguine view. The Dutch divines were naturally more in sympathy with the Dissenters than with the Churchmen of England. They looked on most of the latter (there is at least a touch of personal feeling in Ken's tone which implies that they had so looked on him) as "at least half-papists." At the best they would require deaneries and the like as the price of their compliance. The great difficulty, however, with them, as with the Scotch Presbyterians and the English Nonconformists of the time, was the recognition of their orders. They would not disown their previous ministrations as invalid. They would insist on the Princess recognising their validity by receiving the communion at their hands. That, Ken felt, would be to sacrifice the whole position of the Church of England in Holland and at home. He is unwilling that a controversy which he "had laid to sleep" should be revived and become again a cause of quarrel. How he had quieted and "satisfied" the Dutch divines he does not tell us, but the principles on which he and those who shared his views acted make it probable that he assured them that the Church of England would not insist on a formal condemnation of their previous ministerial labours, but would consent to their acceptance of her ordination, as legitimatising their ministrations under her polity. It was with that reserve that the more moderate Presbyterians of Scotland had been reconciled to the Church, Archbishop Leighton being one of them, and this was the proposal made by Tillotson in the abortive Commission appointed with a view to re-union with the English Dissenters in 1689. The reference to Hooper is significant as showing that Ken had heard his experiences of his life at the Hague before he entered on his own duties as his successor. The " Mr. Benting " of whom Ken speaks is William Bentinck, William's early friend, who had saved his life by sharing his bed in an attack of small-pox. He was made Earl of Portland the day before the Coronation of William and Mary, and received large grants of land. The friendship between the two continued till William's death.]

II. Within a few weeks of these negotiations Ken was able to report the result of his labours in another direction. At a time when the Church of Rome was winning so many proselytes from that of England, it was something to have it in his power to chronicle a conversion in the opposite direction. Among the residents at the Hague was a Colonel Fitz-Patrick,[1] who had been brought up as a Roman Catholic. Three entries in Sidney's Diary (August 23, 28, 31, 1680) record the facts that the Colonel had talked with him about becoming a Protestant, that the Prince had been glad to hear of his intention, that he had brought about a meeting between the Colonel and Ken, which decided the former, after six months' deliberation, to take the final step. The three letters that follow give a full report of this transaction in its several stages :—

LETTER III.

To the Archbishop of Canterbury (Sancroft).

" My very Good Lord,

" I should not dare to make this invasion on Your Grace, but that my duty enforces me, and the ambition I have to send newes, which I know will be extremely wellcome to your Grace, and the rather because it is of a convert to our Church, and of a convert, who is no lesse a persone than Collonell Fitz-Patrick ; who, upon a deliberate enquiry, is so fully satisfy'd with our Church, that he communicates with us next Lord's day in the Princess's Chapell. 'Tis not to be imagined how much both their Highnesses are pleased with the Colonel's happy resolution, and *the Prince comanded me to give my Lord of London a particular account of it, which I have done.* On Mooneday his Highness goes for Germany ; the pretence is hunting ; but the chiefe thing which he proposes to himself, wee

---

[1] Edward Fitz-Patrick, descended from the ancient Irish kings, and nephew of the first Duke of Ormond, was made Colonel of the Royal Fusiliers in 1692, Brigadier-General in 1694, and was drowned in crossing to Ireland in 1696. His brother Richard was created Baron Gowran 1715, and his descendants, the Earls of Upper Ossory, rose into importance later in the eighteenth century by marriages with the great Whig families of Russell, Gower, Petty, and Fox.— (G. H. S.)

understand, is to discourse the Germane Princes about the present posture of Europe, and to take accurate measures to expose the comon enemy.

"I most earnestly begge your Grace's benediction.

"My Good Lord,

"Your Grace's most obedient and most

humble servant,

"THO. KEN."

" Hague, *Sept.* 13*th*, 1680."

[Fitz-Patrick's conversion was clearly looked upon as an event of some importance. The fact that Ken, who had been suspected, and it may be, talked of, by the Dutch divines, as "at least, a half-papist," had brought it about, probably explains the marked improvement in William's treatment of him. We note also Mary's special interest in the matter. The Prince's journey to Germany was connected with his plan for a confederacy, in which the Emperor, the King of Spain, the Electors of Brandenburg and Hanover, were to be prominent, against Louis XIV., who had established a kind of Court at Metz, to which many of the minor German princes flocked to propitiate the great Monarch.]

LETTER IV.

To the Bishop of London (Compton).

"My very Good Lord,

"I need make no apollogy for this present addresse, in regard it brings the most acceptable newes of a convert to our Church, and that of no lesse a one then Collonell Fitz-Patrick. I easily guesse that your Lordshippe will feele a very agreable surprise at that name, and will not be a little curious to know what were the considerations which prevaild with a person of so great estate, interest, and understanding, to make this happy change; and I can with the more confidence give your Lordshippe an account of it, being as well assured my selfe as any one can be of another's inward sentiments, that the whole conduct of this action has nothing in it but what was most worthy of a man of honour and of a good Christian. The first prejudice he entertaind against the Romanists was that peremptory sentence of damnation which they passt on all them who dissented from their communion, and the Coll. had too much judgment and candour not to observe and owne that many Protestants did lead very holy and exemplary lives, and he could not believe that it was consistent with the infinite goodnesse of God to damne any persons of so unreproachable and primitive a piety. The next thing that shockt the Coll. was the Tridentine doctrine of the Priestly intention; and the ill consequence of that he did the more lively apprehend, by calling to mind that, when he himselfe was in Spaine, there was a Roman Priest who was convicted of having been allwayes a Jew, and had taken the Priesthood onely for a disguise ; and what intention that Jew could have, when either he baptisd, or absolvd, or consecrated, he could not comprehend, unlesse it were to expose and invalidate all the meanes of our salvation. Another difficulty which the Coll. could by no meanes digest was the doctrine of Transubstantiation, to believe which he was to disbelieve all his five senses together. To this may be added some judicious reflections, which the Coll. himselfe made, in his reading history, on the frequent and notorious disorders in the Papacy, and in some of the Westerne Councills, which gave him but little hopes of finding Infallibility there.

" These are some of those just exceptions which first began to loosen the Coll. in the Romish Communion, and having about eight moneths since retird to the Hague, he had leasure to make a more accurate enquiry into this religion then formerly he had done.   To this purpose he converst with some divines of that Church, though but with little satisfaction ; nay, so far was he from it, that for owning his doubts to his confessour, he was denyd absolution.   Then he procurd some choice authours, and study'd them, with more than ordinary application of mind.   To reading he joynd frequent fasting, and prayr, and almes, as became an humble and earnest suppliant for the Divine guidance, which God has now gratiously vouchsaft him ; insomuch, that being fully satisfyd that the Church of England has a juster claime to all the advantages of having trueth than that of Rome, he intends next Lords day to receive the holy Sacrament in the Princesses Chappell, to the unspeakable joy of her royall Highnesse, who on all occasions gives demonstrations of her great and zealous concerne for the Protestant Religion.[1]

" The conversion of so eminent a person wee here cannot but hope will open the eyes of severall of our gentry, who are of the Romish persuasion, to looke beyond the prejudices of their education, and not to suffer themselves to be scar'd from an impartiall search after Catholick Truth, which of all things in the world most highly imports them, and for which they must alwayes live martyres in resolution.   Should any well meaning persons but follow so good an example, I question not but they would be blesst with the like successe, and be enabled by God's gratious assistance to renounce

[1] Later on in life, in 1687, Mary, in answering her father's letter, in which he had given her the history of his own conversion, and urged her to follow his example, showed that she had been well instructed, thanks to Hooper and Ken, in the grounds of her Anglican convictions.—Burnet, O. T., B. iv. 1687.

all worldly considerations, which usually impose on our judgments, and this I am verily perswaded the Coll. did, as all intelligent and unbyast persons will confesse. For there are undeniable evidences here, and tis not unknown to your Lordshippe, of how great importance the Coll. has been ever esteemd, and how much courted in the Romish Communion, booth at home and abroad, of how plentifull estate he is master, and how much booth his estate and person are at this present out of danger; adde to this, the disgusts and losse of many of his old friends, from whome it is an affliction to good nature to dissent, the malice and censures, and jealousys of his enemies, all which sufficiently evince that he cannot propose to himselfe to sitt more safe, or more at ease, or to grow richer or greater, or in any the least temporall respect to better his condition by his change, and can have no motive to sway him but his irresistible conviction of conscience, [and] his passionate desires to take the best way to make sure of his title to heaven.

"I must now be so just to the Right Honourable Mr. Sidney, his Majesty's envoye here, as to acquaint your Lordshippe that the Coll. during his sollicitious enquiry after the way of truth, did often ease his mind to him, from whome he receivd all that encouragement which so sincere and generous a friend, and so knowing and firme a Protestant, could suggest.

"More than this, he tooke occasion to discover his thoughts to the Prince of Aurange, who offerd some weighty reasons of his owne to confirme him, and was infinitely affected with the Coll.'s good intentions; and when his Highnesse was afterwards pleasd to relate to me what passt betweene them, he spake of it with a very particular and visible satisfaction, and then commanded me to wait on him, who, I found, had so fully considerd and so judiciously argued all things with himselfe, that there was little need for me to interpose. I cannot omitt to lett your Lordshippe know, that in that short discourse his Highnesse made to me on this subject, he expresst so great a zeal for the Protestant Religion, that I could not but acknowledge the great mercy of God, in raising up, at this time, so powerfull and resolute a Patron of the reformed Church.

"I am sensible how much I have exceeded the bounds of a letter, but the occasion will justify me, and that duty which I am obliged to pay, who am,

"My Good Lord,

"Your Lordshippes most humble
and most obedient servant,

"THO. KEN."

"Hounslerdyke, *Sept.* 13*th*, 1680."

[In writing to Compton, Ken was more expansive than in the first, more official, letter to Sancroft. The account which he gives of the stages of the conversion is interesting, as showing that Ken, in his controversy with the Church of Rome, followed in the footsteps of Chillingworth, and like him, was not ashamed to call himself a Protestant. That Church had not yet unlearnt its sentence of inevitable damnation for all Christians who did not submit to it, and this clashed with men's intuitive conviction of the equity of the Divine judgments. One notes that the natural inference from Ken's language that he, like Walton, would have been unwilling to pass any "peremptory sentence of damnation" on those Romanists who "did lead very holy and exemplary lives." The "peremptoriness" on the Roman side was not toned down then, as it has been since, by the theory of "invincible ignorance." The doctrine of the intention of the priests was still explained so as to cast a doubt over the efficacy of every sacrament, and this, in a system in which salvation was indissolubly connected with sacramental grace, involved entire uncertainty as to whether any man was in a saved state. Ken, it is clear, was not satisfied with the current explanations which Romanist theologians then gave of that theory, and attached weight to the practical corruptions of the Romish Church as an argument against Papal infallibility. Still more noticeable is the way in which, at the close of the letter, he speaks of the Prince. Previous impressions appear to have passed away, and, looking to the great conflict which, in Ken's eyes, was already imminent, he was able to rejoice that God had raised up "so powerful and resolute a patron of the Reformed Church." It will be well to bear those words in mind when we come to some later passages in his life. If I mistake not, Ken really thought better of William than Burnet did.]

Another letter four days later gives an account of the convert's formal reception.

LETTER V.

To the Bishop of London (Compton).

"My very Good Lord,

"In my last, I gave your Lordshippe an account of Collonel Fitz-Patrick's resolution to receive ye Holy Eucharist in o^r Chappell; wch last Lord's Day he did, to ye great satisfaction of the Court. The Prince & Princesse, his Maiesty's Envoye, Mr Sidney, & Monsieure Bentin [*Bentinck*], & severall persons of quality, were at ye Prayers & Sermon; & I question not but you will find ye Coll. extreamely satisfy'd with his change, for I heare he goes for England with Mr Sidney within a few dayes. I cannot give your Lordshippe a greater demonstration of ye Coll.'s sincerity, then to lett you know y^t *he has discourst with some of his Romish friends so effectually, y^t wee are in hopes of more converts to o^r Church, & those considerable ones too.* I am but just come to towne, &, it being post-day, am streitned in time, wch is ye reason I cannot wait on him till to-morrow; & his Hignesse, who went yesterday for Germany, before he lefft Hounslerdȳke, commanded me to pay a visitt to a Lieutenant Coll. who, wee hope, will suddenly embrace oᵣ coᵐunion. I was at her Hignesses Chappell with yᵉ Collonell, but of this person I hope to send a more perfect account by Mᵣ· Sidney.

"My Good Lord,

" Your Lordshippes most humble &
most obedient servant,

"THO. KEN."

" Hague, *Sept.* 17, 1680."

[Colonel Fitz-Patrick's admission to Communion in the Church of England (we note, by the way, the tone of Ken's phraseology " receive the holy Eucharist ") seemed likely, to the sanguine hopes of the preacher on that occasion, to be the first fruits of a plenteous harvest. The new convert had apparently boasted of his influence with his brother officers and other friends. For one who was coming over to England, not altogether without aiming at personal advancement, it would be a gain to appear with letters of commendation from two such opposite quarters as the Prince of Orange and Dr. Ken. The other possible convert I am unable to identify.]

Compton would seem to have reminded Ken, in his reply to this letter, that, according to the statute of Elizabeth, a recusant received into the Church of England ought to have made a formal abjuration of the errors of Rome, and this had not been done in Fitz-Patrick's case. In the letter that follows Ken explains how the omission came about :—

LETTER VI.

To the Bishop of London (Compton).

" My very Good Lord,

" Since my last I waited on yᵉ Collonell, who on second thoughts told me, yᵗ what he first intimated to me, concerning yᵉ Jew in Spaine, who had there Romish orders, he could not peremptorily affirme; and yᵗ, on regard he was then young, but 17 yeares old, & tooke but very little notice of it, & had at this distance but rude notions of it, & he was apprecsive enough yᵗ yᵉ Papists might probably pick a quarell with it. I told him yᵗ though yᵗ particular fact might not be true, yett such things had often happened, & were urged in yᵉ Councell of Trent, & the reason of yᵉ thing held notwithstanding. I confesse I was sorry yᵗ he did not advert [to] yᵉ rectifying this mistake before, when I read the letter over to him ; but if your Lordshippe has it still in your hands, I begge of your

Lordshippe yᵗ my letter may be copied out without yᵗ passage. I am sensible, yᵗ when yᵉ Coll. was received into oʳ Church, by a statute of Queen Elisab., he should have made an abjuration of Popery, but I. having not yᵉ Statute booke here, & not being able any where in yᵉ Hague to procure it, thought it presumption in me to pen any forme of my owne, & I could not expect yᵉ returne of a post, because I did earnestly persuade yᵉ Coll. rather to owne oʳ profession here, than to deferre it till his coming into England, for yᵉ sake of my master & mistresse here.

"My Good Lord,

"Your Lordshippes most humble &
obedient servant,

"THO. KEN.

"*Sept.* 20, 1860.

"I beseech your Lordshippe, yᵗ yᵉ paragraph in my letter may be thus altered. if you judge it fitt :

" 'The next thing yᵗ shockt yᵉ Coll. was yᵉ Roman doctrine of yᵉ priest's intention ; for what intention those priests, who have been convicted of being Jewes, or Atheists, or Magicians, could have when either they baptis'd (or absolved). . . . '

"Mʳ Sidney goes for England on Sunday or Mooneday next, & yᵉ Coll. I believe will accompany him ; & I am extreamely glad of it, because I know he will receive great confirmation from your Lordshippe and my Lord's Grace."

[It will be seen that Ken finds himself obliged to modify a somewhat important statement in his former letter. The Colonel's memory had become hazy, and he would not peremptorily affirm that he had personally known, as stated in a previous letter, a Spanish Jew who had lived as a Romish priest. Ken, with a characteristic scrupulousness as to accuracy, has to make the statement hypothetical, and to assume, what, perhaps, his knowledge of Spanish ecclesiastical history enabled him to affirm, that it was notorious that some priests had been convicted of being Jews or atheists.]

We have seen that Ken had formed a high estimate of his convert's character. That estimate, however, was not shared by all who knew him. Sidney, who narrates the conversion, records[1] also that he had been charged with forging bills of exchange, that Lord Essex, who was then at the Hague, wondered that the Prince would talk with "such a villain," "the worst man in the world," of "so ill a reputation that

[1] *Diary,* i. pp. 163, 179, 183.

everybody was ashamed to appear for him." Whether Essex was prejudiced or Ken deceived, we have, so far as I know, no materials for deciding. The Colonel appears, however, in good company, in 1687, when Evelyn, on May 2nd, records his meeting him at dinner, together with Lord Middleton, Principal Secretary of State, Lord Pembroke, Lord Lumley, Lord Preston, and Sir John Chardin, in the house of Mynheer Diskvelts (Dykvelt) the Dutch ambassador.[1]

The year to which Ken had consented to stay at the Hague was, however, drawing to a close, and within a month he had returned to England. A letter from Lord Arlington, dated October 21, 1680, in the Records of the Lord Chamberlain's office, announcing that he was appointed to preach before the King on the following Sunday, shows that he had taken up his quarters for a time in the house of his old friend, Francis Turner, then a prebendary of St. Paul's, a widower with one infant daughter, in Amen Corner. It is probable that this implies a previous appointment as Chaplain to the King. The registers of the Lord Chamberlain's office show that he was not appointed to that office between the 14th of January, 1677, and the 30th of July, 1680. At this point they become defective, and there is no entry therefore of the precise date of Ken's appointment.[2] It seems likely, however, that the Princess Mary had commended him to the favour both of her uncle and her father, and that this fresh step in the ladder of Court preferment awaited him immediately on his return from Holland. The influence of other friends, such as Lord Maynard and Bishop Morley, may have contributed to the same result. Sidney, who was nephew to Sunderland, may have spoken in his favour. Probably, however, such recommendations were scarcely needed. Ken had already won Charles's respect before he was appointed to the Hague, and the post of a royal chaplain was the natural recognition of services such as he had rendered. The next two years seem to have been passed quietly at Winchester. In the common course of things he would take

---

[1] Later on in the history of the period, Fitz-Patrick received a bribe of one thousand guineas for promoting the Charter of the East India Company (*Strickland*, xi., p. 302). Such gifts were, however, too common then for this to be a proof of any special baseness.   [2] Anderdon, p. 178.

his turn in preaching at Whitehall, but his name does not appear in the special list of Lent Preachers appointed by the King in the *London Gazette* for 1681 or 1682. Morley's increasing infirmities made his visits to Winchester House less frequent, and Ken's time was probably passed tranquilly in the cathedral city. The fury of the Popish-plot storm had spent itself before his return, and he would watch the vehemence with which the Protestant party in the House of Commons pushed the Exclusion Bill, with the dissatisfaction and alarm which were expressed by the bishops and clergy generally, and which were shared, as I have said, by a Whig statesman like Halifax. The Duke of York during the greater part of the year was occupied in repressing Argyle's rebellion in Scotland. The Prince of Orange came over to England in July, but there is no evidence that he and Ken crossed each other's paths.

The summer of 1682 was marked by the loss of one of Ken's earliest and dearest friends. He was summoned from Winchester in June, to attend the death-bed of Lady Margaret Maynard. After an illness at Whitehall, she had removed, after Whitsuntide, to Easton Lodge, "not out of any hope of recovery, but that she might die in a place which she loved, in which God had made her an instrument of so great good to the country." The intimacy which had begun at Little Easton had continued unimpaired. Either when they met in London or by correspondence, of which unhappily not a fragment is known to survive, he had shared her most secret thoughts for twenty years.[1] It must have been a comfort to him to know that she had in her neighbour, Lady Warwick, whose notes of Ken's sermons have been referred to in Chapter VI., one like-minded with herself. The later entries in that lady's diary record more than once how she drove over from her own house, Lees, or Leighs, near Braintree, to Little Easton, and had some hours of sweet converse with her friend.[2] Such portions of the funeral sermon, preached by Ken on June 30, 1682, as were necessary to show what

---

[1] I am indebted to Lady Brooke, the present owner of Easton Lodge, for this negative information.

[2] Lady Warwick's *Diary*, March 26, 1668, Feb. 16, Oct. 19, Dec. —, 1671. She was sister to Robert Boyle.

Lady Maynard's influence had been to Ken, how he saw in her such an ideal of womanhood as he was not likely to find elsewhere, have been already given in Chapter VI. What we note here is the fidelity of Ken's nature to that early friendship. We may believe that when he returned from that funeral, it was with the feeling that life was poorer than it had been, and with a deeper sense of loneliness. The dedication of the sermon to the bereaved husband is, I think, sufficiently characteristic, alike in the humility and in the sensitiveness which it indicates, to find a place here among Ken's letters :—

LETTER VII.

To the Right Honourable William Lord Mainard, Baron of Estains, and Comptroller of His Majesty's Household.

"My Lord,

"Though I am unwilling to decline any service which your Lordship expects from me, yet when you enjoined me the printing of this sermon, I could not obey your command without disputing it. For I considered, that in such an age as this, where an exemplary holiness is very rare, I shall be thought guilty of most gross flattery, in the character I have given of your incomparable lady, now in heaven.

"But knowing I have so many unexceptionable witnesses to attest every line I have said, especially yourself, who best understood her value, and are most sensible of her loss ; and being conscious to myself that I have spoken no other throughout than the words of truth, I soon broke through all the discouragements I had, either from the just censures the world would fix on the meanness of the discourse, or from the unjust ones it might pass on my insincerity ; and resolved to do all that little honour I could to her memory, and to give God the glory of her example ; and I humbly beseech the Divine goodness, that what I now offer to the public, may not be wholly unprofitable to those who read it ; however, I am sure, it will not be unacceptable to your Lordship, or to those who were so happy to know her, which will be satisfaction enough to

"My good Lord, your Lordship's
most humble and faithful servant,
"THO. KEN."

The 23rd of the month of March, 1683, was a day much to be remembered in the history of Winchester. Charles, whose country residence at Newmarket had been nearly burnt to the ground, set his mind on the erection of a new palace at Winchester, which was designed by Sir Christopher Wren, and was intended to rival Versailles in its magnificence. It was to be surrounded with a park, and a stately street was to connect it with the cathedral. It was to contain one hundred and sixty rooms, with a cupola, and a staircase with marble columns. The day above-named was fixed for laying the first stone of the edifice. The park and gardens were to be laid out after plans by Wren.[1] The King and the Duke of York were present, and then, and in the months that followed, the royal visits brought with them crowds of courtiers. While the building was in progress the Bishop's palace and the houses of the dean and prebendaries were in request for the accommodation of the royal party, and that party was a large one. The King could not separate himself from the two mistresses who were then highest in his favour, the Duchess of Portsmouth and Nell Gwyn, and they had to be provided for. The official known as the "harbinger," to whose functions it belonged to assign lodgings for the several members of the Court, fixed on Ken's prebendal house for the last-named personage. It was probably assumed that one who had been recently appointed as a Court chaplain would be subservient after the manner of his kind. With Ken, as we might expect, it was quite otherwise. He met the message with an indignant refusal. "A woman of ill-repute ought not to be endured in the house of a clergyman, least of all in that of the King's chaplain." "Not for his kingdom" would he comply with the King's demands. A local tradition relates that he took a practical way of settling the matter, by putting his house into the builder's hands for repairs and having it unroofed. Mrs. Eleanor Gwyn was, however, at last provided for. The Dean (Dr. Meggot, appointed 1669, d. 1694) was found more compliant than the Prebendary. A room was built for her at the south end of the deanery, and was

[1] The designs are now in the Library of All Souls' College, Oxford. The work was stopped by Charles's death in 1685. Anne thought of it for Prince George, but the carcase remained unfinished. It was used for barracks during the war with France at the close of the last century.—Elmes, *Wren and His Times*, p. 300. (C. J. P.)

known familiarly by her name till it was destroyed by Dean Rennell, perhaps as perpetuating an unsavoury association, about 1835.[1]

In the common calculations as to Court favour, Ken risked his chance of future promotion by this act of boldness. As it was, he rose in Charles's esteem. The King had not yet lost, in the midst of all his profligacy, the power of recognising goodness. The bold faithfulness of Ken as a preacher at White-hall had led the King to say, in words which were remembered afterwards, as he was on his way to the royal closet, " I must go and hear little Ken tell me of my faults." The courage which the chaplain now showed led the way, contrary to the expectations of all courtiers, to a fresh step onwards to the " great things " which Ken did not seek, but which were to be thrust upon him.

One of the incidents which darkened the public history of the year, must, if I mistake not, have touched Ken with a special sorrow. The Rye House Plot, a republican conspiracy which, it was alleged, was aimed at the life of the King and his brother, that Monmouth might take their place as a Protestant king, or that a new Constitution might be framed by a free Parliament, would fill him, as it did most of his order, with horror and alarm. The principles in which he had been trained would lead him to concur, at least generally, in the declaration of the University of Oxford (July 24, 1683) in favour of the doctrines of passive obedience and non-resistance, but he could scarcely remain unmoved by the fate of some of the leading victims of the judicial proceedings connected with that plot. Essex he had known at the Hague; Algernon Sidney was the brother of the Envoy with whom he had been associated there; with William, Lord Russell, there were points of contact of another kind. Ken's friend Dr. Fitzwilliam, who had succeeded him at Brightstone, was the friend and counsellor of the family, and continued to be Lady Rachel's spiritual adviser for years afterwards. Kettlewell also was on terms of intimacy with them, and he and Fitzwilliam were called as witnesses for the defence, to give

[1] The story is told by Hawkins, Ken's great-nephew, but without a date. It may have been either before or after Ken's appointment as Chaplain to the Fleet.

evidence that the idea of complicity with assassination was incompatible with all they had ever known of the character of the accused. Ken must, we may believe, have shared in the sorrow of his friends. Fitzwilliam, who two years later commended Ken's *Practice of Divine Love*[1] to Lady Rachel, as likely to bring a message of comfort to her soul, could hardly fail to tell his friend of her sorrow and to seek for it his sympathy and prayers.

Before the year came to an end Ken was called to work of another kind, in which we have now to follow him.

[1] I assume that this is the book to which Lady Rachel Russell referred as Ken's "*Seraphic Meditations.*"

FAC-SIMILE OF INSCRIPTION REFERRED TO IN PAGE 139.

CHAPTER XI.

> " Or on a voyage, when calms prevail,
>   And prison thee upon the sea,
> He walks the wave, He wings the sail,
>   The shore is gained, and thou art free."
>
> *J. H. Newman.*

CATHARINE of Braganza had brought to Charles II., as part of her marriage dower, the Portuguese settlement of Tangier, on the African coast of the Straits of Gibraltar, as well as that of Bombay, which gave England its first important foothold in India. It was regarded, at the time, in much the same light as the acquisition of Gibraltar itself was at a later period of English history. It commanded the entrance of the Mediterranean, and strengthened the force of the English fleet in its waters. It was handed over to Lord Sandwich on January 30th, 1661, and Lord Peterborough was left as Governor. Its acquisition was supposed, more or less, to balance the discredit of the sale of Dunkirk. The fortifications were strengthened, and a mole of large dimensions was constructed to widen and improve the harbour, at a vast expense. It proved, however, to be a *damnosa hæreditas.* A body of Commissioners, including the Duke of York, Prince Rupert, the Duke of Albemarle and Samuel Pepys, was appointed to govern its affairs, and the *Diary* of the last-named member of the Commission is full of details as to its management. It became the source of a constant drain on the resources of the country, and the House of Commons began to be jealous of the grants that were demanded for it, and suspicious as to the management of its finances. Before long it was regarded with distrust and dis-

like for another reason. Roman Catholics had been sent over
by James as governors and officers in the garrison. It was
believed, in the panic terror of the Popish Plot, that the King
and the Duke were training a Popish army there for later use
in England; that pay was drawn for the troops on the strength
of false muster rolls; that everything was jobbed by engineers
and contractors on a large and lavish scale. Lancelot Addison, the father of the more famous Joseph, was chaplain there
for seven years, and describes the garrison as half-starved.
Idle, vicious, demoralised, in all senses of the word, "their
very hearts were broken with ill success." Some ran away
to the Moors, and became renegades, or ended their lives in
slavery. In the later years of Charles II., when he was trying
to dispense with grants from Parliament, and grudged parting
with the money which he received from Louis XIV. for any
other object than his palaces and his mistresses, he came to
the resolve that he would get rid of the annual expense by
demolishing the mole and fortifications, and leaving the town,
not in the hands of Portugal, from which he had received it,
but to the chance of occupation by the Moors. A naval force
of twenty ships was accordingly dispatched in the summer of
1683, under the command of Lord Dartmouth, for this purpose.

This nobleman, the son of Col. William Legge, who had
assisted Charles I. in his escape from Hampton Court, and
whom that monarch had commended to his successor "as the
faithfullest servant that ever man had," was one of the model
churchmen of the time. His father declined a peerage at the
Restoration, and died in 1672. The son entered the navy and
distinguished himself by his integrity, was high in the Duke
of York's confidence, rose to the position of Admiral, Master
of the Ordnance and Privy Councillor, and was raised to the
peerage in 1682.[1] In his later career he was faithful to his
master's cause in the Revolution of 1688; was Governor of
Portsmouth, and commanded the fleet against the Prince of
Orange. In 1691 he was imprisoned on the charge of being

---

[1] Evelyn (June 11, 1683) reports his election as Master of the Trinity House,
" sonn to George (*William*) Legge, late Master of the Ordnance, and one of
the groomes of the bedchamber; a greate favorite of the Duke's, an active and
understanding gentleman in sea affairs."

implicated in Lord Preston's conspiracy against William III., and died in the Tower on October 25th of that year.

Dartmouth, who seems at all times to have been anxious to raise the moral condition of the navy, looked out for a chaplain for the fleet that now sailed under his command. Ken was recommended to him by Samuel Pepys, who, having been connected both with the Admiralty and the Tangier Commission for many years, was made one of Lord Dartmouth's council in this expedition, and the recommendation was, we may well believe, due to the favour in which Ken stood at Court and to the high estimate that had been formed of his character; probably also to the way in which he had discharged his duties as chaplain at the Hague, and to Pepys's personal knowledge of him. The man who had succeeded in making schoolboys devout was thought likely to exercise an influence for good over the sailors and soldiers that were now committed to his care.[1] Writing at a later date, in 1688, when Lord Dartmouth was in command of the fleet intended to oppose the landing of the Prince of Orange, to Dr. Pechell, Master of Magdalene College, Cambridge, Pepys referred to what he had done on this occasion with self-congratulation. Lord Dartmouth was "in the highest degree solicitous in the choice of a chaplain," and looked for "piety, authority, and learning" as necessary qualifications.[2] These he had found in Ken.

Pepys has, moreover, preserved for us the very letter in which Lord Dartmouth tendered the appointment to Pechell himself, and it is so characteristic of the man, and has so strong a bearing on the reasons which determined his choice of Ken, that it is worth while to quote a few sentences. He thinks it "of the highest importance to have the ablest and best man" he can possibly obtain, "both for the service of God and for the good government of the clergy that are chaplains in the fleet." He begs Pechell "for God's sake" to do him the "honour and favour" to go with him. He feels that "he has to answer to God for the preservation of so many souls as He hath been pleased to place under his care."[3]

[1] For Ken's view of the ideal life of soldiers and sailors see Chap. xxviii.
[2] Pepys' *Life*, ii. 149.
[3] Pepys, *Life*, &c., ii. 149.

It was not an office which presented much outward attraction. The naval chaplains were held in little esteem, and were often men of damaged character. They were hardly classed as officers, and their pay was not more than that of a common seaman. They could not hold a service without the commander's leave, and where the commander was indifferent or undevout, that leave was often withheld, and weeks might pass during which the chaplain's office would be in abeyance, and the common sailors would taunt him with doing nothing for his money—money which, as they believed, was deducted from their own pay. Often they were not provided with Bible or Prayer Book or surplice. Scant provision was made for them on board ship, and they wanted comforts which even a midshipman enjoyed.

Ken's position as Chaplain of the Fleet and Lord Dartmouth's respect for him probably exempted him from many of these discomforts. If he had had to face them, it would probably have made little difference in his decision. As it was the rule of his life to "ask for nothing," so it was also to "refuse nothing" that seemed to come as a call from God, and gave an opening for the service of his Master. He was content to leave the quiet routine of Winchester, to say "good-bye" to Morley, who was now eighty-five, and to Izaak Walton, who was ninety, and to take his chance in the work that lay before him.

For the first and last time in his life Ken was now brought into contact with a Boswell, with the one exception, that the reverence with which Boswell looked on Johnson was not found in the feelings with which Pepys regarded Ken. Bustling, gossiping, egotistic, the counsellor of the Tangier expedition, while he congratulated himself on the pleasant prospect of a voyage "in a good ship, under a very worthy leader, in a conversation as delightful as companions of the first form in divinity, law, physic, and the usefullest parts of mathematics can render it, Dr. Ken, Dr. Trumbull (Judge Advocate of the Expedition), Dr. Lawrence (Physician to Lord Dartmouth), and Mr. Sheres (Engineer)," obviously felt that he was entitled to criticise Ken's sermons, and to argue with him on questions of theology. On such an occasion as this, Pepys naturally reverted to the habits of his early days, intermitted for some years, and kept a diary, and its pages are sufficiently entertaining. He had had to start at forty-eight hours' notice, and probably Ken was not allowed much longer time for preparation. On his way to Portsmouth, Pepys dined "at the College at Winchester,"—probably, therefore, with Ken,—on Aug. 1st, 1683, and reached Portsmouth the same evening. They had to wait for a week till Lord Dartmouth arrived in the *Grafton*, on August 8th, and then they "went on board for good and all." On the 12th Ken read prayers and preached; on the 19th he read prayers twice, but did not preach. Morning prayers were read daily on deck. On Sunday, September 9th, Ken preached again, and "this being the day of Thanksgiving for the King's late deliverance from the Rye-house plot, gave us a very good sermon on the duty of subjects to their Prince." On week days there was much music in the evenings, and Ken's gifts in that line, which had been cultivated in the Musical Society at Oxford, may, perhaps, have been brought under contribution.[1] After supper, the higher officers sat and talked, and Pepys dwells with manifest complacency on a long discussion, in which he and Ken took the leading part. The entries in the Diary stand thus—

"2nd September.—Discourse about Spirits, Dr. Ken asserting there were such, and I, with the rest, denying it."

"11th.—After supper in my Lord's cabin, Dr. Ken and I were very hot in disputes about Spirits."

"12th.—To supper and talk :—Dr. Ken producing his argument for Spirits from the ancient oracles, which I took upon me against the next time to answer."

We are left to conjecture what were the precise points involved in the discussion. Did Pepys go the whole length of the Sadducean denial of either "angels or spirits?" Did Ken, mystically devout, trembling at the very breath of doubt, thinking it better to believe too much rather than too little, assert his belief in ghosts, *i.e.* apparitions of the dead, as well as in good or evil angels? His poems and hymns testify in every page to the latter, but we have no direct evidence from them as to the former. The mention of the ancient oracles suggests the inference that he held, as many of the early Christian writers held, that there was a supernatural power

[1] See p. 52.

of evil in them, underlying the jugglery of priests and sooth-
sayers. We can, at any rate, fancy him arguing, with a certain mixture of irony and indignation, against the shallowness
which refused to believe that there were more things between
heaven and earth than were dreamt of in its philosophy, con-
cluding with Milton that

> " Myriads of spiritual beings walk the earth
>   By us unseen,"

and posing the self-satisfied, but slightly materialistic *soi-disant*
philosopher with questions which he found it hard to answer.
The last trace of the discussion which seems to have begun on
September 2nd, is found in the entry for the 22nd :—

"22 Sept.—Mighty talk [at supper] of spirits in [the] *York
Castle* [one of the ships], mighty noises being heard by the
minister and most intelligent men, and particularly by Dr.
Lawrence [the physician of the Expedition]. He told me how
he now began to be convinced of spirits, this having continued
for some time, and appearing every three or four nights, but
nothing since we came to this 22nd, being Saturday ; a good
argument against Dr. Ken's argument from the silence of
oracles."

It is not easy to enter into the process of reasoning implied
in the last sentence. Ken had apparently urged the tradition,
with which Milton's *Ode on the Nativity*[1] has made us familiar,
that the old oracles of Greece had ceased to give answers at the
birth of Christ, and had pressed the inference that this showed
that there had been a supernatural element at work in them,
which was then restrained in its activities. Pepys may, perhaps, have turned upon him on the strength of the mysterious
voices, and have argued that there were the same unaccount-
able phænomena now, that Ken, who may have shown some
incredulity as to the said noises, was bound either to accept
them also as supernatural, or to give up his belief in the ma-
nifestations of demoniac power in the ancient oracles.

The discussion appears to have ceased at this point. The

---

[1] " The oracles are dumb.
     No voice or hideous hum,
Rings through the hollow roof in words deceiving."

stirring life that followed their arrival at Tangier left, it may be, little leisure for such things. But there is, from this point onward, a certain touch of the irritability of the worsted controversialist in the tone in which Pepys speaks of Ken. The day after this last debate he notes, in a patronising tone, that " Dr. Ken made an excellent sermon, full of the skill of a preacher, but nothing of a natural philosopher, it being all forced meat." On the 30th he records "a very fine and seasonable, but most unsuccessful, argument from Dr. Ken, particularly in respect of the vices of this town. I was in pain for the Governor, and the officers about us, at church; but I perceived they regarded it not." On October 7th he notes that Ken "made a weak sermon on the great business of our being called home." On the following Sunday we have the simple fact, " Dr. Ken gave us a sermon."

Something of the same tone of disparagement appears in his noticing (how far truly we cannot judge) that Ken showed (September 23rd) some symptoms of fear as they rowed across the bay with a rough wind against them. On one point, however, the two men agreed. With all his experience of sea-life among the officers and men, with whom his work at the Admiralty brought him into contact, and of London life in the regions of Whitehall, Pepys had never seen such a hell upon earth as he found in Tangier. Curses and blasphemies and foul words were heard on every side from a drunken soldiery, whom the Governor, Colonel Percy Kirke, of whose work Ken was to see something in his own diocese two years later, did nothing to restrain.[1] Women were sunk to the lowest depths of shamelessness. Pepys, whose nerves were not likely to be over-sensitive on these points, wrote on October 26th that Ken dined with him, and that " we had a great deal of good discourse on the viciousness of the place, and its being time for Almighty God to destroy it." And Ken, as usual, had the courage of his convictions,

---

[1] It is, perhaps, worth noting that when pressure was put upon Kirke to become a Roman Catholic under James II., he pleaded a prior promise to the Sultan of Morocco that, if he ever changed his religion, it would be to turn Mahometan. As it was, he joined William on his landing in Torbay, and was active in his service.—Macaulay, Ch. vi.

and did not confine himself to vexing his soul in secret.
Kirke had put Roberts, a drunken and profligate priest, the
brother of his mistress, into the office of reader in the parish,
or garrison, church, where there was already a decent minister,
and wanted to have made him chaplain on board the *James*,
the ship commanded by Cloudesley Shovel. Ken represented
the case to Lord Dartmouth and the whole company at supper
on October 23rd, and strongly urged another appointment, in
the person of one Mercer, the schoolmaster of the town. A
few days later (Sunday, October 28), Pepys notes the fact that
Ken had preached a sermon on the " excessive liberty of swearing which we observe here," and that this had led to " very
high discourse between him and Ken on the one side and
Kirke on the other." With the exception of an entry on
November 3rd, in which we find that Ken " kept his chamber,
very ill of a headache," probably as much from vexation and
grief of heart as from climate, this is the last notice of him
in the journal.

The proceedings of the Commission dragged on, however, for
some months longer. The fortifications and the mole were destroyed by the middle of January, but a treaty had to be made
for the liberation of Christian slaves who were held in bondage
by the Moors, and terms of compensation secured to the English
and Portuguese settlers for the loss of property sustained by
the evacuation of the town.

On the whole one fancies that the time must have been
passed by Ken somewhat miserably, in spite of the interest with
which he may have watched the new charms of unfamiliar
scenery, the new features of Moorish life, the aspect presented
by yet another of the great religions of the world. Over and
above the pain which he felt at the vices which he could not
check, there were troubles among his associates. Dr. Trumbull did not get on well with either Dartmouth or Pepys, complained that he was losing the practice he might have had in
London, and wanted to go back. Pepys grumbled at his " silli-
ness and poorness of spirit," and even Ken had to confess that
" he was not to be supported." Dartmouth was vexed and out of
temper at the delays of the officials at home and the inade-
quacy of the supplies sent for provisioning the ships. On this

point he had remonstrated before the expedition started, but had been met by Lord Rochester with a sneer, and had been asked angrily whether he wished to go or not. He learnt, as he told Ken (a lesson which later experience probably taught him also), that "a man's courage must be questioned if he lets his prudence say anything."

According to his great-nephew Hawkins, Ken beguiled the weary weeks ("about the time of his voyage") by composing an epic poem, which has been identified by Anderdon with the *Edmund* published after his death with other poems in four volumes. A perusal of that poem, however, shows that it contains allusions to Wells, which could scarcely have been written before his connexion with that diocese. Possibly, of course, these may have been inserted at a later date. An epic poem in thirteen books of rhymed heroic verse is a thing which an author begins, puts by, retouches, and finally re-copies till he leaves it ready for the press. And this was, we may, perhaps, believe, the case with *Edmund*. I reserve an examination of the poem and of the passages above alluded to for a later chapter.[1]

At last the work of the Commission was over, and the ships started for their homeward voyage. Ken was on the Admiral's ship, the *Grafton*, and had to endure Kirke's company, whose occupation as Governor was gone, and who returned to take his place in home service. Whether there was any more "high discourse" between them, or whether Ken withdrew into the solitude of his cabin, vexing his soul with the ungodly deeds and words of his companions; whether he preached "seasonable" but "unsuccessful" sermons on the way home, or contented himself with reading prayers, are questions which must be left to the historical imagination. The one permanent result of the expedition, as far as he was concerned, was, probably, that he secured the friendship and esteem of the Admiral, and learnt, on his side, to trust and honour him. We shall find them later on corresponding on terms of intimacy, and acting together, with one memorable exception,[2] in the political crises in which, before many years were passed, they were destined to bear a part.

The fleet cast anchor off Spithead in the first week of April,

---

[1] See Chap. xxviii.   [2] See Chap. xvii.

1684, and Ken, we may presume, landed at Portsmouth, and made his way to Winchester.[1] On his arrival there he found, if he had not heard it before, that he had lost one whose presence had been interwoven with his earliest memories, and whom he loved with a filial affection. Izaak Walton had passed to his rest on December 15, at the age of ninety, and had been buried in Prior Silkstead's Chapel in Winchester Cathedral. The epitaph which marks his resting-place runs as follows :—

HERE RESTETH THE BODY OF
MR. IZAAK WALTON,
WHO DIED THE 15TH OF DECEMBER,
1683.

Alas, he's gone before,
Gone to return no more!
Our panting breasts aspire
After their aged sire,
Whose well-spent life did last
Full ninety years and past.
But now he hath begun
That which will ne'er be done.
Crowned with eternal blisse,
We wish our souls with his.

VOTIS MODESTIS SIC FLERUNT LIBERI.

I have given the epitaph because it has been ascribed by Bowles and Anderdon to Ken's authorship. To me the con-

---

[1] Evelyn records (May 26) Lord Dartmouth's re-election as Master of the Trinity House, "newly return'd with the fleete from blowing up and demolishing Tangier." He adds that "in the sermon preach'd on this occasion, Dr. Can observed that, in the 27th chapter of the Acts of the Apostles, the casting anchor out of the fore-ship had been cavill'd at as betraying total ignorance : that it is very true our seamen do not do so, but in the Mediterranean their ships were built differently from ours, and to this day it was the practice to do so there." I venture on the conjecture that "Can" may have been written in mistake for "Ken." The records of the Trinity House show that the preacher was appointed by Lord Dartmouth (Mr. A. J. Inglis), and the remark made by the preacher exactly fits in with Ken's recent Mediterranean experiences. Curiously enough, the Churchwarden's Accounts at Frome, even as late as 1776, contain an entry of expenditure for "repairing the palisades round Bishop Can's grave." I am indebted for this information to the Rev. W. E. Daniel, of Frome. There was, however, I believe, a Dr. Cann in or near London at the time, and, of course, he may have been the preacher.

jecture does not seem a very probable one. The lines have not the ring of Ken's verse. They do not contain any of his favourite phrases. I incline to conjecture that they came from the pen of Izaak Walton, jun., and that the son had thus expressed his filial love for his "aged sire."

Walton bequeathed by his will " to my brother, Dr. Ken," a ring, with this motto, ' A Friend's Farewell ; I. W., obiit 15 Dec., 1683." Other rings, with the motto "Love my Memory," were left to other relations, including Ion Ken and his wife, and Mr. Beacham, and friends. Bishop Morley was to have one with the quaint device of "A Mite for a Million," as being the infinitesimally small return for the countless acts of a life-long kindness. Another gift would appear to have come into Ken's hands at his death, not by way of bequest, but as presented to him by Walton's family, who felt that it belonged to him as by a right of spiritual inheritance. When Donne was dying he had by his will ordered rings, such as have been described in Chapter II. (p. 20), to be given to a long list of friends, including Sir Henry Wotton ; Hall, Bishop of Norwich ; Duppa, Bishop of Salisbury ; and King, of Chichester ; and, last but not least, George Herbert. In the last case, indeed, the ring would appear to have been sent before Donne's death, and to have been accompanied by verses which, with Herbert's answer, it seems worth while to print, as showing with what associations Ken would receive the ring, which he wore and used during the remainder of his life.

To Mr. George Herbert.

Sent him with one of my seals of the anchor and Christ.

A sheaf of snakes used heretofore to be my seal, which is the crest of our poor family.

> *Qui prius assuetus serpentum falce tabellas*
> *Signare, hæc nostræ symbola parca domus,*
> *Adscitus domui domini* . . . . . .[1]

> Adopted in God's family, and so,
> My old coat lost, into new arms I go.

[1] In each case apparently, the friends sent the opening words of a Latin poem, which they had intended to write, but which each left in a fragmentary and unfinished state. I print them from Walton's *Life of Donne.*

The Cross, my seal in baptism, spread below,
Does by that form into an anchor grow.
Crosses grow anchors ; bear, as thou shouldst do,
Thy cross, and that cross grows an anchor too.
But He that makes our crosses anchors thus,
Is Christ, who there is crucify'd for us.
Yet with this I may my first serpents hold :
(God gives new blessings and yet leaves the old).
The serpent may, as wise, my pattern be ;
My poison, as he feeds on dust—that's me.
And, as he rounds the earth to murder, sure,
He is my death ; but on the cross my cure.
Crucify nature, then, and then implore
All grace from Him crucified there before.
When all is cross, and that cross anchor grown,
This seal's a catechism, not a seal alone.
Under that little seal great gifts I send,
Both works and pray'rs, pawns and fruits of a friend.
O, may that saint that rides on our great seal,
To you that bear his name large bounty deal.

JOHN DONNE.

IN SACRAM ANCHORAM PISCATORIS
GEORGE HERBERT.

Quod crux nequibat fixa clavique additi,
Tenere Christum scilicet ne ascenderet,
Tuive Christum.   .   .   .   .   .

Although the cross could not here Christ detain,
When nail'd unto't, but He ascends again ;
Nor yet thy eloquence here keep him still,
But only while thou speak'st—this anchor will :
Nor can'st thou be content unless thou to
This certain anchor add a seal, and so
The waters and the earth both unto thee
Do owe the symbol of their certainty.
Let the world reel, we and all ours stand sure ;
This holy cable's from all storms secure.

GEORGE HERBERT.

With this ring Walton's will was sealed, as afterwards was Ken's.   Nearly all his letters to Bishop Lloyd of Norwich and Dr. Thomas Smith bear its impress.[1]

[1] See p. 20.

The following letter belongs to this period. It does not, at first sight, seem to possess any special interest, but experience teaches me that, however commonplace a letter may appear, it may become, under the light of new information, a missing link in a chain of evidence on some important point, and I therefore insert it. In this case it serves to show Ken's intimacy with the family of the "Student-Penitent," who will meet us later on.

LETTER VIII.

To Mr. Grahme, at Lord Dartmouth's House in St. James's Square.

"I received your very kind letter, and yesterday Mr. Smith came to me to know if I had received a bill for the mony. I told him I had received advice of it, but no bill. He replyed, he was sorry I had not, because he staid in the towne on purpose to be rid of his mony, and as soone as he could be eased of that, he would be gone. I answered him that you would be here within a few dayes, and, in the mean time, I would lett you knowe what he said. When my Lord and Lady come to the Hollt I fully intend, God willing, to wait on them, but I must stay here till your coming. I returne you many thankes for your kindnesse to my poore brother, which I shall allwayes gratefully acknowledge. My most humble service to my good Lord and Lady and my hearty respects to Mr. Chettwood.

"*July* 8, 1684."

[The copy sent me from the Historical MSS. Commission Office has no signature, but comes as one of Ken's letters in Lord Dartmouth's MSS. The "Mr. Grahme" is, I can scarcely doubt, the Mr. James Grahme, or Graham, who will meet us afterwards in Chap. xxiv. (see p. 128). The "good Lord and Lady" are probably Lord and Lady Dartmouth. I cannot identify the Mr. Smith, to whose business transactions the letter refers, nor the Mr. Chettwood. Hearne (*Diary*, ii. p. 119, 1886) mentions a Dr. Chetwode who was Chaplain to the Duke of Marlborough, and afterwards Dean of Gloucester. Being of strong Whig principles he would not allow the bells of the Cathedral to be tolled for Bishop Frampton's funeral. The "poore brother" is, probably, Ion Ken, of whose widow and son we hear later on (ii. p. 184). Possibly, however, the phrase may refer to Izaak Walton. I do not know where the "Hollt" is.]

CHAPTER XII

> " Peace-loving man, of humble heart and true!
>   What dost thou here?
>   Fierce is the city's crowd; the lordly few
>   Are dull of ear."
>
> *J. H. Newman.*

BEFORE the year 1684 had ended another link which connected Ken with a past generation was broken.   It was true of Morley and Walton, in their friendship, that as they had been "lovely and pleasant together" in their lives, so "in their death they were not divided."   Towards the close of the October of that year Ken was summoned from Winchester to Farnham to attend the Bishop's deathbed.   With him was his friend Dr. Fitz-william, who had succeeded him at Brightstone, and we learn from a letter of Lady Rachel Russell's, of October 1st, 1684, that he had sent a report of the good Bishop as " probably hastening to the end of his race, which, without doubt, he will finish with joy."   Ken sent off an express to his friend Turner, just translated to Ely, but still, apparently, residing at the old palace of the Bishops of Rochester at Bromley, who reported the tidings to Sancroft in the following letter, which, as embodying Ken's, I print in full :—

                              " BROMLEY, *October 30th*, 1684.

" MAY IT PLEASE YOUR GRACE,

        " Late yesterday I received an express from Dr. Ken, written from Farnham, to inform me that it pleased God to release the good old Bishop out of all the miserys of this life, between two and three of the clock yesterday morning.   So he was gathered under the feet of St. Simon and St. Jude.[1]   I suppose this authen-

---

[1] October 28th is the Festival of St. Simon and St. Jude.

tique intelligence was sent me to Ely House on purpose that I might transmit it to your Grace at Lambeth, together with my truest duty, which I shall present in my personal attendance (if it please God) upon Sunday morning."

Of the earlier life of Bishop Morley some account has been given in Chapter VII. The later years of his life had been clouded over with some sorrows and disappointments which he must have felt keenly. He had seen the Duchess of York, to whom, as Anne Hyde, he had acted as spiritual guide and confessor, whose almoner he had been in works of charity, slip out of his hands into those of the emissaries of Rome. He and Sancroft had made a vain attempt in February, 1678, to win back her husband to the faith of the martyred king whom they had loved and honoured.[1] He had, as we have seen (p. 129), been disturbed by the frequent visits which Charles, surrounded by his ministers and courtiers, had insisted on paying to Winchester and Farnham. He had lost, a few months before his death, in Izaak Walton, one with whom he had lived for more than sixty years in the most close and uninterrupted friendship. All these things were against him. His management of his diocese would seem to have been accepted by Ken as that of a model Bishop. He too, like Ken, had chosen the celibate life, that he might give himself, and all that he had, to his pastoral work. Like Ken, he practised an ascetic austerity, took but one meal a day, and up to his eighty-seventh year rose, winter and summer, at five o'clock, and, on the coldest mornings, was without a fire.[2] He had given largely to the restoration of his cathedral and of his palace (Wolvesey House) at Winchester; had laid out £8,000 on Farnham Castle, had paid £4,000 for Winchester House, Chelsea, to be annexed to the diocese as the Bishop's town residence, and had been one of the most munificent contributors to the new cathedral of St. Paul's. He built and endowed a hospital at Winchester for ten widows of clergymen, and was a benefactor on a large scale to his old college (Christ Church) at Oxford. His will, made when he was eighty-

[1] D'Oyly's *Life of Sancroft*, chap. iv.
[2] Hammond is another instance of the same severe self-discipline as regards both food and sleep.—Fell, *Life of Hammond*, 1662, p. 107. [C. J. P.]

six years old, was obviously written out of the fulness of his heart. In it he describes himself as "Bishop of Winchester, though most unworthy of such an high dignity, charge, and trust in the Church of God," commends his soul into the hands " of my most merciful Creator," asks for pardon "notwith- standing all my former transgressions, rebellions, and back- slidings," pleads "the mediation and intercession of His only Sonne" as the ground of his hope, implores "the Divine Goodness to give me more and more grace during the short remainder of my life, dayly to renew and improve my repent- ance, and more and more to mortify all my evil and corrupt affections." He ends this profession of his faith with a doxology "to the Trinity in Unity and Unity in Trinity," to Whom "whatsoever becomes of all such sinful wretches as I am, be ascribed and given, as is most due, all honour and glory."

The directions of his will are not less characteristic. He is to be buried "without attendance of heralds, or any secular pomp or solemnity," in his own private chapel or in the cathe- dral at Winchester, at or after Evening Prayer, "without any funerall sermon or panegyricall oration, because (besides myne owne being unworthy of any such publicke commemoration) I have observed that *In hujusmodi multiloquiis aut nunquam aut raro deest peccatum.*" No "monument or stately tomb" is to be erected for him; only a black marble slab is to cover his grave, with such an inscription as he shall leave behind him for that purpose. He gives the communion-plate of his private chapel to his successors; his library to the Dean and Chapter of Winchester for the use of the clergy of the diocese; his ordi- nary ecclesiastic habits, "gowns, cassocks, and the like, to such of the poorer clergy as his executor shall think fit." Ken, with the other prebendaries of Winchester, had the legacy of "a ring, of twenty shillings, and mourning," and ten pounds were given "to the poore of the Soake, near Winchester," which had been, it will be remembered, under Ken's special charge. Augmentations of twenty pounds per annum were left to the vicarage of Farnham, and to two churches (to be united into one parish) at Guildford, and of ten pounds to Horswell, in Surrey. In each case the condition was attached that the incumbent was to read daily morning and evening prayers in the parish church. In a codicil, dated six months later, he leaves five hundred pounds to the building of the Military Hospital at Chelsea, "as an humble and grateful acknowledgment of the King's favour and kindnesse, humbly beseeching his Majesty to accept it, as being all, or neare all, I have left to dispose of." [1]

Morley's death led to a great and unlooked-for change in Ken's life. The see of Winchester was filled by the translation of Peter Mews, who in 1672 had succeeded Creighton as Bishop of Bath and Wells. He had been, in earlier life, a chaplain in the army of Charles I., and a black patch over a bullet-wound in his cheek still bears its witness, in his portrait in the town-hall of Wells, that he had risked his life in that cause. He was in personal habits very unlike Morley, ostentatious and extravagant in expenditure, not unfrequently running into debt. [2] When this step was settled, there were the usual floating rumours as to the see which he left vacant. [3] Some talked of Dean Meggot, of Winchester, who had shown himself complaisant in the matter of Nell Gwyn's lodgings; some of Parker, afterwards Bishop of Oxford, and memorable in connexion with the disputes between James II. and the Fellows of Magdalen College. Ken's name was also on the lips of men as not unlikely to be chosen. The King had been impressed by the sermons in which "little Ken tells me of my faults." His work, as chaplain in the Tangier Expedition, had commended him, through Lord Dartmouth, to the notice of the Duke of York. Probably the Princess Mary was known to have formed a high estimate of his character. "Devout and

[1] Anderdon, pp. 219—223.

[2] Shaftesbury, in a letter to John Locke (November 13, 1674), says that "the strong ale which he gave the Somersetshire squires was the only spiritual thing they knew of him."—King, *Life of Locke*, i. 70.

[3] Prideaux, in a letter written just after Morley's death, speaks of Ken and Parker as named even for Winchester. "Whoever fails of that will have Norwich." Parker, as we know, was reserved for Oxford; Norwich was given to Lloyd. Prideaux also states that Morley, in his last illness, had filled up all his leases, so that his nephew received £20,000. This was so utterly unlike Morley that, assuming the fact, the only explanation is, as I have said (p. 85), that his mind was so enfeebled by illness that he signed whatever was put before him.

honourable women" looked to him as the guide of their spiritual life.   The only charge that had been whispered against
him was that he was overmuch inclined to look with favour on
the Church of Rome, and this with the King and his brother
was, of course, not likely to be regarded as a drawback.   According to the current tradition of the time,[1] however, Ken
owed his advancement to that which, in the eyes of courtiers,
would have seemed most likely to hinder it.   When men were
applying to him on behalf of this or that candidate, Charles is
said to have stopped their representations with the declaration,
"Odd's fish !   Who shall have Bath and Wells but the little
black fellow who would not give poor Nelly a lodging?"   Ken's
own friends were told that they need not trouble themselves;
that "Dr. Ken should succeed, but that he designed it should
be his own peculiar appointment."[2]   The rapidity with which
the whole matter was decided was shown by the fact that,
Morley having died on October 29th, Sunderland wrote, on
November 4th, to Mews, to tell him that the King had nominated him for Winchester, and that on the same day Arlington wrote to another of the King's chaplains, informing him
that he was to be in attendance in the following February,
"in the place of Dr. Ken, who is removed to be a Bishop."[3]
Charles showed in this, as in some other instances, that he had
not lost the power of respecting in others the goodness which
he did not pretend to strive after for himself.[4]

And so once more the greatness which Ken would not seek
—we remember that "*Et tu quæris tibi grandia ? Noli quærere*"
(p. 139)—was thrust upon him.   More than twenty years afterwards, in dedicating his *Hymnarium* to his friend and successor,
Hooper, he records the feelings with which he had entered
on his new and, as it proved to be, perilous and troubled
path :—

---

[1] Hawkins, *Life*, p. 5.

[2] Hawkins, p. 5.

[3] Anderdon, p. 228, from Secretary of State's Letter Book.

[4] I follow Anderdon and Markland in quoting from Boswell Johnson's estimate of Charles II.   "He was licentious in his practice, but he always had a
reverence for what was good.   He knew his people and rewarded merit.   The
Church was at no time better filled than in his reign."

> "Among the herdsmen I, a common swain,[1]
> Liv'd, pleas'd with my low cottage on the plain,
> Till up, like Amos, on a sudden caught,
> I, to the past'ral chair, was trembling brought."
>
> *Works* ii., *Hymn*, p. iv.

He had to leave the quiet congenial life, which had grown so dear to him, his boys at Winchester, the poor of his parish of the Soke, and to plunge into a vortex of ever-increasing anxieties, and laden with tremendous responsibilities. For the most part, the appointment was welcomed as the best that could have been made. Burnet, indeed, speaks of it in terms of some disparagement, but the *History of his Own Time* was written, we must remember, after he and Ken had crossed swords in the Non-juring controversy. Probably, however, as I have said (p. 131), the two men had always felt a certain mutual repulsion, and few characters of the time stand out in more marked contrast with each other. Burnet writes thus :—[2]

> "Ken succeeded Mews in Bath and Wells—a man of an ascetic course of life, and yet of a very lively temper, but too hot and sudden. He had a very edifying way of preaching, but it was more apt to move the passions than to instruct, so that his sermons were rather beautiful than solid, yet his way in them was very taking. The King seemed fond of him, and by him and Turner the papists hoped that great progress would be made in gaining, or at least deluding, the clergy. It was observed that all the men in favour among the clergy were unmarried,[3] from whom they (the papists) might more probably promise themselves a disposition to come over to them."

As an example of the art of "damning with faint praise," the paragraph is not unworthy of study. Burnet, the husband of three wives, looks with a glance of suspicion on those who have chosen to remain single, and insinuates that this, and not the general holiness of his character, had commended Ken to

---

[1] The phrase is found also in the Dedicatory Epistle to the *Practice of Divine Love*, Round, p. 210.

[2] *Own Time*, B. iii. 1684.

[3] This was true of Sancroft, and Ken, and Frampton, but Lloyd (of Norwich) was married, and Turner was a widower.

Court favour. The asceticism is admitted, but the admission is qualified by what Burnet had himself experienced, that the man commonly so calm and meek could, on occasion, flash out into a sudden heat of indignation, and write sharp words that went like arrows to their mark.

The Chapter-Acts of Wells record, in their usual order, the several stages that followed on the royal choice. The *Congé d'élire* was received on December 9th. The election, for which the greater Chapter, including the whole body of prebendaries who were not " residentiaries," was summoned, took place on December 16th, and, according to the customary formula, they proceeded to elect, *Spiritu divino, ut sperant, inspirati.* The Dean, Ralph Bathurst, who was also President of Trinity College, Oxford, was not present at any of the proceedings.[1]

The consecration took place in the chapel of Lambeth Palace on St. Paul's-day (January 25, 168⅘). The bishops who took part, besides Sancroft, as Primate, were Compton, of London ; Crewe, of Durham ; Lloyd, of Peterborough ; Turner, of Ely, the friend of Ken's school-days ; and Sprat, of Rochester. The sermon was preached by Edward Young, another college friend, at the time a Fellow of Winchester, and subsequently, first Canon, and then Dean, of Salisbury, and father of the author of the *Night Thoughts.* It contains some passages which, as

---

[1] There would seem, among the inferior members of the Cathedral staff, to have been at least one notable exception to the good-will with which the appointment was generally welcomed. Within three weeks of Ken's election (January 7, 1685), the Chapter Records note the deprivation of Benjamin Whitcare, a vicar-choral, then in his year of probation, partly because he had neglected his duties in the Cathedral on Christmas-day, but partly also because he had sent round letters to his brother vicars, attacking the recently elected Bishop, *verbis dishonestis et insinuationibus immodestis.* The Dean and Chapter do not care to specify what these insinuations were. It is probable, I think, that they were the outgrowths of an ultra-Protestant suspicion. Given a celibate bishop, suspected of a leaning to Popery, and known to act as spiritual director to women, married and unmarried, and the imagination of the average middle-class Englishman will not be slow to picture many things to itself, and to whisper them to others in the closet, or proclaim them on the house-tops. It is worth noting that when Ken came to his diocese he had to live down at least a local slander of this kind, that, for once in his life, he had to pass through the same ordeal as that which had befallen Athanasius, and Hooker, and Molinos, and the saintly Bishop of Alet, Nicolas Pavillon.

practically portraying Ken's character, in describing what a Bishop ought to be, are worth reproducing :—

The preacher speaks of the "pious care of the King" who "chooseth such to lead us, as by their ardent love and zealous contention towards heaven have given a true report of the desireableness of that good land; a truth which, were it not for a few such reports, the world lies always under a propension to mistrust."

*   *   *   *   *

"Pious men, in all ages, have trembled at the thought of *seeking* the Episcopal charge, lest, by running officiously into the obligation of a mighty duty, they might tempt God and provoke Him to withhold that measure of Grace which was necessary for the due discharge of it."   In times of persecution and suffering it might have been otherwise.   "But as soon as it came to be baited with honours and advantages, then all good men became jealous of themselves, lest *in desiring the office of a Bishop they might not so much desire a good work as a good accommodation ;* lest their passions should draw them more prevalently than their conscience, which must necessarily have brought a check upon the Divine blessing; for the want whereof no parts, nor wisdom, nor industry in their administration could ever compensate.   From this pious jealousy of theirs' it followed that the greatest bishops have been not only wisht and nominated, but sought, woo'd, and commanded, out of their retirement, to the undertaking of their charge, where, after they had undertaken it, we find them bewailing themselves upon the tremendous prospect of its duty, and *crying that it was in punishment to their sins that God had committed the Helm of a Diocese into their hands.*"—August. *Ep.* 148, *ad Valer. (Ep.* xxi. *Tom.* ii., p. 25, *ed. Bened.*)

*   *   *   *   *

"And now, if Timothy will stir up this spirit of courage, he must, in the first place, bethink himself well of his undertaking ; he must imagine himself a champion of war entered into the lists, as a David heretofore into the valley of Elah, where he must either conquer, or die, not a single man, but an army; both the Israelites and Philistines surveying him in the mean time, with different hopes and censures, whereof the most (as envy will always have it) are against him.   Some blame his youth, some his confidence, some his want of arms, and some, like Goliath, curse him by their gods; but as these casual forms of popular breath cannot in themselves affect his success, so neither must he suffer them to affect his thoughts."

*   *   *   *   *

"He must set himself to work to check the range of Satan in the world; to awe men out of ill manners; to oppose vice vigorously and impartially, without any glozing or fear of the great, without any unthankful indulgence to benefactor or friend. He must awe it out of countenance, and beat it off the stage, with his looks, intimations, discourses, interests, monitions, and rebukes; and if it bear up its head against all these, he must then separate the leper from the camp, and turn the sacred key against the refractory sinner."

  *   *   *   *   *

And in doing this, he is to remember that the censure must be tempered with love. " Love, condescending from such a height of place, wins and captivates, and makes a man look like God both in temper and beneficence—like God (I say), whose most amiable and endearing character to the sons of men is this, that He is a *Lover of Souls*." Lastly there comes the " sound mind," which is the fruit of the wisdom from above. " He (the Bishop) must be watchful, sagacious, and prudent. While his hands are upon the helm, his eyes must be upon the needle and the chart; he must observe the pointings of Providence, the opportunities of action, the seasons of counsel, the differences of place, the varieties of temper, and the accommodations, that he may ever be *gaining some*."

In conclusion, the preacher turns to the future bishop with a stirring apostrophe :—

" And now, O Timothy, see here are the arts of thy government; *continue in these* and thou needest no other policy. . . . . Do thou stir up the gift of God that is in thee; do thou quicken the divine coal that toucheth thee, and thy coal shall blaze into a flame, and thy flame shall be ennobled into a star, a vast orb of glory, such as shall crown the heads of all those happy men who, by their conduct and example, turn many unto righteousness."

So passed Sunday, January 25th, at Lambeth Palace. An entry in Evelyn's *Diary* shows how it was spent at Whitehall :—

" January 25th, Dr. Dove preached before the King. I saw this evening such a scene of profuse gaming, and the King in the midst of his three concubines, as I had never before seen—luxurious dallying and prophanenesse."

The Sunday that followed was, as the following extract from the same *Diary* shows, like its predecessor :—

" I can never forget the inexpressible luxury and prophanenesse, gaming and all dissolutenesse, and, as it were, total forgetfulnesse of God (it being Sunday evening) which this day se'ennight" [the entry is made on February 8th] "I was witnesse of, the King sitting and toying with his concubines, Portsmouth, Cleaveland, and Mazarin,[1] &c.; a French boy singing love songs, in that glorious gallery, whilst about 20 of the greate courtiers and other dissolute persons were at Basset, round a large table, a bank of at least £2,000 in gold before them, upon which two gentlemen who were with me made reflexions with astonishment. Six days after was all in the dust."

The stroke to which Evelyn refers in the last words was the apoplectic fit that on the morning of Monday, February 2nd, ushered in Charles II.'s fatal illness. Bleeding seemed at first to abate the symptoms, but as the case appeared dangerous, the bishops about the court were summoned to attend the royal sufferer, and Compton, Crewe, Turner, and Ken had to enter on the task of their spiritual ministrations. They were summoned on the Wednesday, and Ken at least remained for three days and nights, consecutively, by the King's bedside. On the Thursday, between six and seven P.M., Turner wrote to Sancroft[2] telling him that some of the physicians thought there was "immediate and extreme danger," that the coming night promised to be a "bad one," that "several lords were asking, Where is my Lord Archbishop?" and Sancroft obeyed the summons. From the first, however, the chief work of exhortation, though he was the junior bishop, fell on Ken.[3] It was thought, apparently, that he had greater gifts as a preacher of repentance than any others, and that Charles would, in sickness as in health, be willing to let "little Ken tell him of his faults," while he might turn a deaf ear to others. Even Burnet admits that

---

[1] The Duchess of Mazarin was niece to the Cardinal. Evelyn (June 11, 1699) mentions her death, and describes her as having been "dissolute, impatient of matrimonial restraint, so as to be abandoned by her husband and banished."

[2] Tanner MSS., xxxii. p. 22, in Anderdon p. 236.

[3] Burnet reports (B. iii. 1685) that the "Bishop of London spoke a little to the King, to which he answered not a word, but this was imputed to the Bishop's cold way of speaking, and to the ill opinion they had of him at Court." Sancroft "made a very weighty exhortation to him, in which he used a good degree of freedom, which he said was necessary, since he was going to be judged by One who was no respecter of persons. To him the King made no answer neither, nor yet to Ken, though the most in favour with him of all the Bishops."

he "applied himself much to the awaking the King's conscience," that "he spoke with great elevation both of thought
and expression, like a man inspired, as those who were present
told me.   He resumed the matter often, and pronounced many
short ejaculations and prayers, which affected all that were
present except him who was the most concerned, who seemed
to take no notice of him and made no answers to him."   One
open scandal Ken was able to repress.   The Duchess of Portsmouth, who seems, from what followed, to have been in alarm
about the King's soul as well as body, came in while Ken was at
his task "suggesting pious and proper thoughts and ejaculations," and "sat on the King's bed taking care of him, as a
wife of a husband."[1]   He prevailed on the King to have her
removed, and took that occasion of representing the wrongs
done to his queen so effectually, that his Majesty was induced to
send for her and ask her forgiveness.   She had been present at
his bed-side till her violent emotion compelled her to withdraw.
When the King asked for her, she sent a message to excuse her
absence and "to beg his pardon, if ever she had offended him
in all her life."   With a touch of conscience which Ken must
have welcomed, he replied, "Alas, poor woman, she beg my
pardon!   I beg hers with all my heart."   This utterance of
something like sorrow for the past may at least help to explain
Ken's later conduct.   Though he did not confine himself to the
use of forms, he thought it right to follow the method of the
Service for the Visitation of the Sick.   He pressed the King
six or seven times to receive the Holy Communion, and reminded
him that he had received it at his hands as recently as the previous Christmas.   Charles seemed lethargic, said he was too
weak, that "there was time," that "he would think of it;" and
though a table was set out with the elements ready for conse-

---

[1] Burnet (*ut supra*).   Anderdon (p. 245) quotes the testimony of Hawkins,
James II., Huddleston, Turner's Chaplain (Ellis, *Letters*, iii. p. 335), Barillon,
and the Earl of Aylesbury on the other side.   The last witness (*Europ. Mag.*,
xxvii. p. 22) is very emphatic, "Burnet is a liar from beginning to end.   My
good King and Master falling upon me in his fit, I ordered him to be blooded,
and then I went to fetch the Duke of York, and when we came to the bed-side
we found the Queen there, and the impostor says it was the Duchess of Portsmouth."   Hawkins's statement that the Duchess came in and was removed, was
probably, however, derived from Ken himself.

cration, they remained unused. The request that he would at
least declare that he desired it, and died in communion with
the Church of England, was met with an apathetic silence.
Then came the effort to lead the sick man to make a confession
of sins. If a detailed confession was impossible, would he generally acknowledge his sinfulness, and desire absolution? By
some broken words, or look, or gesture, the King was supposed
to assent, and the solemn words of absolution were accordingly
pronounced. Ken thought that there was ground for assuming
that the conditions of repentance had been sufficiently, though
imperfectly, fulfilled. He hoped against hope, and uttered the
Absolvo te.[1]

At some stage or other of these proceedings (the days and
hours are not carefully noted in the records) Ken must have
taken part in another scene. The King commended all his
children (with the significant exception of the Absalom of the
Court, the Duke of Monmouth, who was then in exile at the
Hague) to his brother's care, and sent for them that, one by
one, he might give them a parting embrace and blessing. The
bishops seized on the opportunity to try and elicit from him
some expression of his regard for their order and their Church,
and cried out, that "as he was the Lord's anointed and the
father of his country, they also, and all that were there
present, and in them the whole body of his subjects, had a right
to ask his blessing." "They all knelt down ; the King raised
himself on his bed, and very solemnly blessed them all."[2]

So far, though it was not all they could have wished, the
bishops seemed to have gained their point. They were able to
say that Charles had died, as he appeared to have lived, as a

[1] Burnet, after his manner, criticises Ken's action. "He was much blamed
for this, since the King expressed no sense of sorrow for his past life, nor any
purpose of amendment. It was thought to be a prostitution of the peace of the
Church to give it to one who, after a life of sin, seemed to harden himself against
everything that could be said to him." It may be pleaded as Ken's *apologia*
that he was present and Burnet was not, and that in spiritual discernment and
sense of responsibility, he was, to say the least, not inferior to him. James, in
his narrative, distinctly states that his brother said, in answer to Ken's
questions, that he *was* sorry for his sins. The facts are gathered from Hawkins,
pp. 5—6 ; Burnet, *O.T.*, B. iii. A.D. 1685 ; Clarke, *James II.*, i. p. 747.

[2] Narrative by Bishop Turner's chaplain, in Ellis's *Original Letters*, First
Series, iii., pp. 335—338.

member of the Church of England. At the very last the
prize was snatched from their hands, and they were forced to
accept the alternative that his conformity to the Church of
England had been all along false and hypocritical. The last
days of the wretched king were a time of plots and intrigues,
of mining and countermining, which, in spite of the grim,
dread reality of the scene of death, irresistibly remind us of
the light comedy touch with which Lord Beaconsfield, in his
novel of *Lothair*, has painted the struggle of prelates of the
rival churches for the wealthy and powerful noble. And the
agent in bringing about this result was none other than the
Duchess of Portsmouth, whom Ken had excluded from the
dying man's chamber. Her life of splendid shame had not
made her altogether callous or indifferent, and a thrill of
superstitious panic took possession of her soul. She knew that
Charles had been in heart a Romanist. She shuddered at the
thought of what would fall on him, if he should die under
false colours as a member of a heretical sect, and without the
sacraments which the true Church alone could offer him
as a *viaticum* for his perilous journey. She had all along acted
as the agent of the French Court, and so, in her distress, she
turned to the French ambassador, Barillon. "Monsieur
Ambassador," she said to him, "I am going to tell you the
greatest secret in the world, and my head would be in danger
if it were known. The King of England at the bottom of his
heart is a Catholic ; but he is surrounded with Protestant
bishops, and nobody tells him of his condition nor speaks to
him of God. I cannot with decency enter the room ; besides
that the Queen is almost constantly there; the Duke of York
thinks of his own affairs, and has too many of them to take
the care he ought of the King's conscience. Go and tell him
I have conjured you to warn him to think of what he can do
to save the King's soul. He commands the room, and can turn
out whom he will : lose no time, for if it is deferred ever so
little, it will be too late." [1]

---

[1] Dalrymple's *Memoirs*, App. to vol. i., p. 95. Macaulay (c. iv.) quotes from a
broadside in the Somers Collection, which states that James was reminded of his
duty to his brother by P. M. A. C. F. The initials have been identified by
Mr. John Kent and others, whom Macaulay follows, with Père Mansuete, a
Cordelier Friar, who was James's Confessor.

The counsel was acted on ; the command was given, probably by the Duke of York, and the Bishops, and all the courtiers except the Earls of Feversham[1] and Bath, both, it may be noted, Protestants, but trusted as discreet, left the room. Search was made for a priest, and John Huddleston was brought through a back-door into the sick man's chamber. He and the King had met once before under circumstances which gave him a special influence. After the Battle of Worcester, Charles had taken refuge at Boscobel, a lonely country-house in Staffordshire, inhabited by five brothers of the Penderell family. It was while concealed there that he had passed twenty-four hours, when the Parliamentary forces were on his track, in the branches of the tree which, as the Royal Oak, became a name in history, and made oak-apples and branches the received symbol of loyalty on the 29th of May. The Penderell family were Roman Catholics, and Huddleston, as a Jesuit priest, had sought shelter under their roof. So he and Charles were brought together, and he naturally made use of his opportunity, pressed on him the usual arguments of Romish controversialists, gave him books to read, and among others a MS. by a relation of his, Robert Huddleston, of the order of St. Benedict. Charles read, or affected to read, them with attention, and professed that the arguments in them " were so plain and conclusive that he did not conceive how they could be denied."[2]

When the proposal that a Romish priest should be sent for had been made to him by the Duke of York, Charles had assented eagerly. " For God's sake, do, brother, and lose no time." And when Huddleston came in he welcomed him as

---

[1] Louis Duras, by birth a French Protestant, and nephew of Turenne, had married the daughter of the Earl of Feversham, and was created an English peer with that title. (Lingard ix. p. 319) Up to the time of the order thus given, the sick man's room had been filled by five bishops, seventy-five lords and privy councillors, besides surgeons and servants. (*Ibid.* x. p. 107.) The five bishops were Sancroft, Compton, Crewe, Turner, and Ken, the last throughout taking the leading part.—Evelyn, February 4.

[2] The Huddleston MS. was probably the basis of, if not identical with, the two papers that were found in Charles's desk, and which James had printed, and sent to Sancroft and some of the Bishops. The Williams MSS., which have been communicated to me through the kindness of Bishop Hobhouse, contain a copy with an attestation in James's handwriting. Burnet (*O.T.*, B. iii. 1685) supposes they were written by Bristol or Aubigny.

one who, having once had a share in saving his life, had now come to save his soul. The presence of the bishops had become wearisome. He was impatient of the mask which he had worn so long. He proved himself in Huddleston's hands an apt and docile pupil. The Jesuit father may be left to tell his own tale of what followed.

" I was called into the King's bed-chamber, where approaching to the bed-side and kneeling down, I in brief presented his Majesty with what service I could perform for God's honour, and the happiness of his soul, at this last moment on which eternity depends. The King then declared himself: that he desired to die in the Faith and Communion of the Holy Roman Catholic Church ; that he was most heartily sorry for all the sins of his past life, and particularly that he had deferred his reconciliation so long ; and through the merits of Christ's Passion he hoped for salvation ; that he was in charity with all the world ; that with all his heart he pardoned his enemies, and desired pardon of all those whom he had anywise offended, and that, if it pleased God to spare him longer life, he would amend it, detesting all sin. I then advertised his Majesty of the benefit and necessity of the Sacrament of Penance, which advertisement the King most willingly embracing, made an exact confession of his whole life with exceeding compunction and tenderness of heart ; which ended, I desired him, in further sign of repentance and true sorrow for his sins, to say with me this little short act of contrition, ' O my Lord God, with my whole heart and soul I detest all the sins of my life past, for the love of Thee, whom I love above all things ; and I firmly purpose by Thy Holy Grace never to offend Thee more : Amen, sweet Jesus, Amen. Into thy hands, sweet Jesus, I commend my soul ; mercy, sweet Jesus, mercy ! ' This he pronounced with a clear and audible voice ; which done, and his sacramental penance admitted, I gave him absolution. After receiving the Holy Sacrament of the Eucharist, and Extreme Unction, he repeated the Act of Contrition, raising himself up, and saying, ' let me meet my heavenly Lord in a better posture than in my bed,' &c., and so he received his Viaticum with all the symptoms of devotion imaginable." [1]

[1] " *Brief Account of Particulars occurring at the happy death of our late Sovereign Lord, King Charles the Second, in regard to Religion ; faithfully related by his then assistant, Jo. Huddleston,*" 4to, 1685, in Lingard, x. The Huddleston family were of Sawston Hall, Suffolk, where a portrait of the Jesuit priest is still extant. It may be noted that, after Charles's death, he continued to act as Chaplain to the Queen Dowager, that he weathered the storm of the Revolution, and died at Somerset House in 1698.

While this was passing only James was present, and those who had been turned out of the room remained in the ante-chamber, wondering why they had been shut out. Suddenly the door was opened, and a glass of water called for. It was reported afterwards that the King was half-choked with the wafer of the sacred host.

Of the other stories connected with Charles's death, how he gave James some special keys which were taken from his pocket, and the use of which he was supposed to understand; how, with a quaint touch of the old cynical humour, he apologised to the bystanders for being " so unconscionable a time in dying;" how he specially commended the Duchess of Portsmouth and her son to the Duke's care, as those who were dearest to his heart; how the words, " Let not poor Nelly starve," told that he was not forgetful of the mistress of lower rank, it may be enough to give this brief summary.[1] There is no reason to doubt them, but it is not easy to fix their precise place in the order of events which crowded round the death-bed. It is not likely that the bishops who had been shut out were called in again while life yet lingered. They, and Ken among them, had to wait for a while in indignant and sorrowing wonder, and then to learn how they had been tricked and outwitted. To James and Huddleston, and the Duchess, who had prompted the whole movement, there must have been something of the sense of triumph in a successful strategy. We may believe that they had also, according to their light, some feeling of satisfaction of a higher kind. The King had, at least, not passed into the unseen world with a lie in his right hand. He had, to use words which expressed the feeling of the

---

[1] As often happens in the case of royal deaths that are supposed to be convenient for the plans of a party, among the rumours connected with Charles II.'s death, one was that he had been poisoned, and that James was privy to the crime. There is, it need hardly be said, not a shadow of foundation for the charge, but it was prominent in the Duke of Monmouth's proclamation against James (p. 213). Men remembered, perhaps, that the King had taken Jesuit's bark, and sent for a Roman Catholic physician, during the Popish plot, and the fever of suspicion did the rest. (Foley, v. p. 67 ; Evelyn, February 4, 1685.) Burnet, *O.T.* B. iii. 1685, describes symptoms that clearly suggested that conclusion to his own mind, and quotes the testimony of a Roman Catholic physician, Dr. Short, who attended the King, and even of the Duchess of Portsmouth as confirming it.

time, made, before it was too late, the *amende honorable* to God. He had started on his journey duly furnished with the orthodox *viaticum.* They had now good grounds for hoping that all was well with him. As we do not read of any masses having been offered for his soul, it may be inferred that it was believed that he did not need even the discipline of the "milder shades of purgatory." Perhaps, however, under the circumstances it is scarcely safe to rest too much on this merely negative evidence, and Huddleston and others may have said their masses in secret.

The old rule, *Le Roi est mort, vive le Roi!* had, however, to be acted on, and from the chamber of death the new king passed to that of the Council. After a passionate expression of his sorrow, he told his councillors, in words that were afterwards remembered but too well, as contrasted with his actions, that "he would endeavour to follow the example of his predecessor in his clemency and tenderness to his people; that, however he had been misrepresented as affecting arbitrary power, they should find the contrary, for that the laws of England had made the king as great a monarch as he could desire; that he would endeavour to maintain the Government, both in Church and State, as by law established, its principles being so firm for monarchy, and the members of it showing themselves so good and loyal subjects, that he would always take care to defend and support the Church of England, and that as he would never depart from the just rights and prerogatives of the Crown, so would he never invade any man's property; but as he had often adventured his life in defence of the nation, so he would still proceed, and preserve it in all its lawful rights and liberties."[1]

The words were hailed by the Council as a pledge of security for the future, but as they had been spoken and not read, the Solicitor-General (Finch, afterwards Earl of Aylesford) undertook to reproduce them from memory, withdrew to a side-table, and wrote them out in words of which the King approved, and

[1] The declaration was received with unbounded enthusiasm throughout England. For the feelings of the laity see Evelyn, Feb. 8, 1685, Reresby, p. 315. The address from the Bishop and Clergy of the Diocese of Bath and Wells, given in the next chapter, is a fair sample of the feelings of the clergy.

in this form, to which we shall soon see that Ken appealed, the
address was published and circulated throughout England,
giving rise, for a time, to a burst of passionate and loyal enthusiasm in favour of the new monarch,[1] among the earliest
expressions of which, we find an address from the bishops who
were then in town, of whom Ken was one.   They speak of his
"admirable declaration which we ought to write down in letters
of gold and engrave in marble.   We have nothing to ask your
Majesty but that you would be (what you have always been
observed to be) yourself: that is, generous and just, and true
to all you once declare."   It does not appear that Ken or any
of the bishops took part in the funeral on February 14th, in
Henry the Seventh's Chapel.   That ceremony indeed, though
attended by the Privy Councillors and the household and some
of the peers who were in town, was noted at the time as wanting in the usual state ("very obscurely buried," "without any
manner of pomp," was Evelyn's phrase),[2] as if some embarrass-
ment was felt at interring with the rites of the English Church
one whose last act had been to renounce her communion, and
whose successor and chief mourner had renounced it years
before.

One or two facts connected with Ken's new position deserve
a record before we pass on to the work which awaited him in
his diocese.   One was singularly characteristic.   It had been
customary—a custom which he thought more honoured in the
breach than in the observance—for a new bishop to give a consecration dinner, which was commonly on a large and costly
scale.   We have seen (p. 130) how Leighton felt when invited to such a banquet.   To Ken, in his like-mindedness to
Leighton, it must have seemed a singularly inappropriate in-
auguration of the work of a chief shepherd of the flock.[3]   Fell,
Bishop of Oxford, had set an example which Ken followed.
He knew how great an interest his friend Morley had taken in

---

[1] James, in his later years, thought that the reporter had interpolated the
phrase about "defending and supporting" the Church of England.   Evelyn,
however (*Diary*, May 22, 1685), reports James's Speech to his first Parliament,
in which he refers to the declaration on his accession, and reproduces the words
in question.

[2] *Diary*, February 14, 1685.

[3] Burnet, *O.T.*, B. ii. 1061.

the building of the new St. Paul's, and on the day following
his consecration he sent a donation of £100, "in lieu of his
consecration dinner and gloves."[1] Even this, however, would
seem to have been given out of borrowed money. He had
treated his income as Fellow and Prebendary like one who looked
on himself as simply a steward for the poor, and had no cash
in hand to meet the expenses of official fees and the outfit of his
new life, till it was supplied by Francis Morley, the nephew of
his friend the Bishop. It was his excuse, made to one of his
chaplains, Dr. Cheyney, for doing less in his diocese than he
wished to do in the way of giving, that he had the burden of
this debt upon him, and thought it right to be just before he
was charitable.[2] At or about the same time he gave £100 towards the new school-room at Winchester, and £30, together
with some valuable books, to the Cathedral library.[3] His formal
resignation of his fellowship bears the date of January 26th.

While these events were passing in London a solemn ceremony took place at Wells, in which Ken would, in the common
course of things, have been likely to take part. The Dean and
Chapter had fixed February 6th as the day for the new Bishop's
enthronement. The Chapter Acts of that period record, in a
Greek note, the death of his Most Serene Majesty ($\gamma\alpha\lambda\eta\nu\acute{o}\tau\alpha\tauο\varsigma$
$\acute{}\Lambda\upsilon\tauοκρ\acute{\alpha}\tauωρ$) at noon on that very day. As Ken had been in
attendance at Whitehall from the 3rd of February, it was pro-
bably known that he could not come, and it was arranged that
the enthronement should take place by proxy, a proceeding for
which there were many precedents. Thomas Holt, one of the
Canons and Chancellor of the Cathedral, was chosen as the
Bishop's representative, and treated in all respects as if he had
been the Bishop himself, was fetched from the Palace by a

---

[1] It was, I suppose, the custom, as in the still surviving practice at funerals,
for the new Bishop to send gloves to all who officiated at his consecration.

[2] Hawkins, p. 13.

[3] The list of books (for which I have to thank the Dean of Winchester) is interesting, as indicating Ken's line of reading. The selection of elaborate books
of Roman Catholic theology and casuistry is somewhat peculiar. Probably Ken
felt that the arguments of Protestant controversialists were too often based upon
inaccurate and popular prepossessions, and that men ought to read both sides of
the question in works of the highest authority. Schmidius on *Nov. Testamentum* ;
Collegii Salmanticensis Cursus Theologicus, twelve vols. ; Filiucii, *Casus Con-
scientiæ,* two vols. ; Raymundi, *Summa Theologiæ Moralis,* were the works chosen.

verger, and conducted to the Cathedral through the gateway known as Pennyless Porch. After he had knelt down and prayed at the entrance of the west door, he was led to Bishop Bubwith's chantry, and then " to the place where the Litany was wont to be chanted." The necessary documents were then presented by the official persons, and the Procurator took, in the name of the Bishop, the customary oaths. He was then placed in the throne, and a *Te Deum* greeted him from the clergy, and the men and boys of the choir. One sentence of the oath—(I do not know whether it is peculiar to Wells, or obtains in other dioceses)—seems to have impressed itself deeply on Ken's mind and heart. The Bishop swears that he will defend the rights, customs, and liberties of the Cathedral, "*ut bonus Pastor et Sponsus Ecclesiæ.*"[1] The seal which Ken had engraved for his use as Bishop consisted of his own family arms (these, as has been said in p. 10, were identical with those of the Kenns of Kenn Court, in Somerset), impaled with the St. Andrew's cross which belonged to the diocese. The shield thus emblazoned was represented as held by the Good Shepherd, bearing a sheep upon his shoulders.[2] Round the shield ran the motto, *Pastor bonus animam dat pro ovibus.* In the spirit of a half-conscious prophecy, of a very definite and distinct purpose, this was what Ken chose as his watchword when he entered on the duties of his episcopate, as he had chosen his *Noli quærere* when he first stood at the entrance of the path which had led on to it.

The following letter comes in here in order of time. Like that in the preceding chapter, it refers to matters about which it is difficult to obtain accurate information, but which may perhaps receive light through being published.

LETTER IX.

To Lord Dartmouth.

" My very good Lord,

I came last night, blessed be God, to my beloved retreat at Winchester, and enquiring how the election of the towne was like to succeed, I found, by Mr. Lestrange's owne acknowledgement

---

[1] No such phrase occurs in the installation ritual of Salisbury Cathedral, where, if anywhere, looking to the intimate relation between the two bodies from the thirteenth century onwards, we might most have expected to find it.

[2] See the cover of these volumes.

that Mr. Morley's interest was very strong, and more likely to pre-
vaile than Sir John Cloberry's.   Being thus informed, I represented
to Mr. Morley in private how agreeable it was to his Majesty's
pleasure, and how much for his service, that Mr. Lestrange and Mr.
House should be chosen; upon which, in pure obedience to his
Majesty, Mr. Morley promised me to desist, and is to meete Mr.
Lestrange this afternoone to consult how he may best promote his
and Mr. House being chosen.   One thing Mr. Morley complaines
of, that he has been misrepresented to the King, and that words are
imputed to him which he never said, and he vowes that if, when he
mentioned his standing to the King, his Majesty had in the least
measure expresst any dislike of it, he would never have appeared;
and it is an evident instance of the deference he payes to his
Majesty, that having been these four yeares making an interest,
and now having a morall assurance of a major part, he lays all
downe at his Majesty's feet, and he makes it his humble petition
to your Lordshippe, to which I must adde my owne request, to
acquaint his Majesty with the trueth, that he may not lye under his
Royal displeasure; and I doe the more confidently aske this favoure
of your Lordshippe, because I so well know the benignity of your
nature.

" *March* 15, (168⅘.")

[Ken probably took Winchester on his way from London to Wells.   He found
that city in the excitement of a contested election.   Morley, the late Bishop's
nephew, was one of the candidates, and Sir John Cloberry apparently stood with
him.   The Court's Candidates, however, were Roger l'Estrange (James knighted
him after the election) and a Mr. House.   L'Estrange had been prominent as a
High Church and Tory pamphleteer, had been editor of the *Public Intelligencer*,
1663, and was the editor of the *Observator*, the most "thorough" of all the
journals that opposed the Whigs and the Trimmers, often violent, scandalous,
and abusive.   In early days he appears as a friend of Evelyn,[1] with a special
taste for music.   James was obviously bent on his being elected, and Ken, still
relying on the "inviolable word of a king," thought it wise and right to comply
with his wishes and keep him in good temper.   He accordingly used his
influence with Morley (to whose kindness, it will be remembered, he had been
recently indebted), and induced him to withdraw, and so L'Estrange was elected.
On the whole, at the first blush of things, one admires Morley's share in the
transaction more than Ken's, and one is glad that, as it was the first, so also it
was the last, instance in which we find the Bishop mixed up in the secularities
of a contested election.   The *Observator*, it may be added, was suppressed by
James because, after all, it was not thorough enough.   L'Estrange himself was
arrested, in his eightieth year, under William III., as involved in the Assassination Plot.   [The Cloberry and Holt families (p. 202) seem to have been connected.   *Catalogue of Oxford Graduates* (1659) 1850, p. 331.   (J. K.)]

[1] Evelyn, *Diary*, March 4, 1656, May 29, 1654.

CHAPTER XIII

LIFE AT WELLS.

" Had he not of wealth his fill,
  Whom a garden gay did bless,
And a gently trickling rill,
  And the sweets of idleness ?

" I made answer, ' Is it ease,
  Fasts to keep and tears to shed ?
Vigil hours and wounded knees,
  Call you these a pleasant bed ? "

J. H. Newman.

THE part which Ken had taken at the deathbed of Charles II.
brought him prominently before the eyes and thoughts of men.
How would he act? they asked, in the new and embarrassing
position in which he and the other Bishops of the Church of
England now found themselves, with a Roman Catholic sovereign on the throne. He and those who had shared his
ministrations at that deathbed had, at least, no doubt as to the
line which it was right for them to take. Most of them—
though it will be seen, I think, that Ken did not go to
the same lengths as others—had all along opposed the
Exclusion Bill, mainly on the ground that the divine law of
hereditary succession was to prevail against all considerations
of expediency. Subjects were not to choose their king, but to
obey the sovereign whom the providence of God, acting ordinarily according to that law, had placed over them. For
themselves and for the people they must ' accept the inevitable,'
and make the best of the circumstances in which they found
themselves.

Within a few days from the presentation of the address

o 2

BISHOP'S PALACE, WELLS.

given in the last Chapter, Ken, after some formalities, putting
him in possession of the temporalities of his see, which had
been interrupted by the late King's death, had been completed,
proceeded to his diocese, and entered on the occupation of the
stately palace which was, as it may then have seemed to him,
to be his home for the remainder of his life. Few episcopal
residences in England equal it in its picturesque beauty and
historical associations. Begun by Bishop Jocelyn early in the
thirteenth century, enlarged by Bishop Burnell (1275), who
added the beautiful chapel which is still in use, surrounded
with military defences in the shape of walls and towers and a
moat, and a gateway entered by what was then a drawbridge,
it presented, in all their completeness, the main characteristics

of a stately mediæval mansion. Bishop Beckyngton (1443) had
added a tower-gate, by which it was approached from the city,
and had connected the well (St. Andrew's Well), from which the
city takes its name, with a conduit in the market-place which
supplied the citizens with water, flowing in a clear stream on
either side of the High Street.[1]   The palace was surrounded

MARKET PLACE, WELLS.

by a spacious garden, along the south side of which, following
the line of the wall between two corner bastions, runs a
terrace-walk which tradition reports to have been a favourite
resort of Ken's.   If we may not think of him, according to the
local belief, as having there thought out his Morning and
Evening and Midnight Hymns (these were, probably, as will
be shown, composed at Winchester), it is at least likely that

_____

[1] It was part of the conditions of the gift that the citizens of Wells should
meet once a year in the market-place, march in procession to the Cathedral, and
there offer prayers for the Bishop's soul.   This, of course, had lapsed into disuse
after the Reformation.   The present Conduit is a structure of the last century.

some of his other poems, and the works which marked his episcopate, the *Exposition of the Church Catechism*, and his pastoral
Letter on Lent, may have been the fruit of those hours of
meditation, and that the hymns may have been sung in the
early hours of dawn, or as the sun was sinking into the west.
The summer-house, with its inscription from Horace,

> " Ille terrarum mihi præter omnes
> Angulus ridet, ubi non Hymetto
> Mella decedunt, viridique certat
>   Bacca venafro ;
> Ver ubi longum tepidasque præbet
> Jupiter brumas, et amicus Aulon
> Fertili Baccho minimum Falernis
>   Invidet uvis."
>
> *Od.* ii. vi. 5—13.

in which Mr. Anderdon has seen an indication of Ken's classic
tastes, as finding, like Hooker, a solace and recreation, amid
severer cares, in the Odes of the Latin poet, is, it is believed,
of later date, probably of the time of Bishop Law (1825).[1] In
the garden, parallel with the terrace, stood in Ken's time, as
now, the ruins of the magnificent dining-hall, the "Hall of
the Hundred Men," which had once been the glory of the
palace, but which, stripped of its lead by the Protector Somerset, who had taken possession of the Bishop's residence, or by
Sir John Gates who succeeded the Duke in its occupation,
had been allowed to fall into decay. During the Cromwellian
period, one of the commissioners, Cornelius Burgess, once a
chaplain in Charles the First's army, afterwards transferring

---

[1] So the present Bishop thinks, looking to the style of the inscription. Proofs
of Ken's taste for Horace are, however, found in the fact that not fewer than
thirteen editions of that poet are found among his books at Longleat, and that
the fourth volume of his poems (pp. 508—534) contains "imitations" of the
Integer Vitæ, the *Donec gratus eram*, the *Eheu fugaces*, and the *Quem tu, Melpomene*.
They bear the stamp, if I mistake not, of school and college exercises. The
mature Ken would hardly have written of "those pretty babes, this pleasing
wife," as among the blessings which a man must one day leave. So, too, the
line, "No mitre for his brows provide," was obviously written before his episcopate, and the picture of one who delights "to angle for trout, pike, and bream"
throws us back upon his early companionship with Walton.—(C. J. P.)

RUINS OF HALL AT WELLS PALACE.

his allegiance to the Parliament and then to Cromwell, to whom the Deanery had been assigned, had largely plundered this and other portions of the palace for building materials for the work of transforming the old house built by Dean Gunthorpe in 1475, in which he found himself, into one which should be more adapted to the domestic habits of the seventeenth; and Ken's predecessors, Pierce (1632), Creighton (1670), and Mews (1672), had had to spend considerable sums in the work of restoration. The large hall had been the scene of a memorable event which could not have been without its interest for a man like Ken. There the last Abbot of Glastonbury, Whiting, who had refused to render possession of the Abbey to Henry VIII.'s commissioners, had been tried and condemned to death, and the palace contained in Ken's time, as it does now, the chair in which he had sat as abbot. The memory of that faithfulness to conscience must, if I mistake not, have come back to Ken's mind in after years. Of the other associations connected with Wells and Glastonbury, the traditions of

Joseph of Arimathæa, as having planted a Christian Church at both places, of the Arthurian legends of the Isle of Avalon as the burial-place of the British prince, of the foundation of the cathedral by Ina, King of Wessex, of the part which Alfred had played, in the marsh country of what was of old the Isle of Athelney, in defending Somersetshire against the Danes, Ken has shown in his poem of *Edmund* that he knew them, and loved to dwell on them.

Of the Dean and Chapter with whom Ken was now brought into contact there is not much to be told as affecting his life and character. Ralph Bathurst, who had succeeded Creighton as Dean, when the latter was transferred from the deanery to the palace in 1670, was also President of Trinity College, Oxford, and lived for the most part there. The two men, though thus brought into contact by their respective positions, and though they had been contemporaries at Oxford, had but little in common. Bathurst, in a varied career not without interest in its way, had taken the degree of Doctor of Medicine, had practised successfully as a physician in London during the Presbyterian rule at Oxford and under Cromwell, and had acted as chaplain at the ordinations which Bishop Skinner, of Oxford, had held during that period.[1] He was a scholar of some repute, and distinguished himself by writing Latin verses on the marriage of Charles I.'s daughter to the Prince of Orange, on Cromwell's victory over the Dutch, on Charles II.'s marriage with Catharine of Braganza, with an impartiality of allegiance to the powers that be which could scarcely have met Ken's approval. He had obtained his deanery by a panegyric, in the same form, on Hobbes' *Essay on Human Nature*, which had attracted the admiration of the Duke of Devonshire, who was then conspicuous as the patron of the philosopher of Malmesbury.[2] As President of Trinity he had built by subscriptions, to which he largely contributed, a new chapel, after designs by Wren. He was a member of the association of men interested in physical science, known in Oxford as the Virtuosi,

---

[1] It is probable that Ken was ordained by Skinner, and, if so, then the future Dean of Wells may have examined the future Bishop.

[2] Hobbes, it will be remembered, had been recommended by the University of Oxford as tutor to Charles II. His pupil bettered his instructions.

which afterwards developed into the Royal Society.[1] As Vice-Chancellor of the University he had taken one step which must have won Ken's approval, when in 1674 he had issued the edict already mentioned in p. 48, prohibiting secular apparel by the clergy and students in divinity, and condemning, with all the force of Latin superlatives, the slovenly practice of reading sermons. Both at Oxford and at Wells he seems to have been genial and hospitable. In the latter city he appears to have placed his medical skill at the service of the poor, and to have been ready to give advice and medicine gratis. Evelyn speaks of him with manifest respect, both as a preacher and a man, and makes special mention of the kindness which he had shown to his son.[2] On the whole one pictures his character as not without several attractive qualities, but very little capable of sympathising with Ken's devotion or following him in his asceticism.[3] Of the Canons whom Ken found there,

[1] The Society included Locke, Wren, Boyle, and Ant. à Wood. Stahl, a German professor from Jena, was their teacher in chemistry. I do not find Ken named as a member, but his tastes would, I think, have led him to join his friend Turner in attending the classes in chemistry (Wood, *Life*, p. 184), and I find Stahl's *Lectures* among Ken's books at Wells.

[2] *Diary*, April 11, 1666; Jan. 29, Oct. 8, 1667; July 10, 1675; May, 1704.

[3] As one indication of Bathurst's character I insert the opening sentences of his will. It presents, as will be seen, a curious contrast to Ken's, which will meet us further on (ii. p. 209), both in its profession of faith, and in its general tenour. The tone of eighteenth-century rational religion is at least beginning to supersede that of Anglo-Catholic theology.

"Since no man knoweth the time of his dissolution, and it becomes every serious Christian to die, as it were, daily, I, Ralph Bathurst, Doctor of Physick, being at this time (prais'd be God) in perfect health both of body and mind, yet not unmindful of the uncertainties of humane life, and, especially foreseeing that the infirmities of old age are not far off, and this earthly frame of mine must, in a short time, fall to decay and ruin, do commend all that I am, or have, into the hands of God Almighty, who was and is and will be for ever, beseeching Him to pardon and accept me, an unworthy sinner, through His mercies in our gracious Redeemer and Saviour, Jesus Christ, and that, when my change cometh, He will still keep me close unto Himself, even as now I live and move and have my being in Him who is all in all. And first, I do declare and profess myself a true and dutifull son of the Church of England, desiring to live and dye in the faith of that religion which is so happily by law established. And here I cannot but with a thankful heart acknowledge and celebrate that good providence by which I first obtained, and have, through God's goodness, these many years enjoyed a serene and well-established mind, and that the conversation of many learned and ingenuous friends (wherein I have long been exceedingly happy) hath

Richard Busby alone, the well-known Head Master of Westminster (d. 1695), Treasurer of the Cathedral, had established
any claim to a permanent fame.   He had had under him as
pupils John Dryden, and Philip Henry, the Nonconformist.
The fact that Ken's friend, George Hooper, had also been one
of his scholars, may have been a point of contact between
them.   Busby, however, seems to have been seldom at Wells,
and made up for his non-residence by a gift of £100 to the
Cathedral Library.   Two or three minor notables are just
worth naming.   Thomas Holt, Chancellor of the Cathedral,
seems, as we shall see when we come to the events of the summer of 1685, to have been a man of some decision of character.
Robert Creyghton, son of the former Dean and Bishop, Precentor for sixty years (1674—1734), composed chants and anthems,
still in frequent use at Wells and elsewhere, and thus had
tastes which he shared with Ken.[1]   Baptist Levinz, afterwards

carried me far above those anxieties to which myself in time past have not been
a stranger, and under which the greater part of mankind do labour, and,
although I know that human frailty is great, and our fears strong, especially in
times of infirmity and declining strength, neither can any man assure himself
that his reason shall always be firm and constant to him, yet it is my hope and
shall be my endeavour that I may continue the same unto the end.

' *Felix qui rerum potuit cognoscere causas,*
Atque metus omnes et inexorabile fatum
Subjecit pedibus.'

" As for my worldly estate it hath pleased God to give me neither poverty nor
riches, a condition not only suitable to me, but surely in itself most desirable. I
have not made it the labour of my life to live great or dye wealthy ; but have
studiously avoided that vanity and sore travel, to bereave my soul of good by
heaping up riches, not knowing who shall gather them.   Yet, while it has been
my endeavour not to live unprofitably, or dye without being desired, but rather
in an honest calling to do good in my generation, and uphold myself in a way
agreeable to my mind and conditions in the course of my life, something of this
world's good, as we call it, hath cleaved unto me without much design or
contrivance, so that by the good hand of Providence upon me, my cup is not
onely full, but something there is which probably may run over ; which, that it
may be disposed of according to my mind, I have caused this my last will and
testament to be written as follows . . . ."

The foreboding as to the failure of intellect, was, alas! only too fully realised,
and Evelyn describes him, in the last of the entries referred to, as " stark blind,
deaf, and memory lost."

[1] Does the line at the opening of *Hymnotheo*, B. ix., " Music, whose force,
like God himself is trine," refer to Creyghton's celebrated triple time?   In any

President of St. John's, Oxford, must have been nearly contemporary with the Bishop, and, as he had been chosen to play the part of *Terræ Filius* (the licensed jester of the University *Saturnalia*), at the first Act which was held after the establishment of the Presbyterian régime, must have had some reputation for power to conceive, and courage to utter, the somewhat coarse and caustic satire which was normal on that occasion. The appointment of the two who became canons during Ken's episcopate, Thomas Brickenden, Fellow of New College, who was appointed by virtue of a royal mandate of James II., and of Thomas Cheyney, who became Head Master of Winchester School in 1700, having been previously a Fellow, may probably be traced to his influence.[1]

On the whole, however, though Ken never quarrelled with his Chapter as his successor, Kidder, did, he does not seem to have formed any special friendships among them. Not a single letter remains addressed by him to any of them. Out of the whole body of the prebendaries only four followed him in the refusal to take the oaths of allegiance to William and Mary, which led to his and their deprivation.

On the other hand, Ken had scarcely arrived at Wells when the Chapter showed themselves ready to follow his lead in the political complications of the times. The Chapter Acts of March 2nd, 1685, contain an address to the new king, which, as it purports to come, not from them in their corporate character, but from the Bishop and Clergy of the diocese, may fairly be assumed to have been prompted by Ken, and probably to have been written by him. For that reason, and because it may serve as a sample of the style of addresses which the clergy were sending up, it is, I think, worth while to give it *in extenso* :—

---

case, the passage is interesting as throwing light on Ken's musical culture. —[C. J. P.]

[1] The Archdeacons of the diocese in 1685 were (1) Edwin Sandys, of Wells. The name suggests intimacy with Walton (see p. 23), and his appointment (November, 1684) may have been due to Ken's influence. The Bishop frequently visited him at his home after his deprivation. (2) John Sellecke, of Bath, and (3) Edward Maple, of Taunton. Of the last two I know nothing but their names. Cheyney was Ken's chaplain, and Hawkins (p. 13) states that he was indebted to him for many particulars of his *Life* of the Bishop.

" If ever our loyalty could be truly said to sow in tears and to reap in joy, it was that hour when we received the news of our late Dread Soveraigne's death and of your Majesty's peaceable succession.

" But blessed be God, whose propitious Providence made our joys to overbalance our sorrows by soon satisfying us that our King never died, that Hee still lives in you his Rightful Successor, that Hee still lives in you his onely Brother, and, as hee himself on his deathbed often professed, his Dearest Friend, that Hee still lives in you in that Peculiar Graciousness which rendered Him admirable to all mankind and a most tender nursing Father to yᵉ Church and People of England, and which, to our unspeakable consolation does illustriously appear in that Auspicious Promise your Majesty has made, of protecting our Established Religion, the greatest concerne we have in this worlde.

" 'Tis this assures us That the dying Benediction his late Majesty gave to his kingdom is abundantly fulfilled in you, and we securely relye on the sacredness of your Royal Word, which has ever been inviolable, for which wee return our most humble acknowledgment to your Majesty, and offer up our Praises to yᵉ Divine Goodnesse.

" We do with all solemnity vow to teach and to inculcate Allegiance, both in our Discourses and by our Examples, to all your Subjects under our Care, and to encite them to join with us in our fervent prayers That your Majesty may have a happy Reigne here below, and a late Exaltation to your Throne above."

It is obvious that some passages in this document, the references to Charles's deathbed utterances, and to James's declaration to the Privy Council on the day of his accession, have a peculiar force as coming from one who, like Ken, had been at Whitehall at the time, and could report the former, at least, as having himself heard them. Like the address in which he had concurred with Sancroft and other bishops, it practically reminds James of his promise and emphasises his obligation to be faithful to it. As might be expected, it repudiates the policy of the Exclusion Bill, and in the solemn pledge with which it ends we may, without the shadow of a doubt, find the key to Ken's subsequent action. The fact that he had given such a pledge in the face of his diocese, without reservation or conditions, must have seemed to him, over and above his own conviction of the abstract rights of the case, an additional constraint binding him to keep clear of whatever might seem to be at variance with it.

Within a week from the date of this address Ken was in London, taking his turn as a Lent preacher on March 8th, the first Sunday in Lent, at Whitehall. The King, who had recently opened an Oratory at Whitehall for the use of his priests, had ceased to attend these sermons, but the Princess Anne was probably there as usual; and as it was Ken's first sermon since his appointment, the chapel would naturally be full of all but the avowed Romanists of the Court. It does not seem desirable to fill these pages with long extracts from it, but when we have but three extant sermons in the whole life of a man like Ken, it is natural to look on each of them as likely to present some characteristic features which cannot well be passed over. And so it was in this instance. Choosing as his text the words, "O Daniel, a man greatly beloved" (Dan. x. 11), he sketches the character of the prophet as one who, under at least five kings, had been the ideal courtier, favourite, minister. One can hardly help thinking of the grim contrast to that ideal presented by the men to whom Ken was preaching, and wondering whether the preacher was conscious of the irony of the situation. Some, at least, must have winced as they heard Daniel's asceticism pressed on them as " naturally fitting him for his secular employment," and must have seen their own likeness, or that of their fellows, in the words that " nothing more clouds our understandings and indisposes us for business; nothing does more debase a great man, or make a wise man look like a fool, or more exposes them to the mockery and contempt of the meanest of their servants . . . . than the surfeits of intemperance." What he urges is the Daniel fare " for a few weeks, of pulse, not the palatable wines, and the delicacies of fish, and the luxury of banquets," with which both Anglicans and Romanists alike comforted themselves during the forty days of Lent. " Lent, in its original institution, was a spiritual conflict to subdue the flesh to the spirit, to beat down our bodies and bring them into subjection "—a " penitential martyrdom." " A devout soul that is able to observe it, fastens himself to the Cross on Ash Wednesday, and hangs crucified by contrition all the Lent long, ... that he may offer up a pure oblation at Easter and feel the power, and the joys and the triumph of the Saviour's resurrection."

In the picture which Ken draws of the character of Daniel we can scarcely avoid seeing something of an unconscious self-portraiture. This, at least, was the ideal which he had set before himself as a pattern for imitation in the new and difficult position in which he now found himself. "To the Courtier, the Favourite, and the Minister, he added the Ascetic and the Saint." He was a man *greatly beloved* both by God and man; or in the literal rendering of the margin, 'a man of desires!' He was 'the beloved prophet' under the old dispensation, as John was the 'beloved disciple' under the new. Both "engaged young in the service of God, and consecrated their lives by an early piety." "Both had the like intimacy with God, the like admission into the most adorable mysteries, and the like abundance of heavenly visions; both had the like lofty flights and ecstatic revelations." And in the practical counsels which followed from the contemplation of this ideal, we may trace almost something of a half-prophetic character, an indication of the line which the preacher had marked out for himself as the right course to be taken amid the perplexities and intricacies of the time:

"Learn from Daniel a universal obligingness and benignity, an awful love to your Prince, a constant fidelity, an undaunted courage, an unwearied zeal in serving him. Learn from Daniel an equal mixture of the wisdom of the serpent and of the innocence of the dove, an unoffending conversation, a clean integrity, and an impartial justice to all within your sphere. Learn from the man *greatly beloved* to reconcile policy and religion, business and devotion, abstinence and abundance, greatness and goodness, magnanimity and humility, power and subjection, authority and affability, conversation and retirement, interest and integrity, Heaven and the Court, the favour of God and the favour of the King; and you are masters of Daniel's secret; you will secure to yourselves an universal and lasting interest; you will, like him, be greatly beloved both by God and man."

When we think of the courtiers and statesmen who heard that sermon, and read what manner of men they were, in the

journals and letters and history of the time, one fears there
were not many who were roused to strive for the attainment
of this ideal.   When we read what Ken was in action and in
suffering in the year that followed, we are sure that he, at
least, endeavoured to reproduce the pattern which he thus
depicted.   He was, in all senses of the word, " a man of desires,"
and took his place among those who turn many to righteousness, and win the hearts of men in their own and succeeding
generations to reverence and love.

A few weeks later, on April 23rd (St. George's Day seems
to have been selected, as it had been when Charles II. was
crowned, as of good omen), Ken was called up from Wells
to take part in the ceremonial of the coronation.   The service,
as it had been handed down from previous reigns, had to be
adapted to the altered circumstances of the present.   James
and his Queen could not receive the communion of the Anglican ritual, and that had to be omitted.[1]   In the order of the
functions of the day it fell to Ken's lot, in conformity with
an ancient custom, which assigned that position, in conjunction
with the Bishop of Durham (Crewe), to the Bishop of Bath
and Wells, to walk by the King's side under the canopy of
state, in the procession from Westminster Hall, and to support
him on the steps of the throne in the Abbey.[2]   His friend
Turner, recently translated from Rochester to Ely, who had
been chaplain in James's household in the previous reign, was
appointed to preach the coronation sermon.   He took for his
text 1 Tim. ii. 1, and dwelt, as might be expected, on the
favourite dogmas of his school, the divine right of kings, the

---

[1] Sancroft is said, in after years, to have reproached himself for having sanctioned the omission.   One wonders what programme he would have substituted.
Would he have sanctioned an act of " occasional conformity" against the King's
conscience, or administered the communion to all but the King and Queen and
their Roman Catholic officials?

[2] I am unable to trace the origin of the custom, nor have I verified its occurrence in all successive coronations.   Our old records at Wells show that it
existed under Richard I., when Savaric was bishop, and the same order was
observed at the coronation of Queen Victoria.   See Paper by Canon C. M.
Church, *On Bishop Reginald*, p. 24, published by the Antiquarian Society, 1887.
The custom was broken at the coronation of Henry VII., because both bishops
had supported the House of York ; and again at those of William and Mary, and
of Anne.—Stanley, *Memorials of Westminster Abbey*, pp. 75, 98.

iniquity of the Exclusion Bill, and the duty of unquestioning obedience on the part of subjects. James, it was noticed, went through the whole proceedings with an air of studied indifference, never moved his lips for the responses, showed no sign of fervour or devotion, presenting in this respect a marked contrast to his Queen, of whom Bishop Patrick[1] records that, when she was anointed and crowned, he had "never seen greater devotion in any countenance." What impression these things made on Ken we have no means of knowing. One imagines that they must have deepened the sad forebodings with which he looked out upon the impending future. On the other hand, the fact that James was now the anointed of the Lord, solemnly consecrated to his high office, would be, to one of Ken's temperament and convictions, a fresh tie binding him to allegiance, and the memories of the part which he had himself taken in the proceedings of that day may well be thought of as turning the scale, when for one brief moment, in the perplexities of the future, he seemed to halt between two opinions. He and his old school-fellow Turner had been brought together in the ceremonial of James's coronation. He may naturally have shrunk from choosing a different path when the question presented itself, whether the obligations which, as viewed by his judgment, that day recognised and intensified, had been cancelled by the unfaithfulness of the King to whom they had both sworn allegiance.[2]

---

[1] *Autobiog.*, 1839, p. 105.

[2] Among the incidents of the coronation it was noticed that the crown was too large for James's head, and that it nearly fell off. It was held up by Henry Sidney, as Keeper of the Robes. "This," he said, "is not the first time our family has supported the Crown." The irony of history has seldom received a better illustration. Sidney was the foremost among those who invited William, was, in fact, so far as one man could be, the maker of the revolution. (Stanley, *ut supra*, p. 93.)

CHAPTER XIV

" Henceforth, while pondering the fierce deeds then done,
    Such reverence on me shall its seal impress,
    As though I corpses saw, and walked the tomb."
                                    J. H. Newman.

WITHIN little more than two months from the date of the
" Daniel" sermon Ken was to learn something of the meaning
of the text which he had chosen as his motto, *Pastor bonus dat
animam pro ovibus.* His own diocese was the chief scene of a
rash and reckless rebellion, planned without foresight, and executed without wisdom, and when the rebellion was subdued, of
a ruthless policy of vindictive cruelty. The story of that rebellion[1] stands ' writ at large' in every history of England, and it
does not seem necessary here to reproduce fully what has been
told a hundred times before, or to give any lengthened account
of the unhappy pretender whose folly brought so terrible a
destruction upon his followers. I confine myself mainly to the
question, what Ken was likely to feel when the tidings of the
rebellion reached him, what he may have known of the Duke
of Monmouth in earlier years, what part he took in the proceedings that followed on the rebellion.

James Crofts,[2] son of Lucy Walters, *alias* Barlow, the first-
born of Charles's illegitimate children, was a boy of eleven at
the time of the Restoration. He had been brought up at Paris,
under the Queen-Dowager, Henrietta Maria, as a Roman
Catholic. The King was scarcely settled on his throne before
he sent for him. The boy, bright, handsome, engaging, be-

---

[1] The fullest account both of the rebellion itself, and of Monmouth's life
generally, is to be found in Roberts' *Life of the Duke of Monmouth.* 2 vols., 1844.

[2] The name was given because he was brought up by Lord Crofts, and passed
as his relation. His mother was the daughter of Richard Walters, Esq., of
Haverfordwest.

came the idol of his father's heart. Titles, places, honours were lavished upon him with a prodigality which had no parallel in the history of English bastards of royal blood. He was to take precedence of all peers. The hand of the wealthiest heiress in all Scotland, the Countess of Buccleuch, was given to him in 1665, when she was a child of fourteen and he but two years older. As if to remove any impediments to his recognition as a prince of the blood, he was received into the Church of England by Charles's orders. It was scarcely to be wondered at that men should have surmised that there was something more than mere fondness in all these marks of an exceptional favour, and that Charles intended some day, if the temper of his people permitted, to acknowledge him as legitimate. Rumours floated in the air, and before long were eagerly drunk in by the vain empty-headed youth himself, that there had been a secret marriage with his mother.[1]

In the earlier stages of his career, however, before the question of the secret marriage was mooted, he was almost as much in favour with James as with Charles, and the bishops and clergy (Morley, Turner, and others) who were influential at York House, may thus have had some share, as has been already suggested,[2] in the edict which Monmouth issued, as Chancellor of the University of Cambridge, against unclerical costumes and reading written sermons. It was not till James avowed the change in his religion and the Exclusionists found themselves foiled in their efforts to carry their Bill through Parliament, that the Whig and Republican parties began to entertain serious thoughts of setting up Monmouth's claims in opposition to those of James. It was in vain that Charles entered with his own hand in the register of the Privy Council (April, 1680) a declaration that he had never entered into any contract of marriage save with Catharine of Braganza, and had his declaration signed by all the Privy Councillors present, enrolled in Chancery and published in the *Gazette*. Men did not place implicit

[1] According to a current rumour, even Charles's parentage was questioned, and Monmouth was reported to be the son of Colonel Robert Sidney, brother of Algernon and Henry, whom he was said to resemble. His tutor, Ross, when in Paris, during Charles's exile, tried to persuade Cosin, whom Lucy Walters had consulted as a penitent, to sign a certificate of marriage.—Roberts, i. p. 3, 6.

[2] See p. 48, *n*. 3.

reliance on the word of a Stuart, and thought that this repudiation of Monmouth's claims as a matter of policy was outweighed by the favours that had before been spontaneously lavished on him. The young Absalom found his Ahithophel[1] in Shaftesbury, and was for a time the darling of a large section of the people, made royal progresses, notably in Somerset and Devon, visiting Longleat[2] among other noble houses, and was welcomed by thousands as the "Protestant Duke" whom they hoped to see one day on the throne. When these hopes took shape in the Rye House plot, and that plot collapsed, and in its failure brought Russell and Sidney to the scaffold, Monmouth purchased his pardon by a humiliating confession, and by a cowardly abandonment of his associates. He promised that he would never again do anything against the Duke of York. To be banished from the King's presence would be for him the "greatest curse." Charles, however, felt that there was little prospect of quiet or safety, as long as Monmouth remained in England, and he was accordingly sentenced informally to banishment. For some months before Charles's death he had been staying at the Hague, welcomed as an honoured guest with an unusual show of cordiality by both William and Mary.[3] When that death placed the nephew and the uncle in a position of more direct rivalry, and intensified the bitterness with which they looked on each other, it did not fall in with William's policy to keep Monmouth at the Hague. He did not mean to comply with James's request that he would arrest the Duke and send him over to England. He did not wish his own court to be openly the centre of the plots into which it was but too likely that Monmouth would again plunge. He was content, on one view of his conduct, to let Monmouth's attempt at rebellion take its chance, while he played the waiting game of

---

[1] The two names have been immortalised in Dryden's poem, which furnishes, perhaps, the best key to the tangled problems of the time.

[2] See Note, p. 227.

[3] The fact that Mary extended her marked attention even to Lady Henrietta Wentworth, who was living in open adultery with Monmouth, must probably be ascribed to the complete subjugation to which William had brought her. (*Strickland*, x. p. 328.) Lady Henrietta was the only daughter and heiress of the Earl of Cleveland. She superseded another mistress, Mrs. Needham, in the Duke's affection in 1684.

a calmer and more subtle policy. The Duke left Holland for Brussels, and half persuaded himself that he had done with politics and conspiracies, and might, in the society of his mistress, for whom he had abandoned his wife and children, pass the remainder of his life in peace.

It lies in the nature of the case that Ken must have looked on Monmouth's conduct, up to this time, with grave condemnation, mingled, it may be, with some touch of pity for one whose early years had been so fatally wanting in all that educates men for higher things, and so fatally abounding in all examples and influences of evil. We can, in some measure, picture to ourselves what he must have felt when tidings reached London that Monmouth, pushed on by hot-headed and reckless conspirators like Ferguson,[1] and Lord Grey of Wark, and Fletcher of Saltoun, had decided to leave his retirement and to stake all things on the hazard of a rebellion ; that he had landed with about one hundred and fifty followers at Lyme Regis on the 11th of June, 1685. In the proclamation which he issued on landing, drawn up by Ferguson, and, as Monmouth told James after his defeat, signed by him without reading it, he practically cut himself off from all hope of reconciliation or pardon. He charged "James, Duke of York," not only with tyrannical and unconstitutional acts, subversive of freedom and the Pro-

---

[1] The life of *Robert Ferguson the Plotter*, recently published (1887) by Mr. James Ferguson, throws much light on these transactions. "The policy of the Prince of Orange was dark, but the sympathies of the authorities of Amsterdam were open and notorious. They 'wished well to us and our design'" (pp. 205, 206). In a fuller statement made at a later date, Ferguson writes that William deliberately encouraged the scheme. "He (the Duke) was the only deliverer in view, and as long as this idol of the populace was in view, it was impossible for the Pope to make use of his engine, the Prince of Orange ; " and so to remove this impediment "there was all underhand encouragement of him to prepare for an invasion of England" (p. 370). On the night before Monmouth started for his expedition, he had a long interview with William at the Hague, and received from him money for his journey. Shortly afterwards William wrote to James that "Monmouth only came as a suppliant, was shown a little common hospitality, and was sent away." (*Strickland*, x., p. 330.) It is obvious, if we apply the *Cui bono?* principle, that the Prince of Orange was the only person whose position was improved by Monmouth's expedition. (Ferguson, p. 168.) Evelyn (July 18th, 1685) records the fact that William had sent Scotch and English regiments from Holland to assist James, but this would not be inconsistent with Ferguson's hypothesis. He had no wish that Monmouth should succeed, and of course did not desire to appear as sanctioning his rebellion.

testant religion, but with the guilt of having planned the fire
of London, and the murders of Sir Edmundbury Godfrey and
the Earl of Essex, and even with that of having poisoned the
late King, his brother.[1] He asserted his own right to the
Crown as the legitimate heir, and ascribed his father's repudiation of his claims to the malign influence of James and other
Popish advisers. He appealed, in the inflated language of the
fanatics of an earlier day, to the Lord of Hosts, of whom he presented himself as the champion, to decide the issue between them.

The news of his landing reached London, and prompt measures were taken to oppose his progress. An Act of Attainder
was passed rapidly through both Houses of Parliament on
July 2nd, and a reward of five thousand pounds offered for his
person whether alive or dead. Feversham, a naturalised Frenchman,[2] was sent with troops to the West to crush his followers.
Ken was present in the House of Lords when the Act of Attainder was passed, and within a few hours must have heard
news that filled his mind with misgivings and alarm for the
well-being of his diocese. Meanwhile the men of Somerset,
not the gentry, but the miners of the Mendips and the Puritan
traders of Taunton and Bridgwater, rallied round Monmouth's
standard. Women and girls, notably the 'maids of Taunton,'
who afterwards had to pay a heavy ransom to avoid the penalty
of transportation to the West Indies, met him with flowers and
banners.[3] The handsome Protestant Duke, for a few brief days
' King Monmouth,' signing proclamations and writing to
Albemarle as " James R.," touching for the king's evil (results
unrecorded), as if already an anointed sovereign, was during
that week of mad unwisdom as much the darling of Somerset
as " bonnie Prince Charlie " was of the Highlanders in 1745.

It is not without interest to note how all these proceedings
were looked at from the point of view of the Chapter House of
Ken's cathedral city.[4] On the 13th of June, three days after

---

[1] See p. 189, *n.*

[2] See p. 187, *n.* By a singular coincidence Feversham had been a suitor for
the hand of Lady Henrietta Wentworth.—Roberts, ii. p. 85.

[3] Among these, we may note, was Elizabeth Broadmead, who was then fifteen,
and who survived to tell the tale of the rebellion a hundred years later. She
died in 1785. Her portrait may be seen in the Museum at Taunton.

[4] Chapter Acts, 1685.

the landing at Lyme Regis, we find an agitated entry in the Chapter Acts of Wells. Rebellion was spreading far and wide, the King's troops were starving, soldiers were deserting to the enemy. The Chapter could not do otherwise, with that address from the Bishop and Clergy staring them in the face from their own Register,[1] than come to the rescue by voting a grant of £40—or, perhaps, loan : " *accommodare*" is the word used—to the Duke of Somerset as Lord Lieutenant of the county. The days passed on and the 1st of July dawned on the fair 'City of Fountains.' From time immemorial that had been one of the four quarterly meeting days of the Chapter. Dean and Canons and Priest, and lay vicars-choral, were wont to meet solemnly in that stately Chapter House. No such meeting could take place now. The city, the Cathedral itself, was in the hands of the rebels.[2] On that very morning they had rushed into the sacred building with rude hands ready to destroy, had all but broken up the organ, and would have profaned the Holy Table itself, had not Lord Grey stood, with his sword drawn, in front of the altar rails to defend it. The rebels had stabled their horses in the nave on the evening of June 30th. Black-mail was levied on the inhabitants of the Cathedral precincts, and, in particular, as an October entry records, on Mrs. Frideswide Creyghton, wife of the Precentor, to the amount of £20, but for which, according to the testimony of the commissary of the rebels, then a prisoner at Wells, "not only this Cathedral church, but ye Canon's house" (one notes here the somewhat curious climax), "would have suffered the utmost violence." As it was, the silver verge, carried before the Dean (relic of a remote past), was stolen by the rebels, and £4 had to be voted in October for a new one, which is, I presume, that now in use. Repairs were needed for the injuries inflicted on the nave, to the amount of £500.

---

[1] See p. 203.

[2] Macaulay, ch. v. The *London Gazette* reports that they "robbed and defaced the Cathedral, drinking their villainous healths at the altar, plundered the town . . . . and committed all manner of outrages" on men and women. This seems, however, the language of exaggeration. The Cathedral bears no marks of serious injuries beyond those recorded in our Chapter Acts. Perhaps some windows were broken, and, if so, this may be the explanation of the patchwork arrangement of the stained glass now in the Lady Chapel.

In their thankfulness that matters had not been worse, the Dean and Chapter voted £10 to the Sacrist, James Williams (honour to whom honour is due), "for his very honest services in yᵉ preservation of yᵉ ornaments and plate" of the Cathedral on that day of outrage and terror, and so it is that the Cathedral still rejoices in the possession of the flagon, and patens, and chalices which have come down to it from the days of Elizabeth,[1] and were used by Ken during his episcopate.

What could an unhappy Chapter do under circumstances such as these? Bathurst, the Dean, was, as usual, at Oxford. Some of the Canons, it may be, had fled into the country; others bolted and barred themselves in their houses, or paid their ransom, if not, like Mrs. Creyghton, to the extent of £20, yet in the shape of bread and beef and beer to the hungry crowds, to whom those three B.'s were for the time more important even than the claims of the Protestant hero whom they were following to his and their destruction. One Canon, however, rose to the situation. Thomas Holt, Chancellor of the Cathedral, whom we have seen as Ken's proxy on the day of the enthronement, would hold the normal Chapter, though he sat alone in it. With an almost Roman courage he writes in eloquent Latin a record of the work of devastation, as above described, and adjourns the Chapter ("not despairing of the Republic") to that day four weeks, confidently hoping that the nefarious rebellion would be stamped out before that day should come. And when the 29th of July arrived (to anticipate the course of events a little) we note how it was solemnly recorded that the hope of the heroic President of the Chapter had not proved deceitful. The memorable 6th of July had witnessed at Weston Zoyland, in Sedgmoor, the utter defeat of the rebel army, and now the Canons could return to their homes in peace. And so the Chapter Clerk, or perhaps Holt himself, ends with a fervour not common in Cathedral Acts, and with all the emphasis of a reduplication not in the original,

"*Deus, Deus nobis hæc otia fecit.*"

Ken, as we have seen, was in London when his Cathedral

---

[1] The older plate had, probably, either been looted by Sir John Gates under Edward VI., or may have been "defaced" as "before-time used to superstition,"

city was thrown into this wild confusion. No attack appears to have been made upon the palace, partly, perhaps, because its gateways and walls and moat served as a sufficient defence against an irregular attack; partly, it is open to conjecture, because Ken had already become, in some measure, known to his people and found a home in their affections.

In the meantime Ken's predecessor, Peter Mews, of Winchester, had hastened to the scene of action. His old military habits had revived, and, like the war-horse, he smelt the battle from afar, and finding in the battle of Sedgmoor[1] that Feversham and his officers were less expert than himself in the management of artillery, took upon himself the duty of working their guns with a strategical genius which contributed much to decide the issue of the battle.[2] The proceedings that followed on the battle were, it would seem, too much even for him. He had not shrunk from shooting down the stray sheep of his former flock, but when Feversham began to put his prisoners to death in cold blood, with circumstances of aggravated outrage, hanging them naked, without even the form of a trial, he remonstrated on what seemed to him at once illegal and un-English. This was "mere butchery," and he, for his part, would be no sharer in it.[3]

under an order from Elizabeth in 1572, the date, it may be noted, of that now in use.—See "Wells Cathedral and its Deans," in *Contemporary Review* for March, 1888.

[1] I do not dwell on the details of the march or battle. It was characteristic of Ferguson that he preached, the very morning before it, on the text, "The Lord God of gods, the Lord God of gods, he knoweth, and Israel, he shall know; if it be in rebellion, or if in transgression against the Lord, save us not this day" (Joshua, ch. xxii., v. 22). Ferguson, we remember, was afterwards one of William's confidential "secret service" agents in the Revolution, and was rewarded with a sinecure place of £600 a-year in the Customs. He was dissatisfied, thought himself ill-treated, and, still "plotter" to the end, joined the Jacobites, and took an active part in their conspiracies. — *Ferguson the Plotter*, pp. 233, 264.

[2] James presented Mews with a "rich medal" for this service.—Wood's *Ath. Oxon.* iv. 338, in Cassan, *Lives of Bishops of Bath and Wells*, ii. 76.

[3] The credit of this interposition, it should be added, was given by Bishop Kennet, not to Mews, but to Ken, and his narrative has been accepted by some of his biographers. Macaulay (chap. v.), however, urges the fact that Ken, who was in London on July 2nd, was there again with Monmouth on July 14th, the day before his execution, and that it was not likely that he should have travelled down to Wells and then hastily returned. Markland, on the other hand, argues

Before many days had passed Ken was called to bear his part in one of the closing scenes of the tragedy. Monmouth, who, with Lord Grey, a German officer, and others, most of whom took other directions in the course of the flight, had fled from Sedgmoor before the battle was over, belying by this cowardice the promise of courage given in his French campaign, had been taken, after two days' wandering, by the King's troops near Cranbourne Chase, at a spot which still bears the name of Monmouth's Close, lying in a ditch,[1] covered with brambles, half dead with hunger and fatigue, was allowed but a short shrift, and managed to exhibit in the compass of a few days all his characteristic vices of vacillation, falsehood, faithlessness. He pleaded for his life with an abject pusillanimity, threw all the blame on his associates, asserted that he had signed the unpardonable proclamation without reading it, half hinted that he might, if his life was spared, go back to the religion in which his early years had been trained (it was characteristic of both parties to that interview—July 13—that the nephew should have thought this the surest path to his uncle's clemency), grovelled on the ground in prostrate and tearful humiliation, and finally, when all hope was gone, rose, with some touch of the courage of despair, to prepare for the inevitable end. The 15th of July was fixed for his execution.[2] The intervening hours were spent in piteous appeals to the King, the Queen, and ministers, for life on any terms. The only reply was significant enough. Roman Catholic priests were sent to

that there was just time for the double journey, and vindicates for Ken the honour of this interposition. An elegy written on Ken's death by Joseph Perkins, the Latin poet laureate of the period (see ii. p. 262), mentions to his honour that the lives of a hundred prisoners had been spared through his interposition, but he does not specify the circumstances, and this may possibly refer to an incident of later date. On the whole I follow Anderdon in thinking it probable that Kennet or his informants were mistaken, and assigned to Ken what was due to his predecessor. Mews had left the diocese so recently that the country people might easily still speak of him as Bishop of Bath and Wells. He preached at Wells on July 8th.

[1] Reresby (p. 341) reports that when his pockets were searched they were found to be filled "with prayers, and songs, and charms, by which to escape from prison."

[2] He was put to death under the Act of Attainder, but by a special warrant, dispensing with the customary penalties of treason. James's signature to the warrant, now in the State Papers of the Record Office, is firmly written, with careful neat little flourishes [R. C. B.].

prepare him for his death. When he rejected their ministrations, Ken was sent for by James to give such spiritual counsels as the case required,[1] and with him were associated his friends Francis Turner, Bishop of Ely, and George Hooper, now Rector of Lambeth, and at Monmouth's own request, Tenison, afterwards Archbishop of Canterbury. Ken and Turner were with him during the night, and at his wish all four accompanied him to the place of execution. They found it hard to rouse his conscience to activity, or to elicit the full confession which was, in their eyes, the note of a true repentance. He seemed at first insensible to the misery and death that he had brought on his followers, and declared that he " had nothing on his conscience, and had wronged no man." He would not admit that he had been wrong in leaving his wife for Lady Henrietta. He had been forced, when too young to give an intelligent consent, into a marriage which was no marriage. That had led to a reckless license of life, from which he had been rescued by the new attachment for one who was worthy of his love, and to whom he had been faithful.[2]

The divines, who had to do their work in the face of such difficulties, took the somewhat unusual course (probably under orders from the King) of drawing up a formal narrative of their dealings with the condemned man, which was afterwards published by the Government, and as it bears Ken's signature, and his conduct and that of his associates has been made matter for adverse criticism, it seems worth while to give it *in extenso*, as printed in the *Somers Tracts*, pp. 260 *et seq.*

" An Account of what passed at the Execution of the late Duke of Monmouth, on Wednesday, the 15th of July, 1685, on Tower-hill.

"The late Duke of Monmouth came from the Tower to the scaffold attended by the Bishop of Ely, the Bishop of Bath and

---

[1] James remembered, we may believe, how Ken had spoken " like one inspired " at his brother's death-bed.

[2] The Duchess visited him in the Tower the day before his execution. After his death she married Lord Cornwallis. It is said that she never went to William's Court. Of the unhappy mistress who had been left in Holland all we know is that she died—it was said, of a broken heart—on April 23rd, 1686, and that a magnificent monument, which cost £2,000, was erected to her by her mother at Toddington, in Bedfordshire (Roberts, ii. 340).

Wells, Dr. Tennison, and Dr. Hooper, which four the King was graciously pleased to send him as his assistants to prepare him for death, and the late Duke himself entreated all four of them to accompany him to the place of execution, and to continue with him to the last. The two Bishops going in the Lieutenant's coach with him to the bars, made *seasonable* and devout application to him all the way, and *one of them* desired him not to be surprised if *they*, to the very last, upon the scaffold, *renewed* [1] those exhortations to particular repentance which they so often repeated before.

" At his first coming on the scaffold he looked for the executioner, and seeing him, said, ' Is this the man to do the business ? *Do your work well.*' Then the Duke of Monmouth began to speak, some one or other *of the assistants*, during the time, applying themselves to him.

" *Monmouth.*—I shall say but little—I come to die. I die a Protestant of the Church of England.

" *Assistant.*—My Lord, if you be of the Church of England, you must acknowledge the doctrine of non-resistance to be true.

" *Monmouth.*—If I acknowledge the doctrine of the Church of England in general, that includes all.

" *Assistant.*—Sir, it is fit to own that doctrine particularly, *with respect to your case.*

" Here he was much *urged* about the doctrine of non-resistance, but he repeated, in effect, his first answer.

" *Then he began, as if he was about to make a premeditated speech in this manner :*

" *M.*—I have had a scandal raised upon me about a woman, a lady of virtue and honour, the Lady Henrietta Wentworth. I declare she is a very godly and virtuous woman ; I have committed no sin with her ; and that which hath passed betwixt us was very honest and innocent in the sight of God.

" *A.*—In your opinion, sir, as you have been often told (*i.e.* in the Tower); but this is not fit discourse in this place.

" *Mr. Sheriff Gosselin.*—Sir, were you ever married to her ?

" *M.*—This is not a time to answer that question.

" *Mr. Sheriff Gosselin.*—Sir, I hoped to have heard of your repentance for the treason and bloodshed you have committed.

" *Monmouth.*— I die very penitent.

" *Assistant.*—My Lord, it is fit to be *particular ;* and, considering the public evil you have done, you ought to do as much good now as you possibly can, by a public acknowledgment.

" *Monmouth.*—What I have thought fit to say of public affairs is in a paper which I have signed ; I refer to my paper.

---

[1] Italics are printed as in Somers, *l.c.* It is not easy to see their *raison d'être.*

"*Assistant.*—My Lord, there is nothing in that paper about resistance, and you ought to be *particular* in your repentance, to have it well grounded. God give you true repentance!

"*Monmouth.*—I die very penitent; and die with great cheerfulness, for I know I shall go to God!

"*Assistant.*—My Lord, you must go to God in his own way: Sir, be sure you be truly penitent, and ask forgiveness of God for the many you have wronged.

"*Monmouth.*—I am sorry for every one I have wronged—I forgive every body—I have had my enemies—I forgive them all.

"*Assistant.*—Sir, your acknowledgment ought to be public and *particular.*

"*Monmouth.*—I am to die: pray, my Lord:—I refer to my paper.

"*Assistant.*—They are but a few words we desire; we only desire an answer to this point.

"*Monmouth.*—I can bless God that he hath given me so much grace, that for these two years past I have led a life unlike my former course, in which I have been happy.

"*Assistant.*—Sir, was there no ill in these two years? In these years these great evils have happened, and the giving public satisfaction is a necessary part of repentance: be pleased to own a detestation of your rebellion.

"*Monmouth.*—I beg your Lordships that you will stick to my paper.

"*Assistant.*—My Lord, as I said before, there is nothing in your paper about the doctrine of non-resistance.

"*Monmouth.*—I repent of all things a true Christian ought to repent of. I am to die—PRAY, MY LORD.

"*Assistant.*—Then, my Lord, we can only recommend you to the mercy of God, but we cannot pray with that cheerfulness and encouragement as we should if you had made a *particular* acknowledgment.

"*M.*—God be praised, I have encouragement enough in myself; I die with a clear conscience; I have wronged no man.

"*A.*—How, sir, no man? Have you not been guilty of invasion and of much blood that has been shed; and, it may be, the loss of many souls who followed you? You must needs have wronged a great many.

"*M.*—I do, sir, own that; and am sorry for it.

"*A.*—Give it the true name, sir, and call it rebellion.

"*M.*—What name you please, sir; I am sorry for invading the kingdom, for the blood that has been shed, and for the souls that have been lost by my means. I am sorry it ever happened. [This he spoke softly.]

" *Mr. Sheriff Vandeput.*—[To some that stood at a distance.] He says he is very sorry for invading the kingdom.

" *A.*—We have nothing to add, but to renew the frequent exhortations we have made to you, to give some satisfaction for the public injuries to the kingdom. There have been a great many lives lost by this resistance of your lawful prince.

" *M.*—What I have done has been very ill, and I wish with all my heart it had never been; I never was a man that delighted in blood; I was very far from it; I was as cautious in that as any man was; the Almighty knows how I now die with all the joyfulness in the world.

" *A.*—God grant you may, sir; God give you true repentance.

" *M.*—If I had not true repentance, I should not so easily have been without the fear of dying. I shall die like a lamb.

" *A.*—Much may come from natural courage.

" *M.*—I do not attribute it to my own nature, for I am fearful as other men are; but I have now no fear, as you may see by my face; but there is something within me which does it, for I am sure I shall go to God.

" *A.*—My Lord, be sure upon good grounds : Do you repent you of all your sins, known or unknown, confessed or not confessed ; of all the sins which might proceed from error in judgment?

" *M.*—In general for all; I do with all my soul.

" *A.*—God Almighty, of his infinite mercy, forgive you. Here are great numbers of spectators; here are the sheriffs, they represent the great city; and in speaking to them, you speak to the whole city; make some satisfaction, by owning your crime before them. [*He was silent here.*]

" [*Then all went to solemn commendatory prayers, which continued for a good space; the late Duke of Monmouth and the company kneeling, and joining in them with great fervency.*

" *Prayers being ended, before he, and the four who assisted him, were risen from their knees, he was again earnestly exhorted to a true and thorough repentance.*

" *After they were risen up, he was exhorted to pray for the king; and was asked, Whether he did not desire to send some dutiful message to his majesty, and to recommend his wife and children to his majesty's favour.*]

" *M.*—What harm have they done? Do it, if you please; I pray for him, and for all men.

" [*Then the Versicles were repeated.*]

" *A.*—O Lord, show thy mercy upon us.

" *M.*—[*He made the Response.*]   And grant us thy salvation.

" *A.*—[*It followed.*]   O Lord, save the king.

" *M.*—And mercifully hear us when we call upon thee.

" *A.*—Sir, do you not pray for the king with us?   [*The Versicle was again repeated.*]   O Lord, save the king.

" *M.*—[*After some pause he answered.*]   Amen.

" [*Then he spoke to the executioner concerning his undressing, &c., and he would have no cap, &c., and at the beginning of his undressing, it was said to him on this manner.*]

" *A.*—My Lord, you have been bred a soldier, you will do a generous, Christian thing, if you please to go to the rail, and speak to the soldiers, and say, That here you stand a sad example of rebellion, and entreat them and the people to be loyal and obedient to the king.

" *M.*—I have said I will make no speeches : I will make no speeches : I come to die.

" *A.*—My Lord, ten words will be enough.

" *M.*—[*Then calling his servant, and giving him something, like a tooth-pick case.*]   Here (said he) give this to the person to whom you are to deliver the other things.

" *M.*—[*To the Executioner.*]   Here are six guineas for you ; pray do your business well ; do not serve me as you did my Lord Russell ; I have heard, you struck him three or four times.   Here (*To his Servant*) take these remaining guineas, and give them to him if he does his work well.

" *Executioner.*—I hope I shall.

" *M.*—If you strike me twice, I cannot promise you not to stir.

" [*During his undressing and standing towards the block, there were used by those who assisted him diverse ejaculations proper at that time, and much of 51st Psalm was repeated, and particularly,* ' Deliver me from blood-guiltiness, O God, thou God,' *&c.*]

" *Then he lay down, and soon after he raised himself upon his elbow, and said to the executioner,* Prithee let me feel the axe : (*He felt the edge, and said*) I fear it is not sharp enough.

" *Executioner.*—It is sharp enough, and heavy enough.

" *Then he lay down again.*

" *During this space many pious ejaculations were used by those that assisted him with great fervency,* Ex. Gr. God accept your repentance ; God accept your repentance ; God accept your imperfect repentance ; My Lord, God accept your general repentance ; God Almighty shew his omnipotent mercy upon you ; Father, into thy hands we commend his spirit, &c. ; Lord Jesus receive his soul.

" *Then the executioner proceeded to do his office.*

" A copy of the Paper, to which the late Duke of Monmouth referred him-
self in the Discourses held upon the Scaffold.

"I declare, That the title of king was forced upon me; and that
it was very much contrary to my opinion when I was proclaimed.
For the satisfaction of the world, I do declare, That the late king
told me, he was never married to my mother. Having declared
this, I hope that the king, who is now, will not let my children
suffer on this account. And to this I put my hand this fifteenth
day of July, 1685.

"MONMOUTH.

"This is a true account, witness our hands,

"FRANCIS ELY,   THOMAS TENNISON,
"THOMAS BATH AND WELLS.   GEORGE HOOPER,
        "WILLIAM GOSSELIN, ⎞ Sheriffs."
        "PETER VAN DE PUT,⎠

The reader will see from this what measure of truth there is
in Burnet's judgment that the two bishops "did certainly very
well in discharging their own consciences and speaking so
plainly to him; but they did very ill to talk so much of this
matter" (the connexion with Lady Henrietta) "and to make
it so public as they did, for divines ought not to repeat what
they say to dying penitents, no more than what the penitents
say to them." It is not without significance, as bearing upon a
later incident in Ken's life, that Burnet adds that Monmouth
was "better pleased with Dr. Tenison as speaking in a softer
and less peremptory manner," and "leaving the points on
which he could not convince him to his own conscience."[1] The
memories of that 15th of July may have been present to our
Bishop's mind when, on reviewing Tenison's ministrations at
another royal death, he charged him with want of faithfulness as
a preacher of repentance, with speaking smooth things and pro-
phesying deceits.[2] It was natural enough that a man like Charles
Fox[3] should judge of the action of the bishops on this occasion
from a somewhat secular standpoint, and one is scarcely surprised to find him censuring them for their want of "compas-
sion" and "complaisance," for worrying their "illustrious

[1] Burnet, *O. T.*, B. iv., 1685.
[2] See Note on Ken's *Letter to Tenison*, at the end of ch. xxi.
[3] *History of James II.*, p. 250.

penitent" with "controversial altercations," for being far more
solicitous to make him profess what they deemed the true creed
of the Church of England (the doctrine of non-resistance) "than
to soften and console his sorrows, or to help him to that compo-
sure of mind so necessary for his salvation."[1]   It may be added
that Ken's great-nephew and earliest biographer, Hawkins, in
noticing like reflections which had appeared in a pamphlet
under the title of *A Secret History*, &c., and in which Ken was
singled out for special censure on these very grounds, expressly
states "that our Bishop never acted or assisted there but in the
devotional part only.   And this, though a negative, may be
proved to satisfaction."   The authoritative tone in which this
statement is made suggests the conclusion that he must have
had it from Ken's own lips, and, as Anderdon remarks, it
receives some confirmation from Ken's statement in his letter
to Burnet in 1689 that " passive obedience " was a subject with
which he had very rarely meddled.[2]

   To this tragic close had come the career of the Absalom
of English history.   To Ken, as to us, it must have seemed
the sad end of an evil and recklessly wasted life.   But the
handsome Duke, with his graceful manner and kindly smile,
was still the darling of the people.   Those who witnessed his
execution dipped their handkerchiefs in his blood, and cherished
his memory as that of a Protestant martyr.   Among those who
had not witnessed it the belief lingered for at least two or
three years, in Somerset and elsewhere, that he was still alive,
that another criminal had died in his stead, and that he would
one day reappear as the champion of their liberties.[3]

   As soon as this melancholy task was over Ken hastened to
his diocese, and the spectacle which met him on his arrival was

---

[1] Evelyn (July 15th, 1685) records a visit to Tenison, in which that divine told
him that he and the bishops had refused to administer the Holy Communion to
Monmouth because he would not acknowledge his sin in the matter of Lady
Henrietta.

[2] See ii. 48.

[3] Francis Turner, writing to Bishop Lloyd, of Norwich, in 1687, mentions that
when one of his attendants visited his friends in Derbyshire, he was questioned
by all the Dissenters of the neighbourhood, who could scarcely be made to believe
that Monmouth had really been executed.   (*Tanner MSS.*, xxix., f. 64, in the
Bodleian Library.) Macaulay (chap. v.) gives other instances of the same belief.

sufficiently appalling. The "quarters" of the rebels who had
been executed after Sedgmoor, smeared with tar and impaled
on high stakes, poisoned the air. The prisons at Wells and
elsewhere were crowded with rebels, who were left half starved,
waiting for their trial in the Bloody Assize. The Bishop,
backed by Sir Thomas Cutler, then in command at Wells, lost
no time in interceding with the King, and apparently succeeded
in stopping the brutalities of the martial law which Feversham
and Kirke (Ken's old acquaintance at Tangier) had, by order
from James and his ministers, executed with a ruthless severity.[1]
James is said to have complied with their request, and to have
thanked them afterwards for their interposition, and it is
probably to this that Perkins refers in his statement that a
hundred prisoners had been saved by Ken from death.[2] The
tender mercies of James were, however, cruel enough. Jeffreys
was sent to the West to stamp out the last embers of the
rebellion, and entered on his task of blood with all his wonted
ferocity. He wrote exultingly to Sunderland that he would
" pawn my life, and what is dearer to me than life, my honour,
that before I have done my work, Bristol shall be taught its
duty to. its King and to its God."[3] Kirke and his " lambs "
were still in the West, to support him in his task of repression.
Peter Mews had preached in the cathedral at Wells on July 8th,
on the duty of subjects to their king, and after the service five
of the rebels were hanged.[4] The result of the assize at Wells,
in September, tried under a special commission and without a
jury, was that out of 500 prisoners 97 were condemned to death
and 385 to transportation. Ken in vain remonstrated with

In 1698 a pseudo-Monmouth was accepted by many of the yeomen and peasants
of Sussex, and was tried and found guilty at Horsham. Voltaire (*Dict. Philos.*)
thought it necessary, some years after the accession of George III., to refute the
notion that Monmouth had been the " Man in the iron mask," which had been
maintained by St. Foix in a pamphlet in 1762. For other examples see Roberts,
ii. pp. 166—168.

[1] Lord Lonsdale's *Memoirs of the Reign of James II.*, 1808, p. 12, and Routh's
edition of Burnet's *James II.*, p. 73.

[2] The Latin Poet Laureate, under Anne. See p. 217; ii. p. 262.

[3] *State Papers*, 1685. From the same source we learn that he wrote again
(September 22) to Sunderland, begging that the King may not be surprised
into pardoning any rebels till he (Jeffreys) has kissed hands. [R. C. B.]

[4] Wayless, *Hist. of Devizes*, p. 319.

VOL. 1.   Q

Jeffreys on the illegality and cruelty of his proceedings. Finding his efforts to stop them fruitless he gave himself to the more congenial task of ministering to the prisoners at Wells, and Taunton, and Bridgwater, relieving their bodily wants with food and clothing, and giving them, as far as opportunities allowed, such spiritual counsel and comfort as they would receive. For the most part Ken was reticent, like other men of the same stamp, as to his good deeds, and hardly allowed his left hand to know what his right hand had done; but on this, long years afterwards (April, 1696), his lips were unsealed, and we have the statement of what he then did embodied in his own words. He had been charged, under William III., with the seditious act of joining other non-juring Bishops in issuing a paper inviting subscriptions for their deprived brethren. He vindicated his action by pleading what he had done for those who were far more guilty in the eyes of the law than the non-juring clergy. " My Lords," he said, addressing the Privy Council, " in King James's time there were about a thousand or more imprisoned in my diocese who were engaged in the rebellion of the Duke of Monmouth, and many of them were such which I had reason to believe to be ill men and void of all religion; and yet, for all that, I thought it my duty to relieve them. It is well known to the diocese that I visited them day and night, and I thank God I supplied them with necessaries myself as far as I could, and encouraged others to do the same." [1]

Yet another instance of Ken's action has been brought to light within the last few months, by the publication of a letter from George Hickes, Dean of Worcester, and afterwards eminent as a leading Non-juror.[2] His brother, John Hickes, was a Nonconformist minister, and had joined Monmouth at Shepton Mallet. It was for receiving him that Alice Lisle was beheaded—the original sentence passed by Jeffreys was that of being burnt alive—at Winchester. Hickes himself was executed on October 6th at Glastonbury. The Dean, writes to one of

[1] See ii. 99. On the supposition that Ken was the author of the *Royal Sufferer*, published as by him, what he says in it of the conduct of James's Government in repressing the Monmouth rebellion has a special interest. (See Note at end of chapter xxii.)

[2] *English Historical Review*, October, 1887, p. 753.

Ken's chaplains, Robert Eyre, and, after thanking him for his personal kindness towards "my late wretched brother," goes on as follows :—

"I must also entreat you to return my most humble duty and thanks to my good Lord Bishop, for his eminent condescension and charity towards him in praying with him and for him, and for suffering so unworthy a body to be interred in Glassenbury (*Glaston-bury*) Church. I take this last great respect of my Lord's to be done to myself, and desire in a particular manner to be thankful for it."

The rest of the letter contains expressions of regret that the prisoner had persisted in his nonconformity, and inquiries as to the circumstances of his death. What had Jeffreys said to him at his trial? Was his body 'given whole' to his friends? Had he left "any message to his children that they should live in the communion of our Church?" Had he "desired, and received the Holy Sacrament, or, if not, whether he refused it, or it was refused to him," as "persisting in schisme"?[1]

---

[1] It may be noted as not without interest that Hickes sends his "particular respects" to Dr. Creighton, of Wells, and the "good dean" (Bathurst).

[NOTE ON LONGLEAT (p. 211).—Longleat, afterwards to be, for so many years, Ken's home, was, at the time of Monmouth's progress, in the possession of Thomas Thynne, commonly known, from his general popularity, as "Tom of Ten Thousand," who was a prominent member of the Whig party and an intimate friend of Monmouth. He was murdered on February 12th, 1682, at the instigation of Count Konigsmark, who had been a rival suitor for the hand of Lady Ogle, heiress of the house of Percy. The actual assassins were found guilty and executed, but the Count himself was acquitted. His brother was afterwards famous as the reported lover of Sophia Dorothea of Zell, the wife of George I. Thomas Thynne's tomb in Westminster Abbey presents the story of the murder in relief. He was succeeded by Ken's friend, at the time Sir Thomas Thynne, who was, in the same year (December, 1682), raised to the peerage as Viscount Weymouth.]

Two additional facts of interest may fitly find a place here :—(1) Jeffreys, when Sharp visited him in the Tower (ii. 27), threw all the blame on James, and said that he was urged on "by ———, who is now the darling of the people." He obviously meant William (Routh's Burnet, *l.c.*). (2) A medal in the museum at Taunton commemorates Monmouth's defeat. The obverse gives the Duke's head, the reverse represents a man falling, in the act of climbing a rock, at the top of which are three crowns, with the legend, *Superi Risere*.

CHAPTER XV.

THE PASTOR AND HIS FLOCK.

" When foemen watch their tents by night,
  And mists hang wide o'er moor and fell,
  Spirit of Counsel and of Might,
  Their pastoral warfare guide Thou well."
                                    John Keble.

THE execution of the Duke of Monmouth took place on July 15, 1685. The following letter shows that on August 5th Ken was at Winchester. The address has been lost, but as it is found among the Longleat papers there can be little doubt that it was addressed to Thomas Thynne, Viscount Weymouth, the owner of that mansion. It will be seen that its contents lead naturally to the same conclusion :—

LETTER X.

TO VISCOUNT WEYMOUTH.

" MY VERY GOOD LORD,

" All Glory be to God. Amen.

" I am extreamely ashamed that I should suffer a letter of your Lordshippe's to lye by me so long, without making any returne, but ye person you sent stay'd so little with me y^t I did not advert to aske him how I might addresse my answer, for wch I humbly beg your pardon. I was ready to have dispacht your Clerk imediately, but that my Secretary was gone to Wells, though had he then been with me, I found afterwards, I could not have done it; there having been two Caveats enter'd, wch would force me to retard ye Institution. I had a designe to have waited on your Lordshippe before this time, to have made my excuse, and had come as far as

Winchester, but the circumstances of my condition are such y^t they necessitate my stay here, till towards the end of ye month, though very much against my Inclinations, which all draw me towards my flock. In the meantime I have sent your Lordshippe some of ye poore provision I have made for you; wch I beseech you to accept of, for ye sake of the subject treated of, wch is Divine Love. God of His Infinite Goodnesse preserve yourselfe and your Family in His Favour, wch is of all things in the world ye most desirable.

"My Good Lord,

" Your Lordshippe's most humble and faithful Servant,

"THO. BATH & WELLS.

" Winch. Coll., *Aug. 5th*, 1685."

[The letter has the interest of being the earliest extant connected with a friendship which began early and lasted till the close of Ken's life. Thomas, son of Sir Henry Frederick Thynne, had been a student of Christ Church in Ken's Oxford days. They had both been members of the same Musical Society. His education had been mainly directed by Hammond and Fell, on the lines of sober Anglicanism. His aunt, Lady Pakington, was the supposed, and perhaps actual, author of *The Whole Duty of Man.* He had married Lady Frances Finch, daughter of Heneage, second Earl of Winchelsea, had been M.P. for the University of Oxford in 1673—4, and afterwards for Tamworth, and on December 11th, 1682, had been created Viscount Weymouth (see Note, p. 227). His wealth and high character gave him great influence both in the country and in the circle of the Court. Longleat was not in Ken's diocese, but it was sufficiently near (within twenty miles from Wells) to lead naturally to a renewal of the old Oxford friendship, and much of Lord Weymouth's property lay actually within the limits of the diocese, in which also he held the patronage of some livings. The letter seems connected with the institution of some one not named, but probably the Mr. King mentioned in later letters, to one of them.

Two passages of the letter suggest inferences of some interest. (1) Ken is at Winchester, more or less against his wishes, which would have led him to return at once to his diocese, then, as we may well believe, in all the suffering and confusion consequent on the Duke of Monmouth's rebellion, much in need of his presence for comfort and counsel. Circumstances necessitated his stay there till the end of the month. It seems a probable hypothesis that he stayed there to see if he could be of any use to those who were to be tried by Jeffreys for their share in the rebellion. Among the prisoners indicted and condemned there was Dame Alice Lisle, who, on August 27, was found guilty of treason for having given shelter to John Hickes, one of the rebels who had fled after the defeat at Sedgemoor. He, as has been stated (p. 226), though a Nonconformist and a rebel, was brother to George Hickes, Dean of Worcester, afterwards, as we shall see, conspicuous among the Nonjurors. Ken may have remained to watch the issue of her trial, and to see if he could do anything to avert or mitigate the penalty. The letter from Dean Hickes, quoted in p. 227, shows that the Bishop ministered to his brother. (2) The last sentences of the letter refer to the first of Ken's publications as a

Bishop, his *Practice of Divine Love, being an Exposition of the Church Catechism.* The *Imprimatur* of that book bears date August 9th, 1685. As the letter bears date August 5th, the volume sent to Lord Weymouth must have been one of the "early copies," sent to the Bishop for private presentation, before it was issued to the public.]

An examination of the *Practice of Divine Love* leads to the conclusion that it must have been begun almost as soon as Ken entered on the duties of his episcopate. This was as the first-fruits of his work as the shepherd of his flock. What he had seen of the ignorance of the peasantry of Somerset during his short stay among them, or in his ministration to the rebels, an ignorance which the succeeding age did little to remove,[1] may well have led him to hasten its publication. This was to show how he loved and cared for them. It was also to be a manifesto of the principles by which he sought to guide his course amid the "unhappy divisions and confusions of the time."[2]

The book is from first to last pre-eminently characteristic of Ken's mind, and calls for a brief analysis of its contents. It is addressed as follows :—

"To the inhabitants within the diocese of Bath and Wells, Thomas, their unworthy Bishop, wisheth the knowledge and the Love of God."

It opens with reproducing the Rubric that follows the Catechism in the Prayer-book, and laments the "gross ignorance and irreligion" which, "our woeful experience shows us abound where catechising is neglected."

It is probable enough that such neglect had prevailed for many a long year throughout the whole of Ken's diocese. Not to speak of the interruption to all pastoral work caused by the

---

[1] Readers of Hannah More's Life will remember the crass, heathen ignorance in which she found the inhabitants of Cheddar and Wrington. It is to be recorded to Bishop Law's and Dean Ryder's honour that they were among her warm supporters, when the squires, farmers, and not a few of the clergy, were fierce in their opposition.

[2] Ken's book had had predecessors in Hammond's *Practical Catechism* and Lancelot Addison's *Primitive Institution, or a Seasonable Discourse of Catechising.* Probably the "expounding" at Ely House, which the Princess Anne wished to hear (p. 271), was a catechetical instruction.

civil wars, and by the temporary disestablishment of the Church under the Commonwealth, there is nothing to show that any one of the Bishops of Bath and Wells since the Restoration, Pierce, or Creighton, or Mews, had exerted any personal influence, by precept or example, on the religious training of the younger members of their flock. It was not in Ken's nature, however, to dwell on the short-comings of others. He starts with what concerns himself :—

"Since, then, the providence of God, who is wont to glorify his strength in the weakness of the instrument he uses, has caught me up from among the meanest herdmen into the pastoral throne, and has been pleased to commit you to my care; the love I ought to pay to the chief Shepherd obliges me to feed all his lambs and his sheep, that belong to my flock, and, according to my poor abilities, to teach them the knowledge and the love of God, and how they may make them both their daily study and practice." [1]

He " passionately " exhorts and beseeches all the adult members of his flock of either sex, to help in this good work by " bringing all children under their care to catechising and confirmation."

The characteristic feature of the *Exposition* throughout is that the Catechism is turned in all its parts into a manual of devotion. The revelation of God in Christ is presented as the manifestation of an infinite and eternal love. Creation, redemption, sanctification, are all proofs of that love. In words which remind us of those of Ignatius,[2] Christ himself is " love, afflicted and compassionate love, love bleeding, and crucified, and agonised." Each step in the history of the Passion is brought before the reader, and every sentence opens with the

[1] Compare the passage from Ken's poems quoted in p. 179. The words were, we may well believe, more than the formal utterance of a feigned humility. There had been a true *Nolo Episcopari* at the very moment of his acceptance of his high office, but his natural human will had yielded to the sense of a divine calling.

[2] Ὁ ἐμὸς ἔρως ἐσταύρωται. (Ignatius, *Ep. ad. Rom.* c. 7.) The words are found written in Ken's hand, on the flyleaf of a copy of Andrewes's *Preces Privatae* at Longleat. Compare the *original* refrain of Wesley's Hymn 28, " My Lord, my Love is crucified."

words, " I grieve and I love." His experience at Winchester
had apparently taught Ken that it was well to pitch the note of
devotion high, and not to descend to the lower keys of controversial bitterness or conventional morality. Some passages,
bearing on Ken's relation to the leading controversies of the
time, though not controversial in their tone, are worth quoting
in extenso, as exhibiting the main aspects of his theology. He
is expounding the article of the Creed on " The Holy Catholic
Church :"—

"I believe, O blessed and adorable Mediator, that the Church is
a society of persons, founded by thy love to sinners,[1] united into
one body, of which thou art the head,[2] initiated by baptism,[3]
nourished by the Eucharist,[4] governed by pastors commissioned by
thee, and endowed with the power of the keys,[5] professing the doctrine taught by thee,[6] and delivered to the saints,[7] and devoted to
praise and to love thee.

"I believe, O holy Jesus, that thy Church is holy, like thee its
author; holy, by the original design of its institution ;[8] holy, by
baptismal dedication ; holy, in all its administrations, which tend
to produce holiness ;[9] and though there will be always a mixture of
good and bad in it in this world,[10] yet it has always many real saints
in it ; and therefore, all love, all glory be to thee.

"I believe, Lord, this Church to be Catholic or universal, made
up of the collection of all particular Churches ; I believe it to be
catholic in respect of time, comprehending all ages to the world's
end, to which it is to endure ;[11] catholic in respect of all places, out
of which believers are to be gathered ;[12] catholic in respect of all
saving faith, of which this creed contains the substance, which shall
in it always be taught ;[13] catholic in respect of all graces, which
shall in it be practised ; and catholic in respect of that catholic war
it is to wage against all its ghostly enemies for which it is called
militant. O preserve me always a true member of thy Catholic
Church, that I may always inseparably adhere to thee, that I may
always devoutly praise and love thee.

"Glory be to thee, O Lord my God, who hast made me a member
of the particular Church of England, whose faith, and government,

[1] Matt. xvi. 18 ; Eph. v. 25.   [2] Col. 1, 18.   [3] Matt. xxviii. 19.
[4] Matt. xxvi. 26.   [5] Ibid. xviii. 18 ; John xx. 22, 23.   [6] Acts ii. 41, 42.
[7] Jude 3.   [8] 2 Tim. i. 9.   [9] 2 Tim. ii. 19.   [10] Matt. xiii. 24.
[11] Matt. xvi. 18 ; xviii. 20   [12] Matt. xxviii. 19.   [13] John xvi. 13.

and worship are holy, and Catholic, and Apostolic, and free from the extremes of irreverence or superstition ; and which I firmly believe to be a sound part of thy Church universal, and which teaches me charity to those who dissent from me ; and therefore, all love, all glory, be to thee.

"O my God, give me grace to continue stedfast in her bosom, to improve all those helps to true piety, all those means of grace, all those incentives of thy love, thou hast mercifully indulged me in her communion, that I may with primitive affections and fervour praise and love thee.

" ' THE COMMUNION OF SAINTS.'

" *Communion.*

" I believe, O King of Saints, that among the saints on earth, whether real, or in outward profession only, there ought to be a mutual Catholic participation of all good things,[1] which is the immediate effect of Catholic love. Thou, O God of love, restore it to thy Church.

" I believe, O thou God of love, that all the saints on earth, by profession, ought to communicate one with another in evangelical worship, and the same holy sacraments, in the same divine and apostolical faith ;[2] in all offices of corporal[3] and spiritual charity,[4] in reciprocal delight in each other's salvation, and in tender sympathy as members of one and the same body ;[5] O God of peace, restore in thy good time this Catholic communion, that with one heart, and one mouth, we may all praise and love thee.

" O my God, amidst the deplorable divisions of thy Church, O let me never widen its breaches, but give me Catholic charity to all who are baptised in thy name, and Catholic communion with all Christians in desire. O deliver me from the sins and errors, from the schisms and heresies, of the age. O give me grace to pray daily for the peace of thy Church,[6] and earnestly to seek it, and to excite all I can to praise and to love thee.

" I believe, O most holy Jesu, that thy saints here below have communion with thy saints above,[7] they praying for us,[8] in heaven, we here on earth celebrating their memorials, rejoicing at their

---

[1] John i. 7. [2] Acts ii. 42, 46. [3] Gal. vi. 10.
[4] Rom. xii. 9, &c. ; 1 Thess. v. 14 ; Heb. x. 25. [5] 1 Cor. xii. 13, 26.
[6] Ps. cxxii. 6. [7] Heb. xii. 22.
[8] "That they pray for us, while we celebrate their memories, congratulate their bliss," &c. 1st Ed. Compare p. 79.

bliss, giving thee thanks for their labours of love, and imitating their examples; for which, all love, all glory, be to thee.

"I believe, O gracious Redeemer, that thy saints here on earth have communion with the holy angels above; that they are 'ministering spirits,'[1] sent forth to minister for them who shall be heirs of salvation,' and watch over us;[2] and we give thanks to thee for their protection, and emulate their incessant praises, and ready obedience; for which, all love, all glory, be to thee.

"I believe, O my Lord, and my God, that the saints in this life have communion with the Three Persons of the most adorable Trinity,[3] in the same most benign influences of love, in which all three conspire; for which, all love, all glory be to thee, O Father, Son and Holy Ghost, world without end.

"Glory be to thee, O Goodness infinitely diffusive, for all the graces and blessings in which the saints communicate, for breathing thy love into thy mystical body, as the very soul that informs it, that all that believe in thee may love one another, and all join in loving thee."

From the devotions that follow on the second commandment I take the prayer:—

"O my God, O my Love, for thy dearest sake, give me grace to pay a religious, suitable veneration, to all sacred persons, or places, or things, which are thine by solemn dedication, and separated for the uses of Divine love, and the communications of thy Grace, or which may promote the decency and order of thy worship, or the edification of faithful people."

His thoughts on the Sabbath question are suggestive:—

"We Christians, O Lord God, following the moral equity of thy command, and authorised by apostolical practice, celebrate 'the Lord's Day,' 'the first day of the week,' in memory of our redemption, in memory of thy resurrection from the dead, O most beloved Jesu, when thou didst rest from the labours and sorrows of the new creation: O may I ever remember thy day and thee!

"Glory be to thee, O my God, my Love, who hast under the Gospel delivered us from the rigours but not from the piety of the Jewish Sabbath."

---

[1] Heb. i. 14.   [2] Ps. xxxiv. 7.   [3] 1 John i. 3; Phil. ii. 1.

So, among the sins forbidden by the fourth commandment we have :—

"All profanations of thy hallowed day, and of all other holy times dedicated to thy praise and thy love.

"All Judaizing severities, all worldly-mindedness and unnecessary business, or not allowing those under my care liberty and leisure for thy service on thy day.

"All unmercifulness to my very beasts."

That Ken should accept the sacramental teaching of the Catechism in its simplest and most natural meaning was, of course, to be expected, but it is well, for the sake of completeness, to give his very words, in which, as was his wont, dogma is translated into devotion :—

"Glory be to thee, O Jesu, who, from our 'death to sin' in our baptism, dost raise us to a new life, and dost breathe into us the breath of love; 'tis in this 'laver of regeneration,'[1] we are 'born again by water,[2] and the Spirit,' by a 'new birth unto righteousness:' that as the natural birth propagated sin, our spiritual birth should propagate grace; for which all love, all glory, be to thee.

"Glory be to thee, O most indulgent Love, who in our baptism dost give us the holy Spirit of love, to be the principle of new life, and of love in us, to infuse into our souls a supernatural, habitual grace, and ability to obey and love thee; for which all love, all glory, be to thee."

In his teaching as to the other sacrament Ken saw reason to alter in the subsequent editions of his book the language which he had used in the first. As the controversies of the time thickened round him, it became necessary to be more wary and cautious in his language, to give no handle to the adversaries on either side, so to maintain the doctrine of the Eucharistic Presence that it might be kept clear of the subtleties of Romish scholasticism, or the practices of Romish superstition. The nature of the change will be best appreciated by comparing the two statements as they stand side by side :—

[1] Tim. iii. 5.   [2] John iii. 5.

First Edition.

"O God incarnate, how thou canst give us thy flesh to eat, and thy blood to drink; how thy flesh is meat indeed, and thy blood is drink indeed; how he that eateth thy flesh and drinketh thy blood, dwelleth in thee, and thou in him; how he shall live by thee and be raised up by thee to life eternal; how thou who art in heaven art present on the altar, I can by no means explain; but I firmly believe it all, because thou hast said it, and I firmly rely on thy love, and on thy omnipotence to make good thy word, though the manner of doing it, I cannot comprehend."

Later Editions.

"O God incarnate, how the bread and the wine, unchanged in their substance, become thy body and thy blood; after what extraordinary manner thou, who art in Heaven, art present throughout the whole sacramental action, to every devout receiver; how thou canst give us thy flesh to eat, and thy blood to drink; how thy flesh is meat indeed, and thy blood is drink indeed; how he that eateth thy flesh, and drinketh thy blood, dwelleth in thee, and thou in him; how he shall live by thee, and be raised up by thee to life eternal;[1] I can by no means comprehend; but I firmly believe all thou hast said, and I firmly rely on thy omnipotent love, to make good thy word; for which all love, all glory, be to thee."

It will be noted that every alteration involves a definite protest against the most distinctively Romish dogma. The insertion of the words "unchanged in their substance" repudiates transubstantiation. The Christ who had been spoken of at first as "present on the altar," as with a materialised and localised presence, is, on maturer thought, defined as "present throughout the whole sacramental action," but only "to every devout receiver," and so there is an implied protest against the ritual which assumes that there is a presence of another kind. It is a singular fact in the history of two men who, like Ken and Keble, have so much in common, that each should have been led to alter the devotional language in which they had spoken of the Eucharistic presence. It is, perhaps, even more singular that these alterations should have been made in opposite directions, that Ken should have moved towards the more Protestant

---

[1] John vi. 54.

theory, while Keble receded from it. One wonders whether the act of the earlier poet was present to the mind of the later, when he decided on a change which to most members of the English Church seems, to say the least, matter for regret.[1]

The *Practice of Divine Love* was followed rapidly by a work of a yet humbler and simpler type. The first edition of *Directions for Prayer for the Diocese of Bath and Wells* appeared in 1685. It can hardly be doubted that it was the direct outcome of Ken's ministrations to the prisoners whom he visited on his return to Wells, and in whom he had found a "lamentable ignorance and forgetfulness of God." "Some never pray at all, pretending they were never taught, or that their memories are bad, or that they are not book-learned, or that they want money to buy a book, and by this means they live and die rather like beasts than men." He has to write now to those of whom many were " wholly ignorant " even of the Catechism. He must treat them "as children in understanding though not in age;" must feed them with milk before they can be capable of strong meat. The teaching of the Catechism, in a simpler form than that of *The Practice of Divine Love*, forms naturally the basis of his instruction. The prayers which he entreats them to use are often hardly more than ejaculations. These they are to teach their children as well as themselves. Instead of "idle tales and songs," they are to store their children's minds and their own with short psalms, which they are to repeat when they lie awake at night. Those that have families are to use the prayers of the Prayer Book "as being most familiar and of greatest authority withal." One of those which he thus commends to their use is the first of the two prayers for the King in the Communion Service. "This," he says, "I exhort you never to omit, because you know that the country wherein you live was the only seat of the late rebellion, and the tares of sedition have been industriously sown among you, and you have the greater reason to pray that you may be firm in your allegiance."

[1] The line in the *Christian Year* which had stood during multitudinous editions of the book during the author's life-time, as " Not in the hands, but in the heart," appeared after his death (it was stated by his directions) in the form " As in the hands, so in the heart."

Yet another Manual of Devotion belongs probably to the same year, and marks Ken's unwearied care for the souls of his people. Under the Restoration the tide of fashion was beginning to set in at the first of the two cities which gave his diocese its name, and though its stately streets and terraces and crescents belong to a later period, it had become the resort of men and women of wealth and rank. Both sexes bathed together in a somewhat barbarous and promiscuous fashion, as they do, or did till lately, in the baths of Leuk, in Switzerland.[1] There was much of the "idleness and fulness of bread" which were the fruitful parents of scandals. The ordinary parochial ministrations of the Church failed to meet the spiritual needs of the mixed multitude that were thus brought together. The Queen, who in September, 1687, came to the baths in the hope that an heir to the throne might be given her, and the question of succession be so far settled, brought with her chaplains, among whom there were many active propagandists, such as one whom we shall find publishing a letter to Ken a little later on. Whatever devotional feeling there might be among the visitors of Bath was likely enough to run in that direction. Looking at these things, Ken thought himself bound, as a good shepherd, here also to come to the rescue. It bears the characteristic heading of *All Glory be to God*, which he was beginning now to use as the superscription of every letter. It comes, as the two other Manuals had done, from "Thomas, unworthy Bishop of Bath and Wells, to all Persons who come to the Baths for cure." He "wisheth for them from God the Blessings of this Life and of the Next." The work is too purely devotional to present many passages for quotation. It is characteristic of Ken that he presses the claims of the poor and needy on those who too often gave way to the selfishness of suffering. They were to do (as, we may add, he himself did), and to support their brethren and sisters in need who had come, as they had come, to use the waters of healing.[2]

[1] A book recently published under the title of *The Bathes of Bathe's Ayde*, by Charles E. Davis, Bath, 1883, reproduces the scene in the King's Bath from an old drawing.

[2] The fact is stated in Thomas Guidott's *Register of Bath*, quoted by Gough, *British Topography*, 1780, ii. pp. 197—8. (Anderdon, p. 311.) It may be noted

For the sake of completeness in this survey of Ken's pastoral addresses to his people, I anticipate the strict chronological order of events and pass to an encyclical letter which he issued to the clergy of his diocese in April, 1686.

LETTER XI.

A Letter Exhorting the Clergy of the Diocese of Bath and Wells to Collect in Behalf of the French Protestants.

" All Glory be to God.

" Sir,

" His majesty in these his letters patent, which I now send you, having given a fresh and great assurance of his graciousness to his own subjects, in showing himself so very gracious to Protestant strangers, and having required me to give *a particular recommendation and command* to my brethren of the clergy within my diocese, *to advance this so pious and charitable a work;* I think it my duty, with my utmost zeal to further so godlike a charity; and I do therefore strictly enjoin you, that you most *affectionately and earnestly persuade, exhort, and stir up all under your care to contribute freely and cheerfully to the relief of these distressed Christians,* and to do it with as well tim'd an expedition as you can. And that his majesty's royal goodness may have its full effect, I beseech you, for the love of God, to be exemplarily liberal towards them yourself, according to your ability: remembering how blessed a thing it is to be brotherly kind to strangers, to Christian strangers, especially such as those whose distress is very great, and is in all respects most worthy of our tenderest commiseration, and how our most adorable Redeemer does interpret and does proportionably reward all the good we do to them as done to himself. God of his infinite mercy inspire this fraternal charity into your own soul, and into the souls of all your parish.

" Your affectionate friend & brother,

" THO. BATH & WELLS.

" Wells, *April 15th,* 1686."

In the Edict of Nantes (April 13, 1598) Henry IV. had secured for the Huguenots of France the free exercise of their

that one of Ken's most illustrious predecessors, Bishop Reginald, of Bath, had, in 1180, founded a hospital of St. John the Baptist for the benefit of the sick and aged poor. I do not know, however, whether this was with special reference to their use of the waters.

worship, and of their rights and liberties as French subjects.
They prospered as landowners, merchants, manufacturers.
Their ministers were conspicuous for learning and for piety.
They attracted the sympathy even of the highest Anglicans.
Cosin did not hesitate to join in communion with them.
What Ken had seen of them in his travels in France had
probably led him also to look on them as his brethren in Christ,
as not involved in the guilt of heresy or wilful schism. On
September 6, 1666, at the close of the war of the Fronde,
Louis XIV. had acknowledged their loyalty, and had solemnly
promised that they should live on terms of equality with his
other subjects. The 'grand Monarch,' however, under the
influence of Madame de Maintenon and his priestly counsellors,
had fixed his mind, in the devoteeism of his later years, on
being the restorer of Catholic unity in France, and after an
irregular persecution, in 1681, when Poitou was laid waste by
dragonnades, and many thousands took refuge, as exiles, in
England and elsewhere, he formally revoked the Edict of
Nantes on October 18, 1685. On the former of these occasions
Charles II. had yielded to the current of popular Protestant
feeling, and by an Order in Council issued letters of denization
to more than a thousand of the refugees, had promised the
further benefit of naturalisation, and had taken measures for their
relief by all officers, civil and military, at whatever port they
landed. Letters were also addressed by him to Compton,
Bishop of London, directing collections to be made for them,
"not only as distressed strangers, but also as persecuted Christians," and the Lord Mayor was stirred to a like activity on
their behalf.[1] With Charles of course this was only part of the
game which he found it convenient to play, so as to calm the
præternatural suspicions which had shown themselves in the
Popish Plot and the Exclusion Bill. Probably enough, in his
heart of hearts, he thought his most Christian brother of France
a little over-hasty, and was tempted to say, in substance, what
was the rule of his own life, *Surtout, point de zèle.* The great
body of the English clergy and people, however, were in
earnest in the matter then. They were still more in earnest
when the new persecution drove fresh exiles to their shores,

[1] Smedley, *Hist. of Reformed Religion in France*, iii. 261, in Anderdon, p. 320.

sufferers for conscience' sake, their very flight from persecution (they were forbidden to leave France) being a fresh crime, beggared and starving. From all classes of men there came memorials urging active measures on their behalf. James found himself halting between two opinions. He would, and he would not. He had all along, as later, in 1687 and 1688, in his Declaration of Indulgence, avowed himself an advocate of the largest toleration. His personal experience as a sufferer for conscience' sake had probably made that theory part of his convictions. It would be confirmed by his conversations with the two men with whom, outside the range of Roman Catholic advisers, he was most in sympathy, with Ken on one side, with William Penn on the other. So far as he was capable of aiming at an ideal at all, he pictured himself as a patriot king, influencing the Church of England and the Universities by his appointments of men with Catholic sympathies, till they were ripe for a spontaneous reunion with Rome, and in the meantime protecting Romanists and Dissenters alike against the intolerant Acts of Charles II.'s Parliaments. His aim, partly realised by the two Lord Baltimores, as Roman Catholic Governors of the colony of Maryland, from 1632 onwards, was to show that the Catholicism of Rome was compatible with the widest toleration of other forms of Christianity.[1] On the other hand, he was reluctant to take any action which would seem to imply a censure on the King on whom he counted for support, or to condemn an act which the 'Vicar of Christ,' Innocent XI., had solemnly approved and welcomed with a *Te Deum* throughout the Roman States. And so it was that his action was wavering and uncertain. The letters of Lady Rachel Russell, whose relationship to Ruvigny[2] gave her a natural promi-

---

[1] The limitation must be noted. The laws of Maryland inflicted severe penalties on those who denied or blasphemed the faith of Christians.—Anderson, *Colonial Church*, chap. xiv.

[2] Lady Rachel's mother, wife of Thomas Wriothesley, Earl of Southampton, was sister of Daniel, Seigneur de Ruvigny. He and his brother, the Marquis de Ruvigny, took refuge in England from the persecutions in France. The latter supported William III., and his son was created Earl of Galway. The Marquis de Ruvigny settled at Greenwich, was the first governor named in the charter of Greenwich Hospital, and founded, in 1714, the Hospice for French Protestants, in Old Street, St. Luke's, now rebuilt in Victoria Park. [G. H. S.]

nence in the movement, record the delays and disappointments which brought delay where the proverb *Bis dat qui cito dat* was above all things applicable, and vexed the heart of the sufferers with the sickness of hope deferred.

In November, 1685, she heard that the King had given leave for a collection ; on January 15, 1686, the brief for the collection was put aside by Jeffreys in the Council Chamber with words of contemptuous indifference. A week later she records that private applications to the Chancellor had met with a reception that was not encouraging. The French Ambassador was naturally busy in obstructing the collection. It was not till March 29th that the brief was read in the London churches, and when it came, it was accompanied by measures which went a good way in diminishing its helpfulness.[1]

The higher Anglicans were afraid at the prospect of the English Dissenters being reinforced by so formidable an addition, and Sancroft brought a Bill into the House of Lords which, while it assigned the refugees a place of worship in the city, restricted them to the use of a French translation of the Book of Common Prayer, and to the ministrations of clergy in English orders.[2] The brief commanded the clergy to content themselves with reading it, and not to preach on the sufferings of the exiles. Ken, however, who took his turn as a Whitehall preacher on March 14th, 168⅚, probably before the brief was formally issued, did not feel himself bound by any such restriction. He preached what Evelyn describes as "a most excellent and pathetic discourse" on John vi. 17 ; and "after he had recommended the duty of fasting and other penitential duties, he exhorted to constancy in the Protestant religion, detestation of the unheard-of cruelties of the French, and stirring up to a liberal contribution." He adds, and his language is significant as showing the feelings about Ken which were floating

[1] *Letters* xxvii., xxviii., xxx.

[2] The offered boon might seem marred in the giving. It may be remembered, however, that the ground on which English Churchmen of the school of Sancroft, such as Cosin, entered into communion with Huguenot ministers in France, might seem to involve reciprocity. The French Protestants, being in England, and in communion with the Church of England, might be expected to surrender some prepossessions, and to accept her polity and ritual. A more liberal policy would, perhaps, have been wiser, but that actually adopted admitted of a fair defence.

in men's minds, that "this sermon was the more acceptable, as it was unexpected from a bishop who had undergone the censure of being inclined to Popery, the contrary whereof no man could show more." "This, indeed," he goes on to say, "did all our bishops, to the disabusing and reproach of all their delators, for none were more zealous against Popery than they were." Ken's conduct in thus speaking was all the more noticeable from the fact that James had complained to Sancroft of the overbold language in defence of the Church of England, which had been used on the previous Sunday by Bishop Frampton of Gloucester.[1]

Ken lost no time, as we have seen, in commending the good work of relieving the Huguenots of his diocese. He set an example of the scale on which he thought men ought to contribute by giving great part of a fine on the renewal of a lease, amounting to £4,000, to the collection.[2] It was probably the largest sum received by the treasurers of the fund. The King had given £1,500, others of high rank sums varying from £1,000 downwards. Sir William Coventry, uncle to Lord Weymouth (here we may probably trace Ken's influence), who died in the summer of 1686, left £3,000 to redeem slaves (probably the Christian slaves in Algiers), and £2,000 to the French refugees. Ken's munificence was all the more striking from the fact that he had to borrow money from Morley's nephew for the fees and other expenses connected with his appointment as Bishop. Nor was the see which he filled one of those conspicuous for its wealth. When the seven Bishops divided the

[1] Frampton's letter to Sancroft, defending himself against the charge of having consciously spoken a single word that could give the King offence, is dated March 27th, and possibly therefore Ken may not have heard of the matter. Rumours of a King's displeasure, however, soon find their way into circulation among Court whisperers. Till then Frampton had been one of the King's favourite Bishops, and he placed him on the same high level as Ken, as the best among the preachers of the English Church. (Evans, *Life of Frampton,* pp. 145-149.) Evelyn (Dec. 20th, 1685) records a sermon by Dr. Turner, brother to the Bishop of Ely, preached at Whitehall, on the submission of Christians to their persecutors, which seems to have spoken slightingly of the French Protestants and to have thrown cold water on the measures for their relief. "Some passages," Evelyn says, "were indiscreet enough, considering the time, and the rage of the inhumane French tyrant against the poore Protestants."

[2] Hawkins, p. 13.

costs of their trial amongst them in proportion to their incomes.
Ken was assessed at £850, as compared with the £4,000 of
Canterbury and the £2,000 of Ely above him, with Chichester
at £770, Peterborough at £630, and Bristol at £350 below.[1]
The Dean and Chapter seconded Ken's effort by a grant of
£40. The amount seems at first somewhat small as compared
with the Bishop's munificence, but it may be pleaded on their
behalf that they were at the time saddled with heavy expenses,
amounting to over £500, for repairing the injuries done to
the Cathedral by the Monmouth rebels.[2] The collections from
Somersetshire parishes do not seem to have been much above
the average level of those which were commonly the result of
a King's brief.[3]

Yet another Pastoral Letter was issued by Ken to his clergy,
"concerning their behaviour during Lent." It bears date,
"From the Palace in Wells, Feb. 17, 1687," but as the date
on the title-page is 1688 I incline to think that Ken, as was
his custom, followed the old reckoning, according to which
the year began on March 25th, and the letter belongs, therefore, to the latter year, and this conclusion is confirmed by the
agitated and distressed tone which pervades it, and which presents a striking parallel to the sermon which Ken preached at
Whitehall on April 1st of that year, and which will come
before us later on. Troubles were thickening round the
Church. It seemed to him that there were dark days coming,
in which it would be difficult for men to see their way clearly,
"a day of trouble and rebuke and blasphemy," of abortive plans
and frustrated aspirations, the "children come to the birth"

---

[1] Gutch, *Miscell. Curiosa*, ii. 368.

[2] *Wells Chapter Acts*, 1685.

[3] Those at Swanswick, near Bath, amounted to £10 19s. 2½d., from twenty-
six persons; at North Curry, one of the Chapter livings, they reached the
sum of £2 19s. 11d. At Frome there is an entry of £1 1s. 2d. for an earlier
Brief for French Protestants in 1682, in 1688 for £9 18s. 0d., and in 1689 for two
collections for Irish Protestants of £18 17s. 0d. and £9 7s. 10½ respectively. At
Wroxall there are entries of collections for a second Brief for the French Protestants in 1694, and for the "French Vaudois" in 1699. The collections were
apparently continued under William. Others of like character are at Dinder
for building a church at Malting, in Curland, in 1709, and for "Palatines who
came to England, being 8,000 families," in 1710. Similar facts are reported from
South Shields and elsewhere. Newbury seems to have been conspicuous for its
liberal contributions.

with "no strength to bring forth." It seemed to him also that the time needed not the wrath of men, but the righteousness of God. Confession, penitence, intercession, charity, these were the elements of the temper in which such a time should be met. The whole letter is so characteristic that I print it *in extenso*, as helping us to understand Ken's feelings and the principles which guided him in his action.

LETTER XII.

"All Glory be to God.

"REV. BROTHER,

"The time of Lent now approaching, which has been anciently and very Xtianly set apart, for penitential humiliation of soul and body, for fasting and weeping and praying, all which you know are very frequently inculcated in Holy Scripture as the most effectual means we can use, to avert those judgments our sins have deserved; I thought it most agreeable to that character which, unworthy as I am, I sustain, to call you and all my brethren of the clergy to mourning; to mourning for your own sins, and to mourning for the sins of the nation. In making such an address to you as this, I follow the example of St. Cyprian, that blessed Bishop and Martyr, who from his retirement wrote an excellent epistle[1] to his clergy, most worthy of your serious perusal, exhorting them, by publick prayers and tears to appease the anger of God, which they then actually felt, and which we may justly fear. Remember that to keep such a fast as God has chosen, it is not enough for you to afflict your own souls, but you must also according to your ability, 'deal your bread to the hungry:'[2] and the rather, because we have not only usual objects of charity to relieve, but many poor Protestant strangers are now fled hither for sanctuary, whom as brethren, as members of Christ, we should take in and cherish. That you may perform the office of a publick intercessor the more assiduously, I beg of you to say daily in your closet, or in your family, or rather in both, all this time of abstinence, ye 51st Psalm, and the other prayers that follow it in the Commination. I could wish also that you would frequently read and meditate on the Lamentations of Jeremy, which holy Gregory Nazianzen was wont to doe,[3] and the reading of which melted him into the like lamentations as affected the prophet himself when he pen'd them.

[1] Ep. iv., edit. Oxon.   [2] Isa. lviii. 5. 7.   [3] Orat. xii.

But your greatest zeal must be spent for the publick prayers, in the
constant and devout use of which, the publick safety, both of
Church and State, is highly concerned : be sure then to offer up to
God every day the Morning and Evening Prayer, offer it up in
your family at least, or rather, as far as your circumstances may
possibly permit, offer it up in the Church, especially if you live in a
great town, and say over the Litany every morning during the
whole of Lent.   This I might enjoin you to doe, on your canonical
obedience, 'but for love's sake, I rather beseech you,' and I cannot
recommend to you a more devout and comprehensive form of penitent and publick intercession than that, or more proper for the
season.   Be not discouraged, if but few come to the 'solemn
assemblies,' but go to the 'House of Prayer,' where 'God is well
known for a sure refuge;' go, though you go alone, or but with
one besides yourself ; and there, as you are God's 'remembrancer,
keep not silence, and give him no rest till he establish, till he make
Jerusalem a praise in the earth.'[1]   The first sacred council of Nice,
for which the Xtian world has always had a great and just veneration, ordains a provincial synod to be held before Lent, that all
dissentions[2] being taken away, a pure oblation might be offer'd up
to God, namely of prayers, and fasting, and alms, and tears, which
might produce a comfortable communion at the following Easter ;
and that in this diocese we may in some degree imitate so primitive
a practice, I exhort you to endeavour all you can to reconcile differences, to reduce those that go astray, to promote universal charity
towards all that dissent from you, and 'to put on as the elect of
God,'[3] holy and beloved, bowels of mercies, kindness, humbleness
of mind, meekness, long-suffering, forbearing one another and for-
giving one another, even as Christ forgave you.'[4]   I passionately
beseech you to reade over daily your ordination vows, to examine
yourself how you observe them ; and in the prayers that are in that
office, fervently to importune God for the assistance of His good
Spirit, that you may conscientiously perform them.   'Teach publickly, and from house to house, and warn every one night and day
with tears;' 'warn' them to repent, to fast and to pray, and to
give alms, 'and to bring forth fruits meet for repentance;' 'warn'
them to continue steadfast in that 'faith once delivered to the
saints;' in which they were baptiz'd 'to keep the word' of God's

---

[1] Isa. lxii. 6, 7.

[2] Can. v. Ken paraphrases the Canon, giving "dissentions" for the two
Greek words φιλονεικία and μικροψυχία. A second Synod was to be held in
autumn. Both were to regulate the discipline and penance of the excommunicated.

[3] Col. iii. 12.   [4] Col. iii. 12.

patience, that God may keep them in the hour of temptation;
'warn' them against the sins and errours of the age; 'warn' them
to deprecate publick judgments, and to mourn for publick provo-
cations.   No one can reade God's holy word but he will see, that
the greatest saints have been the greatest mourners; David 'wept
whole rivers;'[1] Jeremy 'wept sore, and his eyes ran down in
secret places day and night like a fountain;'[2] Daniel 'mourned
three full weeks, and did eat no pleasant bread, and sought God by
prayer and supplications, with fasting, and sackcloth and ashes;'[3]
St. Paul was humbled, and bewailed and wept for the sins of
others;'[4] and our Lord himself, when he 'beheld the city, wept
over it.'[5]   Learn then of these great saints, learn of our most compassionate Saviour, to weep for the publick, and weeping, to pray
that 'we may know in this our day, the things that belong to our
peace, lest they be hid from our eyes.'   To mourn for national
guilt, in which all share, is a duty incumbent on all, but especially
on priests, who are particularly commanded 'to weep and to say,
Spare thy people, O Lord, and give not thine heritage to reproach,
that God may repent of the evil and become jealous for his land
and pity his people.'[6]   Be assured that none are more tenderly
regarded by God than such mourners as these; there is 'a mark'[7]
set by him on 'all that sigh and cry for the abominations of the
land;' the destroying angel is forbid to 'hurt any of them,' they are
all God's peculiar care, and shall all have either present deliverance, or such supports and consolations as shall abundantly endear
their calamity.   'Now the God of all grace, who hath called you
unto his eternal glory by Christ Jesus, make you perfect, stablish,
strengthen, settle you' in the true Catholick and Apostolick Faith,
profess'd in the Church of England, and enable you to adorn that
apostolick faith with an apostolick example and zeal, and give all
our whole Church that timely repentance, those broken and contrite
hearts, that both priests and people may all plentifully sow in tears,
and in God's good time, may all plentifully reap in joy.

"Your affectionate friend and Brother,
"THO. BATH & WELLS.

" From the Palace in Wells,
    Feb. 17*th*, 1687."

[It will be noted that the Huguenot refugees are still, two years after his first
appeal, prominent in Ken's thoughts. The Protestant strangers are still

[1] Psal. cxix. 136.   [2] Jer. ix. 1; xiii. 17.   [3] Dan. ix. 3; x. 2.
[4] 2 Cor. xii. 21.; Phil. iii. 18.   [5] Luke xix. 41.
[6] Joel ii. 17, 18.   [7] Ezek. ix. 4.

recognised as "brethren, members of Christ whom we should take in and cherish." Anticipating Sancroft's action, who urged the clergy in his pastoral letter (July 27, 1688) to have "a special and tender care for their brethren, the Protestant Dissenters," Ken exhorts the clergy of his diocese to "endeavour all you can to reconcile differences, to reduce (*i.e.* bring back) those that go astray, to promote universal charity towards all that dissent from you." To "mourn for national guilt, in which all share," was "a duty incumbent upon all, especially on priests." They were to warn their people to continue steadfast in that faith once delivered to the saints, in which they were baptized. We note, as characteristic, the earnest exhortation to daily public prayer, however scanty might be the attendance of the people.]

Lastly, among the documents which bear on Ken's work in his diocese we have what chronologically comes first in order, the *Articles of Visitation and Enquiry*,[1] exhibited to the ministers, churchwardens, and sidesmen of every parish in the first year of his episcopate. These are, for the most part, of a formal character, and therefore I do not reproduce them. Some inferences may, however, be drawn, on the principle applicable to all such documents, that men do not inquire about remote or imaginary evils, and these are worth noting, as showing the state of things which Ken found on entering upon his office, and which he had to strive, as far as might be, to remedy. I note accordingly—

(1.) That there were churches not provided with a decent Communion-table in the chancel. The Puritan domination led, in not a few places, to the replacement of the Table in the body of the church.[2]

(2.) That some churches were not provided with a surplice, or the Authorised Version, or the Prayer-book of 1662, or the Table of Prohibited Degrees, or the Book of Canons.

(3.) That some were "without a chalice with a cover, and one or more flagons," and that where they were found they had often been "prophaned by common use."

---

[1] Round gives them as printed in 1683, but Ken was not consecrated till January 25th, 168⅘. The probable explanation is that the Articles had been printed after a consultation between Sancroft and the Bishops for general use, and this may account for the earlier date being attached to them.

[2] So in 1687 Cartwright, Bishop of Chester, gives orders for moving the Table to the East end. (*Diary*, p. 79.) The ante-communion service, when there was no celebration, was often read from the reading-desk.—Richard Hart, *Parish Churches turned into Conventicles*, 1683; in Overton, *Life in English Church*, c. iv.

(4.) That some churches were not "in good and sufficient repair," and that, in some cases, part had been pulled down, and the lead, timber, &c., embezzled or sold.

(5.) That the careful registration of births, deaths, and marriages, "according to the ancient use," was often neglected.

(6.) That strangers were admitted to preach with no record of their names and licenses.

(7.) That the churchyards were in some cases left unfenced and not decently kept, and were subject to encroachments, and that parsonages were not always kept in good repair.

(8.) That non-residence was still a crying evil, as it had been in the days of the *Expostulatoria*, in its earlier form of *Ichabod* (1663), that the curates were not always in holy orders, or if so, "not allowed by the Ordinary." (See p. 56.)

(9.) That the rubrics of the Prayer-book of 1662 were not uniformly observed, and that sins of omission and commission still prevailed, that the surplice, *e.g.*, was not always worn at the reading of divine service, or even in administering the sacraments.

(10.) That in some parishes there was not one sermon, or even a homily, on Sunday.

(11.) That there was much negligence as to catechising, preparing candidates for confirmation, visiting the sick, and baptizing, infants being baptized without sponsors, or their parents admitted, contrary to the canons, to that office.

(12.) That the publication of banns was neglected, and that marriages were celebrated in private houses, and outside the canonical limits of time, which were from eight to twelve in the morning.

(13.) That adultery, fornication, incest, drunkenness, swearing, blasphemy, railing, unclean and filthy talking, sowing sedition or faction among neighbours were common offences.

(14.) That marriages were celebrated within the prohibited degrees, and that some who were lawfully married and not separated or divorced by course of law, did not live together.

(15.) That some parishioners refused to pay Easter offerings and church-rates.

(16.) That new pews were erected without leave from the

Ordinary, and that strife and contention about seats and pews were common evils.[1]

(17.) That men kept school, practised physic or chirurgery, and that women exercised the office of a midwife, without license from the Ordinary.

All these things must have grieved the soul of one who entered on his office with an ideal standard of completeness, and sought to bring his diocese nearer to that standard than he found it. It remains for us to see what steps Ken took personally to attain that end.

If I mistake not, our cathedral chronicles show some traces of the revival of church discipline under Ken's influence. They record in 1686 that Elizabeth L., having borne a bastard child, was sentenced by the Chapter to do public penance in the Cathedral.[2] I do not find any like entry, since the Reformation, before Ken's time or after it.

Of his direct action in the work of instruction we have an account, not so full as might be wished, in the short life by his great-nephew and executor, William Hawkins, prefixed to his sermons :—

"He had a very happy way of mixing his spiritual with his corporal alms. When any poor person begged of him, he would examine whether he could say the Lord's Prayer or the Creed, and he found so much deplorable ignorance among the grown poor people that he feared little good was to be done upon them; but he said he would try whether he could not lay a foundation to make the next generation better. And this put him upon setting up many schools in all the great towns of his diocese for poor children to be taught to read and say their catechism . . . . and the ministers of the parishes were by him furnished with a stock of necessary books for the use of children."

I assume, in the absence of evidence to the contrary, that these schools, like the charity schools which were about the

---

[1] Our records at Wells present a striking illustration of the evil. A woman was summoned before the Dean and Chapter for chiding and brawling with another woman as to her right to a seat in the Cathedral, " striking her in the mouth and making it bleed, during divine service" (Hist. MSS. Comm. Report, p. 252). This, however, was in 1626.

[2] *Chapter Acts*, 1686. I suppress the name, as descendants of the family are still to be found in Wells.

same time founded in many parts of London,[1] were for the free
education of the poor, and that they were dependent on endowments or voluntary contributions for their support.   Hawkins
adds further that "in the summer time" (travelling in Somerset was not easy in winter) "he went often to some great parish,
where he would preach twice, confirm, and catechise."   The
great preacher, who drew crowds of the noble and wealthy to
Whitehall or St. Martin's, found, as others have found before
and after him, a greater attraction in the work of preaching the
gospel to the poor.   *Pasce agnos meos* was still his rule of life.

What one may call the socialist element of Christianity, the
Christ-like sympathy with those who are oppressed, and who,
while on the side of their oppressors there was power, found
no comforter, was, as in others in whom we recognise alike
the primitive and the mediæval type of Catholic sanctity,
strongly developed, as might be expected, in Ken's character.

"He often deplored the condition of the poor at Wells (who were
very numerous), and, as he was charitably disposed, so he was very
earnest in contriving proper expedients of relief; and thought no
design could better answer all the ends of charity than the setting
up a workhouse in that place.   But judging it not practicable without the advice, or, at least, the assistance of the gentlemen, he
therefore often met and consulted with them, but not finding any
suitable encouragement, he was forced to desist.   In this he had a
double view, to rescue the idle from vicious practice and conversa-

[1] The so-called Charity Schools of London are said to have originated in the
foundation of a school by Tenison, then rector of St. Martin's-in-the-Fields, to
counteract the influence of a Roman Catholic School which had been opened by
the Jesuits in the Savoy, under James II., under the title of the Blue Coat
School, in St. Margaret's, Westminster.   The work was extended, towards the
end of William III.'s reign, and under Anne; Ken's friends, Lord Weymouth
and Robert Nelson, being most active in the cause.   In 1712, there were 117
such schools in London, and the children educated in them had an anniversary
meeting at St. Paul's (discontinued in 1878).   In other parts of England and
Wales 500 schools had been established.   They were founded, it need scarcely
be said, on strictly Church principles.   (Secretan, *Life of Nelson*, pp. 118, 119.)
I have not succeeded in tracing any of the village libraries which Ken is said to
have started.   It would be interesting to learn what books he was specially
anxious that his people should read, and I shall welcome any information on
the subject.   He left, as has been said (p. 93), his French, Italian, and Spanish
books to the Library at Bath, presumably, as the books were placed there by
Lord Weymouth, to that in the Abbey Church.   Readers will recollect Dr. Bray's
efforts to found parochial libraries in all important towns.

tion, and the industrious from the oppression of the tradesmen
who, to use his own expression 'did grind the face of the poor
growing rich by their labour, and making them a very scanty
allowance for their work.'" [1]

The *animus* indicated by this extract is plain enough.   To us
the projected remedy of "setting up a workhouse" may at first
be somewhat hard to understand.   At that time, however, the
term had not acquired the meaning with which we are now
familiar.   It was used by the philanthropists of the period for
industrial institutions, to be maintained by voluntary contributions, where the unemployed were to get a fair day's wages
for a fair day's work, and where the regulations of the place
were to guard against drunkenness and vice.   It was, that is, an
attempt, like the *Monts de piété* of France and Italy, like Louis
Blanc's *Ateliers Nationaux*, to deal with the labour market on
other principles than those of supply and demand.   Defoe,
with his vigorous, incisive common-sense, attacked it as likely
to cause more evils than it cured, and the attempt proved
abortive.[2]   It was left for another generation to apply the
principles of what Frederick Maurice in 1848 rightly called
"Christian Socialism," under the wiser and more practicable
form of co-operation, and even that, as we know, has been
only a partially successful experiment.

Ken's sympathy with the poor was, however, shown in
another way, in which he reproduced, as a bishop, what had
entered, as we have seen, into George Herbert's ideal of a
"country parson:"—

"When he was at home on Sundays, he would have twelve poor
men or women to dine with him in his hall, always endeavouring
while he fed their bodies, to comfort their spirits by some cheerful
discourse, generally mixt with some useful instruction.   And when
they had dined, the remainder was divided among them to carry
home to their families." [3]

Dinner parties of that kind were, we may well believe, something new in the experience of the good people of Wells.
Peter Mews had "entertained the gentry" with a liberal hos-

[1] Hawkins, p. 9.

[2] *Giving Alms no Charity*, 1704 ; *Works* (ed. 1869), pp. 539—547.

[3] Hawkins, p. 8.

pitality, but to act on the letter of the words of the Master whom Christians own, and to invite " the poor, the lame, the halt, the maimed," who could render no recompense but that which should be given in the resurrection of the just, was at least unconventional. It may have seemed to many, like Ken's celibacy, suspicious and unprotestant. Would it not have been safer and better to do as other bishops of the time did, to invite Dives and leave Lazarus at the gate? At any rate, it would be felt by many that this and Ken's celibacy went together. A married bishop of that age with a family might do much that was good, kindly, generous. He would hardly have spent his Sundays in such a way as this.[1]

Anyhow, the picture remains to live in our memories as a thing that has actually been seen, once at least, in the history of the English Church. We can picture the good Bishop acting as a courteous host to these his guests, bringing to bear all that he had learnt of culture and refinement from his intercourse with the noblest in the land, all the meekness and lowliness which had come to him from a higher source, to make the meal a pleasant one. Each Sunday probably brought with it a different set of guests. Each carried away with him, besides the " fragments that remained," the memory of some kindly word, of some warm hand-grasp which raised him in his self-respect. One wonders whether they felt the change when Kidder took Ken's place.

And through all this, we must remember, there was probably the same ascetic life as we have seen in Ken's earlier years at Winchester, the one meal a day, after Morley's example, the one slumber at night, the Midnight Hymn, as well as those for Morning and Evening, in constant use, sung when he woke and rose in the small hours of the night. He was probably a total abstainer (he identifies the vine in his *Hymnotheo* with the forbidden fruit which " brought death into the world and all our woe "), and his only luxury was the coffee which he may have learnt to take at Oxford, and which appears, from the fact that

---

[1] In this, as I have noted in p. 22, Ken was following in George Herbert's footsteps. Frampton is reported to have done the same after his deprivation in his parish of Standish. [Many Puritans gave a Sunday meal to worshippers from a distance. (See Clark's *Lives of Dod and others.*—J. K.)]

his silver coffee-pot was the only article of plate he left behind
him, to have been his favourite beverage till the end (ii. p. 208).

I insert here some hitherto unpublished letters which bear
on Ken's work during this period of his life.

LETTER XIII.

To Viscount Weymouth.

"All Glory be to God.

"My very good Lord,

"I am extreamely sorry yᵗ Mr. King should once more goe away
from hence, without yᵉ dispatch of his affaire, but it is not in my
power at present to helpe him. Your Lordshippe's favourable
acceptance of so inconsiderable a testimony of my respect as I was
able to send, encourages me to send two more, one for yᵉ young
gentleman, and yᵉ other for yᵉ young Lady, wᶜʰ I now understand
are with you, and are the Pledges of God's favour with wᶜʰ He has
been pleased to bless you. I return your Lordshippe all due acknowledgements for your most obliging Invitation, but it goes
against me to wait on my Lord Weymouth in my passage onely. I
reserve the Satisfaction for a journey on purpose, and when I am
not Streightened in time. God of His Infinite Goodnesse keep
yourselfe and your good Lady and your family in His Reverentiall
Love.

"My Good Lord,

"Your Lordshippe's most affectionate humble Servant,

"THO. BATH & WELLS.

"*Oct.* 21*st*, 1685."

[Mr. King had been nominated by Lord Weymouth to the living of Mers-
tham Bigott, in Ken's diocese. There had apparently been some unavoidable
delay in his institution, owing to some one, probably an "aggrieved parishioner,"
having entered a *caveat* in the Bishop's Court. (See Letter XIV.) The "young
gentleman" is probably Henry Thynne, Lord Weymouth's son, born February 8,
1675, who married Grace, daughter of Sir George Strode, of Leweston, and
died before his father; the "young lady," his daughter, Frances, who afterwards married Sir Robert Worsley. The gifts sent to them are obviously two
more copies of the *Practice of Divine Love*, with which their father seems to have
been pleased. We note that Ken is already welcome at Longleat as an honoured
guest. The letter gives no date of place, but was probably written at Wells,
where he had been ministering to the five hundred prisoners who were waiting
for their trial at the Bloody Assize, and, as we have seen, to John Hickes at

Glastonbury, on October 6. Jeffreys' "bloody assize" in that city ended September 20th. His ministrations included, as we shall see (ii. p. 99), the relief of bodily necessities as well as spiritual comfort and counsel.]

LETTER XIV.

To Viscount Weymouth.

"All Glory be to God.

"My very good Lord,

"Your Lordshippe had great reason to blame ye custome of ye Court here, as it was represented to you, and for my owne part, though such Courts are called ye Bishoppe's Courts, yett your Lordshippe judges rightly, y^t we have little to do in them, and we often see things in them y^t we may deplore, but cannot remedy. Upon enquiry I find y^t ye trouble wch Mr. Furze has created, was onely to get mony, y^t he might be bought off; and therefore, upon ye reading of your Letter, I resolved to give Mr. King Institution, wch having now done, I hope his adversary will forbeare to molest him. I doe withal returne your Lordshippe many thanks, for bringing such a person into my Diocesse. What little observation I have hitherto been able to make convinces me y^t it is a Benefaction to the Country, to send an able and a good man among them.

"God of His Infinite Goodnesse, multiply His blessings on yourselfe and Family.

"My Good Lord,

"Your Lordshippe's very humble and affectionate Servant,

"THO. BATH & WELLS.

"*Oct.* 28, 1685."

[The difficulties connected with Mr. King's institution have apparently been surmounted. Furze seems to have entered a *caveat* which led to proceedings in the Court of the Chancellor of the Diocese, proceedings with which the Bishop had little or nothing to do, and with which he could not personally interfere. Ken now felt himself, after due inquiry, free to disregard the threats which originated in nothing better than a desire to extort black-mail of some kind. The Registry of the Diocese shows that he followed Ken in not taking the oath, and was deprived in 1691.]

LETTER XV.

To Viscount Weymouth.

"All Glory be to God.

"My very good Lord,

"I can now, God's holy name be prais'd, give your Lordshippe a better account of the Good Lady than I did in my last. She is now in all appearance past danger, and sleepes well, and eats an egge, and sits up for two or three houres, and has taken Steele (*word omitted*) a weeke wch agrees very well with her, so that she recovers dayly, and it is visible in her lookes. She has a great mind for Asparagus, and there is none in all ye Country. If your Lordshippe has any, this messenger will wait on you tomorrow, and they will be a most acceptable present; and the Physicians doe very gladly indulge her y^t sort of Diett. She presents her humble service to yourselfe and to my Lady, with abundant acknowledgements of your great concerne for her. I cannot yett be permitted to leave Her; onely I made an excursion to Wells for two nights, and I am very glad Mr. King came not thither.

"God of His infinite goodnesse multiply His blessings on yourselfe, on my Lady, and on your family.

"My Good Lord,

"Your Lordshippe's most humble & affect. Servant,

"THO. BATH & WELLS."

[The letter is undated, but the mention of Mr. King and of asparagus points to the early spring of 1686. I cannot identify the "good lady" on whose behalf Ken writes. Apparently she was not resident at Wells. I conjecture that she may have been one of Ken's Winchester friends or relations, or, possibly, one of the Misses Kemeys of Naish. The letter has, in any case, the interest of showing that Ken's sympathy with sufferers extended even to the capricious variations of their appetite. He who would ask nothing for himself would write to a friend in high position for asparagus for a sick woman. The cultivation of asparagus was common enough in Ken's time, but he was probably asking for it before the usual season, and the forcing houses at Longleat might have been able to supply what was wanting in the garden of the Palace at Wells.]

LETTER XVI.

To ——.

"All Glory be to God.

"SIR,

"Since my last y^r Tenant has been here, & this weeke my Steward to comply with him went to Wintescombe (Winscombe?) to meet him, and when things are truely stated to you, you will find so little difference between your officer's accounts & mine, that you will then be convinced that I have great reason to adhere to my first proposal, *as I doe, resolving not to recede from it.* I must needs let you know that y^r Officer had a great advantage of my Steward when they mett, for he could summon what Tenant he pleased to make good his surveigh, whereas my Steward could call none to justify mine, because he would not expose them to yᵉ displeasure of their imediate Landlord, and yett, though wee lay under that disadvantage, yʳ own valuation serves very much to confirm ours.   Let me then begg of you to present my due respects to yʳ Co-exectᵐ and to acquaint them with my finall answer, which is, *That things standing as they doe,* I expect what I first proposed. Some accidents may make me heighten my demands, but I am satisfyed that there can be no just reason to lessen them. If you are pleased to accept of my Conditions, my Steward shall wait on you at London. If not, I shall acquiesce ; for the future onely, if we doe agree, I forewarne you of one difficulty, wᶜʰ I am told you may meet with, that it will be a troublesome thing to get all the Tenants to surrender, partly because they would have the lease run out that they might hold of me ; partly, because upon surrendering they have been ill used.

"The blessing of God rest upon you & yʳ family.

"Good Sir,

"Your affectionate faithfull Servant,

"THO. BATH & WELLS.

" *October 2nd,* 1686."

[There is no address to the letter. It refers apparently to some negotiations about the renewal of a lease. It is, I think, the only letter extant which brings out Ken's character as a man of business. It will be seen that, when occasion called for it, he could be at once clear-sighted in his proposals, and sufficiently firm in adhering to them. The "acquiescence" probably means that he would take no action, but let the lease run out. The following passage in Hearne's *Diaries* (ch. xciv. 132, Bodleian Library) is, I think, worth inserting as bringing out the same element in Ken's character :—" I have heard the impropriation there (Glastonbury) is in the Bishopric of Bath and Wells, and the Church served by a Curate or Vicar at a very small allowance, that Bishop Ken resolved to increase it upon renewing with his tenant, but they could not agree, and the tenant tempted him often with the fine, before his deprivation, to no purpose. His successor, Kidder, took it, without any further provision for the Church."]

NOTE TO CHAPTER XV.

KEN AND NICOLAS PAVILLON.

I have suggested (p. 110 *n.*) the probability of Ken's having come, during his travels in 1675, within range of the reputation and influence of the good Bishop of Alet who bore this name. The study of the *Statuts Synodaux* of that diocese, published in that very year, which I find among the books left by Ken to the library at Bath Abbey, leads me to the conclusion that his administration of his own diocese was largely modelled after the pattern of what he had thus seen. Whether we regard him as the author of *Ichabod* or not,—and I have, I believe, shown that there is a balance of probability in favour of that authorship,—we must, at any rate, think of him as starting on his travels with a keen sense of the shortcoming of the pastoral work of the English Church, such as he had seen and known it. He would naturally ask himself whether he could find things better ordered elsewhere. As a whole, he would seem to have sympathised more with the Protestants than with the Roman Catholics of France. But at Alet he would find one who would seem to him, as he did to others, to revive the simplicity and earnestness of the days of the Apostles, and to combine it with an organizing power of which the dioceses of England, at that time, presented few examples. He would admire the rules by which Pavillon sought to check non-residence (p. 9), secular dress (p. 14), or secular amusements (p. 20); the systematic provision for catechising all classes down to the poorest and most ignorant (pp. 37, 39); the stress laid on teaching children and those who could not read, short forms of prayer and praise, for morning and evening, and on other occasions during the day (pp. 159—162), and on a brief epitome of Christian doctrine as a basis for catechising, after due preparation (p. 155); the establishment of schools for both boys and girls under masters and mistresses appointed by the bishop (pp. 171—176); the conferences, such as we should call ruri-decanal, held once a month in each of the seven districts into which the diocese was divided, discussing pastoral questions, cases of conscience, and the like (pp. 30—35); the discipline enforced on negligent or scandalous priests (pp. 13—20); the standard of a devout daily life, beginning at 4 A.M. winter and summer, each hour of the day having its appointed work, of worship, or meditation, or study, or visiting the sick, or teaching, or gardening, all done as in the presence of God and from the motive of the love of God (pp. 163—167); all this which we find in the *Statuts*, we find also in Ken's life and action, and as far as he had the power to enforce them, in his directions to his clergy. The case for derivation, as distinct from that of a natural resemblance between two men working on the same lines, is strengthened by the fact that Pavillon (pp. 23, 166) more than once recommends special books to his clergy, and that among these the writings of Louis of Granada, and of the author of the *Imitatio Christi*, occupy a high place. I find both these among Ken's books. I imagine that not many Anglican divines of the time were conversant with the former.[1]

A friend (C. J. P.) suggests that the *Devout Life* of S. Francis de Sales, or the *Recollections* of him published by his disciple and friend the Bishop of Bellay, may also have had much influence on Ken's character, and says with truth that the *Practice of Divine Love* is throughout permeated with the spirit of the Bishop whose favourite maxim was *Mourir ou Aimer*. I admit the resemblance. I think it certain that there was influence, but I do not find in this case the marks of derivation which seem to me so strong and clear in the case of Pavillon. De Sales's *Introduction* is, however, among Ken's books at Wells.

---

[1] For a fuller account of Pavillon see the *Life, by a Layman*, Oxford (1869), and the *Tour to Alet*, in Mrs. Schimmelpenninck's *Memoirs of Port Royal*. The work of the "Regents" of Alet, devout women who did the work of Sisters of Charity, but not under the obligation of vows, reminds one strongly of the "Protestant nunnery" of Ken's friends, the Misses Kemeys of Naish Court. (See chap. xxiv.)

The catalogue of Ken's books at Bath Abbey gives the following works by Louis de Granada : (1) *Doctrina Christiana*, 1657 ; (2) *Primera Parte de la Introduccion del Symbolo de la Fe*, 1672. The writer was born in 1504 at Granada, and died at Lisbon in 1582. At the age of twenty-four he entered the Dominican Monastery of Scala Cœli, near Granada, and was much influenced by the writings of Pedro d' Alcantara, the spiritual master of St. Theresa, born 1515, died 1582, canonised 1622. Following in his steps, he wrote a *Treatise on Prayer and Meditation* (1544), and a *Guide of Sinners* in 1556. The latter work was placed in the *Index* by the Inquisition, the ban being, however, removed in 1570. The former work took its place with Boethius and Augustine among Charles V.'s favourite books in his retreat at Yuste. At the request of St. Charles Borromeo, Gregory XIII. congratulated him on his *Larger Catechism* (1582). He takes his place among the noblest, and yet safest, of the Spanish mystics. Among other books of like character, I note the *Vida e Obras* (vol. i. 1618) of Juan de Avila (born 1500, died 1569), also one of St. Theresa's guides, and those of Juan de la Cruz (born 1542, died 1591, canonised 1674), who also forms one of the same group. It is noticeable that many of the works of all these writers were at first placed in the *Index*. For a fuller account of the School to which they all belonged, see Rousselot, *Mystiques Espagnols*, 1869. Ken's books also include the *Lettres Chrétiennes* of St. Cyran, and Pascal's *Lettres Provinciales*.

CHAPTER XVI.

"'Not so,' He said: 'hush thee, and seek,
    With thoughts in prayer and watchful eyes,
    My seasons sent for thee to speak,
    And use them as they rise.'"

J. H. Newman.

WE are drawing near the scene in which the two men who, strongly contrasted with each other, played their part in the drama of life in more or less close association, were brought face to face in what was for each the great crisis of his life. It will help us to understand that crisis, and to enter more fully into the life and character of each, if we can arrive at any definite impression as to the relations in which Ken and James stood to each other, before there was as yet any cause of conflict between them; and this will accordingly be the chief subject of the present chapter.

I enter on the inquiry with some reluctance, but with a strong feeling of its importance. I am compelled to note as defective the treatment which it has received at the hands of Ken's previous biographers, and of most, if not all, popular historians. They have written as if Ken looked on James as Macaulay and Hume have taught us to look on him, as a contemptible mixture of profligate and bigot, showing perhaps a little honesty and capacity for business in its details, but narrow-minded, vindictive, and superstitious, delighting in cruelty for its own sake,[1] perhaps the least loveable character

---

[1] Macaulay, *e.g.* (following Burnet, *O. T.*, B. ii., 1684), represents him as gloating over the sufferings of the Covenanters in Scotland, when they were subjected to the "boot"—a statement for which the authority is, to say the

in the long list of English sovereigns. They look on Ken's
adherence to his cause as simply an instance of his devotion to
the principle of divine hereditary right, and of faithfulness to
his oaths of allegiance, uninfluenced by any personal attachment.

I have been led to a conclusion so different from this that I
will state it clearly at the outset, and then submit to the judgment
of my readers the evidence on which it rests. To me it seems
that no explanation of Ken's conduct is adequate which does
not include the element of a strong personal attachment between
the two men, sincere and loyal, in its way, on the part of James,
and on Ken's part, in proportion to the greater fervour and
spirituality of his character, deepening into an affectionate
interest, as of one who, being a lover of souls, cared for that of
his friend, as one who was worthy of his love, with a deeper
feeling than the loyal obedience of a subject. For him, I cannot doubt, the intercessions for the King, which he used himself
and urged on others to use daily, were something more than
"State Prayers." During the period of his Non-juring life he
inserted such prayers in his *Manual for Winchester Scholars*, not
merely on principle as a protest against William's usurpation,
but because these were the prayers that came from his own lips
and heart. If I were to illustrate my meaning by analogies
more or less applicable, I should say that, *mutatis mutandis*, Ken
felt towards James as Wilberforce felt towards Pitt, and Lord
Shaftesbury towards Palmerston.[1] All this is, of course, very
different from the tone and temper of the Whig historian, sitting
on his seat of judgment, like Dante's Minos, and sentencing
the men and women who came before him, according to their

least, in the highest degree doubtful. (See Strickland, *Queens*, ix. p. 125.)
Burnet himself admits that James, on his first visit (1680—81), adopted a far
gentler policy than Lauderdale, and was accordingly popular.—*O. T.*, B. ii., 1682.

[1] I note, though I cannot follow up the inquiry, that the same strong tie of
personal affection is also found in the relations between James and William Penn.
It is impossible to read the letters of the latter without seeing in them the tone of
a real friendship. There must, I take it, have been something loveable in a man
who won the regard of two men who, like Ken and Penn, standing at opposite
poles of religious thought, had yet this in common, that each followed conscience
and sought after holiness. I refer to the letters in Janney's *Life of Penn* (Philadelphia), for my knowledge of which I am indebted to the Right Hon. John
Bright. Mrs. Penn was a frequent visitor, after James's exile, at St. Germain's.

merits, to the pits of Malebolge, in which, if not in the lower depths of Antenóra or Caïna, James is to find his place. I submit that the view which I have taken is more in accordance with the evidence, more in harmony with all we know of the temper and character of a man like Ken, and I await the verdict of my readers with equanimity.

Let it be remembered, then, on James's side, that he had known something of Ken almost ever since the Restoration, through his intimacy with Morley. He had learnt to think of him and Frampton, Bishop of Gloucester, as the best preachers among the English clergy.[1] Ken's ascetic purity of character, his freedom from all worldly aims, would impress itself on the King's mind as being after the pattern which, both before and after his conversion to Rome, he had been taught to reverence.[2] He had not lost the capacity, which even Charles, with his more careless cynicism, retained, of admiring in others the virtues in which his own life was conspicuously wanting. He could scarcely fail to have had a share in Ken's appointment as chaplain to his daughter at the Hague, and in the expedition to Tangier. In spite of the difference in their creeds he must have listened, without being offended, to Ken's earnest pleadings with his dying brother, and recognised that they had, at least, prepared the way for what, from his point of view, were Huddleston's more availing ministrations. His choice of Ken, as one of those who were to attend the wretched Monmouth at his execution, may well be traced to his sense of his fitness for the work of a confessor. When, at his interview with the Seven Bishops, he turned round and said that he "did not expect such usage from the Church of England, especially from some of the petitioners," we can scarcely doubt that he spoke from the bitterness of his heart, as feeling that he was thwarted by one who had been his familiar friend.

And putting ourselves, as far as is possible, in Ken's position,

---

[1] A. à Wood, in Bowles, ii., 69 ; *Life of Frampton*, Evans, p. 45.

[2] James, in his letter to his daughter Mary, gives the greater holiness which he found in the Church of Rome, as the chief ground of his conversion. Another influence was that of a nun in a monastery of Flanders who advised him " to pray every day that if he was not in a right way, God would set him right, which did make a great impression on him."—Burnet, *O. T.*, ii., 1662.

we must remember that, over and above the feeling of gratitude
for the confidence thus shown in him, there were elements in
James's character on which he could scarcely fail to look with
interest and hope. He must have recognised the conscientious-
ness which led him, at the risk of exclusion from the throne,
the certainty of loss of office, to avow the change in his convictions, instead of wearing, as Charles did, the mask of Protestantism even to the end. He would seem to Ken to stand far
above the French King, who was the world's hero, and who had
changed his creed because "Paris was well worth a mass." And
besides this proof of his sincerity there were even then, struggling
through the habitual sensuality of his life, the germs of that
ascetic devotion which was afterwards developed in the seclu-
sion of St. Germain's and of La Trappe. Burnet found him,
in 1675, reading Nieremberg *On the Difference of Things
Temporal and Things Eternal,*[1] and ready to enter into conversation on topics which that work suggested as to the vanity
of the world and its pleasures. Charles's sneer at his brother's
choice of unbeautiful mistresses as an act of penance commanded by his confessor, would have obviously had little
point, had it not been well known that James was in the habit
of self-inflicted chastisement, even to the discipline of the
scourge. At the time, too, of which I now speak, 1685—6, he
had made a spasmodic effort after a greater purity of life, had
condemned the prevailing license of his courtiers, and had
emancipated himself (alas! only for a time) from his thraldom
to Catherine Sedley, afterwards Countess of Dorchester (was
the title offered by way of *solatium ?*), the last of the "unbeautiful." Ken's sympathies at such a time would rather
be with Petre and James's confessor, who had urged this
reform of manners, than with Rochester, who, in spite of his
own somewhat effusive religiousness, sought to keep James in
constitutional courses through the influence of a mistress.[2]

[1] Burnet, *O. T.,* B. iii., 1675. It is a curious coincidence that Ken probably
derived his story of "The Monk and the Bird" (ii. p. 249), which has, after passing through many hands, been popularised by Longfellow, from this very work
of Nieremberg. We ask, "Did James recommend the work to Ken, or Ken to
James?" We have, at any rate, a proof of sympathy. The volume is found in
the Ken Library at Longleat.

[2] Macaulay, ch. vi. ; Reresby, p. 356.

Were I free to assume, as I am inclined to do (I shall give reasons for my judgment at a later stage), the genuineness of two works which most of Ken's biographers reject as apocryphal, I should have a comparatively easy task. It is impossible to mistake the tone of personal affection which breathes, from first to last, through the *Royal Sufferer.* Differences of creed have not impaired the writer's power of sympathy in spiritual things with the sufferer to whom he writes. He enters on a task which was nothing less than that of supplying the exiled king with an *Icon Basilike,* like that which had endeared the memory of Charles I. to so many thousands of his subjects, and invested him in their eyes with the character of a saint and martyr.[1]   He apologises for his acts of misgovernment, such as the cruelties of the Bloody Assize and his interference in the Magdalen College election, on the ground that he was misguided by his counsellors. He hopes that he may be guided through the changes and chances of life to a crown of "immarcescible glory." Nor is the evidence of the *Letter to Archbishop Tenison* less conclusive.   The point on which the writer of that letter lays most stress, in indicting that prelate for his want of faithfulness in his ministrations at Mary's deathbed, is that he had not exhorted her to repentance for her needlessly undutiful conduct to her father, for her treatment of those who were loyally attached to her, and whom she had treated as her enemies simply because they were her father's friends.   Had Ken been at her deathbed, he would have pleaded for that father's claim on his daughter's affection, with the warmth of personal attachment.   Even on the assumption of the spuriousness of the works which I have named, it remains, as a fact not without weight, that this was what the authors of the apocryphal publications thought they could safely present to the public, as being what Ken was likely to have thought and written.[2]

I pass to less controverted indications of Ken's feeling towards James in the language of devoted and confiding loyalty which breathes through the address from the Bishop

---

[1] I may note, in passing, the dedication of churches at Plymouth and Tunbridge Wells to St. Charles the Martyr. There are, I believe, four others.

[2] See Notes to chaps. xxi. and xxii.

and clergy of his diocese, quoted in chap. xiii., and which pervaded the Coronation sermon preached by his dearest friend and old school-fellow Francis Turner. The same warm regard is traceable in the portrait of Daniel, more or less unconsciously a self-portraiture, in the memorable Lent sermon preached at Whitehall in 1685. "He did greatly love, and therefore he was greatly beloved; that was all the court cunning, all the philtre that Daniel had." "None can serve the prince well, but he does serve the people too, and Daniel served his prince and not himself." "You have seen how love was reciprocal, how Daniel greatly loved the king and the people; and this was the secret he had, which naturally attracted so universal a love." "Learn from Daniel a universal obligingness and benignity, an awful love to your prince, a constant fidelity, an undaunted courage, an unwearied zeal in serving him." Even the stress which Ken lays on the higher obligations of conscience, as illustrated in Daniel's refusal to obey the decree of Darius, is best understood when we see in it a forecast of the choice, which even then he felt he might before long have to make, between his personal affection for the king and his duty to his God.[1]

And as yet James had not laid aside the moderation that might deceive more discerning eyes than Ken's. When Ken wrote to him, in conjunction with Sir Thomas Cutler, then in command at Wells, to remonstrate against the cruelty of Feversham and his officers, and pleaded for the extension of the royal mercy to them, their request was granted without any signs of reluctance. The King thanked Sir Thomas for his intercession, expressed how agreeable it was to him, and wished that the like humanity had engaged others to act in the same way.[2] A month or two later Ken met James at Winchester, where he had probably waited to renew his intercession for the

---

[1] The sermon presents an interesting parallelism with St. Francis de Sales. "No holy person can love God to that degree, without passionately desiring to love Him more and more" (Round, p. 172). "If you want to love God, go on loving Him more and more; never look back, press forward continually." (Camus's *Spirit of St. Francis,* i.) The fact that Ken had De Sales' *Guide to a Devout Life* in his library makes it probable that this was more than a coincidence of thought. (See p. 206 for a fuller account of the sermon.)

[2] *Reflections upon Dr. Burnet's Posthumous History,* p. 100; Routh, p. 73.

rebels,[1] while Jeffreys was opening his "campaign," and Evelyn records a conversation on September 16, 1685 :—

"*Sept.* 16. The next morning setting out early, we arriv'd soon enough at Winchester to waite on the King, who was lodg'd at the Dean's (Dr. Meggot). I found very few with him besides my Lords Feversham, Arran, Newport, and the Bishop of Bath and Wells. His Majesty was discoursing with the Bishop concerning miracles, and what strange things the Saludadors would do in Spaine, as by creeping into heated ovens without hurt, and that they had a black crosse in the roofe of their mouthes, but yet were commonly notorious and profane wretches ; upon which his Majesty further said, that he was so extreamly difficult of miracles, for feare of being impos'd upon, that if he should chance to see one himselfe, without some other witness, he should apprehend it a delusion of his senses. Then they spake of the boy who was pretended to have a wanting leg restor'd him, so confidently asserted by Fr. de Sta. Clara and others. To all which the Bishop added a greate miracle happening in Westminster[2] to his certaine knowledge, of a poor miserably sick and decrepit child (as I remember, long kept unbaptiz'd), who immediately on his baptism recover'd ; as also of the salutary effect of K. Charles his Majesty's father's blood, in healing one that was blind.

" There was something said of the second sight happening to some persons, especially Scotch ; upon which his Majesty, and I think Lord Arran, told us that Mons. ——————, a French nobleman, lately here in England, seeing the late Duke of Monmouth come into the play-house at London, suddenly cried out to somebody sitting in the same box, *Voilà Monsieur, comme il entre sans tête.* Afterwards his Majesty spoke of some reliques that had effected strange cures, particularly a piece of our Bl. Saviour's Crosse, and healed a gentleman's rotten nose by onely touching ; and speaking of the golden crosse and chaine taken out of the coffin of St. Edward the Confessor at Westminster, by one of the singing men, who, as the scaffolds were taking down after his Majesty's coronation, espying a hole in the tomb, and something glisten, put his hand in and brought it to the Deane, and he to the King ; his Majesty began to put the Bishop in mind how earnestly the late King (his brother) called upon him, during his agonie, to take out what he had in his pocket. I had thought, said the King, it had been for some keys, which might lead to some cabinet that his Majesty would have me

---

[1] See Letter x. p. 228.

[2] Probably a mistake of Evelyn's for Winchester (see p. 91).

secure; but, says he, you well remember that I found nothing in any of his pockets but a crosse of gold, and a few insignificant papers; and thereupon he shew'd us the crosse, and was pleas'd to put it into my hand. It was of gold, about three inches long, having on one side a crucifix enamell'd and emboss'd, the rest was grav'd and garnish'd with goldsmiths' work, and two pretty broad table amethists (as I conceived), and at the bottom a pendant pearle; within was inchas'd a little fragment, as was thought, of the true Crosse, and a Latine inscription in gold and Roman letters. More company coming in, this discourse ended. I may not forget a resolution which his Majesty made, and had a little before enter'd upon it at the Council Board at Windsor or White-hall, that the Negroes in the Plantations should all be baptiz'd, exceedingly declaiming against that impiety of their masters prohibiting it, out of a mistaken opinion that they would be *ipso facto* free; but his Majesty persists in his resolution to have them christen'd, which piety the Bishop blessed him for."

It will be admitted that the tone on both sides in these conversations is that of men who respected and confided in each other, who felt that they had much in common in their religious convictions, and as to the rest, might well be content to differ. Ken's story of the cure, which seemed to him to have a quasi-miraculous character, could scarcely fail to impress itself on a man like James. The King's zeal for the baptism of the negroes in our plantations, his feeling that for them also Christ had died, and that for them was the kingdom of heaven, would touch the deepest chords in the heart of the Bishop.

Before long, however, the nation gazed, with wonder and alarm, on a more rapid development of James's plans. Romish controversialists circulated their pamphlets broadcast in coffee-houses and other places of resort, and entered into discussions with passengers in stage-coaches to Windsor and elsewhere. The Pope's Nuncio, Count Ferdinand d'Adda, who had arrived in London in November, 1685, after being consecrated in James's Chapel as Archbishop of Amasia, was received in state at Windsor on July 3rd, 1687.[1] In Ireland the Romish bishops

---

[1] Two bishops, Crewe and Cartwright, were subservient enough to attend the ceremonial. The Duke of Somerset was dismissed from his posts at court because he refused to attend on the occasion. Amasia was in Bithynia, a see *in partibus.*

were authorised to hold a convention on May 15th, 1686. The Irish judges were dispensed from taking the oath of supremacy. Nineteen Romanists were sworn in Privy Councillors; in Ireland the corporations were filled with them. Three hundred Protestant officers and five thousand soldiers were dismissed from their regiments, and their places were filled up by Papists. Romish priests were appointed military chaplains. The comparatively cautious policy of Lord Clarendon (brother of the Earl of Rochester) as Viceroy was overridden by the more 'thorough' action of the Earl of Tyrconnel, who at last formally superseded him. In Scotland (March 2nd, 1686) the King issued his first declaration of indulgence in favour of his Romish subjects, but did not extend it to the Presbyterians. A collusive trial, in the case of Sir Edward Hales, who, being a Roman Catholic, had been appointed Lieutenant of the Tower, had, in the hands of subservient judges, established the King's dispensing power. Under the King's first Declaration of Indulgence in 1687 many thousand Papists and twelve thousand Quakers had been released from prison. In England a revived Court of Ecclesiastical Commission, with vague, undefined powers in dealing with offences, was created (July 14th, 1686) by royal edict, in defiance of an Act of Parliament. Jeffreys was its leading mind. Sancroft had been placed on it, but declined to act, pleading the infirmities of age, and was consequently informed that the King no longer desired his attendance at Court. Crewe, Bishop of Durham, and Sprat of Rochester, however, consented to take the place assigned to them. The other members were Sunderland, Rochester, and Herbert, Chief Justice of the Common Pleas.[1] Compton was brought before the Court, in August, 1686, for not having suspended Sharp, Dean of Norwich, and rector of St. Giles-in-the-Fields, for preaching a controversial sermon in spite of the King's proclamation forbidding all controversy. The officers of the Household were sent for to the King's closet, and offered their choice between accepting his policy or dismissal. It must have been a satisfaction to Ken to find that his old friend Lord Maynard, who filled the post of Comptroller of the Household,

---

[1] The Court was not inaptly described as the College *de Propaganda Fide*, transferred from Rome to London.

stood firm under this pressure, as he had done forty years before, when impeached by Parliament for his adhesion to James's father, and, with less wavering and delay, did as Rochester had done, and resigned his office.

So matters were going on when it came to Ken's turn to preach again at Whitehall, on the fifth Sunday in Lent, 1687. The King, of course, never attended these sermons, but the Princess Anne was there, and "at least thirty of the greatest nobility," and the chapel was crowded. Ken did not publish the sermon, and all that we know of it is to be found in Evelyn's *Diary* of March 10, 1687. His text was St. John viii. 46, " Which of you convinceth me of sin ?   And if I say the truth, why do ye not believe me ?" :

"Most of the greate Officers, both in the Court and Country, Lords and others, were dismiss'd, as they would not promise his Majesty their consent to the repeal of the Test and penal Statutes against Popish Recusants. To this end most of the Parliament men were spoken to in his Majestys closset, and such as refus'd, if in any place or office of trust, civil or military, were put out of their employments. This was a time of greate trial, but hardly one of them assented, which put the Popish interest much backward. The English Cleargy everywhere preach'd boldly against their superstition and errors, and were wonderfully follow'd by the People. Not one considerable proselyte was made in all this time. The party were exceedingly put to the worst by the preaching and writing of the Protestants in many excellent treatises, evincing the doctrine and discipline of the Reform'd Religion, to the manifest disadvantage of their adversaries. To this did not a little contribute the sermon preach'd at White-hall before the Princesse of Denmark and a great croud of People, and at least 30 of the greatest Nobility, by Dr. Ken, Bishop of Bath and Wells, on 8 John 46 (the Gospel of the day) describing thro' his whole discourse the blasphemies, perfidy, wresting of Scripture, preference of tradition before it, spirit of persecution, superstition, legends and fables of the Scribes and Pharisees, so that all the auditory understood his meaning of a parallel between them and the Romish Priests, and their new Trent Religion. He exhorted his audience to adhere to the written Word, and to persevere in the Faith taught in the Church of England, whose doctrine for Catholic and soundness he preferr'd to all the Communities and Churches of Christians in the world; con-

cluding with a kind of prophecy, that whatever it suffer'd, it should
after a short trial emerge to the confusion of her adversaries, and
the glory of God."[1]

This was followed up on the following Palm Sunday by
a sermon at St. Martin's-in-the-Fields. I again quote from
Evelyn, noting only that Ken's reverence for the day led him in
this instance to eschew all controversy, and to confine himself
to the mysteries of the Passion :—

" *March* 20.—The Bishop of Bath and Wells (Dr. Ken) preach'd at
St. Martines to a crowd of people not to be express'd, nor the wonderful eloquence of this admirable preacher ; the text was 26 Matt. 36
to verse 40, describing the bitterness of our Bl. Saviour's agony, the
ardour of his love, the infinite obligations we have to imitate his
patience and resignation : the means by watching against tempta-
tious, and over ourselves, with fervent prayer to attaine it, and the
exceeding reward in the end. Upon all which he made most pa-
theticall discourses. The Communion followed, at which I was
participant. I afterwards din'd at Dr. Tenison's with the Bishop
and that young, most learned, pious and excellent preacher, Mr.
Wake."

It is the first recorded interview between the model bishop
and the model layman, but, looking to the number of their
common friends, it is probable enough that they were already
acquainted, and that they were invited by Tenison, then Rector
of St. Martin's, to meet each other for that very reason.

During these visits to London he seems to have been the
guest of his old schoolfellow, Francis Turner, at Ely House,
near Holborn, and an undated letter from the Princess Anne
to that bishop probably belongs to this period :—

---

[1] An earlier sermon had been preached by Ken on March 14th, 168¾, Evelyn's
report of which has been given in p. 242. What strikes one in the sermons of
this period is that the necessities of the time forced him against his will, and against
the usual tenor of his life, into the attitude of a controversialist, and that he did
not shrink from speaking the truth with boldness, precisely at the time when that
boldness was certain to bring him into disfavour with the prince, whom he not
only respected as a king, but also loved as a friend. He, at all events, would
not tune his voice according to the time, and be like the Proteo of his own
Edmund (see ii. p. 243).

"I hear the Bishop of Bath and Wells expounds[1] this afternoon at your Chapel, and I have a great mind to hear him; therefore I desire you would do me the favour to let some place be kept for me, where I may hear well, and be the least taken notice of: for I will bring but one body with me, and desire I may not be known. I should not have given you the trouble, but that I was afraid if I sent any body, they might have made some mistake. Pray let me know what time it begins."

The Bishop's sermons were obviously making a sensation in London, and the suspicions previously entertained as to his Protestantism probably increased the interest with which men now listened to him. On the 4th of April, 1687, the King issued his first English Declaration of Indulgence.[2] The nature of that document and its effect on the action of Ken and the other bishops will come under our notice at a later stage. Here I content myself with printing it *in extenso*, as a State paper of the first order of historical importance.[3] For the most part, English historians give little more than the briefest possible summary of it. The biographer of Ken may well think himself bound to bring before his readers the very words on which the Bishop had to form a judgment, which were to him and those who acted with him the occasion of the great crisis of their lives:

His Majesties' Gracious Declaration to all His Loving Subjects for Liberty of Conscience. James R.

"It having pleased Almighty God, not only to bring Us to the Imperial Crown of these Kingdoms, through the greatest difficulties, but to preserve Us by a more than ordinary Providence upon the Throne of Our Royal Ancestors, there is nothing now that We so earnestly desire, as to Establish Our Government on such a Foundation as may make Our Subjects happy, and unite them to Us by Inclination as well as Duty; Which We think can be done by no means so effectually as by

---

[1] The word suggests that it was in the nature of a catechetical lecture rather than of a formal sermon. Ken's gifts would seem to have lain emphatically in this direction. The letter appears in the *Gentleman's Magazine* for March, 1814, as communicated by Richard Fowke.—Round, p. 208.

[2] The theory of toleration was at least no new thing with James. "He assured us (Burnet and Stillingfleet) he desired nothing but to follow his own conscience, which he imposed on nobody else. He did very often assure me that he was against all violent measures, and all persecution for conscience' sake."—Burnet, *O. T.*, B. iii., 1673.

[3] Miscellaneous Printed Papers. Ashmole, 1818. Bodl. Libr. Howell, *State Trials*, pp. 234—8.

granting to them the free Exercise of their Religion for the time to come, and add that to the perfect Enjoyment of their Property, which has never been in any Case Invaded by Us since Our coming to the Crown : Which, being the two things Men value most, shall ever be preserved in these Kingdoms, during Our Reign over them, as the truest Methods of their Peace and our Glory. We cannot but heartily wish, as it will easily be believed, that all the People of Our Dominions were Members of the Catholick Church, yet We humbly thank Almighty God, it is, and hath of long time been, Our constant Sense and Opinion (which upon diverse Occasions We have declared) that Conscience ought not to be constrained, nor People forced in matters of meer Religion : It has ever been directly contrary to Our Inclination, as We think it is to the Interest of Government, which it destroys by spoiling Trade, depopulating Countreys, and discouraging Strangers ; and finally, that it never obtained the End for which it was employed. And in this We are the more Confirmed by the Reflections We have made upon the Conduct of the four last Reigns. For after all the frequent and pressing Endeavours that were used in each of them, to reduce this Kingdom to an exact conformity in Religion, it is visible the Success has not answered the Design, and that the difficulty is invincible ; We therefore out of our Princely Care and Affection unto all Our Loving Subjects, that they may live at Ease and Quiet, and for the increase of Trade, and incouragement of Strangers, have thought fit by vertue of Our Royal Prerogative, to issue forth this Our Declaration of Indulgence ; making no doubt of the Concurrence of Our Two Houses of Parliament, when We shall think it convenient for them to Meet.

" In the first Place We do Declare, That We will Protect and Maintain Our Arch-Bishops, Bishops, and Clergy, and all other Our Subjects of the Church of *England*, in the free Exercise of their Religion, as by Law Established, and in the quiet and full Enjoyment of all their Possessions, without any Molestation or Disturbance whatsoever.

" We do likewise Declare, That it is Our Royal Will and Pleasure, That from henceforth the Execution of all and all manner of Penal Laws in Matters Ecclesiastical, for not coming to Church, or not Receiving the Sacrament, or for any other Non-conformity to the Religion established, or for, or by Reason of the Exercise of Religion in any manner whatsoever, be immediately Suspended ; And the further Execution of the said Penal Laws and every of them is hereby Suspended.

" And to the end that by the Liberty hereby granted, the Peace and Security of Our Government in the Practice thereof, may not be indangered, We have thought fit, and do hereby straitly Charge and Command all Our Loving Subjects, That, as We do freely give them Leave to Meet and Serve God after their own Way and Manner, be it in Private Houses or Places purposely Hired or Built for that use; so that they take especial care, that nothing be Preached or Taught amongst them, which may any ways tend to Alienate the Hearts of Our People from Us or Our Government ; And that their Meetings and Assemblies be peaceably, openly, and publickly held, and all Persons freely admitted to them ; And that they do signifie and make known to some one or more of the next Justices of the Peace, what Place or Places they set apart for those uses.

" And that all Our Subjects may enjoy such their Religious Assemblies with greater Assurance and Protection, We have thought it requisite, and do hereby Command, That no Disturbance of any kind be made or given unto them, under Pain of Our Displeasure, and to be further proceeded against with the utmost severity.

" And forasmuch as we are desirous to have the Benefit of the Service of all Our Loving Subjects, which by the Law of Nature is inseparately annexed to and inherent in Our Royal Person : And that none of our Subjects may for the future be under any Discouragement or Disability (who are likewise well inclined and fit to serve Us) by Reason of some Oaths and Tests, that have been usually Administered on such Occasions : We do hereby Declare, That it is Our Royal Will and Pleasure, That the Oaths commonly called, *The Oaths of Supremacy and Allegiance*, and also the several Tests and Declarations, mentioned in the Acts of Parliament made in the 25th and 30th years of the Reign of Our late Royal Brother, King *Charles* the Second, shall not at any time hereafter be required to be Taken, Declared, or Subscribed by any Person or Persons whatsoever, who is or shall be Imployed in any Office or Place of Trust, either Civil or Military, under Us or in Our Government, And We do further Declare it to be Our Pleasure and Intention from time to time hereafter, to Grant Our Royal Dispensations under Our Great Seal to all Our Loving Subjects so to be Imployed, who shall not take the said Oaths, or Subscribe, or Declare the said Tests or Declarations in the above-mentioned Acts and every of them.

" And to the end that all Our Loving Subjects may receive and enjoy the full Benefit and Advantage of Our Gracious Indulgence hereby intended, and may be Acquitted and Discharged from all Pains, Penalties, Forfeitures, and Disabilities by them or any of them incurred or forfeited, or which they shall or may at any time hereafter be liable to, for or by reason of their Non-conformity, or the Exercise of their Religion, and from all Suits, Troubles, or Disturbances for the same; We do hereby give Our Free and Ample Pardon unto all Non-Conformists, Recusants, and other Our Loving Subjects, for all Crimes and Things by them committed or done contrary to the Penal Laws formerly made relating to Religion and the Profession or Exercise thereof. Hereby Declaring, That this Our Royal Pardon and Indemnity shall be as Good and Effectual to all Intents and Purposes, as if every Individual Person had been therein Particularly named, or had particular Pardons under Our Great Seal, which We do likewise Declare shall from time to time be granted unto any Person or Persons desiring the same : Willing and Requiring our Judges, Justices, and other Officers to take Notice of and Obey Our Royal Will and Pleasure herein before Declared.

" And although the Freedom and Assurance We have hereby given in relation to Religion and Property, might be sufficient to remove from the Minds of Our Loving Subjects all Fears and Jealousies in relation to either; yet We have thought fit further to Declare, That We will Maintain them in all their Properties and Possessions, as well of Church and Abbey-Lands,[1] as in any other their Lands and Properties whatsoever.

" *Given at Our Court at* Whitehall *the Fourth Day* of April, 1687. *In the Third Year of Our Reign.*

" By His Majesties special Command.

" *London*, Printed by *Charles Hill*, *Henry Hill*, and *Thomas Newcomb*, Printers to the King's Most Excellent Majesty, 1687."

---

[1] The mention of the Abbey lands was noted as significant. " It looked as if the design of setting up popery was thought very near being effected, since otherwise there was no need of mentioning any such thing."—Burnet, *O.T.* B. iv., 1687.

VOL. I.   T

It may be noted that the declaration seemed at first likely to accomplish its purpose. Addresses poured in from Anabaptists, Quakers, and other bodies of Nonconformists, thanking James for his indulgence. Some of the Bishops who were his subservient instruments, Chester, Durham, Lincoln, Lichfield and Coventry, and St. David's, presented like addresses, signed by many of their clergy. The Bishop of Peterborough, however, who had been invited and expected to join, would have nothing to do with it, and the leading Dissenters of London, as well as the clergy of the Diocese, held aloof. Ken's own diocese was not free from the infection. Three addresses of warm and fulsome thanks were presented to the King from the Dissenters at Taunton, the Dissenting ministers of the county of Somerset, and from Presbyterian ministers at Bath. On the other hand, the magistracy of Bristol, as reported by Trelawney, the Bishop of that diocese, in a letter to Sancroft, July 1, 1687, set themselves against "the fanatical mode of addressing," and only two of his clergy had attached their signatures. Trelawney himself declared that he was "not to be forced from the interest of the Church of England by the terrors of R. (Royal) displeasure or death itself." Another letter, now without an address, but very probably written to Ken himself, may for that reason be printed *in extenso* :—

"MOST DEARE FREIND,

"I sent you my hearty respects last weeke from Norwich, where I was uppon a visitt to that excellent good Prelate,[1] with whom I long'd to discourse uppon the publick affaires. I left him in expectation of being suddenly presst afresh on the matter of addressing. I am very full of hopes that, since tis putt so hard uppon the Citty of London to give thankes (not for any gratious expressions in the Declarations, but) for the indulgence its selfe, nothing less will be demaunded or accepted of us, and then we may fairly and flatly decline it, when once it resumes its first ugly shape, and is taken out of the palliating dress which has made it the greater snare to many. Wee must be call'd ungratefull, if we do not make express

---

[1] The Bishop of Norwich referred to (William Lloyd) was of all the Bishops the most in Sancroft's confidence, and carried on a constant correspondence with him, as afterwards with Ken himself. (See chap. xxiii.)

acknowledgments for this great Grace of letting loose the King's and Churche's enemys. I would faine hear from you how the Westerne Bishops and the rest in his Majesty's Progress have scaped at their enterviews.

"Your most affectionate friend and Servant,

"FRAN. ELY."[1]

"Ely, *Aug.* 25th, 1687."

In the meantime, after the issue of the Declaration of Indulgence, but before the date of these two letters, Ken had found another opportunity, this time in his own diocese, of preaching a sermon which was of the nature of a manifesto.[2] The Queen, who had not abandoned the hope of giving birth to an heir to the throne, and so strengthening her husband's position, had gone to Bath with the Princess Anne to drink the waters. She was accompanied by her court ladies, officials, and priests. Ken preached on Ascension Day (May 5th), in the Abbey church of Bath, and took for his text Ps. xlvii. 8, "*God is gone up with a shout, the Lord with the sound of a trumpet.*" The sermon was not printed, but we are able to judge of its character from a pamphlet dedicated to the King and published "with allowance," with the title of *Animadversions by way of Answer to a Sermon preached by Thomas Kenne, D.D., Lord Bishop of Bath and Wells.* The writer concealed his name, but gave his initials F. I. R., and described himself as "a most loyal Irish subject, of the Company of Jesus." He was probably one of the priests attached to the Queen's household, sufficiently conspicuous for the initials to tell their tale to those who cared to inquire.[3] The tone of the pamphlet is that of somewhat supercilious praise. He had long wished to hear one who had the "parts of an

---

[1] Tanner MSS., vol. xxix. fol. 64, in Anderdon, p. 364.

[2] The fact is recorded in a poem by Perkins, the Latin Poet Laureate, written on Ken's death in 1711.

> "When to the Bath Her Royal Highness came,
> "Ken made the Abbey Church resound his fame;
> "Floods of grave eloquence from him did fall;
> "Ken in the pulpit thundered like St. Paul."

[3] Anderdon (p. 243) suggests that he may be identified with Father Jo. Reed, who is mentioned in Anthony A Wood's *Life* as living in 1671, and who became a Benedictine. But qu. Would a Benedictine be also a Jesuit? Wood met him in company with Hugh, *alias* Serenus, de Cressy (see p. 105).

T 2

orator," who would have been "an evangelical one too" had
he been reared in the bosom of the true Church. He is surprised that Ken began his sermon without making the sign
of the cross, and he tells us that it was an hour and a half
long. He notes that Ken had "given a fling at the Pope's
supremacy, to which he had "show'd all imaginable aversion,"
that he had spoken " with much vehemency against the Real
Presence," had told his hearers that "Christ was not to be
found on this altar or on that altar, but that he was actually in
heaven ;" that he had "protested mightily against Roman
Catholics for coining and forging new Articles of Faith, as
well in relation to Transubstantiation as the Spiritual Supremacy, &c." He quotes the words of the Bishop's *Exposition
of the Catechism* on the Sacramental Presence as inconsistent
with the language of the sermon. Finally, he intimates that
the sermon was probably preached "in order to take away all
suspicion of your being Roman Catholickly inclined." " Those
suspicions rested," he says, on the fact of "your Lordship's
living, as Seneca saith, *sine impedimento*, that is, without a
wife, and having the reputation of living morally well, which
is enough for the Rabble to say you are Popishly affected,"[1]
and therefore the Bishop "undertook that day's work to take
away the scandal, which had no other ground than your good
works." He adds, and the addition is significant, that the
Bishop had preached again the next day, and had dwelt on the
doctrine of justification by faith as illustrated in the case of
Abraham. To this the pamphleteer replies by referring him
to "the west window of that cathedral" (Bath Abbey), in
which he would find "in capital letters, his own judgment
drawn out of James ii. 26, ' For as the body without the
spirit is dead, so faith without good works is dead also.' "[2]

Ken did not allow himself to be drawn by this challenge into
a controversial discussion with his opponent. Few things, I
imagine, would have been more repellent to his nature than a
prolonged dispute after the Chillingworth type, pamphleteer
answering pamphleteer, paragraph by paragraph, with endless

---

[1] See Evelyn, *Diary*, March 14th, 1686, in Note, p. 270.

[2] The words are not found in the west window now, but I am unable to say
when they were removed.

iteration of time-worn and threadbare arguments. The press of London was teeming with such publications, and Ken's books at Wells contain some twenty volumes of them. What he actually did, and it sufficiently indicates the temper of his mind at this crisis, was to alter the sentence in the *Practice of Divine Lore* with which his opponent had taunted him so as to avoid the possibility of a Romish interpretation.[1]

As yet, however, the part which Ken had taken does not seem to have given offence to the King. After dissolving Parliament in the hope that, by manipulating the elections, he might obtain a House of Commons more disposed to compliance with his wishes and to accept the Declaration of Indulgence, and after having received at Windsor the Pope's nuncio, Ferdinand d'Adda, Archbishop of Amasia, with great pomp (no such ceremony had been witnessed in England for a hundred and fifty years), James started on a state progress through the western counties, accompanied, of course, by his household, by his chaplains, by Father Petre, and (the juxtaposition is sufficiently strange) by William Penn.

In the course of that progress James came to Bath, where his Queen was still staying, and there he and the Bishop met under somewhat trying conditions. The King, remembering probably the effect that had been produced by Monmouth's "touching" for the king's evil, and probably enough, really holding this to be among his most precious privileges as an anointed King, determined to hold a function of like character with all imaginable stateliness. It is difficult for us to realise the feelings which led to the long continuance of that ceremonial through the movements of the Reformation and the great Puritan rebellion, which might have seemed likely to bring about its natural death. To us it seems almost the *ne plus ultra* of a sickly superstition; and yet it held its ground through all the chances and changes of history, from the days of Edward the Confessor, with whom it originated, and to whose canonisation it had contributed. Not bishops and divines only proclaimed its efficacy, but men of reputed science accepted its supernatural cures. The work, in the words of John Browne, one of Charles II.'s "Chirurgeons in Ordinary,'

---

[1] See p. 236.

"carried more of Divinity than Majesty in it. The art of physick
was non-plus'd, and Chirurgery tied up; all chirurgeons whatsoever must truckle to the balsamic power; more souls have
been healed by His Majesty's Sacred hand in one year than
have been cured by all the physicians and chirurgeons of his
Three Kingdoms since his happy Restauration."[1]

One of the features of the ceremony naturally made it attractive to real or pretended sufferers from scrofula. Each of
those who came to the healing was presented with a gold coin,
known from the device on it as an "angel," strung upon a white
silk ribbon, which was hung round the patient's neck by the
royal hands. It was natural, under such conditions, that the
ceremonial should be well attended. Evelyn records (March
28th, 1684) that six or seven persons were crushed to death in
the crowds at Whitehall in Charles II.'s reign. It was equally
natural that the sufferers should often discover that their
cure was not complete without a second application of the same
talisman, and that the talismans themselves should sometimes
find their way to the goldsmiths' shops. If, as recorded,
Charles II. had "touched" some ninety-two thousand persons
in the course of his reign, the ceremonial must have been a
somewhat serious drain on the royal treasury. A special
service, often printed and bound up with the Book of Common
Prayer, in which bishops and chaplains took part, was used on
the occasion. It is significant that William III. discontinued
the practice as a silly superstition, that it was revived under
Queen Anne (Samuel Johnson was "touched" by Queen Anne
in his early childhood; unfortunately, in his case, the cure was
all too imperfect), and since the accession of the House of
Brunswick the practice has happily become entirely obsolete.[2]
On this occasion the ceremonial was one of singular magnificence, and the circumstances were such as must have impressed
themselves on the minds of all beholders. Of all the many
acts, insolent and insidious, by which James, as if possessed by

[1] Browne's *Adenochoirodelogia : Treatise on King's Evil Swellings.* 8vo, 1684,
quoted by Anderdon, p. 374. See Pettigrew: *Superstitions connected with Medicine*, 1844, pp. 117—154.

[2] The Jacobites of the time, of course, looked on the disuse as a practical confession that one of the special gifts attached to the Divine Right of kings was
wanting to the then wearer of the crown.

the *dementia* in which the mediæval proverb recognised the note
of a fore-ordained, self-wrought destruction, brought about his
own ruin, this, though it finds no place in the long list of offences
which enter into Macaulay's narrative as counts in the indictment
against James, and, though it was less violent and oppressive
than his treatment of the two Magdalen Colleges or of Bishop
Compton, seems to me at once the most insolent and insidious.
The "touching" was to take place in the Abbey Church, which
was popularly known as one of the two cathedral churches of
Ken's diocese, and which, though it had no dean and chapter, was
the church in which the Bishop had his *cathedra*, or throne, and
was so far entitled to the name. Ken was himself at Bath, and
no notice was given to him of the intended ceremonial. The
altar was decked and the ritual ordered by Huddleston, who
had successfully interposed between Ken and the soul that he
was seeking to win and save as a member of the English Church.
According to a Bath tradition, Huddleston took the opportunity to make a proselytising address to the crowds that filled
the Abbey, exhorting them to return to the Church of their
forefathers.[1] A new form of service, reviving the order used
under Henry VIII., was printed by the King's order for the
occasion, distinctively Romish in character, in which the King
was made to say, "I confess to God and the blessed Virgin
Mary, to all saints and to you, that I have sinned in thought,
word, and deed through my fault. I pray holy Mary, and all
the saints of God, and you, to pray for me."[2]

One cannot help thinking that James ventured deliberately

[1] According to one form of the same tradition Ken was present, and, as soon as
Huddleston had finished, "mounted the pulpit and exposed his fallacies in a
strain of such expressive eloquence as astonished and delighted his congregation,
and confounded Huddleston and the royal bigot" (Warner, *History of Bath*,
p. 257). I incline, however, with Markland and Anderdon, to think that this was
improbable, and was a distorted version of the course which Ken reports that he
actually took.

[2] The City Records of Bath (for extracts from which I am indebted to Mr. B.
H. Watts) throw no light on the Abbey scenes; but the Council Books of
that city of August 23rd, 1687, show that the King took the opportunity of
"commanding" the Council to elect Francis Carne as Master of the Free
School. I surmise that the man was either a Papist or a Popishly inclined teacher,
and that James was playing at Bath the same game as at Oxford. William E.
Guest was also made a freeman of the city by the King's command. Both cases
were probably intended to illustrate the Declaration of Indulgence.

on this audacious defiance of decency as calculating on Ken's non-resisting meekness. To some extent he was not disappointed. Ken (as we see from his own account of the transaction) made no public protest at the time. It did not seem to him expedient to condemn a ceremonial which, after all, he had no power to prevent, and which seemed to his people to be connected with a work of charity. What he actually did, and his *apologia* for it, we find stated with sufficient clearness in the following letter :—

LETTER XVII.

To Archbishop Sancroft.

" All Glory be to God.

" My very good Lord,

"Though I have always been very tender of giving your Grace any trouble, yett I thinke it my duty, having this opportunity of a safe conveyance, to acquaint you with one particular, which happened at Bath, and to begge your advice for the future. When His Majesty was at Bath, there was a great healing, and without any warning, unlesse by a flying report: the office was performed in the Church, between the houres of prayer. I had not time to remonstrate, and if I had done it, it would have had no effect, but only to provoke : besides I found it had been done in other churches before, and I know no place but the Church which was capable to receive so great a multitude as came for cure : upon which consideration I was wholly passive. But being well aware what advantage the Romanists take from the least seeming complyances, I took occasion on Sunday from the Gospell, the subject of which was the Samaritan, to discourse of Charity, which, I said, ought to be the religion of the whole world, wherein Samaritan and Jew were to agree, and though we could not open the Church-doores to a worship different from that we paid to God, yett we should alwayes sett them open to a common work of Charity, because, in performing mutuall offices of Charity one to another, there ought to be an universall agreement.

"This was the substance of what I said upon that action, which I humbly submit to your Grace's Judgment; and it was the best expedient I could thinke of, to prevent giving scandall to our owne people, and to obviate all the misrepresentations the Romanists might make of such a connivance. I am very sensible of your Grace's burthen, and doe beseech Almighty Goodnesse to support you under it. And I earnestly crave your Blessing, being ambitious of nothing more than to be one of the meanest of your Companions in the Kingdome and Patience of Jesus.

"My good Lord,

" Your Grace's most obedient Son and

humble Servant,

"THO. BATH & WELLS.[1]

" *Aug.* 26*th,* 1687."

[It will be noted (1) that Ken did not trust the post with his letter, but waited till he could send it, without risk of its being tampered with, by a private hand. (2) That, though this was on a more conspicuous scale, there had been like services held in other churches before. I have not been able to trace where. Macaulay (ii. 794) says vaguely that " James visited Portsmouth, walked round the fortifications, and touched some scrofulous people." (3) The phrase as to charity being " the religion of the whole world " is singularly characteristic.]

James seems to have started immediately afterwards on a further progress, went to Gloucester, Worcester, Chester,[2] was joined at the last-named city by Penn, and made his way to Oxford, where he bullied and threatened the Fellows of Magdalen, and found that his threats were fruitless.[3] He went away in a rage, and rejoined his Queen at Bath.

It was within that week that we find Ken writing another letter, which exhibits him in a state of some perplexity. Assuming the rumour of which he speaks to have had some foundation, James may probably have been tempted by his compliant silence at Bath, to think that he would find him in all things subservient to his wishes. Ken, he knew, had personal friends among the Fellows of Magdalen, and notably

[1] Bodleian Tanner MSS., vol. xxix. p. 65.

[2] The King 'touched' at Chester, as he had done at Bath, but there Cartwright was Bishop, and, of course, there was nothing said by way of protest. (Cartwright's *Diary,* p. 74.) It was at Chester too that he went, by way of a practical illustration of the Declaration of Indulgence, to hear Penn hold forth in a conventicle, after attending mass in the Shire-hall, fitted up for the purpose, in the morning. (*Ibid.*)

[3] It is significant that one of James's reproaches at Oxford was that in his father's time " Catholicks and Protestants " used to live peaceably together, and now it was otherwise. He bade his hearers remember that he, for his part, was determined that he would have this altered. His filling Magdalen with a President, Fellows, and Demies, all of whom were Romanists, was, apparently, his first great step in that direction. Why should men grudge one college to the members of the King's Church ?—A. à Wood, *Life,* pp. 361—363.

Thomas Smith and John Fitzwilliam (both of whose names
will meet us again), and he may have hoped that Ken would
exercise his influence over the rebellious college, and persuade
it to submission.   In any case his visiting the Bishop in his
own palace would impress the public mind with the conviction that he was in full accord with the King's proceedings.
Mingled with this there may have been (we cannot, I fear, get
out of the region of conjecture) a feeling of personal affection,
and a wish to see something of the Bishop's saintly life in his
own home.

LETTER XVIII.

To Lord Dartmouth.

" All Glory be to God.

" My very good Lord,

" Having been in that part of my Diocesse which is neere Bristoll,
and passing through the City towards Wells, I mett with a report
that his Majesty was goeing for the West and would probably call
at Wells: I was extreamely surprised at the newes. I know not
what measures to take; for to pretend to give the King such an
entertainment, which is in some way sutable, is more than it is
possible for me to doe at so short a warning, besides I doe not
know whether he will passe through our towne, or on what daye.
In this great perplexity betwoen my desire of doeing my utmost
duty and the difficulty of doeing it, I begge your Lordshippe's
advice in a line or two, that I may know his Majesty's pleasure and
what is expected from me. Let me then beseech your Lordshippe
to lay my most humble duty at the King's feet, and to assure his
Majesty that I shall esteeme it a very great honour if he conde-
scends to grace my house, and to endure such an extemporary
reception as I can at so short a warning contrive for him. I wait
for your Lordship's directions not without some impatience.

" *Sept. 6th* (1687)."

[Reading the letter in the light of recent events we can well understand that
Ken was indeed "extremely surprised" at the rumours which had reached him.
He felt, perhaps, as he remembered Morley's princely hospitality at Farnham,
that his own lowlier style of living was little suited for a royal guest.   On the
other hand the letter shows a lingering affection, and he probably waited, after
his manner, for the providential guidance of events, not, perhaps, without hope
that, if the King came, he might find an opportunity for saying some words of

much-needed counsel. I have not been able to ascertain whether the King carried his supposed intentions into effect. This is indeed the only mention of his purpose. The visit referred to in the opening words of the letter was probably to the Misses Kemeys of Naish Court (Chap. xxiv.).]

Two other letters belonging to the later months of the same year have to be interpreted as we best can:—

LETTER XIX.

To Archbishop Sancroft,

" All Glory be to God.

" Most Reverend Father and my very good Lord,

" I had made my acknowledgments sooner to your Grace, for the favour of your letter, but that I delay'd them on purpose, hoping to have sent them by another hand. In the affair I mentioned in my last, I acted according to the best of my judgment, and that I might give no occasion to any more of those misrepresentations, under which I have so often, and so undeservedly, lay'n. The copy which I have by me, I will take care to send by my secretary, who, God willing, is to be in Towne at the Terme. There are some particulars, especially those, which relate to Faculties, which by experience, I find not practicable, and many of the cures in my diocesse are so very small, that I am very glad to gett a sober person to supply them, though he is not a graduate, but as for ordinations, your Grace may be assured that I endeavour all I can to lay hands suddenly on no man. I am very sensible of the charitable opinion you are pleased to have of me, and the favourable construction you make of my actions; God grant I may in some measure answer your Grace's just expectations. I beseech God of his infinite goodnesse, and in mercy to his poore Church, to give you a supereffluence of his H. Spirit, to assist and support you, and I humbly begge your benediction.

" My good Lord,

" Your Graces most obedient son and Servant,

"THOS. BATH & WELLS."

" *Oct.* 1*st* (1687)."

[The " affair mentioned in my last " is probably the Bath incident. We note the Bishop's sensitiveness to the " misrepresentations," against which he was anxious to guard. The rest of the letter refers apparently to some regulations which Sancroft had issued for the guidance of the Bishops of his province. There had apparently been some complaints, in reply to which Ken makes his *apologia*, that he had admitted " literate persons," both to Holy Orders and to livings, but, as Ken pleads, not without sufficient reason. The reader of *Expostulatoria* (alias *Ichabod*) will remember that *Undue Ordination* was one of the five "Complaints of the Church" on which the writer emphatically dwelt as tending to her discredit and decay (see p. 56). We may well believe that Ken sought earnestly to be free from that guilt himself.]

LETTER XX.

To Archbishop Sancroft.

"All Glory be to God.

"My very good Lord,

"The entire veneration I have ever had for your Grace, makes your displeasure the more afflicting, especially so great a displeasure against me, as your letter expresses, and that too for such a crime which I abhorre, no lesse than insincere dealing, and in the whole, I am so unhappy as to be supposed guilty by your Grace, and to be treated by you as if I were. But I hope your Grace will have that charity for me, as to believe me, when I with all humble submission acquaint you, that I never had the originall you mention. And if I had had it, I know not the least temptation imaginable I could have had to have detained it. The onely copy I had, I have sent, and I thought it was the same you meant, having, as I understood your letter, lost the other; and I sent it to the Bishop of Ely, because I was tender of giving you the trouble of a letter which might be spared, and I sent it with a particular circumstance of duty to your Grace, that my old friend must needs be very forgettfull, if he gave no better account who it was that brought it, or how it came to his hands. I confesse I should have sent your paper sooner, and so I had done, had not the persons with whome my secretary was to transact businesse disappointed us, and this, if it be a fault, I presume is a veniall one. But how much soever assured I am of my owne innocence, rather than tyre you with a tedious vindication of myselfe I choose to begge your pardon, as well as your benediction.

"My good Lord,

"Your Graces most obedient son and Servant,

"THO. BATH & WELLS.

"*Inc. 5th*, 1687."

[The sensitiveness, noticeable in the previous letter, is seen here in yet stronger colours. Sancroft had apparently written accusing him of "insincere dealing," connected with some important document of which he thought Ken had kept the original. What this was we can only conjecture, possibly some circular letter which Sancroft had written to his suffragans on the character of James's policy.

[Did he suspect that Ken had shown it to the King ? D'Oyly's *Life of Sancroft* (p. 146) shows that the Archbishop, about this time, received an important letter from the Princess Mary which he answered on November 3rd. Could this be the document referred to ?]

So the year 1687 closed in darkness and gloom, which must have filled Ken's mind with sad and anxious forebodings. The King pursued his infatuated course without scruple and without fear.   The Fellows of Magdalen were deprived by a Royal Commission packed for the purpose, of which a bishop of the English Church, Cartwright of Chester, was base enough to act as President. Compton continued under the suspension inflicted by the Court of Ecclesiastical Commission. Sancroft was still excluded from the King's presence for his refusal to attend that Court.   All the Lord Lieutenants who would not lend themselves to the King's schemes for securing a servile majority in the next House of Commons were summarily dismissed. " Regulators " were appointed under the new charters, who exercised their powers by dismissing all Church of England functionaries, aldermen, and others, from the Tweed to the Land's End, and filling their places with Papists, or with Presbyterians, Independents, and Baptists, who had joined in addresses to the King, thanking him for his Declaration of Indulgence. Men as they looked before and after might well " prognosticate a year of sects and schisms," even more appalling than that of the forecast of which Milton wrote.

The date of the following letter leads me to insert it here, though it has no special connexion with the events related in the chapter :—

LETTER XXI.

To Viscount Weymouth.

" All Glory be to God.

" My very good Lord,

" Your Lordshippe was pleased to offer me a generous kindnesse by Dr. Bellsted, wch I am very confident you design'd I should make use of : and it is upon the strength of that, I have sent my Servant to begge halfe a buck. My Lord Mainard has been with me this fortnight, very neer, and intends to returne the beginning of next

weeke, and I have engaged to wait on him at Longleat.   I beseech
your Lordshippe to present my humblest service to my Lady.   God
of His Infinite Goodnesse multiply His blessings on yourselfe &
family, & fill you with ye perfect Love wch casteth out all feare.

"My Good Lord

"Your Lordshippe's most humble &

affectionate Servant

"THO. BATH & WELLS.

"*July* 26*th*, 1687.

"The two Manuals are for ye young Lady and Master."

[I have not been able to learn who Dr. Bellsted was, or to what kindness Ken
refers.   Possibly it may have been the supply of some dainties for his patients,
like the asparagus mentioned in Letter xv., p. 256.   Lord Maynard, it will be remembered, had recently been expelled from his office in James's household because
he would neither turn Romanist nor comply with James's general policy (p. 269.)
It is interesting to find the widower turning to his old friend for comfort and
counsel in the troublous times through which both were passing.   The two
"Manuals" were probably copies of the Prayers for Winchester scholars, for the
son and daughter of Lord Weymouth, to whom he had before sent his *Exposition of the Church Catechism* (see p. 229).]

CHAPTER XVII

THE PETITION OF THE SEVEN BISHOPS.

" So works the All-wise ! our services dividing
      Not as we ask ;
  For the world's profit, by our gifts deciding
      Our duty task.
  See in kings' courts loth Jeremiahs plead,
  And slow-tongued Moses rule by eloquence of deed."

J. H. Newman.

THE year 1688 opened upon Ken with sufficiently gloomy prospects. Without were fightings and within were fears. The King, for whom he still cherished a lingering and loyal affection, for whom he yet hoped against hope, was rushing on in his infatuated career. It was difficult for a true churchman and a true patriot to see his way clearly in the tangled labyrinth of the politics of the time. We have to draw a very different picture of the Bishop's life from the idyllic scene which at first presents itself to us, and in which he appears as sitting in the arbour, or walking up and down the terrace, in the Palace Gardens, singing his own hymns, or reading the Odes of Horace. One or two lines of those Odes may indeed have been often in his thoughts as reminiscences of his boyhood. He may have thought of the *cultus instantis tyranni*, of the *ardor civium prava jubentium*. He might have resolved that he at least would not accept the *arbitrium popularis auræ* as the standard of his conduct. If I were to conjecture—and here the conjecture would have at least the basis of fact—I should think of him as occupying himself with very different studies, reading the books on Moral Theology and Cases of Conscience, on the limits of the authority of the Church and State, of the *Regale* and *Pontificale*, of kings and subjects, in which his library was exceptionally rich, perhaps recalling

the action of Nicholas Pavillon, when he found himself constrained to disobey Louis XIV.'s command to sign the condemnation of the Jansenist propositions.[1] And, to add to his
troubles, he found himself misunderstood and misrepresented
suspected not only by the "rabble" but by a man like
Sancroft, of "insincere dealing." How was he to clear his
character, to define his position, to "walk warily" in such
" dangerous days " ?

If I am right in assigning his Lenten address to his clergy to
the spring of 1688, as I have done in p. 244, it throws light on
the state of his mind at this period. I have printed that address
as connected with his pastoral work, and do not see sufficient
reason for altering the arrangement, but it reflects, if I mistake
not, the depression and agitation of his mind at this period, and
it shows in what he had found strength and peace. Only by
penitence, and prayer, and intercession for the Church and the
nation and their rulers, was there any hope for the future. The
closing words of the letter would at least serve to make his own
position clear. His prayer was that he and those to whom he
wrote might be settled " in the true Catholick and Apostolick
Faith profess'd in the Church of England." So, adorning
" that apostolick faith with apostolick zeal," it might be granted
to them that " both priests and people may all plentifully sow
in tears, and in God's good time may all plentifully reap in joy."

A few weeks after this pastoral letter Ken found himself
named, probably much to his surprise, for a Lent sermon at
Whitehall. The appointment must have had the King's
sanction, even if it was not, as I think probable, his own direct
nomination, and Ken did not shrink from the responsibility
which it imposed. His preaching turn was fixed for the
afternoon of Passion Sunday, April 1st, 1688. Evelyn's account,
in his entry for that day, shows that the announcement had
excited men's expectations far and wide. Stillingfleet preached
in the morning. The service was followed by the celebration
of Holy Communion. The sermon was " so interrupted by the
rude breaking in of the multitude," who came " from all
quarters," " jealous to hear " the afternoon preacher, that " the

---

[1] Palafox y Mendoza, *Historia Real Sagrada* ; Fr. de Quevedo Villegas, *Politica
de Dios* at Bath Abbey, *cum multis aliis* at Longleat and Wells.

holy office could hardly be heard, or the sacred elements be distributed without great trouble." Ken entered the chapel to find every eye fixed on him in eager expectation. The King, of course, was not there, but the Princess Anne was in the royal box. As usual he preached without book, possibly repeating a written sermon from memory, after the manner of the great French preachers, but possibly also, one delivered with no other preparation than that of much careful thought, and reduced to writing afterwards for future publication. The style of the sermon and the occasional repetitions in it seem to me in favour of the latter view. He preached, Evelyn adds, " with his accustomed action, zeal, and energy." Of all his sermons it had most the character of a manifesto. It occupies thirty 8vo pages, and must have taken about an hour and a half in delivery. The text which he chose was fitted to stimulate the eager desire of his hearers to learn what part he was going to take in the struggle which even then was seen to be impending. It was from Micah vii. 8, 9.

"Rejoice not against me, O mine enemy : when I fall, I shall arise ; when I sit in darkness, the Lord shall be a light unto me. I will bear the indignation of the Lord, because I have sinned against him, until he plead my cause, and execute judgment for me : he will bring me forth to the light, and I shall behold his righteousness."

The words would naturally suggest, and were probably intended to suggest, to those who knew under what circumstances Ken was preaching, a directly personal application. This was his answer to those who might examine him. It was not Ken's purpose, however, otherwise than by that suggestion, to make a personal *apologia ;* and he proceeded at once to his exposition, every step of which must have kept his hearers on the *qui vive* of expectancy. The prophet spoke of the " *reformed* church of Judah. . . . . It was a bold undertaking to denounce God's judgments to the King and to the Court . . . . but true prophets, in the delivery of their messages, fear none but God, and dare say anything that God commands them. And there are times when prophets cannot, must not, keep silence." They must speak, as Amos did, even 'in the King's Chapel and in the King's Court.' " Happy was it for the King," in the case of Micah, " that he so devoutly attended to the prophet ; happy for the prophet that he had the opportunity of preaching to the King himself." Otherwise " what tragical relations had been made of his sermon " by those who came " on purpose to wrest his words, and with thoughts against him for evil ! " Three times in the course of the sermon does the preacher dwell, in this half-aggrieved, half-pathetic tone, on the King's absence, and I can hardly help surmising that Ken had ventured to hope that the King would break through his usual rule, and come and hear his sermon, as he had heard Penn's, and that his disappointment gave to what he said a greater flavour of despondency, if not of bitterness.

Yes. The prophet's message was to the " reformed Church of Judah," but that reformation had been incomplete. The righteous were but a remnant. Men might be "reformed in their faith and in the public worship, but the generality of them were still unreformed in their lives." And the "enemies" of that Church (he abruptly changes the singular into the plural) were the Babylonians, the type of the " man of sin," of the mystical Babylon of the Apocalypse, which was identified with the Antichrist ; and the Edomites were "originally of the same blood and of the same religion with Judah, though they had revolted from the Church of God." Now they were allied with the Babylonians, in revenge for the loss of their birthright. Both took up their parable against Judah, and taunted her with being abandoned by the Lord in Whom she trusted, in words which, as Ken uttered them, must have seemed to his hearers almost as an echo of those which were constantly in the mouth of Petre and his cabal, and of the Dissenters who were associated with them. Then came the preacher's forecast of the future. He saw no prospect of any near change for the better. For the " reformed Church[1] of Judah " (his hearers would read " of England " between the lines) there might possibly be the discipline of a seventy years'

---

[1] We note Ken's general use of the term " reformed " (1) as a protest against the omission of that term in James's Declaration (see Evelyn's letter of October 10th, 1688, ii. p. 20) ; (2) as probably chosen as indicating more sympathy with the Huguenots of France than with the Lutherans of Germany.

captivity. And Edom would share in that suffering. "Had Judah and Edom both joined for the common safety, both might have preserved their liberty, but Edom will be an easy prey to the Babylonian, now her neighbour, Judah, is led captive." Where, then, was the hope of Judah? It was to be found only in the "righteous remnant," in "the watchmen who were God's remembrancers." Discipline might at last do its work, and then "not only seventy years of Babylon, but seventy times seven, would be welcome." God could make "the hearts of the very Babylonians to relent towards her." And the duty of "reformed Judah" was to hasten the coming of that good time by patient submission to her King—to "subject their persons to the Babylonish government, but not to prostitute their consciences to the Babylonish idolatry, whensoever the commands of God and of the King of Babylon stood in competition." [1] It would be their wisdom to renounce "all carnal expedients" and "the arm of flesh." "The true Israelites would always be martyrs, but never rebels." Those who were corresponding, or planning correspondence, with William of Orange, would understand the suggestive hint that the decree of Cyrus for the restoration of Judah was not to be looked for till the expiration of the seventy years.

So far all was so plain that he that ran might read. It did not require much of the spirit that 'understands all parables' to discern the meaning of the historic parallel. Towards the end of the sermon, however, there came a singular passage which must have disappointed not a few of those who had listened with rapt attention to the earlier strains of eloquence. The preacher warns his hearers, "since we have not the happiness

---

[1] The whole passage is worth quoting, as expressing the temper of Ken's mind as he faced the crisis in which he found himself:—"If this be captivity, by becoming a Babylonish slave to become the Lord's freeman, O may my captivity last, not seventy, but seventy times seven years! No time, O Lord, is long; eternity itself is not tedious that is spent in Thy fruition. O Almighty Goodness, Thou only canst make captivity desirable; welcome then darkness; there will I sit, desiring to see no light but what comes from Thy countenance, for Thou art light and liberty and joy, and all in all to those who for Thy sake are content for a while to sit in darkness." What Ken anticipated was clearly the triumph of Rome for a time, perhaps for two or three generations. He pictured himself, perhaps, as the Daniel or Jeremiah of the period. His lot was to be far different from that.

which Micah had, to have the King himself for an auditor, in
whose royal candour a faithful preacher might be secure"
against possible misrepresentations which might be made by
" insidious men," that the prophecies as to the mystical Babylon
were open to so many interpretations, some of them so uncertain and some so forced, that he had to confess that he did not
understand, and, therefore, forbore to apply them.   He would
not fix on any particular Church as *the* Babylon of the Apocalypse.   And as to Edom, personified in Esau, "a profane
person, an apostate, one hated by God and a reprobate," "God
forbid that I should bestow such names as these upon any one
communion of Christians whatsoever!"   All that he meant was
that so far as any professing Christians identified themselves
with the characters of Babylon and Edom, to that extent
they would be partakers of their plagues.   And even of
such as these it was true that the right way to encounter
them was that which the Saviour had taught : "Love your
enemies ; bless them that curse you ; do good to them that hate
you ; and pray for them which despitefully use you and perse-
cute you."   "Judah has taught all the faithful how to weather
out a captivity under them ; by repentance and submission."

At first sight this looks, it must be admitted, somewhat like
a rhetorical artifice, a parliamentary formula disclaiming a
natural inference from what had been said before; a plea for
the defence, in the event of the preacher being called to account
for the boldness of his utterance.   Some might even go farther
than this, and suspect even now the "insincere dealing" with
which Sancroft had reproached him.   "See," they would say,
"even he is 'trimming;' he disavows the natural inference
from his own language ; he equivocates and leaves a loophole."
It would, I am persuaded, be altogether unjust to Ken to put
this interpretation on his words.   What I see in them is the
struggle between righteous indignation and personal affection,
between the zeal of the prophet and the all-embracing charity of
the saint.   He has, like Izaak Walton, and like Hooker, known
Romanists whose holiness of life he reverenced; he cannot
think even of James himself as altogether 'in the gall of
bitterness and the bond of iniquity.'   He has known Dissenters in whom there was nothing of the Edom temper.   He

is therefore not afraid to risk being misunderstood in his thoughts of charity, and is content to bear the reproach of those whose zeal was at once narrower and more bitter than his own. Such, I take it, was now, as ever, the mind of Ken, almost eager, as it were, to forfeit the confidence of both prince and people, rather than to incur the reproaches of his own conscience by courting the praise of either. Men might call him a "trimmer": he was willing to "become all things to all men, if by any means he might save some." And, like St. Paul, he had, as might be expected, his reward both for evil and for good.

One immediate result he probably anticipated. The King heard of the sermon, and, as Ken's great-nephew records,[1] sent for him to his closet, and reproached him for the controversial bitterness with which he had spoken. The Bishop's reply was simply that, "if his Majesty had not neglected his own duty of being present, his enemies had missed this opportunity of accusing him," and with this he was dismissed. The answer was, in two ways, significant. It indicated the same sense of soreness at the King's non-attendance which had shown itself once and again in the sermon. It confirms the conclusion to which I have been already led that the sermon was an unwritten one. The natural defence against the charge of disloyalty would have been to produce the MS. It was not printed by way of defence till after his death.

Ken went back to his diocese, and within a month from the date of his sermon, possibly as a direct consequence of the irritation it had caused, the King issued, on April 25th, his second Declaration of Indulgence. It reproduces almost verbatim the earlier Declaration of April 4, 1687, given in the preceding chapter, and I therefore do not reprint it *in extenso*, but its opening words indicate a temper of increased impatience and provocation.

" Our conduct," the King says, " has been such at all times as ought to have persuaded the world that we are firm and constant in our resolutions ; yet that easy people may not be alarmed by the malice of crafty, wicked men, we think fit to declare that our intentions are not changed since the 4th of

[1] Hawkins, p. 17.

April, 1687, when we issued our Declaration for Liberty of Conscience." It then recites that declaration, and adds as follows :—

"Ever since we granted this indulgence, we have made it our principal care to see it preserved without distinction, as we are encouraged to do daily by multitudes of addresses, and many other assurances we receive from our subjects of all persuasions, as testimonies of their satisfaction and duty, the effects of which we doubt not but the next parliament will plainly shew ; and that it will not be in vain that we have resolved to use our uttermost endeavours to establish liberty of conscience on such just and equal foundations as will render it unalterable, and to secure to all people the free exercise of their religion for ever ; by which future ages may reap the benefit of what is so undoubtedly for the general good of the whole kingdom. It is such a security we desire, without the burden and constraint of oaths and tests, which have unhappily been made by some governments, but could never support any Nor should men be advanced by such means to offices and employments, which ought to be the reward of services, fidelity and merit We must conclude, that not only good Christians will join in this, but whoever is concerned for the increase of the wealth and power of the nation. It would perhaps prejudice some of our neighbours,[1] who might lose part of those vast advantages they now enjoy, if liberty of conscience were settled in these kingdoms, which are above all others most capable of improvements, and of commanding the trade of the world. In pursuance of this great work, we have been forced to make many changes both of civil and military offices throughout our dominions, not thinking any ought to be employed in our service, who will not contribute towards the establishing the peace and greatness of their country, which we most earnestly desire, as unbiassed men may see by the whole conduct of our government, and by the condition of our fleet, and of our armies, which, with good management, shall be constantly the same, and greater, if the safety or honour of the nation require it. We recommend these considerations to all our subjects, and that they will reflect on their present ease and happiness, how for above three years, that it hath pleased God to permit us to reign over these kingdoms, we have not appeared to be that prince our enemies

---

[1] This alludes, obviously, to the Dutch, who were, at that time, conspicuous among the nations of Europe for their general toleration of diversities in religion, and for their consequent commercial prosperity.

would have made the world afraid of, our chief aim having been not to be the oppressor, but the father of our people, of which we can give no better evidence than by conjuring them to lay aside all private animosities, as well as groundless jealousies, and to choose such members of parliament as may do their part to finish what we have begun, for the advantage of the monarchy over which Almighty God hath placed us, being resolved to call a parliament, that shall meet in November next at farthest." [1]

Many things, of which no one then dreamt, were to come to pass before that November in which Parliament was to be summoned. We must, for the present, endeavour to place ourselves mentally in the position of Ken and others when they read or heard of the Declaration in the early days of May, 1688.

The general principles of toleration stated in what we may call the preamble of the Declaration have taken their place in the creed of all Liberal statesmen, among the platitudes of all Liberal rhetoric. It is only fair to James to remember that he had, from the first days of the Restoration onwards, contended for them, when he stood almost alone, that in the long struggles of the Popish plot and the Exclusion Bill he had been a confessor, almost a martyr, in defending them. He probably thought that such a declaration by a king, in the full plenitude of his power, was needed to balance the effect produced on the minds of his people by Louis XIV.'s revocation of the Edict of Nantes. Men should see that a Roman Catholic sovereign could be tolerant in proportion to the extent of his prerogative. England should follow, in spite of Parliamentary opposition, or, as he persuaded himself that his management of the elections might succeed in effecting it, with the consent of Parliament, the example that had been set by Lord Baltimore, in the Roman Catholic colony of Maryland. It is of course easy to point to James's action at the very time when he thus stood forward as the apostle of toleration, and to question alike his consistency and his sincerity. Was he not imposing the test of conformity with his own plans, if not with his own religion, upon almost every holder of important office, military or civil? Were not Protestants in every branch of the government service cashiered and their places filled by Romanists? Was he

[1] 12 Howell's State Trials, pp. 234—8.

not forcing Romanists on both Cambridge and Oxford? Had not
Rochester been dismissed because he would not be converted,
would not even express approval of the Declaration of Indulgence? Could James's word be trusted when this was the fulfilment of the pledge given to his council on the word of a king that
he would protect the Church of England in the enjoyment of all
its rights? I may seem to be maintaining a paradox, but I am
disposed to think, and I believe Ken would have thought with
me, that James was not consciously insincere, nor even conscious of his inconsistency. He did not impose the acceptance of
the Mass as a qualifying test for the Privy Council, or for command in the army and navy, or for magisterial offices. A king
was surely—his enemies themselves being judges—entitled to
choose his immediate servants, in his household and his councils,
among those he could most trust, and it was natural that he
should trust members of his own Church more than those of a
rival and hostile communion. Did he not show enough comprehensiveness when he admitted Penn and other Nonconformists to his favour? Was it not natural that he should
look with a certain indignant intolerance on those who were
the persistent opponents of toleration? James's ideal of a
patriot King was, I fancy, that of a monarch presiding over a
Privy Council in which Church of England men, Roman
Catholics, and Dissenters sat on equal terms, all equally ready
to register his decrees, and to give him their best advice as to
carrying his intentions into effect. If it were compatible with
the dignity of history to compare great things with small, I
should be tempted to say that his mental attitude was like that
of the schoolmaster of Orbilian fame (was it Busby or Keate?)
of whom it is related that he once addressed his scholars,
"Boys, it's your duty to love one another, and if you don't,
I'll flog you till you can't stand." [1]

---

[1] James's words to the Vice-Chancellor at Oxford, in 1687, are really hardly
more than a paraphrase of these words: "Of all things I would have you
avoid Pride, and learne the Vertue of Charitie and Humilitie. There are a host
of People among you that are Wolves in Sheep's Clothings; beware of them,
and let them not deceive you and corrupt you. . . . Let not, therefore,
your Eye be evil, and mine be good, but love one another and practise Divinity;
do as you would be done to, for this is the Law and the Prophets."—Ant. à
Wood, *Life,* p. 363.

And then as to the dispensing power. Had not subservient lawyers assured him that it came within the limits of his prerogative? Had not the Court of King's Bench ruled, in the case of the collusive action against Sir Edward Hales, who, being a Roman Catholic, had been appointed as Lieutenant-Governor of the Tower, that he had a right to dispense with the tests imposed by Parliament in each individual case in which he chose to exercise that right, and if so, where was the line to be drawn? Could he not do in all cases what he might rightly do in any one?

Had the King confined himself to publishing this second Declaration of Indulgence, as he had done the first, in the *London Gazette*, it is possible that it might have been little more than a nine days' wonder. Laymen might have talked and shrugged their shoulders; bishops might have sighed; Parliament, when it met in that promised session of November, might, or might not, have remonstrated, according to the success of the manipulating manœuvres of the "regulators;" [1] but there would probably have been no concerted opposition. Happily for the liberties of England, the King was bent on bringing matters to a more speedy issue. The Declaration of April 25th was followed up by an Order in Council of May 4th, which directed the Bishops to send it to their several dioceses, and to have it read during divine service, on the 20th and 27th, in all churches and chapels in London and Westminster, and within a distance of ten miles, and elsewhere throughout the kingdom on the 3rd and 10th of June. [2]

Matters now began to look serious. The mere command to read a royal declaration in church was, of course, not illegal in

[1] The name was given to the official personages appointed to manage the new corporations, the old charters having been in most instances revoked by the Crown, with a view to securing a government majority. (Macaulay, chap. viii.) Even the Lord-Lieutenants of Counties "were ordered to examine the gentlemen and free-holders as to their parliamentary action; which they did very lukewarmly."—Burnet, *O.T.*, B. iv., 1687.

[2] It may be noted as one of the proceedings which tempted James to persevere, that Cartwright had drawn up a form thanking the King for the Declaration, which was signed by himself, Parker, of Oxford, and Sprat, of Rochester. White, of Peterborough, asked for a day to deliberate and then utterly refused.—Cartwright, *Diary*, p. 47.

itself; it was clearly within the range of the rubric that follows the Nicene Creed in the Communion Service.   It had been done once and again under Charles II.   Sancroft himself had moved in Council that that King's proclamation, in 1681, dissolving the Oxford Parliament, should be published by the clergy in all churches.   James probably persuaded himself that though the pill was a bitter one, as he meant it to be, the Bishops could not, in face of these precedents, refuse, and would, though not without some remonstrances and wry faces, ultimately swallow it.   He had failed to lay to heart the advice which Bishop Morley had sent him from his deathbed, through Lord Dartmouth, that "if ever he depended on the doctrine of non-resistance he would find himself deceived.   The clergy might not think proper to contradict that doctrine in terms, but he was very sure they would in practice."   To James that seemed the counsel of "a very good man, but grown old and timorous;" and he was genuinely surprised as well as indignant when Morley's prophecy was fulfilled.

Sancroft, in spite of his age and infirmities, rose to the emergency of the crisis.   A memorandum, found among his papers,[1] probably gives the first result of his deliberations with his own reason and conscience, and was put on paper for his own guidance and that of others.   We can scarcely doubt that it formed the basis of all his subsequent deliberations with his colleagues.

"REASONS FOR NOT PUBLISHING THE DECLARATION.

"1. I am not averse to the reading the King's Declaration for Liberty of Conscience for want of due tenderness towards Dissenters; in relation to whom I[2] shall be willing to come to such a temper[3] as shall be thought fitt, when that matter comes to be considered and settled in Parliament and Convocation.

"2. The Declaration, being founded on such a Dispensing Power, as may at pleasure set aside all laws Ecclesiastical and Civil, appears

_____

[1] The memorandum is in the Tanner MSS. in the Bodleian Library, and is here reproduced in fac-simile.

[2] Sancroft's leniency to Dissenters, as compared with Sheldon's conduct is noticed by Overton (*Life in E. C.*, p. 57). Compare his language in July, 1688, urging the clergy "that they have a very tender regard to our brethren the Protestant Dissenters."—D'Oyly, *Life*, chap. vii.

[3] "Temper" in the old sense of compromise or settlement.

to me illegal; and did so in the Parliament both in the year 1662, and in the year 1672, and in the beginning of his Majesty's reign, and it is a point of such consequence that I cannot so far make myself a party to it, as the reading of it in the Church in the time of Divine Service will amount to."

[Facsimile.]

Sancroft, it is clear, had not forgotten the memorable scene in the Council Chamber, in 1672,[1] when Charles II., yielding to

[1] It was this declaration, we may remember, that set Bunyan free after his twelve years' imprisonment in Bedford gaol, and released thousands of other Dissenters, including Quakers, from like sufferings.

the pressure put on him by his Parliament, had with his own
hands torn up the Declaration in which he had, to some extent,
anticipated James's action.   Like the Duke of Somerset, when
he refused to introduce the Pope's Nuncio, the Primate felt
that, though the King might be above the law, he was not
Prudence, as well as conscience, dictated a policy of non-com-
pliance, which, as he was prepared to suffer the consequences,
was, from his point of view, quite compatible with the theory
of *passive* obedience.   The time was short, and it was not easy
to take adequately concerted action.   The wiser and less servile
Dissenters addressed many of the London clergy, imploring
them not to read the Declaration.   The London clergy themselves held a meeting, at which fifteen Doctors of Divinity were
present, and resolved, chiefly under the influence of a manly
utterance from Dr. Edward Fowler, Vicar of St. Giles', Cripplegate, a Churchman of the school of Tillotson, afterwards Bishop
of Gloucester, on Frampton's deprivation in 1691, that they
would not read it.   Their resolution was signed by all who
were present, including Tillotson, Patrick, Sherlock, and Stillingfleet.   Sancroft, meantime, was not idle.   He called a meeting
at Lambeth on May 12th, at which Compton, Bishop of London,
Turner, of Ely, White, of Peterborough, and Tenison, rector of
St. Martin's, were present.   Cartwright, Bishop of Chester, the
most subservient of James's instruments (he had been President
of the Magdalen Commission) came, probably uninvited, and as
a spy.   Clarendon gave the conference the benefit of his official
experience.   They waited till Cartwright had left, before speaking their minds openly.   A man who joined Tyrconnel in his
drinking bouts, and spent his Sunday afternoons in consultation
with Father Petre, was not one whom they desired to admit
into their counsels.   Tyrconnel had told him that he hoped,
before long, to see him Archbishop of Canterbury,[1] and with
that prize before him, he was apparently willing to do James's
dirtiest work.   The Archbishopric of York was actually vacant
at the time, and that would not be a bad stepping-stone.   After
his departure the Bishops resolved that other prelates of the
province of Canterbury, whose names would carry weight with
them, should be taken into counsel.   Special messengers were

[1] Cartwright, *Diary*, pp. 44, 73, 91.

sent with the letters to country post-towns, near their several residences, in order to avoid the risk of their being opened in the London Post-office. It was probably, therefore, on the 14th or 15th of May that Ken received the following letter at Wells:—

"My Lord,

"This is only in my own name, and in the name of some of our Brethren, now here upon the place, earnestly to desire you, immediately upon the receipt of this letter, to come hither with what convenient speed you can, not taking notice to any that you are sent for. Wishing you a prosperous journey, and us all a happy meeting, I remain

"Your very loving Brother,

"WILLIAM CANTUAR."

The letter was sufficiently mysterious in its vagueness to give rise to many anxious conjectures. The journey might not be without other dangers than that of perils of robbers. For Ken, however, the path of duty was clear, and as he arrived in London, where he stayed at the house of his friend Hooper, who was Rector of Lambeth, on the evening of the 17th of May, he had probably started without an hour's delay, and made his way to London with utmost speed.[1]

On the following day another conference was held at Lambeth. Besides the six Bishops who with Sancroft signed the petition which was the outcome of their deliberations, Compton was again present, but, being under a sentence of suspension, did not sign. Mews, Bishop of Winchester, was detained by illness. Frampton arrived a day or two afterwards. The letter to Lloyd, Bishop of Norwich, had miscarried through the country post-office. Tillotson, Stillingfleet, Patrick, Tenison, Sherlock, Master of the Temple, and Grove, Rector of St. Andrew's Undershaft, were also present. Sancroft's memo-

---

[1] I think it probable that he made the journey on horseback, as Frampton did. Perkins, in his poem on Ken's death, notes the characteristic fact that, while other Bishops went "in a grand carosse," he, when in London, was commonly seen on foot (ii. 263). The later practice of posting was then unknown. Cartwright took the stage to Chester (*Diary*, p. 9), as did Sir J. Reresby, to London, his servants following on horseback.—See Markland, in *Archæologia*, xx., 443. Evelyn's journey to Althorp, in two coaches hired for him by the Countess of Sunderland, was probably exceptionally magnificent (August 15th, 1688).

randum served as the basis of their counsels, and the petition
on which they ultimately agreed embodied, as will be seen on
comparing the two documents, many of its expressions.   The
language of the petition was carefully considered and toned
down, as is shown by the interlineations and corrections in
Sancroft's rough draft,[1] to the last degree of moderation compatible with firmness.   The deliberations lasted till a late hour
in the evening, and it was not till 10 P.M. that the six Bishops
who were to present it (Sancroft had been under orders, ever
since he refused to act on the Ecclesiastical Commission Court,
not to appear at Whitehall) started in the Archbishop's barge.

The petition is, I think, worthy of being printed *in extenso*.
It is high time in this bi-centenary of the trial of the seven
Bishops that men should know the facts of the case somewhat
more accurately than is common.   Those who read Ken's *Life*
should have before them the very words to which he attached
his signature.

" To THE KING'S MOST EXCELLENT MAJESTY.

"The humble Petition of William Archbishop of Canterbury,
and of divers of the suffragan Bishops of that Province (now
present with him), in behalf of themselves and others of
their absent brethren, and of the Clergy of their respective
Dioceses,

" HUMBLY SHEWETH ;

" That the great averseness they find in themselves to the distributing and publishing in all their churches your majesty's late
Declaration for Liberty of Conscience, proceedeth neither from any
want of duty and obedience to your majesty, (our holy mother the
Church of England being both in her principles and in her constant practice, unquestionably loyal ; and having, to her great
honour, been more than once publicly acknowledged to be so by
your gracious majesty), nor yet from any want of due tenderness to
Dissenters, in relation to whom they are willing to come to such a
temper, as shall be thought fit, when that matter shall be considered
and settled in Parliament and Convocation ; but amongst many
other considerations, from this especially, because that Declaration

1 The draft is reproduced in fac-simile, as frontispiece to Vol. ii., from the
original in the Tanner MSS. in the Bodleian Library.   See Note at end of
chapter.

is founded upon such a Dispensing power, as hath been often declared illegal in parliament, and particularly in the years 1662, and 1672, and the beginning of your majesty's reign; and is a matter of so great moment and consequence to the whole nation, both in Church and State, that your Petitioners cannot in prudence, honour, or conscience, so far make themselves parties to it, as the distribution of it all over the nation, and the solemn publication of it once and again, even in God's house, and in the time of his divine service, must amount to, in common and reasonable construction.

" Your Petitioners therefore most humbly and earnestly beseech your Majesty that you will be graciously pleased not to insist upon their distributing and reading your Majesty's said Declaration.

" And your Petitioners (as in duty bound) shall ever pray, &c.[1]

> " Signed.
>
> | | |
> |---|---|
> | " W. Cant. | Tho. Bath & Wells. |
> | S. Asaph. | Tho. Petriburgens. |
> | Fran. Ely. | Jon. Bristol. |
> | Jo. Cicestr. | |

With a view to a like completeness it will, I think, be worth while to give a few pages to the lives and characters of the six prelates who, on that memorable evening, more fateful than any of them then dreamt, were dropping down the silent river from Lambeth bearing with them, though they knew it not, the fortunes of the English nation. A full biography of each does not, of course, come within the limits of such a work as this. But what it is important to remember is that they, one and all, like the venerable Primate whom they had left at Lambeth, were men who had special claims on James's confidence. This has been made clear already as regards Ken. (1) Lake, of Chichester, had in early life served in Charles I.'s army at Basing House, Wallingford, and had refused to take the Covenant or the

---

[1] On two other copies of the above petition, one of which is in the Archbishop's hand, are the following subscriptions :

> Approbo.　H. London.　May 23, 1688.
> 　　　　　William Norwich.　May 23.
> 　　　　　Robert Gloucester.　May 21, 88.
> 　　　　　Seth Sarum.　May 26.
> 　　　　　P. Winchester.
> 　　　　　Tho. Exon.　May 29, 1688.
> 　　　　　　　　Gutch, *Collectanea Curiosa*

Engagement.   When he returned to his college (St. John's, at
Cambridge), he was "gated" as a suspected person for many
months and not allowed to go outside the college, and he ran the
risk of taking orders in 1647 from one of the deprived Bishops,
probably Skinner.   He was promoted through various stages of
preferment after the Restoration.   He officiated at the marriage
of Evelyn's friend, Margaret Blagge, who had been maid of
honour to James's first wife, and Godolphin.   As Archdeacon
of Cleveland and Prebendary of York, he had taken a prominent part (1680) in suppressing disorders in the Cathedral.[1]
He resigned his prebend for the see of Sodor and Man with a
much smaller income.   He was recommended by Turner (Ken's
friend) to the then Duke of York in 1684, and by him to
Charles, for the Bishopric of Bristol.   While there he had
taken an active part in the suppression of Monmouth's rebellion
in 1685.   James translated him to Chichester in the October
of that year.

(2) Thomas White, of Peterborough, had also been brought
into personal contact with the King.   He had shown his personal
prowess in knocking down a trooper who had insulted him and
the Bishop of Rochester, and Charles, delighted with the story,
had first told him that he should impeach him for high treason,
for assaulting the King's soldiers, and had afterwards thanked
him for teaching the fellow better manners.   On the marriage
of the Princess Anne with Prince George of Denmark, he
had been made,—her father must surely have had a hand in
the appointment,—one of her domestic chaplains, and the King
had been so satisfied with him that he had named him for the
bishopric which he now filled in October, 1685.   (3) Francis
Turner, of Ely, had been more closely connected with James's
household.   He had been with Ken at Winchester and New
College.   Later on in life (1669) he was elected Master of St.
John's College, Cambridge.[2]   He was the friend of Peter Gunning, his predecessor at Ely, was chosen by the Duke of York,
after his conversion to Rome, as a chaplain in his household,

---

[1] On one occasion he left his stall in the Minster, went down the nave, and
knocked off the hats of the loungers to right and left.—Strickland, *Lives of
Seven Bishops*, p. 110.

[2] See p. 72.

and attended him during his exile in Scotland in the time
of the Exclusion troubles in England.   Charles II., on the
Duke's recommendation, made him Dean of Windsor and Lord
Almoner (1683).   In the same year he was made Bishop of
Rochester, and in 1684, on Gunning's death, was translated
to Ely.   James, as we have seen, had chosen him to preach his
coronation sermon, and had assigned to him, in conjunction
with Ken and Hooper and Tenison (the last, however, at Monmouth's request) the painful duty of attending the Duke on
his execution.   (4) Lloyd, of St. Asaph, though less distinctively
Anglican than the others (he had accepted a living from the
Presbyterians at Oxford in 1654,[1] and had satisfied the "triers"),
had risen into high favour on the Restoration and been rapidly
promoted, chiefly on the strength of a book, more or less
biographical, in which he had set forth the saintliness of
the great English Catholics, such as Andrewes, Ussher, Taylor,
and those of whom Walton wrote, and this had drawn forth
James's praise (before his conversion to Rome) as " an excellent
book by a learned and very worthy man."   He was named
chief chaplain in the household of the Princess Mary on her
marriage.   His old Puritan leanings showed themselves, however, in his allowing the Princess to attend the chapel of English, or Dutch, Congregationalists at the Hague, a habit which
Hooper had some difficulty in breaking, and in the part he took in
a furious anti-papal sermon on the murder of Sir Edmondbury
Godfrey, and in otherwise backing Oates and the other contrivers
of the Popish Plot agitation.   Charles II. had, perhaps, sent him
to St. Asaph to get him out of the way.   He was, probably, of
all the six, the least acceptable to James.   He maintained with
great vehemence, as Burnet did, the spuriousness of the so-called
Prince of Wales, was among the most active Churchmen in
William's support, and was appointed almoner to Mary.   A
little later he got entangled in apocalyptic studies, and fixed
the date of the end of all things as near at hand.

[1] See p. 61 for some incidents of his Oxford life.   He had also held services at
the Embassy Chapel at Paris during the Commonwealth, where Morley, Cosin,
Earle and others preached, and where the Dukes of York and Gloucester worshipped (Evelyn, October 1st, 1651, *n.*).   Evelyn mentions with high praise
the moderation of his sermon on Romanism preached before Charles II. (November 23rd, 1679).

Lastly, there was (5) Trelawney, of Bristol, representing one of the most ancient and most loyal of Cornish families. His father had been in James's household when he lived at Deptford, in the early days of the Restoration, and he had distinguished himself in suppressing the Western rebellion. His sister Anne was brought up with the Princess Mary and accompanied her, as her chief maid of honour, to the Hague. In 1685 he was selected for the see of Bristol, but he found the income of that see inadequate (he says it was only £300 a year), and begged hard, through the Earl of Rochester, for a better bishopric. He was consecrated on November 9th, and was introduced into the House of Lords by Ken. As yet his application had not been successful, and the disappointment was keenly felt. It will be seen later on that he and Lloyd were the only two out of the seven petitioners who took the oaths of allegiance to William, and whose names were coupled together in the Jacobite saying, that "the King had sent the seven to the Tower to be tried in the fire, that the others had proved to be as the fine gold, but they had turned out to be Prince's metal."[1]

Such were the six men who landed at Whitehall Stairs on that memorable evening of May 18th. The tale of what followed has been often told, but the scene was one in which Ken bore so prominent a part that I cannot do otherwise than reproduce it. I follow Macaulay in the main narrative, with some side lights from an unpublished letter, without a signature, to Lord Weymouth, dated May 24, in the Longleat MSS.

Lloyd, on landing, left his five companions at the house of Lord Dartmouth, near the Palace, and, probably as senior Bishop, went straight to Sunderland. Would he read the petition, and ask the King whether he would receive it? The Minister shrank from the responsibility of complying with the first half of the request, but went at once to the King and informed him of the arrival of the Bishops. James, we may well believe, felt no uneasiness when he knew who the Bishops were. What he had heard from Cartwright had prepared him to expect, perhaps, some application for a

---

[1] The point of the saying lay, of course, in the fact of the close local connexion of the Tower and the Mint. "Prince's metal" derived its name from Prince Rupert.

little longer time, some request for a modification of one or
two phrases in the Declaration. Late as the hour was, he
graciously consented to receive them. They came and knelt
before him. He bade them rise, and took the petition from
Lloyd's hands, who, as the senior bishop, took the leading
part. He recognised the familiar handwriting. "This," he
said, "is my Lord of Canterbury's hand," and Lloyd admitted
that it was. As he read it his face darkened, and the portraits
of James show that, under such conditions, he could look sufficiently fierce. He grew "heartily angry." "This," he said,
"is a standard of rebellion." [1] He repeated part of his Oxford
speech ("I am king; I will be obeyed. Is this your Church
of England loyalty?") "This is a great surprise to me. I
did not expect this from your Church, especially from some of
you," and, as he spoke, he "looked more sternly than ordinarily"
on Trelawney. The Bishops passionately professed their loyalty, but the King, after his manner, went on harping on the
phrase, "This is a standard of rebellion." At last Trelawney
lost his self-command and burst out. He fell on his knees, and
told the King "that he presumed he was not of that opinion
when he sent him into the West, when he had like to have fallen
into the enemy's hands; and asking if he thought fit to persist
in his opinion," he added, "If some of my family had proved
rebellious to the Crown I should not have much stood in need
of your favour or protection." When James repeated the
charge of rebellion, he flatly contradicted him: "Sir, with
submission I speak it, you know to the contrary." We can
scarcely wonder that James should have said afterwards, that
of all the Bishops he of Bristol was the "most saucy." The
other five Prelates may well have stood aghast as they listened
to this altercation. They endeavoured to pacify the King's
wrath. "We put down the last rebellion," said Lake, who
had been Bishop of Bristol at the time, "and we shall not

[1] Clarendon, who must have had the report from one of the Bishops (probably
Turner or Ken), gives the phrase as "the standard of Sheba," referring of
course to the history of 2 Sam. xx. Probably it was altered in the published
report, as being too obscure an allusion for common readers, or James may have
used both phrases. Assuming him to have used this, it is curious to find him
beginning and ending the interview with an allusive reference to Old Testament
history.

raise another." " We rebel ! " exclaimed Turner ; " we
are ready to die at your Majesty's feet." Ken's words were
calmer and more characteristic : " Sir," said he, " I hope
that you will grant to us that liberty of conscience which
you grant to all mankind." Still James went on, " This is
rebellion. This is the standard of rebellion. Did ever a
good Churchman question the dispensing power before ? Have
not some of you preached for it and written for it ? It is a
standard of rebellion ; I will have my Declaration published."
" We have two duties to perform," answered Ken ; " our duty
to God and our duty to your Majesty. We honour you ; but
we fear God." " Have I deserved this ? " said the King,
surprise and disappointment adding bitterness to his wrath ;
" I, who have been such a friend to your Church ! I did not
expect this from some of you. I will be obeyed. My Declaration shall be published. You are trumpeters of sedition. What
do you do here ? Go to your dioceses and see that I am
obeyed. I will keep this paper ; I will not part with it. I will
remember you that have signed it." " God's will be done,"
said Ken, and White, of Peterborough, echoed the words.
" God has given me the dispensing power," replied James,
" and I will maintain it. I tell you that there are still seven
thousand of your Church who have not bowed the knee to
Baal."

With this somewhat strange application of the words heard
by Elijah, as the King's last utterance, the Bishops had to be
content and they respectfully retired. They returned to Lambeth, as they had come, by water,[1] and so they were spared, for
the moment, the shock of consternation which they would have
felt on hearing the document, which they had looked on, as in
the highest degree, private and confidential, hawked about the
streets of London, read and discussed, even at that late hour
(it must then have been near midnight), in every coffee-house.
Everywhere the people rose from their beds, and came out to
stop the hawkers. Who had been the traitor is one of the
unsolved problems of history. Sancroft, whose veracity is
unimpeachable, declared that he had taken every precaution
against publication. He knew of no copy (*i.e.* no fair copy,

---

[1] There was no Westminster Bridge, it must be remembered, till 1730.

for the rough draft remained, as we have seen, among the Sancroft MSS.) but that which the Bishops had taken with them.[1]   Macaulay thinks it " by no means impossible that some of the divines who assisted in framing the petition may have remembered so short a composition accurately, and may have sent it to the press.   The prevailing opinion, however, was that some one about the King had been indiscreet or treacherous."   Sunderland himself was suspected of having played a double part, at one and the same time urging the King on his career of violence, and inflaming popular indignation against him.   It is, however, against this theory that Sunderland, as we have seen, would not read the petition, that the King said he would not part with it, and that there was scarcely time to get it printed after the Bishops took their departure.

I confess that I am reluctantly compelled to suspect Compton of the breach of confidence.   It would have been easy for him to write the words of the petition, while it was under discussion, clause by clause.   He was deeply implicated in the negotiations with William, which were carried on by Henry Sidney, with whom he was in constant communication, and the prevaricating answer which he gave, when James questioned the Bishops as to their share in these negotiations, shows that he was not a man of very scrupulous conscience.   I surmise that he went straight to Sidney on leaving Lambeth, and that they decided on immediate publication.   If so, he may probably have had some hand in the letter which, on the very next day, was sent by the post and by carriers to every clergyman in England, exhorting them in the strongest terms not to read the Declaration, and which some ascribed to Sherlock and some, including Prideaux, Dean of Norwich, who was a principal agent in distributing it, to Halifax.[2]

The story of the Sunday that followed has been told by all historians.   In the whole city of London the Declaration was

---

[1] A fair copy, in Lloyd's hand (or, perhaps, Ken's), is, however, found in the Tanner MSS., and is reproduced in Cardwell's *Documentary Annals*, ii. 316.

[2] I quote one pregnant sentence from the letter.   " If we read the Declaration, we fall to rise no more.   We fall unpitied and despised.   We fall amidst the curses of a nation whom our compliance will have ruined."—Macaulay, ch. viii.

read in four churches only.   It was read in the Chapel Royal
at Whitehall, though not in that of St. James's, in spite of the
Lord Chamberlain's express orders.   Sprat began it at Westminster, and every one left the Abbey except the singing men
and choristers.[1]   Samuel Wesley, the father of John and
Charles, preached on the answer of the three Jews to the
Chaldæan tyrant: "Be it known unto thee, O King, that we
will not serve thy God, nor worship the golden image which
thou hast set up."   We may be quite sure that it was not read
in the chapels at Lambeth Palace or Ely House, nor in the
Parish Church at Lambeth, which Ken probably attended, and
of which Hooper was rector.   In the course of the following
week the petition received the signatures, with an *Approbo*, of
the bishops whose names will be found attached to it (p. 303).[2]
The Longleat letter states that it would be signed by all the
Bishops except the few who were conspicuously subservient to
James's policy, Crewe, of Durham; Sprat, of Rochester; Cartwright, of Chester; Croft, of Hereford; and Watson, of St.
David's.   Barlow, of Lincoln, is named as doubtful.   Parker, of
Oxford, would probably have found a place with Crewe and Cartwright, but he had died on March 20th, and the see was still vacant.   During that week there was abundant discussion as to the
line the King would take.   On the 24th, the date of the Longleat
letter, it was generally believed that the judges were in favour
of separate prosecutions (qu. before the Ecclesiastical Commission Court?) against each particular Bishop, as guilty of a misdemeanour.   Finally, on Jeffreys' advice, who thought it more
prudent to keep to constitutional forms of legality, and felt
sure that the Judges and Crown Counsel could not fail to obtain a verdict (juries were not uncommonly fined, as in Penn's
trial, for a verdict against the Crown), and was probably not

---

[1] The Longleat letter, however, already quoted, says that Sprat, who had declined, when asked, to sign the petition, left town on the Saturday, giving orders
that it should be read the following day.   Lord Dartmouth's statement quoted
in Stanley's *Memorials of Westminster* (p. 452), is, however, decisive.   He was at
Westminster School at the time, and heard it.   Stillingfleet and Tillotson went
to their country houses.   (Clarendon, *State Letters*, ii. 198.)

[2] Mews accompanied his signature by a "very handsome letter," sending his
opinion "so fully and warmly that he has gott a world of reputation."—Longleat
Letter.

unwilling to transfer the responsibility of presiding at the trial to the Lord Chief Justice, it was decided to prosecute them collectively for publishing a seditious libel (the presentation constituting the publication, for it was impossible to prove any complicity, on the part of the Bishops, with the issue of the printed copies), and the Bishops (Sancroft with them) received notice, on May 27th, that they were to appear before the King in Council on the 8th of June.

Enough had passed since the former interview to embitter James's feelings. Never had there been a greater *fiasco* than that unhappy Order in Council of May 4th. It had proved an utter failure in London and Westminster on the two appointed Sundays. There had been time for tidings to arrive from all parts of England that it had been equally inoperative throughout the country. The mind of London was excited to the utmost point. Other bishops, as we have seen, had given an *ex post facto* adhesion to the petition. The Bishops appeared in the Council Chamber,[1] Sancroft this time accompanying them.

---

[1] I am enabled through the kindness of Mr. C. L. Peel, C.B., Clerk of the Privy Council, to give the list of those members who were actually present, and who, according to the practice which then obtained, must have been specially summoned for this purpose. It is significant that Father Petre was thus invited to sit in judgment on Bishops of the English Church. He, however, did not sign the warrant for their committal to the Tower, nor did the Earl of Berkeley. Arundel of Wardour, Melfort and Castlemaine also were Romanists. It must have been, I imagine, a special grief to Ken and the other Bishops, to find the signature of Lord Dartmouth on the warrant which sent them to the Tower.

EXTRACT FROM THE COUNCIL REGISTER,
8TH JUNE, 1688.

"At the Court at Whitehall.
"Present,
"The King's most Excellent Majesty.

" Lord Chancellor (Jeffreys).	Earle of Middleton.
" Lord President (Sunderland).	Earle of Melfort.
" Lord Privy Seale (Arundel of Wardour).	Earle of Castlemain.
" Marquiss of Powis.	Viscount Preston.
" Lord Chamberlain.	Lord Dartmouth.
" Earle of Huntington.	Lord Godolphin.
" Earle of Peterborow.	Lord Dover.
" Earle of Craven.	Mr. Chancellr. of ye Excheqr.
" Earle of Berkeley.	Lord Chief Justice Herbert.
" Earle of Moray.	Sir Nicholas Butler.

" Mr. Petre."

The King presided in person.   Jeffreys was there to direct the
law proceedings.   The Bishops were not accompanied by
counsel, but it is natural to believe that they had been in
consultation with some of those who afterwards conducted
their defence, with Sawyer[1] and Finch, with Pemberton and
Lewis, with Treby and Somers.[2]   They had come fortified by
the rules of action which counsel, in such a case, would be
sure to give.   They were to admit nothing, but leave the
whole *onus probandi* to the prosecution.   Above all, they were
not to criminate themselves.   Accordingly, when Jeffreys
began by taking up the petition, which was lying on the
table, and asking Sancroft whether that was the paper which
he had written, and which the Bishops had presented, the
Archbishop declined to answer.   It was with pain and regret
that he found himself in the position of an accused person.
Being in that position, he must claim its privilege, and be
cautious in answering questions.   No man was bound to answer
questions that might tend to the accusing of himself.   That,
Lloyd added, was the opinion of "all divines, as well as of all
lawyers."   To the King this seemed the "mere chicanery" of a
pettifogging lawyer.   "Were they going to deny their own
hands?"   Sancroft, on being further pressed, said, "Sir, I am
not bound to accuse myself.   Nevertheless, if your Majesty
positively commands me to answer, I will do so, in the confidence that a just and generous prince will not suffer what I say
in obedience to his orders to be brought in evidence against
me."   Jeffreys roughly interposed, "You must not capitulate
with your sovereign."   James added that he would give no such
command.   "If you choose to deny your own hands, I have
nothing more to say to you."

Jeffreys was clearly nonplussed.   The King could not be
placed in the witness-box, and unless they relied on the evidence
of experts in handwriting—a kind of proof at that time little
recognised in the courts of law—they had no other proof that

[1] Sir Robert Sawyer, who was owner of Highclere, may have known Ken
personally when he was rector of Woodhay, which was in closest neighbourhood
to Highclere.   Clarendon relates, in his *Diary* (ii., p. 200), that on June 5th
he had seen Ken and Turner, and that he " had advised them to consult the best
lawyers, and to be ready for all questions."

[2] Anderdon, p. 449.

the accused were responsible for the petition. The Bishops were ordered to withdraw to the ante-chamber once and again, and on each return to it a like altercation ensued. At last the King positively commanded them to answer, and then, either as thinking that he did so under the implied condition on which they had insisted, or believing that the time for passive obedience, at any risk of suffering, had come, or, it may be, weary of taking a line which, though advised by counsel, must obviously have been uncongenial to men who were ready, if not eager, to act the part of martyrs or confessors, they gave way, and when called in for the third time, acknowledged their respective signatures. The result showed that they were in the presence of men sufficiently unscrupulous. They were now asked whether any others had been present when the petition was framed, whether they knew anything of the letter which had been circulated with the petition through the length and breadth of England. Here, as men with a conscience and a sense of honour, they felt that they must draw the line.

"It is our great infelicity," remarked Sancroft, "that we are here as criminals; and your Majesty is so just and generous that you will not require me to accuse either ourselves" (he must mean, of course, as regards the other matters as to which they had been questioned) "or others." Jeffreys tried what could be done with the rough side of his tongue, "fell into anger and reproaches," dwelt on the tendency of what had been done "to diminish the King's authority and disturb the peace of his kingdom." On this point, however, they stood firm, and there was nothing more to be said. They were formally told that they would be prosecuted for a misdemeanour and must give their own recognisances to appear in the Court of King's Bench.[1] Sir Robert Sawyer and the peers with whom they had taken counsel (Clarendon probably among them) had prepared them for that stage in the proceedings. They declined. They stood, they said, on their privilege as peers,

---

[1] Compton, writing to Sancroft, the day before the Meeting of the Council, tells him that he had heard that the Clerks of the Council were to be made Justices of the Peace in order to take their recognisances, so that the Bishops were forewarned and forearmed on this point.—Gutch, *Collect. Curiosa*, i., p. 313.

who were not bound, like other accused persons, to enter into recognisances. They would give their word of honour to appear, but nothing more. They were resolved "to maintain the rights of the Peerage as well as those of the Church; being equally bound to oppose all innovations, both in Government and religion." Here again the Council was taken by surprise. Jeffreys lost his temper or his head. "In that case, unless they would immediately recant and withdraw the petition, he would send them at once to the Tower." They answered calmly, in the tone of the three 'children' of the Book of Daniel, that "they were ready to go whithersoever the King might please to send them, that they hoped that the King of kings would be their protector and their judge; they feared nothing from men; for, having acted according to law and their own consciences, no punishment should be ever able to shake their resolution." After much wrangling on this point they were again ordered to withdraw.[1]   When they came back the King

---

[1] Gutch, i., p. 351, prints the following dialogue, as having passed between the King and the Bishops at some stage of the proceedings, from the Tanner MSS. in the Bodleian Library.

"*King.*—What brought you to London? What is the temper you are ready to come to with the Dissenters?

"*Answer.*—We refer ourselves to the Petition.

"*King.*—What mean you by the Dispensing Power being declared illegal by Parliament?

"*Answer.*—The words are so plain that we cannot use plainer.

"*King.*—What want of prudence or honour is there in obeying the King?

"*Answer.*—What is against conscience is against prudence and honour too, especially in persons of our character.

"*King.*—Why is it against your conscience?

"*Answer.*—Because our consciences oblige us, as far as we are able, to preserve our Laws and Religion according to the Reformation.

"*King.*—Is the Dispensing Power then against Law?

"*Answer.*—We refer ourselves to the Petition.

"*King.*—How could the distributing or reading the Declaration make you parties to it?

"*Answer.*—We refer ourselves to the Petition, whether the common and reasonable construction of mankind would not make it so?

"*King.*—Did you disperse a printed letter in the Country, or otherwise dissuade any of the Clergy from reading it?

"*Answer.*—If this be one of the Articles of Misdemeanour against us, we desire to answer with the rest."

It is probable, I think, that this represents the substance of the last interview

had vanished, apparently content to leave Jeffreys in the chair as master of the situation. He "used them very roughly." At last the final step was taken. They withdrew for the last time. The Earl of Berkeley came from the Council Chamber, and once more tried to persuade them to yield as to the point of recognisances. They, however, stood firm, and soon the Sergeant-at-Arms came with a warrant signed by fourteen hands to take them as prisoners to the Tower. Another with nineteen signatures was sent to the Lieutenant of the Tower to keep them in safe custody. The Attorney-General (Powys) and Solicitor (Williams) were ordered to conduct the prosecution. To prevent the tumult that might be caused by their passage to the Tower through the streets they were sent by water in one of the King's barges.

It is a singular instance of the perpetuation of a popular, but false, impression that it was believed then, and has been generally believed since, that the seven Bishops were sent to the Tower, because they refused to read the Declaration of Indulgence and to withdraw their petition. As the history of the proceedings shows, they were sent there because they stood firm on the purely technical point of their privilege as peers, and refused to enter into recognisances. A week later, when they appeared before the Court of King's Bench, and the point, after being argued by their counsel, was decided by the Court against them, they were content to waive their right and gave the recognisances which were required. It was, of course, a splendid piece of strategy as regards its effect on the minds of the people. They, unaccustomed to the nice questions of constitutional law, saw the concrete fact that seven Bishops were committed to the Tower after they had presented their petition against the Declaration, and that was enough to lead them to the conclusion that they were committed because they had petitioned. But it is not less true that they had forced the King's hand, aided by Jeffreys's hot-headedness, and so had led, as James afterwards complained, to a step which more than anything

before the King's withdrawal, but I have thought it better to give it as a separate document rather than to attempt to interweave it with the continuous narrative given by other authorities. It was probably Sancroft's report.

else roused the passions of the people against him. One of them at least (Turner, of Ely) in after years, when he saw to what all this had led, looked back with regret on the course they had been advised to take as "a wrong step, and an unnecessary punctilio of honour in Christian bishops." [1]

[1] Strickland, *Bishops,* p. 197. Something of the same feeling is traceable in Ken's language in the *Royal Sufferer,* assuming that book to be his, when he says that, though he "did indeed soon perceive of what ill consequence" the part taken by the Bishops "would be to his Majesty," he had acted "without any evil design," and that it "was not in his power to help it" (p. 74).

[NOTE ON THE DRAFT PETITION, p. 302.—Most of the alterations made by the Bishops in the process of revision are simply verbal, but two are sufficiently important to call for special notice :—

(1). The Draft describes the "dispensing power" upon which the Declaration of Indulgence was founded as being "such as may at pleasure set aside all our laws, both ecclesiastical and civil, which appears to them most manifestly illegal."

(2). The language of the prayer of the petition is much stronger in the Draft than in the form in which it was presented to the King.

"Your petitioners, therefore, most humbly beseech your Majestie that you will be graciously pleased to supersede and revoke the (———?) Order of Council by which this heavy burthen is imposed upon them, of proclaiming Liberty of Conscience to your other subjects, even to their enemies, with the manifest violation of their own, who have been always, in the highest and most hazardous instances, and resolve, by the grace of God, ever to continue your Majestie's most faithfull, loyal, and obedient subjects and servants, the Clergy of the Church of England by Law established."

It would seem from the opening and closing words as if the petition was originally intended to be signed by many other bishops on behalf of the clergy at large, but for this, manifestly, there was no time. It will be seen that the thoughts embodied in the omitted passages crop out more than once in the dialogue between the Bishops and the King (pp. 307—8).

The Draft is found among Sancroft's papers (Tanner MSS., Bodleian Library), and is believed to be in his hand. (See Cardwell's *Documentary Annals,* ii. 316.)]

END OF VOL. I.

PRINTED BY J. S. VIRTUE AND CO., LIMITED, CITY ROAD, LONDON.

www.ingramcontent.com/pod-product-compliance
Lightning Source LLC
Chambersburg PA
CBHW020938030726
47496CB00005B/1255